Red Cavalry

ISAAC BABEL

EDITED BY NATHALIE BABEL

TRANSLATED WITH NOTES BY
PETER CONSTANTINE

INTRODUCTION BY MICHAEL DIRDA

W. W. NORTON & COMPANY
NEW YORK LONDON

To the memory of my father,
Isaac Emmanuelovich Babel,
and of my mother,
Evgenia Borisovna Babel.

Compilation, Preface copyright © 2002 by Nathalie Babel
Translation copyright © 2002 by Peter Constantine
Introduction copyright © 2003 by Michael Dirda
Chronology copyright © 2002 by Gregory Freidin

All photographs courtesy of Nathalie Babel
Frontispiece photograph: Isaac Babel, circa 1931, Molodenovo
Chronology photograph: Isaac Babel, July 1930, previously unpublished in book form,
sent by Isaac Babel to his sister in Brussels with the handwritten inscription,
"My life is spent fighting this man."

Manufacturing by LSC Harrisonburg
Book design by Mary Wirth
Cartography by Jacques Chazaud
Production manager: Anna Oler

Library of Congress Cataloging-in-Publication Data

Babel', I. (Isaak), 1894–1941.
[Konarmiëiia. English.]
Red Cavalry / Isaac Babel ; edited by Nathalie Babel ; translated with notes
by Peter Constantine ; introduction by Michael Dirda.
p.   cm.
Includes bibliographical references.
ISBN-13: 978-0-393-32423-5
ISBN-10: 0-393-32423-0
I. Babel, Nathalie. II. Constantine, Peter, 1963– III. Title.
PG3476.B2K613 2003
891.73'42—dc21   2003000682

W. W. Norton & Company, Inc., 500 Fifth Avenue, New York, N.Y. 10110
www.wwnorton.com

W. W. Norton & Company Ltd., 15 Carlisle Street, London W1D 3BS

CONTENTS

Contents

The Red Cavalry Cycle: Additional Stories 171

1920 Diary 199

Sketches for the Red Cavalry Stories 295

INTRODUCTION

by Michael Dirda

"The orange sun is rolling across the sky like a severed head." So writes Babel on the very first page of *Red Cavalry*—but the sentence might well be a stage direction for Peckinpah's *The Wild Bunch* or Kurosawa's *Seven Samurai* or Coppola's *Apocalypse Now*. The world of *Red Cavalry* is one we recognize from late-twentieth-century film. Violence and brutality mingle with a surreal, sometimes poetic beauty. The established order of things has been interrupted, and we enter a stark theater of wild gesture, one where a man goes into battle with a quip—"Let's go die for a pickle and World Revolution"—or meets his end with a laconic courage that the ancient Spartans might envy. Write this in the letter to my mother, whispers a dying Cossack: "The regimental captain sends his regards, and don't cry."

First published in Soviet magazines in the mid-1920s and gathered together in 1926, the stories of *Red Cavalry*—set during the period of civil war following the 1917 Bolshevist coup—established Isaac Babel's reputation, and for many readers remain the author's most powerful achievement. Blending fact and fiction, personal history and military history, they mainly depict the triumphs and disasters of the Cossack army on the Polish frontier as it attempts to export the Revolution to Eastern Europe. (Babel himself actually covered this campaign as a reporter for *The Red Cavalryman*.) Each story is a short, sharp shock, a slice of life cut with a saber: "The previous night, six Makho fighters raped a maid. When I heard this the following morning, I decided to find out what a woman looks like after being raped six times." Most could be dubbed vignettes, ranging from 500 to 1,500 words, the length of news stories, dispatches from the front lines where the blood is spilled and the atrocities covered up:

> Right outside the house a couple of Cossacks were getting ready to shoot an old silver-bearded Jew for espionage. The old man was screeching, and tried to break free. Kudrya from the machine gun detachment grabbed his head and held it wedged under his arm. The Jew fell silent and spread his legs. Kudrya pulled out his dagger with his right hand and carefully slit the old man's throat without spattering himself. Then he knocked on one of the closed windows.
>
> "If anyone's interested," he said, "they can come get him. It's no problem."

In war, men and women display courage, self-control, loyalty, and, depending on circumstances, may appear vile or heroic. In "Squadron Commander Trunov," the eponymous "hero" skewers an old man with his sword and then shoots a young man in the head with his Japanese rifle. Without a second thought. The pair were enemies—even if they had surrendered. With the same nonchalance the squadron commander accepts his own death moments later. First making sure his men are safely hidden in the forest, he quickly appoints his successor, gives away the new boots on his feet, and then prepares to take on four approaching airplanes with a machine gun.

In these pages the world is turned upside down. A police-officer father fighting for the counterrevolutionary White Army hacks his Communist son to death, and is himself killed by one of his other sons. Language itself grows Boschian: "Blue roads flowed past me like rivulets of milk trickling from many breasts." "The sponge cakes had the aroma of crucifixion." Like Fabrice at the Battle of Waterloo in *The Charterhouse of Parma* or the young soldier in *The Red Badge of Courage*, the reader is whirled precipitously into uncertainty and bewilderment. "Which is the revolution and which the counterrevolution?" asks one casualty of the war.

Yet Babel depicts this disordered realm with lyricism and a grotesque good humor. "The earth lay in its April wetness. Emeralds glittered in the black ditches. Green shoots hemmed the soil with cunning stitches." "Her breasts, bobbing on her high heels, squirmed like an animal in a sack." Now and again, the extravagant similes even recall the arch noir voice of Raymond Chandler: "The moon hung over the yard like a cheap earring." "His long legs looked like two girls wedged to their shoulders in riding boots."

This juxtaposition of an elevated literary style with coarse soldier's talk, of strikingly original analogy with harsh naturalistic observation, lies at the heart of Babel's achievement. In every way the stories yoke together opposites—Jew and Cossack, Russian and Pole, warrior and intellectual—and these natural polarities generate an explosive imaginative power. "Looking at them, I understood the fiery history of these faraway hinterlands, the stories of Talmudists who leased out taverns, of rabbis who dabbled in moneylending, of girls who were raped by Polish mercenaries and for whom Polish magnates shot themselves." In the original collection's final story, "The Rabbi's Son," the narrator packs up the belongings of a dead Jewish soldier, one who has zealously embraced Communism, and implicitly describes his own all-embracing artistry:

> I threw everything together in a jumble, the mandates of the political agitator and the mementos of a Jewish poet. Portraits of Lenin and Maimonides lay side by side—the gnarled steel of Lenin's skull and the listless silk of the Maimonides portrait. A lock of woman's hair lay in a book of the resolutions of the Sixth Party Congress, and crooked lines of Ancient Hebrew verse huddled in the margins of Communist pamphlets. Pages of *The Song of Songs* and revolver cartridges drizzled on me in a sad, sparse rain.

Religion and revolution. Love and war. Nobility and tawdriness. An account of one battle, that around the village of Czesniki, focuses mainly on a slatternly nurse's stratagem to have her mare serviced by the division commander's thoroughbred stallion. After this sexual sideshow, the actual military conflict appears as little more than an afterthought in the last sentence of the last paragraph: "And at a sign from the division commander, we launched our attack, the unforgettable attack on Czesniki." That's it. But nothing more is needed. The unforgettable attack, we later learn, resulted in a shameful rout.

In the midst of carnage, the narrator—a bespectacled Babel look-alike—at one point chats in a quiet kitchen with an itinerant folk painter: "What do we converse about? About the romantic days of the Polish nobility, the fanatical frenzy of women, the art of Luca della Robbia, and the family of the Bethlehem carpenter." Outside stretches a landscape "where dead mice floated down the roads. Autumn surrounded our hearts with traps. Trees, upright naked corpses, stood swaying at crossroads."

In American literature *Red Cavalry* is probably closest to the early Hemingway of *In Our Time*—the same paratactic sentences, the affectless description, the fierce desire to get things right. Like Hemingway, Babel also sets up connections between his stories, ironic echoes, repeating characters. When a woman looks forward to sleeping with a nice clean young man named Sashka, the reader remembers that in an earlier story this same Sashka and his stepfather caught syphilis from an old whore.

It's been said that Babel revised some of his pages forty or fifty times. The care results in a collection that never shirks the filth and gruesome savagery of war but cannot avoid conveying an almost epic sense of its harsh grandeur too. "And on the graves of Polish officers lay horse's skulls." The Red Cavalry—captained by "the willful Pavlichenko and the captivating Savitsky"—sweeps across a battleground that Homer would recognize, one of petty bickering and blood baths, of rape and self-sacrifice, of mud, stars, and sudden death. Babel's astonishing, unflinching language—his very periods like iron spikes to the heart—makes you see it all.

MICHAEL DIRDA
Washington, D.C.
November 2002

PREFACE

by Nathalie Babel

So, who was Isaac Emmanuelovich Babel? Was he a Soviet writer, a Russian writer, or a Jewish writer?

As a Soviet writer, he shows and experiences a profound dichotomy between acceptance of the ideals of the Revolution and repulsion for its methods. As a Russian writer, he expresses both nostalgia for the old world and desire for the new. As a Jewish writer, he was well versed in Hebrew and the Talmud. Yet he wrote in Russian. His work reveals what many have called a "Jewish sensibility." However, when he used the typical Jewish themes found in Yiddish literature, they were always interwoven with Russian cultural archetypes.

Babel's work defies categorization. Simply put, in my personal view, the juxtaposition of compatibles and incompatibles keeps Babel's prose in a state of constant tension and gives it its unique character. Approaching Babel with expectations based on traditional Russian literature might lead either to disappointment or to a feeling of discovery. His prose does not merely draw on past themes and forms, but is the forging of a new manner of writing, which reflected new times. Babel's readers are not only students of Russian literature and history or of the Russian Revolution. They belong to different cultures, different religions, and different social classes. They have no single national tradition.

Critics have taken various positions and a great deal of research and passion has been invested in solving questions of Babel's personal convictions and literary style. Actually, the critical literature on Babel's works fills bookcases, compared to the mere half shelf of his own writings. Babel started writing as an adolescent, but he himself considered that his career as a man of letters, writing "clearly and concisely," began only in 1924. It was then that his stories, which were to become the volumes entitled *Red Cavalry* and *The Odessa Stories* started to appear. The young writer burst upon the literary scene and instantly became the rage in Moscow. The tradition in Russia being to worship poets and writers, Babel soon became one of the happy few, a group that included Soviet writers, who enjoyed exceptional status and privileges in an otherwise impoverished and despotic country. He was allowed to travel abroad and to stay in Western Europe for relatively long periods of time. In the late 1930s, he was given a villa in the writers' colony of Peredelkino, outside Moscow. No secret was ever made of his having a wife and daughter in Paris. At the same time, hardly anyone outside of Moscow knew of two other children he had fathered. As a matter of fact, Babel had many secrets, lived with many ambiguities and contradictions, and left many unanswered questions behind him.

During his lifetime, Babel was loved, admired, and respected as a writer. The following entry from the first volume of the second edition of the *Small Soviet Encyclopedia* of March 1937 provides an insightful description of the man and the writer. I will quote from this article, since I find it well documented, critically sound, and psychologically perceptive. It shows what Babel was striving for and what he in fact achieved. Moreover, it is astonishing to note the date of publication, the year 1937, when the ground was very shaky for Jews and intellectuals. It seems that when the books were already printed in March 1937, the publishers did not have time to revise the contents of the encyclopedia according to the Party's latest interpretations of Soviet history. They did, however, manage to glue by hand an addendum of "corrections" into each of the sixty-one thousand copies of the first volume before they were distributed, explaining the need for the revision of several of the articles. Fortunately for us, the entry on Babel was neither "corrected" nor removed.

Babel, Isaac Emmanuelovich (born 1894)—Soviet writer; son of an Odessa merchant. His first stories appeared in 1916, although the height of his literary activity occurred during the years 1923–1924. Babel's literary output is small in volume. His basic genre was the "novella" or short story, most of which can be grouped into three thematic cycles: "Odessa Stories," mainly about the exploits of the gangsters of Odessa (the film scenario of "Benya Krik" and the play "Sunset" also fall under this theme); the collection of stories "Red Cavalry"—impressions of the 1920 campaign of the army of Budyonny, in which Babel took part; and autobiographical stories ("The Story of My Dovecote," etc.). . . .

An aesthete with a heightened interest in all the colorful revelations of the human character, inclined towards the abstract intellectual humanism and to romanticism, expressing through his whole life and work the agonizing sensation of his own dilettante weaknesses, Babel admired the heroic spirit of the Revolutionary and saw the Revolution as essentially elemental, accepting it without fear.

In his portrayal of Red Cavalry soldiers, as with the gangsters of Odessa, Babel expresses both admiration and horror of their strength and natural daring, through his own intellectual's skeptical irony. This creates an original combination of heroics and humor. Characteristically, in his book "Red Cavalry," Babel focuses his attention less on the colorful episodes of military life, and more on the wild escapades of the partisans.

Typical for Babel is his primordial florid imagery, his original synthesis of romanticism and sharp naturalism, of the physiological and the erotic, which at times becomes pathological. His great mastery is in his concise picturesque story telling, his bright and witty communication of local color and life (for example—the subtly humorous depiction of Jewish life in "Odessa Stories").

The stories which he published after his long silence in 1931–1932, including the fragment "Gapa Guzhva"—which touches separately on the theme of collectivization, are similar in nature to his earlier literary work.

L. KAGAN

Indeed, the author of this "politically incorrect" article was on dangerous ground. One wonders whatever happened to Mr. Kagan.

By this time, the Great Purges were in full swing. Stalin held the country in his fist. His Revolutionary comrades, his generals, writers, anarchists, so-called Trotskyites, and their associates were arrested, tortured, and shot. The political terror penetrated all spheres of life, including literary and cultural circles. It was only a matter of time before my father's turn would come. He surely must have known that he himself had been under the vigilant surveillance of the secret police for some years.

On May 15, 1939, Babel was arrested. He disappeared. Not a trace, not a word. He vanished. His lodgings were searched and every scrap of paper was confiscated—correspondence, drafts, manuscripts, everything. None of it has ever resurfaced. His name, his works, were officially erased as though he had never existed. There was only silence. How could a man so friendly, so socially astute, so famous, not be able to pass a word to the outside? And so the guessing began, and slowly, a sort of myth emerged. He never existed, but by his nonexistence, he became famous. I have been asked many times in my life, "Do you know how he died? Do you know where? Do you know why?" There is another question also often asked. "Why did he go back to the Soviet Union? The times were already bad. Didn't he know it? Why didn't he stay in Paris with his family?" Babel came to Paris in the summer of 1935, as part the delegation of Soviet writers to the International Congress of Writers for the Defense of Culture and Peace. He probably knew this would have been his last chance to remain in Europe. As he had done numerous times for some ten years, he asked my mother to return with him to Moscow. Although he knew the general situation was bad, he nevertheless described to her the comfortable life that the family could have there together. It was the last opportunity my mother had to give a negative answer, and she never forgot it. Perhaps it helped her later on to be proven completely right in her fears and her total lack of confidence in the Soviet Union. My mother described to me these last conversations with my father many times.

So, why did he go back to Moscow in 1935? For many years, Babel had battled with the dilemma of his life situation. During his lengthy visits to Paris dating from 1926, he could express his thoughts without fear of possible betrayal. According to his close friend Boris Souvarine,[*]

---

[*]Boris Souvarine (1895–1984), historian and writer of Russian origin, who settled in Paris. On Lenin's personal recommendation, he became a member of the Committee for the Third International (1919), later a member of the Executive Committee of the Komintern (1921-1924), and a member of the French Communist Party, which he helped to create and from which he was expelled in 1924. Author of *Staline: Aperçu historique du Bolchevisme* (1935), the first biography and historical study of Joseph Stalin, and *Dernières conversations avec Babel*, Ed. Counterpoint, 1979, later a chapter in his book *Souvenirs sur Panait Istrati, Isaac Babel, et Pierre Pascal*, Ed. Gérard Lebovici, Paris, 1985. Souvarine was considered the foremost French specialist on Kremlin politics. The first monograph on his life and work, *Boris Souvarine: le premier désenchanté du communisme,* by Jean Louis Panné, was published in Paris in 1993 by Robert Laffont. The title speaks for itself.

for example, Babel had a great knowledge of high political spheres in the Soviet Union, of its plots, manipulations and daily practices. He knew very well the nature of Stalin's character and private life, and had no illusions about Stalin's monstrous intentions and crimes.

Another person with intimate knowledge of Babel's political views at the time was Yuri Annenkov.* In his memoirs, Annenkov wrote of his many encounters with Babel in Paris and of the letters he received from him through the early 1930s. In 1932, Babel returned to Paris to visit his family, after an absence of three years. Annenkov wrote, "Babel's moods had changed significantly in the past months. It's true, he was still a big joker, but his topics of conversation were different. The last stay in the Soviet Union and the growing repression of creative art through the demands and instructions of the State had completely disillusioned him. To write within the framework of 'the barrack mentality of Soviet ideology' was intolerable for him, yet he didn't know how he could manage to live otherwise."†

Annenkov described another visit with Babel in 1932, noting that the conversation had just one subject: how to manage to live further.

"I have a family: a wife and daughter," said Babel, "I love them and have to provide for them. Under no circumstances do I want them to return to Sovietland. They must remain here in freedom. But what about myself? Should I stay here and become taxi driver, like the heroic Gaito Gazdanov? But you see, he has no children! Should I return to our proletarian revolution? Revolution indeed! It's disappeared! The proletariat? It flew off, like an old buggy with a leaky roof, that's lost its wheels. And it stayed wheelless. Now, dear brother, it's the Central Committees that are pushing forward—they'll be more effective. They don't need wheels—they have machine guns instead. All the rest is clear and needs no further commentary, as they say in polite society. . . . Maybe I won't become a taxi driver after all, although, as you know, I passed the driving test long ago. Here a taxi driver has more freedom

---

*Yuri Pavlovich Annenkov (1889–1974), famous Russian portraitist, painter, printmaker, scientific draftsman, theater designer, cartoonist, writer, critic, stage manager. Left the USSR in 1924 and settled in Paris. His memoirs of his meetings with well-known artists, writers, and political figures were published in 1996 (*People and Portraits: A Tragic Cycle*, Vols. 1–2, published by the Inter-Language Literary Associates, New York, 1996).

†Annenkov, pp. 305–306.

than the rector of a Soviet university. . . . Driver or no driver, I'm going to become a free man.*

On July 27, 1933, Babel wrote to Annenkov that he had received a strange summons from Moscow and was departing immediately, "in the most dramatic conditions and no money and a lot of debts everywhere. . . . Live well without me. Don't forget Evgenia Borisovna† while I'm gone. . . . I kiss you. I'm glad that I'm going to Moscow. All the rest is bitter and uncertain."**

This turned out to be the last letter Yuri Annenkov ever received from my father. In their correspondence, Babel sounds to me like a man divided in his heart, a man pulled with equal force in two different directions.

In 1933, Babel still had a powerful political protector, his beloved mentor Alexei Maximovich Gorky. Gorky had played a critical and irreplaceable role in Babel's life. Babel wrote in 1924, "At the end of 1916, I happened to meet Gorky. I owe everything to this meeting and to this day speak the name of Alexei Maximovich with love and reverence. He published my first stories in the November 1916 issue of *Letopis*. Alexei Maximovich taught me extremely important things and sent me into the world, at a time when it was clear that my two or three tolerable attempts as a young man were at best successful by accident, that I would not get anywhere with literature, and that I wrote amazingly badly."††

During a trip to Italy in the spring of 1933, shortly before returning to the Soviet Union, my father visited Gorky in Sorrento. His death in 1936 was a great personal loss for Babel and signaled the inevitable coming tragedy.

One of Babel's main preoccupations was money. All his adult life, Babel had money problems and worried about them. Not that he did not make money. On the contrary, he made a lot of money. In the 1920s, his stories were published and republished in book form. In one year (1924–1925), four collections of stories and two screenplays were

---

*As above.

† Evgenia Borisovna Babel, born Gronfein. My parents were married on August 9, 1919, in Odessa.

**Annenkov, p. 307.

†† Excerpt from an autobiographical sketch by Babel that appeared in Lidin, Vladimir (ed.), "*Pisateli: avtobiografii i portrety sovremennykh russkikh prozaikov*" ("Authors: Autobiographies and Portraits of Contemporary Russian Writers") Sovremennyie Problemi (Contemporary Problems), Moscow, 1926, pp. 27–29.

published. He also received payment for foreign editions. In the 1930s, he worked for film studios in Moscow, Kiev, and Leningrad and was extremely well paid for his efforts. He not only wrote original scripts, but also revised the screenplays of others, without attribution to himself. Apparently, he was the main author of *The Gorky Trilogy*, which appeared only after his arrest and without his name in the film credits.

Babel's problem was not the absence of money, but his inability to manage it. Above all, he felt the obligation to take care of his relatives abroad. His sister Meri Emmanuelovna Chapochnikoff had left in 1924 to join her fiancé, who was studying medicine in Belgium; my mother Evgenia Borisovna had left in 1925, taking with her a lifelong hatred of the Bolsheviks; and his mother, the last one to leave, joined her daughter in Brussels in 1926.

As I noted in my introduction to *The Lonely Years*, "Money matters tormented him. To make more money, he had to work under increasingly difficult conditions. Moreover, the impractical Babel would let his generosity run away with him. Whether he was in Moscow or in Paris, distant relatives, friends and friends of friends were continually imploring him for financial assistance. A few weeks after his return to the Soviet Union from a trip abroad, he would find himself totally impoverished, his Soviet friends having finished the job that had begun in Paris. Above all, Babel feared that his economic position would affect his work. His life centered on writing."*

His inability to imagine himself as anything but a writer played a critical role in his refusal to leave the USSR. His stays abroad made him understand that he could not make a comfortable living as an émigré writer.

As Cynthia Ozick observed in a review of Babel's *1920 Diary*, "By remaining in the Soviet Union and refusing finally to bend his art to Soviet directives, Babel sacrificed his life to his language."†

Souvarine remembers what he called Babel's leitmotiv, "I am a Russian writer. If I did not live with the Russian people, I would cease being a writer. I would be like a fish out of water."** Actually, my mother

---

Isaac Babel: The Lonely Years 1925–1939. Unpublished Stories and Private Correspondence. Edited with an Intoduction by Nathalie Babel, published by Farrar, Straus and Co., 1964.

†Cynthia Ozick, "The Year of Writing Dangerously," *The New Republic*, May 8, 1995.

**Boris Souvarine, *Souvenirs sur Panait Istrati, Isaac Babel, et Pierre Pascal*, Ed. Gérard Lebovici, Paris 1985, p. 34.

would use these words almost verbatim to explain my father's absence and why I had no brothers and sisters, whom I had always wanted. This romantic ideal of the writer, which was only part of the story, stayed with me for a very long part of my life. It took many years to let it go.

For Babel, it is clear that there was no one ideal solution. In the end, a man's destiny is his own.

In 1954, after many years of official silence, Babel's name was heard again. A typed half sheet of ordinary paper, accepted as an official document, declared, "The sentence of the Military College dated 26 January 1940 concerning Babel I. E. is revoked on the basis of newly discovered circumstances and the case against him is terminated in the absence of elements of a crime." The news took a couple of years to leak out of Moscow to the rest of Europe. Several decades later in the early 1990s, following the breakup of the Soviet Union, some brave souls were able to get access to the KGB's archives on Babel. Minute records had been kept about the arrest and interrogations of the accused.

As we now know, his trial took place on January 26, 1940, in one of Lavrenti Beria's private chambers. It lasted about twenty minutes. The sentence had been prepared in advance and without ambiguity: death by firing squad, to be carried out immediately. Babel had been accused and convicted of "active participation in an anti-Soviet Trotskyite organization" and of "being a member of a terrorist conspiracy, as well as spying for the French and Austrian governments."

Babel's last recorded words in the proceedings were, "I am innocent. I have never been a spy. I never allowed any action against the Soviet Union. I accused myself falsely. I was forced to make false accusations against myself and others. . . . I am asking for only one thing— let me finish my work." He was shot the next day and his body was thrown into a communal grave. All of this horrific information was revealed in the early 1990s, a relatively short time ago.

Considering that revelations about my father have been coming to light for almost fifty years, a large portion of my life, I understand why it has never been possible to put an end to grieving. For many years now, I have been involved with attempting to bring together and to light what is recognized as the body of Babel's work. I hope the present book, along with the *Complete Works* it is drawn from, will provide further insights into his personality, as well as a greater knowledge and appreciation of his literary legacy.

NATHALIE BABEL
Washington, D.C.
March 2001

FOREWORD

by Peter Constantine

*O*ne of the great tragedies of twentieth century literature took place in the early morning hours of May 15, 1939, when a cadre of agents from the Soviet secret police burst into the house of Isaac Babel in Peredelkino, arrested him, and gathered up the many stacks of unpublished manuscripts in his office. From that day on, Babel, one of the foremost writers of his time, became a nonperson in the Soviet Union. His name was blotted out, removed from literary dictionaries and encyclopedias, and taken off school and university syllabi. He became unmentionable in any public venue. When the film director Mark Donskoi's famous Gorky trilogy premiered the following year, Babel, who had worked on the screenplay, had been removed from the credits.

Babel was executed in 1940. It was only in 1954, fourteen years later, that he was officially exonerated, but his books were only warily republished in the Soviet Union, and in censored form. And yet today, sixty-two years after his arrest and the subsequent silence surrounding his name, Babel is considered, both inside and outside Russia, to be among the most exciting—and at times unsettling—writers of the twentieth century.

Babel is one of the great masters of the short story, and for the translator a great and challenging master of style. It has been fascinating to see his style change from work to work. We are familiar with terms such as Proustian, Chekhovian, and Nabokovian, but, as I soon realized, the term "Babelian" is harder to define.

Babel burst onto the literary scene after the Bolshevik Revolution of 1917, becoming within a few years one of Russia's most original and highly regarded authors—"the best Russia has to offer," as Maxim Gorky wrote to André Malraux in 1926. Babel began his career during a time when Russian culture, society, and language were in total upheaval. World War I, the February and October Revolutions of 1917, and the Civil War left in their wake poverty, hunger, and social instability. At the same time, the promise of limitless change was in the air. The people of Russia felt that they were being given the opportunity to participate in an exhilarating and unprecedented social experiment which, if World Communism was to have its way, would be a global one.

The abrupt social changes on all levels, the abolition of imperial censorship, and the new feeling of liberty drove writers of Babel's generation—Mayakovsky, Pasternak, Zamyatin, Bulgakov—to write in new ways about new topics with an unprecedented vigor. Babel did this with a vengeance. His themes were steeped in the brutal realism of the times: In the arctic night of Petersburg a Chinese man, seeing a desperate prostitute, holds up a loaf of bread—"With his blue fingernail he draws a line across the crust. One pound. Glafira [the prostitute] raises two fingers. Two pounds." A teenage girl tries to help her younger sister abort her baby with a clothes hanger—their mother walks in on them just in time. The morgues of Petersburg are filled with corpses—the narrator gazes at a dead aristocratic couple and, looking at the noblewoman, thinks, "In death she keeps a stamp of beauty and impudence. She sobs and laughs disdainfully at her murderers." Starving wet nurses feeding undersized infants in state-run maternity wards beg the narrator for a crust of bread.

These were contemporary topics that before Babel nobody had dared touch. When the valiant Red Cavalry rode into Poland, in what was intended to be the first step that would carry the glories of Communism to Europe and the world, Babel rode along. He brought back with him a series of stories that presented a literary portrait of war that has awed and haunted readers for almost eighty years.

The *Red Cavalry* stories are, stylistically speaking, astonishingly varied. There is the "I" of Isaac Babel and the "I" of Kiril Lyutov, the very Russian war correspondent (who might go as far as admitting that his mother is Jewish). "Lyutov" was also the identity that Babel assumed in real life as a way of surviving among the fiercely anti-Semitic Cossacks of the Red Cavalry. There are also other narrators, such as the murderous Cossack Balmashov. When these characters are the narrators, the tone, style, and grammar in the stories begin to go awry. Babel is a master at re-creating the Cossacks' wild, ungrammatical speech filled with skewed and half-understood Communist doctrine. In "Salt," for instance, the entire story is narrated in the voice of a Cossack whose ranting jumble ranges from Communist jargon to folk verse:

> I want to tell you of some ignorant women who are harmful to us. I set my hopes on you, that you who travel around our nation's fronts have not overlooked the far-flung station of Fastov, lying afar beyond the mountains grand, in a distant province of a distant land, where many a jug of home-brewed beer we drank with merriment and cheer.

I have found in translating other authors, such as Anton Chekhov and Thomas Mann, that after a few stories I was steering toward a Chekhovian or Mannian style I felt worked in English. Not so with Babel. Each of the texts in this volume had to be treated on its own terms. Babel is not only one of the greatest storytellers of European literature, but also one of its greatest stylists.

PETER CONSTANTINE
New York
March 2001

ACKNOWLEDGMENTS

The realization of this volume, and the larger *Complete Works* it draws from, has been a long-term dream and struggle. The struggle has been made easier by my good fortune in working with Peter Constantine, who took it upon himself to translate anew all available original manuscripts and the first publications in Russian—a long and arduous task. As this is the first time that a single person has translated all of Babel's work into English, this volume has a unique coherence and consistency that I believe is true to Babel's voice in Russian. Peter was not only meticulous in his choice of words and phrasing, but also in his research in order to clarify the text and provide notes where necessary. He also was of great help to me in organizing and editing this large and unwieldy collection of materials, and in supporting me with frequent practical advice and unflagging enthusiasm.

I approached Gregory Freidin without warning to request that he prepare a biographical and literary chronology of Babel's life and works. Gregory's exceptional knowledge allowed us to sort out many conflicting or incomplete items of information. I thank him for his graciousness in completing this task.

Special thanks are also due to Robert Weil, my editor at W. W. Norton, who embraced the challenge of giving new life to Babel's work through what he knew would be a difficult project. His editorial advice and his steadfast guidance have earned my heartfelt gratitude. Without the professional perseverance and affectionate encouragement of my friend and literary agent, Jennifer Lyons, this work would not have been completed. I thank her warmly. I also cannot hope to acquit my debt merely with thanks, or even the feelings of profound gratitude and affection that I feel for my friend Christine Galitzine. As she became more and more interested in this project, she also became more indispensable to my being able to advance it. Through her knowledge of English, French, and Russian, as well as her own literary and administrative gifts, she was able to understand my thoughts and sentiments deeply and to help me render them onto the printed page. Indeed, her involvement in this work has been invaluable.

This publication is also the realization of a dream of my husband, Richard Harvey Brown, who for over thirty years has hoped that I would be able to master my memories sufficiently to bring this volume to print. His benevolence and loving support throughout these struggles also should be publicly acknowledged.

NATHALIE BABEL BROWN

I would like to thank Nathalie Babel for offering me this project, and for her constant support and encouragement. I owe particular thanks to my Russian editor, Anneta Greenlee, for her tireless checking of my translation against the Russian original for stylistic nuance. My translation owes much to her specialized knowledge of early-twentieth-century Russian language and literature. I am also grateful to Katya Ilina for her help in editing Isaac Babel's *1920 Diary*, and for the weeks she spent studying the many editions of Babel works, checking for editorial variations and instances of Soviet censorship.

I am also indebted to my editor at Norton, Robert Weil, for his insightful and knowledgeable editing and particularly for his expertise in American and European Jewish literature. I am also grateful to Jason Baskin and Nomi Victor, editors at Norton, and to David Cole for copyediting the manuscript.

I am indebted to Professor Gregory Freidin for his help and advice, and for his specialized knowledge of Isaac Babel's life and works, and to Christine Galitzine for her knowledge of pre-Revolutionary Russia.

I am thankful to Peter Glassgold for his initial suggestion that I translate Isaac Babel, and for his helpful editorial advice. I am thankful also to my agent, Jessica Wainwright, for her encouragement and constant support as I worked on the translation. I also wish to thank Jennifer Lyons, the agent of the Babel estate, for her help and input.

I am deeply indebted to the resources of the New York Public Library, where I did all my research and annotation. I owe special gratitude to Edward Kasinec, curator of the Slavic and Baltic Division, for his erudite advice and for the many times he personally located materials for me that were hidden in obscure Soviet publications of the 1920s and 1930s. I am also grateful to Tanya Gizdavcic, librarian of the Slavic and Baltic Division, for her help in locating material, and to Serge Gleboff, Robert Davis, Lev Chaban, and Hee-Gwone Yoo for their help and advice.

I would like to thank Paul Glasser at YIVO for his helpful explanations of Yiddish expressions. I would also like to express my appreciation to Karina Vamling from the Linguistics Department of the University of Lund, Sweden, for her explanations of Georgian expressions in Isaac Babel's texts and the information she provided on aspects of Georgian and Caucasian politics that Babel referred to, and to Peter

Gasiorowski of the University of Poznan, Poland, for his linguistic advice on expressions used in the *1920 Diary*. I am also grateful to Thomas Fiddick for his help—I benefited greatly from his books and articles on the Russian-Polish war of 1920. I found the extensive annotations in the German translation of the *1920 Diary* by Peter Urban very helpful, as I did the scholarly and bibliographical work on Babel by Efraim Sicher.

My very special thanks to Burton Pike, who inspired, helped, and advised me throughout the project.

PETER CONSTANTINE

RED CAVALRY

The Red Cavalry Stories

In late May 1920, the First Cavalry of the Soviet Red Army, under the command of General Budyonny, rode into Volhynia, today the border region of western Ukraine and eastern Poland. The Russian-Polish campaign was under way, the new Soviet government's first foreign offensive, which was viewed back in Moscow as the first step toward spreading the doctrines of World Revolution to Poland, then to Europe, then to the world.

Babel chronicled this campaign in his RED CAVALRY stories, later to become the most well-known and enduring of his literary legacy. These loosely linked stories take the reader from the initial triumphant assault against the "Polish masters" to the campaigns of the summer of 1920, and the increasingly bitter defeats that led to the wild retreat of the cavalry in the autumn. Babel blends fiction and fact, creating a powerful effect that is particularly poignant in his rendering of the atrocities of war. The stories were published in magazines and newspapers between 1923 and 1926; the reading public was torn between delight at Babel's potent new literary voice and horror at the brutality portrayed in the stories. In 1926, thirty-four of the stories were included in the book KONARMIA (translated into English as

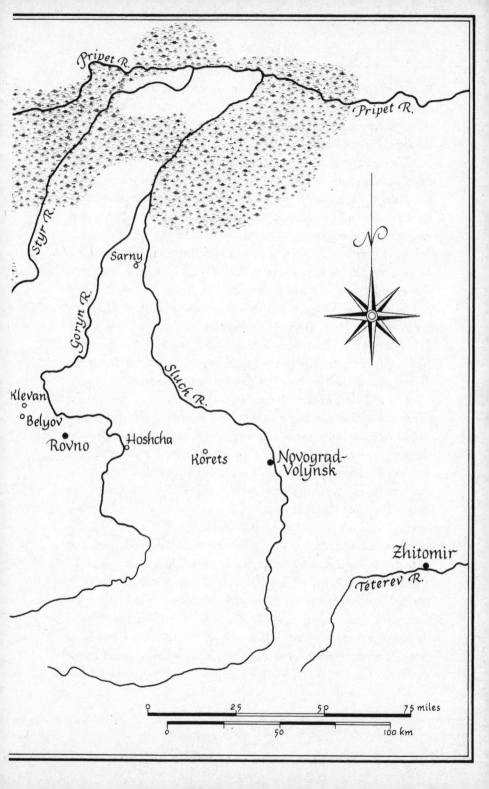

RED CAVALRY), *which quickly went into eight editions and was translat-ed into English, French, Italian, Spanish, and German. It immediately turned Babel into an international literary figure and made him into one of the Soviet Union's foremost writers.*

The stories, as Babel himself repeatedly stressed, were fiction set against a real backdrop. Literary effect was more important to Babel than historical fact. Babel might also have felt more comfortable reconfiguring military strat-egy that might still have been classified when the stories began appearing in newspapers and magazines in the first years after the war. Novograd-Volynsk, for instance, the town in the first story, lies on the river Slucz, not on the Zbrucz as the story indicates. (The Zbrucz runs along the western frontier of Volhynia, along the former border between the kingdom of Poland and Russia.) Also, Novograd-Volynsk was not occupied by the Red Cavalry, but by the Soviet 14th Army. As the historian Norman Davies has point-ed out, a high road from Warsaw to Brest had been built by serfs under Nicholas I, but it lay two hundred miles beyond the front at Novograd-Volynsk, and so could not have been cluttered by the rear guard.

One of Babel's strategies for creating a sharper feeling of reality in his stories was to mix real people with fictional characters. This was to have serious repercussions. General Budyonny, for instance, the real-life com-mander of the cavalry, often comes across in the stories as brutal, awkward, and irresolute. Babel makes fun of his oafish and uneducated Cossack speech. In the story "Czesniki," Budyonny is asked to give his men a speech before battle: "Budyonny shuddered, and said in a quiet voice, 'Men! Our situa-tions . . . well, it's . . . bad. A bit more liveliness, men!' "

Babel had, of course, no way of knowing that General Budyonny was to become a Marshal of the Soviet Union, First Deputy Commissar for Defense, and later "Hero of the Soviet Union." Another real character in the stories, Voroshilov, the military commissar, also does not always come across particularly well. The implication in "Czesniki" is that Voroshilov overrode the other commanders' orders, resulting in an overhasty attack that led to defeat. Voroshilov happened to be a personal friend of Stalin; he had become the People's Commissar of Defense by the time the RED CAVALRY *collec-*

tion was in print, and was destined to become Head of State. These were dangerous men to cross.

In these stories Babel uses different narrators, such as Lyutov, the young intellectual journalist, hiding his Jewishness and struggling to fit in with the Cossacks, and Balmashov, the murderous, bloodthirsty Cossack.

The Soviet Union wanted to forget this disastrous campaign, its first venture at bringing Communism to the world. Babel's Red Cavalry stories, however, kept the fiasco in the public eye, both in the Soviet Union and abroad, throughout the 1920s and 1930s, and ever since.

CROSSING THE RIVER ZBRUCZ

*T*he commander of the Sixth Division reported that Novograd-Volynsk was taken at dawn today. The staff is now withdrawing from Krapivno, and our cavalry transport stretches in a noisy rear guard along the high road that goes from Brest to Warsaw, a high road built on the bones of muzhiks by Czar Nicholas I.

Fields of purple poppies are blossoming around us, a noon breeze is frolicking in the yellowing rye, virginal buckwheat is standing on the horizon like the wall of a faraway monastery. Silent Volhynia is turning away, Volhynia is leaving, heading into the pearly white fog of the birch groves, creeping through the flowery hillocks, and with weakened arms entangling itself in the underbrush of hops. The orange sun is rolling across the sky like a severed head, gentle light glimmers in the ravines among the clouds, the banners of the sunset are fluttering above our heads. The stench of yesterday's blood and slaughtered horses drips into the evening chill. The blackened Zbrucz roars and twists the foaming knots of its rapids. The bridges are destroyed, and we wade across the river. The majestic moon lies on the waves. The water comes up to the horses' backs, purling streams trickle between hundreds of horses' legs. Someone sinks, and loudly curses the Mother of God. The river is littered with the black squares of the carts and filled with humming, whistling, and singing that thunders above the glistening hollows and the snaking moon.

Late at night we arrive in Novograd. In the quarters to which I am assigned I find a pregnant woman and two red-haired Jews with thin necks, and a third Jew who is sleeping with his face to the wall and a blanket pulled over his head. In my room I find ransacked closets, torn pieces of women's fur coats on the floor, human excrement, and fragments of the holy Seder plate that the Jews use once a year for Passover.

"Clean up this mess!" I tell the woman. "How can you live like this?"

The two Jews get up from their chairs. They hop around on their felt soles and pick up the broken pieces of porcelain from the floor. They hop around in silence, like monkeys, like Japanese acrobats in a circus, their necks swelling and twisting. They spread a ripped eiderdown on the floor for me, and I lie down by the wall, next to the third, sleeping Jew. Timorous poverty descends over my bed.

Everything has been killed by the silence, and only the moon, clasping its round, shining, carefree head in its blue hands, loiters beneath my window.

I rub my numb feet, lie back on the ripped eiderdown, and fall asleep. I dream about the commander of the Sixth Division. He is chasing the brigade commander on his heavy stallion, and shoots two bullets into his eyes. The bullets pierce the brigade commander's head, and his eyes fall to the ground. "Why did you turn back the brigade?" Savitsky, the commander of the Sixth Division, shouts at the wounded man, and I wake up because the pregnant woman is tapping me on the face.

"*Pan*,"* she says to me, "you are shouting in your sleep, and tossing and turning. I'll put your bed in another corner, because you are kicking my papa."

She raises her thin legs and round belly from the floor and pulls the blanket off the sleeping man. An old man is lying there on his back, dead. His gullet has been ripped out, his face hacked in two, and dark blood is clinging to his beard like a clump of lead.

"*Pan*," the Jewess says, shaking out the eiderdown, "the Poles were hacking him to death and he kept begging them, 'Kill me in the backyard so my daughter won't see me die!' But they wouldn't inconvenience themselves. He died in this room, thinking of me. . . . And now I want you to tell me," the woman suddenly said with terrible force, "I want you to tell me where one could find another father like my father in all the world!"

* Polish for "Sir" or "Mr."

THE CHURCH IN NOVOGRAD

*Y*esterday I took a report over to the military commissar who had been billeted to the house of a Catholic priest who had fled. In the kitchen I was met by *Pani** Eliza, the Jesuit's housekeeper. She gave me a cup of amber tea and some sponge cake. Her sponge cakes had the aroma of crucifixion. Within them was the sap of slyness and the fragrant frenzy of the Vatican.

In the church next to the house the bells were howling, tolled by the crazed bell ringer. It was an evening filled with the stars of July. *Pani* Eliza, shaking her attentive gray hair, kept on heaping cookies on my plate, and I delighted in the Jesuitical fare.

The old Polish woman addressed me as "*Pan*," gray old men with ossified ears stood to attention near the door, and somewhere in the serpentine darkness slithered a monk's soutane. The *Pater* had fled, but he had left behind his curate, *Pan* Romuald.

Romuald was a eunuch with a nasal voice and the body of a giant, who addressed us as "Comrade." He ran his yellow finger along the map, circling the areas where the Poles had been defeated. He counted the wounds of his fatherland with rasping ecstasy. May gentle oblivion engulf the memory of Romuald, who betrayed us without pity and was then shot without so much as a second thought. But that evening his tight soutane rustled at all the portieres and swept through all the corridors in a frenzy, as he smiled at everyone who wanted a drink of vodka. That evening the monk's shadow crept behind me

*"Mrs." in Polish.

wherever I went. *Pan* Romuald could have become a bishop if he had not been a spy.

I drank rum with him. The breath of an alien way of life flickered beneath the ruins of the priest's house, and *Pan* Romuald's ingratiating seduction debilitated me. O crucifixes, tiny as the talismans of a courtesan! O parchment of the Papal Bull and satin of women's love letters moldering in blue silken waistcoats!

I can see you now, you deceptive monk with your purple habit, your puffy, swollen hands, and your soul, tender and merciless like a cat's! I can see the wounds of your God, oozing with the seed, the fragrant poison that intoxicates young maidens.

We drank rum, waiting for the military commissar, but he still hadn't come back from headquarters. Romuald had collapsed in a corner and fallen asleep. He slept and quivered, while beyond the window an alley seeped into the garden beneath the black passion of the sky. Thirsting roses swayed in the darkness. Green lightning bolts blazed over the cupolas. A naked corpse lay on the embankment. And the rays of the moon streamed through the dead legs that are pointing upward.

So this is Poland, this is the arrogant grief of the Rzeczpospolita Polska!* A violent intruder, I unroll a louse-ridden straw mattress in this church abandoned by its clergymen, lay under my head a folio in which a Hosanna has been printed for Jozef Pilsudski,[†] the illustrious leader of the Polish nobility.

Hordes of beggars are converging on your ancient towns, O Poland! The song of all the enslaved is thundering above them, and woe unto you, Rzeczpospolita Polska, and woe unto you, Prince Radziwill, and you Prince Sapieha,** who have risen for an hour.

My military commissar has still not returned. I go look for him at the headquarters, the garden, the church. The doors of the church are wide open, I enter, and suddenly come face-to-face with two silver skulls flashing up from the lid of a shattered coffin. Aghast, I stumble

---

* Poland's official name after 1918.

[†] Jozef Klemens Pilsudski, 1867–1935, the first Chief of State of Poland after its independence from Russia in 1918, and commander-in-chief of the Polish army.

** Janusz Radziwill, 1880–1967, politician belonging to an important Polish-Lithuanian princely family; Eustachy Sapieha, 1881–1963, was Polish envoy to London in 1919–20 and Polish Foreign Minister in 1920–21. Later he was a leader of the monarchist movement.

back and fall down into the cellar. The oak staircase leads up to the altar from here, and I see a large number of lights flitting high up, right under the cupola. I see the military commissar, the commander of the special unit, and Cossacks carrying candles. They hear my weak cry and come down to haul me out from the basement.

The skulls turn out to have been carved into the church catafalque and no longer frighten me. I join the others on their search of the premises, because it turned out that *that* was what they were doing in the church, conducting a search, as a large pile of military uniforms had been found in the priest's apartment.*

With wax dripping from our hands, the embroidered gold horse heads on our cuffs glittering, we whisper to one another as we circle with clinking spurs through the echoing building. Virgin Marys, covered with precious stones, watch us with their rosy, mouselike eyes, the flames flicker in our fingers, and rectangular shadows twist over the statues of Saint Peter, Saint Francis, Saint Vincent, and over their crimson cheeks and curly, carmine-painted beards.

We continue circling and searching. We run our fingers over ivory buttons and suddenly icons split open, revealing vaults and caverns blossoming with mold. This church is ancient and filled with secrets. Its lustrous walls hide clandestine passages, niches, and noiseless trapdoors.

You foolish priest, hanging the brassieres of your female parishioners on the nails of the Savior's cross! Behind the holy gates we found a suitcase of gold coins, a morocco-leather sackful of banknotes, and Parisian jewelers' cases filled with emerald rings.

We went and counted the money in the military commissar's room. Columns of gold, carpets of paper money, wind gusts blowing on our candle flames, the raven madness in the eyes of *Pani* Eliza, the thundering laughter of Romuald, and the endless roar of the bells tolled by *Pan* Robacki, the crazed bell ringer.

"I have to get away from here," I said to myself, "away from these winking Madonnas conned by soldiers."

---

* The humorous implication here is that when the narrator first saw the Cossack commanders carrying candles, he had assumed that these hard-line Communist fighters had come to the church to pray.

A LETTER

*H*ere is a letter home dictated to me by Kurdyukov, a boy in our regiment. This letter deserves to be remembered. I wrote it down without embellishing it, and am recording it here word for word as he said it.

Dearest Mama, Evdokiya Fyodorovna,

I hasten in these first lines of my letter to set your mind at rest and to inform you that by the grace of the Lord I am alive and well, and that I hope to hear the same from you. I bow most deepest before you, touching the moist earth with my white forehead. (There follows a list of relatives, godfathers, and godmothers. I am omitting this. Let us proceed to the second paragraph.)

Dearest Mama, Evdokiya Fyodorovna Kurdyukova, I hasten to inform you that I am in Comrade Budyonny's Red Cavalry Regiment, and that my godfather Nikon Vasilich is also here and is at the present time a Red Hero. He took me and put me in his special detachment of the Polit-otdel* in which we hand out books and newspapers to the various positions: the Moscow ZIK *Izvestia*,† the Moscow *Pravda*, and our own merciless newspaper the *Krasny Kavalerist*,** which every fighter on the front wants to read and then

---

* A political organ of the new Soviet government charged with the ideological education of the military during the Russian Civil War and the Russo-Polish War of 1920.

† The newspaper published by the Central Executive Committee, which was the executive branch of the new Bolshevik government.

** *The Red Cavalryman.*

go and heroically hack the damn Poles to pieces, and I am living real marvelous at Nikon Vasilich's.

Dearest Mama, Evdokiya Fyodorovna, send me anything that you possibly in any way can. I beg you to butcher our speckled pig and make a food packet for me, to be sent to Comrade Budyonny's Politotdel unit, addressed to Vasily Kurdyukov. All evenings I go to sleep hungry and bitterly cold without any clothes at all. Write to me a letter about my Stepan—is he alive or not, I beg you to look after him and to write to me about him, is he still scratching himself or has he stopped, but also about the scabs on his forelegs, have you had him shod, or not? I beg you dearest Mama, Evdokiya Fyodorovna, to wash without fail his forelegs with the soap I hid behind the icons, and if Papa has swiped it all then buy some in Krasnodar, and the Lord will smile upon you. I must also describe that the country here is very poor, the muzhiks with their horses hide in the woods from our Red eagles, there's hardly no wheat to be seen, it's all scrawny and we laugh and laugh at it. The people sow rye and they sow oats too. Hops grow on sticks here so they come out very well. They brew home brew with them.

In these second lines of this letter I hasten to write you about Papa, that he hacked my brother Fyodor Timofeyich Kurdyukov to pieces a year ago now. Our Comrade Pavlichenko's Red Brigade attacked the town of Rostov, when there was a betrayal in our ranks. And Papa was with the Whites back then as commander of one of Denikin's companies. All the folks that saw Papa says he was covered in medals like with the old regime. And as we were betrayed, the Whites captured us and threw us all in irons, and Papa caught sight of my brother Fyodor Timofeyich. And Papa began hacking away at Fyodor, saying: you filth you, red dog, son of a bitch, and other things, and hacked away at him until sundown until my brother Fyodor Timofeyich died. I had started writing you a letter then, about how your Fyodor is lying buried without a cross, but Papa caught me and said: you are your mother's bastards, the roots of that whore, I've plowed your mother and I'll keep on plowing her my whole damn life till I don't have a drop of juice left in me, and other things. I had to bear suffering like our Savior Jesus Christ. I managed to run away from Papa in the nick of time and join up with the Reds again, Comrade Pavlichenko's company. And our brigade got the order to go to the town of Voronezh to get more men, and we got more men and horses too, bags, revolvers, and everything we needed.

About Voronezh, beloved Mama Evdokiya Fyodorovna, I can describe that it is indeed a marvelous town, a bit larger I think than Krasnodar, the people in it are very beautiful, the river is brilliant to the point of being able to swim. We were given two pounds of bread a day each, half a pound of meat, and sugar enough so that when you got up you drank sweet tea, and the same in the evenings, forgetting hunger, and for dinner I went to my brother Semyon Timofeyich for blini or goose meat and then lay down to rest. At the time, the whole regiment wanted to have Semyon Timofeyich for a commander because he is a wild one, and that order came from Comrade Budyonny, and Semyon Timofeyich was given two horses, good clothes, a cart specially for rags he's looted, and a Red Flag Medal, and they really looked up to me as I am his brother. Now when some neighbor offends you, then Semyon Timofeyich can completely slash him to pieces. Then we started chasing General Denikin, slashed them down by the thousand and chased them to the Black Sea, but Papa was nowhere to be seen, and Semyon Timofeyich looked for him in all the positions, because he mourned for our brother Fyodor. But only, dearest Mama, since you know Papa and his stubborn character, do you know what he did? He impudently painted his red beard black and was in the town of Maykop in civilian clothes, so that nobody there knew that he is he himself, that very same police constable in the old regime. But truth will always show its head—my godfather Nikon Vasilich saw him by chance in the hut of a townsman, and wrote my brother Semyon Timofeyich a letter. We got on horses and galloped two hundred versts—me, my brother Semyon, and boys which wants to come along from the Cossack village.

And what is it we saw in the town of Maykop? We saw that people away from the front, they don't give a damn about the front, and it's all full of betrayal and Yids like in the old regime. And my brother Semyon Timofeyich in the town of Maykop had a good row with the Yids who would not give Papa up and had thrown him in jail under lock and key, saying that a decree had come not to hack to pieces prisoners, we'll try him ourselves, don't be angry, he'll get what he deserves. But then Semyon Timofeyich spoke and proved that he was the commander of a regiment, and had been given all the medals of the Red Flag by Comrade Budyonny, and threatened to hack to pieces everyone who argued over Papa's person without handing him over, and the boys from the Cossack villages threatened them too. But then, the moment Semyon got hold of Papa, Semyon began whipping him, and lined up all the fighters in the yard as befits military order. And then Semyon splashed water all over Papa's beard and the color flowed from the beard. And Semyon asked our Papa, Timofey Rodyonich, "So, Papa, are you feeling good now that you're in my hands?"

"No," Papa said, "I'm feeling bad."

Then Semyon asked him, "And my brother Fyodor, when you were hacking him to pieces, did he feel good in your hands?"

"No," Papa said, "Fyodor was feeling bad."

Then Semyon asked him, "And did you think, Papa, that someday you might be feeling bad?"

"No," Papa said, "I didn't think that I might be feeling bad."

Then Semyon turned to the people and said, "And I believe, Papa, that if I fell into your hands, I would find no mercy. So now, Papa, we will finish you off!"

Timofey Rodyonich began impudently cursing Semyon, by Mama and the Mother of God, and slapping Semyon in the face, and Semyon sent me out of the yard, so that I cannot, dearest Mama, Evdokiya Fyodorovna, describe to you how they finished off Papa, because I had been sent out of the yard.

After that we stopped at the town of Novorossisk. About that town one can say that there isn't a single bit dry anywhere anymore, just water, the Black Sea, and we stayed there right until May, and then we set off for the Polish Front where we are slapping the Polish masters about in full swing.

I remain your loving son, Vasily Timofeyich Kurdyukov. Mama, look in on Stepan, and the Lord will smile upon you.

This is Kurdyukov's letter, without a single word changed. When I had finished, he took the letter and hid it against the naked flesh of his chest.

"Kurdyukov," I asked the boy, "was your father a bad man?"

"My father was a dog," he answered sullenly.

"And your mother?"

"My mother's good enough. Here's my family, if you want to take a look."

He held out a tattered photograph. In it was Timofey Kurdyukov, a wide-shouldered police constable in a policeman's cap, his beard neatly combed. He was stiff, with wide cheekbones and sparkling, colorless, vacant eyes. Next to him, in a bamboo chair, sat a tiny peasant woman in a loose blouse, with small, bright, timid features. And against this provincial photographer's pitiful backdrop, with its flowers and doves, towered two boys, amazingly big, blunt, broad-faced, goggle-eyed, and frozen as if standing at attention: the Kurdyukov brothers, Fyodor and Semyon.

THE RESERVE CAVALRY
COMMANDER

A wail spreads over the village. The cavalry is trampling the grain and trading in horses. The cavalrymen are exchanging their worn-out nags for the peasants' workhorses. One can't argue with what the cavalrymen are doing—without horses there can be no army.

But this isn't much of a comfort to the peasants. They are stubbornly gathering outside the headquarters, dragging behind them struggling old nags tottering with weakness. The muzhiks' breadwinners have been taken away from them, and with a surge of bitter valor, aware that this valor will not last long, they hurry to rant despairingly at the authorities, at God, and at their bitter lot.

Chief of Staff Z.* is standing on the front porch in full uniform. His inflamed eyelids half closed, he listens to the muzhiks' complaints with evident attention. But his attention is only a ploy. Like all disciplined and weary bureaucrats, he has a knack for shutting down all cerebral activity during empty moments of existence. During these moments of blissful empty-headedness our chief of staff recharges his worn-out instrument.

And this is what he is doing this time too, with the muzhiks.

To the soothing accompaniment of their desperate and disjointed clamor, Chief of Staff Z. cautiously follows his brain's soft wisps, those precursors of clear and energetic thought. He waits for the necessary pause, grasps the final muzhik sob, yells in a commanderial fashion, and returns to his office to work.

* Konstantin Karlovich Zholnarkevich, the staff commander in the *1920 Diary*.

But on this particular occasion even yelling would not have been necessary. Galloping up to the porch on an Anglo-Arabian steed came Dyakov,* a former circus rider and now commander of the Reserve Cavalry—red-faced with a gray mustache, a black cape, and wide red Tatar trousers with silver stripes.

"The Father Superior's blessing on all the honest filth of the earth!" he shouted, reining in his horse in front of the porch, and at that very instant a shabby little horse that had been given in exchange by the Cossacks collapsed in front of him.

"There, you see, Comrade Commander!" a muzhik shouted, slapping his thighs in despair. "There you have what your people are giving our people! Did you see what they've given us? And we're supposed to farm with that?"

"For this horse," Dyakov proclaimed distinctly and momentously, "for this horse, my highly esteemed friend, you have every right to request fifteen thousand rubles from the Reserve Cavalry, and if this horse were a trifle livelier, you, my dearest of friends, would be entitled to twenty thousand rubles. Just because a horse falls does not mean it's *factual*! If a horse falls but then gets up—that is a horse. If, to invert what I am saying, the horse does not get up—then that is not a horse. But I do believe I can make this lively little mare spring to her feet again!"

"Lord in Heaven and Mother of God!" the muzhik cried, throwing his hands up in the air. "How is this poor thing supposed to get up? It's on its last legs!"

"You are insulting this horse, my dear fellow!" Dyakov answered with fierce conviction. "Pure blasphemy, my dear fellow!" And he deftly swung his athlete's body out of his saddle. Splendid and deft as if in the circus ring, he stretched his magnificent legs, his trousers girded by cords around the knees, and walked up to the dying animal. She peered at him dolefully with a severe, penetrating eye, licked some invisible command from his crimson palm, and immediately the feeble mare felt bracing power flow from this sprightly, gray, blossoming Romeo. Her muzzle lolling, her legs skidding under her, feeling the whip tickling her stomach with imperious impatience, the mare slowly and deliber-

* For Dyakov, see *1920 Diary*, entries 7/13/20, and 7/16/20.

ately rose onto her legs. And then we all saw Dyakov's slender hand with its fluttering sleeve run through her dirty mane, and his whining whip swatting her bleeding flanks. Her whole body shivering, the mare stood on all four legs without moving her timid, doglike, lovestruck eyes from Dyakov.

"So you see—this is a horse," Dyakov said to the muzhik, and added softly, "and you were complaining, my dearest of friends!"

Throwing his reins to his orderly, the commander of the Reserve Cavalry jumped the four stairs in a single leap and, swirling off his operatic cloak, disappeared into the headquarters.

PAN APOLEK

he wise and wonderful life of *Pan* Apolek went straight to my head, like an exquisite wine. Among the huddling ruins of Novograd-Volynsk, a town crushed in haste, fate threw at my feet a gospel that had remained hidden from the world. There, surrounded by the guileless shine of halos, I took a solemn oath to follow the example of *Pan* Apolek. The sweetness of dreamy malice, the bitter contempt for the swine and dogs among men, the flame of silent and intoxicating revenge—I sacrificed them all to this oath.

* * *

An icon was hanging high on the wall in the home of the Novograd priest, who had fled. It bore the inscription: "The Death of John the Baptist." There was no doubt about it: in the portrayal of John I saw a man I had seen somewhere before.

I remember the gossamer stillness of a summer morning hung on the bright, straight walls. The sun had cast a ray straight on the foot of the icon. Sparkling dust swarmed in it. The tall figure of John came straight at me from the blue depths of the niche. A black cape hung triumphantly on that inexorable, repulsively thin body. Droplets of blood shone in the cape's round buckles. His head had been hacked diagonally off the flayed neck. It lay on an earthen platter that was held by the large yellow fingers of a warrior. The face of the dead man seemed familiar. I was touched by a mysterious premonition. The hacked-off head on the earthen platter was modeled after *Pan* Romuald, the curate of the priest who had fled. Out of his snarling mouth curled the tiny body of a snake, its scales shining brightly. Its head, a tender pink, was bristling with life, and stood out powerfully against the deep background of the cape.

I was amazed at the painter's artistry, his dark inventiveness. I was even more amazed the following day when I saw the red-cheeked Virgin Mary hanging above the matrimonial bed of *Pani* Eliza, the old priest's housekeeper. Both paintings bore the marks of the same brush. The meaty face of the Virgin Mary was a portrait of *Pani* Eliza. And this is where I found the key to the mystery of the Novograd icons. And the key led me to *Pani* Eliza's kitchen, where on fragrant evenings the shadows of old servile Poland gather, with the holy fool of a painter at their center. But was *Pan* Apolek a holy fool, peopling the local villages with angels, and elevating lame Janek, the Jewish convert, to sainthood?

Pan Apolek had come here thirty years ago on a summer day like any other with blind Gottfried. The two friends, Apolek and Gottfried, had gone to Shmerel's tavern on the Rovno high road, two versts from the edge of the town. In his right hand Apolek was holding a box of paints, and with his left hand leading the blind concertina player. The melodious tread of their reinforced German boots echoed with calmness and hope. A canary-yellow scarf hung from Apolek's thin neck, and three chocolate-brown feathers swung on the blind man's Tyrolean hat.

The newcomers had placed the paints and the concertina on a windowsill in the tavern. The artist unwound his scarf, which was neverending, like a fairground magician's ribbon. Then he went out into the yard, took off all his clothes, and poured freezing water over his thin, feeble, pink body. Shmerel's wife brought them raisin vodka and a bowl of meat cutlets stuffed with rice. Gottfried ate his fill, and then placed his concertina on his bony knees. He sighed, threw his head back, and flexed his thin fingers. The chords of the Heidelberg songs echoed against the walls of the Jewish tavern. With his scratchy voice Apolek accompanied the blind man. It was as if the organ had been brought from the Church of Saint Indegilda to Shmerel's tavern and the muses, with their quilted scarves and reinforced German boots, had seated themselves in a row upon this organ.

The two men sang till sunset, then they put the concertina and the paints into canvas sacks. *Pan* Apolek bowed deeply and gave Brayna, the taverner's wife, a sheet of paper.

"My dear *Pani* Brayna," he said. "Please accept from the hands of a wandering artist, upon whom the Christian name of Apollinarius has been bestowed, this portrait as a sign of our most humble gratitude for your sumptuous hospitality. If the Lord Jesus Christ sees fit to lengthen my days and give strength to my art, I will come back and add color to this portrait. There shall be pearls in your hair and a necklace of emeralds upon your breast."

Drawn on a small sheet of paper with a red pencil, a pencil red and soft like clay, was *Pani* Brayna's laughing face, surrounded by a mass of copper curls.

"My money!" Shmerel shouted when he saw his wife's portrait. He grabbed a stick and started running after the two men. But as he ran, Shmerel remembered Apolek's pink body with water splashing all over it, the sun in his little courtyard, and the soft sound of the concertina. The taverner's soul drooped, and, putting the stick down, he went back home.

The following morning, Apolek showed the priest of Novograd his diploma from the Munich Academy, and laid out before him twelve paintings with biblical motifs. They had been painted with oil on boards of thin cypress wood. On his table the *Pater* saw the burning purple of cloaks, the emerald sparkle of fields, and blossoming blankets of flowers flung over the plains of Palestine.

Pan Apolek's saints, a multitude of simple, jubilating elders with gray beards and red faces, were encircled by streams of silk and potent evening skies.

That same day, *Pan* Apolek was commissioned to do paintings for the new church. And over Benedictine wine, the *Pater* said to the artist: "Sancta Maria! My dear *Pan* Apollinarius, from what wondrous realms has your joyous grace descended upon us?"

Apolek worked with great zeal, and within a month the new church was filled with the bleating of herds, the dusty gold of setting suns, and straw-colored cow udders. Buffaloes with worn hides struggled under their yokes, dogs with pink muzzles trotted in front of the large flocks of sheep, and plump infants rocked in cradles that hung from the trunks of tall palm trees. The tattered brown habits of

Franciscan monks crowded around a cradle. The group of wise men stood out with their shining bald heads and their wrinkles red like wounds. The small, wrinkled old face of Pope Leo XIII twinkled with its fox-like smile from the group of wise men, and even the priest of Novograd was there, running the fingers of one hand through the carved beads of a Chinese rosary while with his other, free hand, he blessed the infant Jesus.

For five months Apolek inched along the walls, the cupola, and the choir stalls, fastened to the wooden scaffolding.

"You have a predilection for familiar faces, my dear *Pan* Apolek," the priest once said, recognizing himself among the wise men and *Pan* Romuald in the severed head of John the Baptist. The old *Pater* smiled, and sent a tumbler of cognac up to the artist working beneath the cupola.

Apolek finished the Last Supper and the Stoning of Mary Magdalene. Then one Sunday he unveiled the walls. The distinguished citizens the priest had invited recognized Janek the lame convert in the Apostle Paul, and in Mary Magdalene Elka, a Jewish girl of unknown parentage and mother of many of the urchins roaming the streets. The distinguished citizens demanded that the blasphemous images be painted over. The priest showered threats over the blasphemer, but Apolek refused to paint over the walls.

And so an unprecedented war broke out, with the powerful body of the Catholic Church on one side, and the unconcerned icon painter on the other. The war lasted for three decades. The situation almost turned the gentle idler into the founder of a new heresy; in which case he would have been the most whimsical and ludicrous fighter among the many in the slippery and stormy history of the Church of Rome, a fighter roaming the earth in blessed tipsiness with two white mice under his shirt and with a collection of the finest little brushes in his pocket.

"Fifteen zloty for the Virgin Mary, twenty-five zloty for the Holy Family, and fifty zloty for the Last Supper portraying all the client's family. The client's enemy can be portrayed as Judas Iscariot, for which an extra ten zloty will be added to the bill," *Pan* Apolek informed the peasants after he had been thrown out of the Novograd church.

There was no shortage of commissions. And when a year later the archbishop of Zhitomir sent a delegation in response to the frenzied epistles of the Novograd priest, they found the monstrous family portraits, sacrilegious, naive, and flamboyant, in the most impoverished, foul-smelling hovels. Josephs with gray hair neatly parted in the middle, pomaded Jesuses, many-childed village Marys with parted knees. The pictures hung in the icon corners, wreathed with garlands of paper flowers.

"He has bestowed sainthood upon you people during your lifetime!" the bishop of Dubno and Novokonstantinov shouted at the crowd that had come to defend Apolek. "He has endowed you with the ineffable attributes of the saints, you, thrice fallen into the sin of disobedience, furtive moonshiners, ruthless moneylenders, makers of counterfeit weights, and sellers of your daughters' innocence!"

"Your holiness!" lame-footed Witold, the town's cemetery watchman and procurer of stolen goods, then said to the bishop. "Where does our all-forgiving Lord God see truth, and who will explain it to these ignorant villagers? Is there not more truth in the paintings of *Pan* Apolek, who raises our pride, than in your words that are filled with abuse and tyrannical anger?"

The shouts of the crowd sent the bishop running. The agitation in the villages threatened the safety of the clerics. The painter who had taken Apolek's place could not work up the courage to paint over Elka and lame Janek. They can still be seen today above a side altar of the Novograd church: Janek, as Saint Paul, a timorous cripple with the shaggy black beard of a village apostate, and Elka as the whore from Magdala, decrepit and crazed, with dancing body and fallen cheeks.

The battle with the priest lasted three decades. Then the Cossack flood chased the old monk out of his aromatic stone nest, and Apolek— O fickle fortune!—settled into *Pani* Eliza's kitchen. And here I am, a passing guest, imbibing the wine of his conversation in the evenings.

What do we converse about? About the romantic days of the Polish nobility, the fanatical frenzy of women, the art of Luca della Robbia,* and the family of the Bethlehem carpenter.

"There is something I have to tell you, Mr. Clerk," Apolek tells me secretively before supper.

---

* Luca della Robbia, 1399–1482, Florentine sculptor.

"Yes," I answer. "Go ahead, Apolek, I'm listening."

But *Pan* Robacki, the lay brother of the church—stern, gray, bony, and with large ears—is sitting too close. He unfolds a faded screen of silence and animosity before us.

"I have to tell you, *Pan,*" Apolek whispers, taking me aside, "that Jesus Christ, the son of Mary, was married to Deborah, a Jerusalem girl of low birth—"

"*O, ten czlowiek!*"* *Pan* Robacki shouts in despair. "This man not dies in his bed! This man the peoples will be killing!"

"After supper," Apolek murmurs in a gloomy voice. "After supper, if that will suit you, Mr. Clerk."

It suits me. Inflamed by the beginning of Apolek's story, I pace up and down the kitchen waiting for the appointed time. And outside the window night stands like a black column. Outside the window the bristling, dark garden has fallen still. The road to the church flows beneath the moon in a sparkling, milky stream. The earth is covered with a dismal sheen, a necklace of shining berries is draped over the bushes. The aroma of lilacs is clean and strong as alcohol. The seething oily breath of the stove drinks in this fresh poison, killing the stuffy resinous heat of the spruce wood lying about the kitchen floor.

Apolek is wearing a pink bow tie and threadbare pink trousers, and is puttering about in his corner like a friendly graceful animal. His table is smeared with glue and paint. He is working in quick small movements. A hushed, melodic drumming comes drifting from his corner: it is old Gottfried tapping with his trembling fingers. The blind man is sitting rigidly in the greasy yellow lamplight. His bald head is drooping as he listens to the incessant music of his blindness and the muttering of Apolek, his eternal friend.

". . . And what the priests and the Evangelist Mark and the Evangelist Matthew are telling you, *Pan* Clerk, is not truth. But truth can be revealed to you, *Pan,* for I am prepared for fifty marks to paint your portrait in the form of Saint Francis on a background of green and sky. He was a very simple saint, *Pan* Francis was. And if you have a bride in Russia, *Pan* Clerk, women love Saint Francis, although not all women, *Pan.*"

And from his spruce-wood-scented corner he began telling me the

* Polish: "Oh, this man!"

tale of the marriage of Jesus to Deborah. According to Apolek, Deborah already had a bridegroom, a young Israelite who traded in ivory. But Deborah's wedding night ended in bewilderment and tears. The woman was grabbed by fear when she saw her husband approach her bed. Hiccups bulged in her throat and she vomited all the food she had eaten at the wedding table. Shame fell upon Deborah, on her father, her mother, and on all her kin. The bridegroom abandoned her with words of ridicule, and called all the guests together. And Jesus, filled with pity at seeing the anguish of the woman who was thirsting for her husband but also fearing him, donned the robes of the newlywed man and united himself with Deborah as she lay in her vomit. Afterward she went out to the wedding guests, loudly exulting like a woman proud of her fall. And only Jesus stood to the side. His body was drenched with mortal sweat, for the bee of sorrow had stung his heart. He left the banquet hall unnoticed, and went into the desert east of Judea, where John the Baptist awaited him. And Deborah gave birth to her first son. . . ."

"So where is that son?" I yelled.

"The priests have hidden him," Apolek said with gravity, raising his thin, cold finger to his drunkard's nose.

"*Pan* Artist!" Robacki suddenly shouted, stepping out of the shadows, his gray ears quaking. "What you saying? But this is outrage!"

"*Tak, tak,*" Apolek said, cringing and grabbing hold of Gottfried. "*Tak, tak, panie.*"*

Apolek pulled the blind man toward the door, but stopped by the doorpost and beckoned me with his finger.

"Saint Francis with a bird on your sleeve," he whispered, winking at me. "A dove or a goldfinch, you can choose, *Pan* Clerk!"

And he disappeared with his blind eternal friend.

"Oh, what foolishness!" Robacki, the church lay brother, said. "This man not dies in his bed!"

Pan Robacki opened his mouth wide and yawned like a cat. I wished him a good night, and went home, to my plundered Jews, to sleep.

The vagrant moon trailed through the town and I tagged along, nurturing within me unfulfillable dreams and dissonant songs.

---

* Polish: "Yes, yes, gentlemen."

ITALIAN SUN

*Y*esterday I was sitting once more under a heated garland of green spruce twigs in *Pani* Eliza's servants' quarters. I sat by the warm, lively, crackling stove, and then returned to my lodgings late at night. Below, in the ravine, the silent Zbrucz rolled its glassy, dark waves.

The burned-out town—broken columns and the hooks of evil old women's fingers dug into the earth—seemed to me raised into the air, comfortable and unreal like a dream. The naked shine of the moon poured over the town with unquenchable strength. The damp mold of the ruins blossomed like a marble bench on the opera stage. And I waited with anxious soul for Romeo to descend from the clouds, a satin Romeo singing of love, while backstage a dejected electrician waits with his finger on the button to turn off the moon.

Blue roads flowed past me like rivulets of milk trickling from many breasts. On my way back, I had been dreading running into Sidorov, with whom I shared my room, and who at night brought his hairy paw of dejection down upon me. That night, luckily, harrowed by the milk of the moon, Sidorov did not say a single word to me. I found him writing, surrounded by books. On the table a hunchbacked candle was smoking—the sinister bonfire of dreamers. I sat to the side, dozed, dreams pouncing around me like kittens. And it wasn't until late that night that I was awakened by an orderly who had come to take Sidorov to headquarters. They left together. I immediately hurried over to the table where Sidorov had been writing, and leafed through his books.

There was an Italian primer, a print of the Roman Forum, and a street map of Rome. The map was completely marked up with crosses. I leaned over the sheet of paper covered with writing and, with clenched fingers and an expiring heart, read another man's letter. Sidorov, the dejected murderer, tore the pink cotton wool of my imagination to shreds and dragged me into the halls of his judicious insanity. I began reading on the second page, as I did not dare look for the first one:

· · ·

. . . shot through the lungs, and am a little off my head, or, as Sergey always says, flying mad. Well, when you go mad, idiotically mad, you don't go, you fly. Anyway, let's put the horsetail to one side and the jokes to the other. Back to the events of the day, Victoria, my dear friend.

I took part in a three-month Makhno campaign*—the whole thing a grueling swindle, nothing more! Only Volin is still there. Volin is wearing apostolic raiment and clamoring to be the Lenin of anarchism. Terrible. And Makhno listens to him, runs his fingers through his dusty wire curls, and lets the snake of his peasant grin slither across his rotten teeth. And I'm not all that sure anymore if there isn't a seed of anarchy in all this, and if we won't wipe your prosperous noses for you, you self-proclaimed Tsekists from your self-proclaimed Tsekhs,† "made in Kharkov," your self-proclaimed capital.** Your strapping heroes prefer not to remember the sins of their anarchist youth, and now laugh at them from the heights of their governmental wisdom! To hell with them!

Then I ended up in Moscow. How did I end up in Moscow? The boys had treated someone unjustly, something to do with requisitions or something. Well, fool that I am, I defended him. So they let me have it, and rightly so. My wound was not even worth mentioning, but in Moscow, O Victoria, in Moscow I was struck dumb by the misery all around. Every day the hospital nurses would bring me a nibble of kasha. Bridled with reverence, they brought it in on a large tray, and I despised this shock-brigade kasha, this unregimented

---

* Nestor Ivanovich Makhno, 1889–1934, the Ukrainian anarchist leader.

† A pun: the Tsekists are members of the Tseka, the Central Committee of the Bolshevik Party. A "tsekh," however, is a simple guild.

** Today, Kharkiv, a city in northeastern Ukraine. The "self-proclaimed" capital in the sense that Kharkiv replaced Kiev as the capital of the Ukrainian S.S.R from 1917 until 1934.

treatment in regimented Moscow. Then, in the Soviet Council, I ran into a handful of anarchists. All fops and dithering old men! I managed to get all the way to the Kremlin with my plan for some real work. But they patted me on the back and promised to give me a nice deputy position if I changed my ways. I did not change my ways. And what came next? Next came the front, the Red Cavalry, and the damn soldiers stinking of blood and corpses.

Save me, Victoria! Governmental wisdom is driving me insane, boredom is inebriating me. If you won't help me I will die like a dog without a five-year plan! And who wants a worker to die unplanned? Surely not you, Victoria, my bride who will never be my wife. See, I'm becoming maudlin again, damn it to hell!

But let's get to the point now. The army bores me. I cannot ride because of my wound, which means I cannot fight. Use your connections, Victoria, have them send me to Italy! I am studying the language, and I'll be speaking it within two months. The land down there is smoldering, things there are almost ready. All they need is a few shots. One of these shots I shall fire. It is high time that their King be sent to join his ancestors. That is very important. He is a nice old fellow who plays for popularity and has himself photographed with the tamer socialists for family magazines.

But don't say anything about shots or kings at the Tseka or the People's Commissariat for Foreign Affairs. They will pat you on the head and coo: "What a romantic he is!" Just tell them plain and simple: "He's sick, he's angry, he's drunk with depression, he wants some Italian sun and he wants some bananas! Does he deserve it, or doesn't he? He'll recuperate, and *basta*! And if not, then send him to the Odessa Cheka.* They're very sensible there!"

The things I am writing you are so foolish, so unfairly foolish, Victoria, my dear friend.

Italy has seeped into my heart like an obsession. Thinking about that country that I have never seen is as sweet to me as a woman's name, as your name, Victoria. . . .

I read the letter through and then went to lie down on my dirty, crumpled bed, but sleep would not come. On the other side of the wall the pregnant Jewess was crying heartfelt tears, her lanky husband

---

* The Odessa branch of the "Extraordinary Commission" set up in 1917 to investigate counterrevolutionary activities. The Cheka later became the KGB.

answering with mumbling groans. They were lamenting the things that had been stolen, and blaming each other for their bad luck. Then, before daybreak, Sidorov came back. The dwindling candle was expiring on the table. He pulled another candle end out of his boot and pressed it with unusual pensiveness onto the drowned wick. Our room was dark, gloomy, everything in it breathed a damp, nocturnal stench, and only the window, lit up by the fire of the moon, shone like salvation.

He came over, my agonizing neighbor, and hid the letter. Bending forward, he sat down at the table and opened the picture album of Rome. The magnificent book with its gilt-edged pages stood opposite his expressionless, olive-green face. The jagged ruins of the Capitol and the Coliseum, lit by the setting sun, glittered over his hunched back. The photograph of the royal family was also there. He had inserted it between the large, glossy pages. On a piece of paper torn from a calendar was the picture of the pleasant, frail King Victor Emmanuel with his black-haired wife, Crown Prince Umberto, and a whole brood of princesses.

It is night, a night full of distant and painful sounds, with a square of light in the damp darkness, and in this square is Sidorov's deathly face, a lifeless mask hovering over the yellow flame of the candle.

GEDALI

On the eve of the Sabbath I am always tormented by the dense sorrow of memory. In the past on these evenings, my grandfather's yellow beard caressed the volumes of Ibn Ezra. My old grandmother, in her lace bonnet, waved spells over the Sabbath candle with her gnarled fingers, and sobbed sweetly. On those evenings my child's heart was gently rocked, like a little boat on enchanted waves.

I wander through Zhitomir looking for the timid star.* Beside the ancient synagogue, beside its indifferent yellow walls, old Jews, Jews with the beards of prophets, passionate rags hanging from their sunken chests, are selling chalk, bluing, and candle wicks.

Here before me lies the bazaar, and the death of the bazaar. Slaughtered is the fat soul of abundance. Mute padlocks hang on the stores, and the granite of the streets is as clean as a corpse's bald head. The timid star blinks and expires.

Success came to me later, I found the star just before the setting of the sun. Gedali's store lay hidden among the tightly shut market stalls. Dickens, where was your shadow that evening?† In this old junk store you would have found gilded slippers and ship's ropes, an antique compass and a stuffed eagle, a Winchester hunting rifle with the date "1810" engraved on it, and a broken stewpot.

Old Gedali is circling around his treasures in the rosy emptiness of

* The Star of David.
† A reference to Charles Dickens's novel *The Old Curiosity Shop*.

the evening, a small shopkeeper with smoky spectacles and a green coat that reaches all the way to the ground. He rubs his small white hands, tugs at his gray beard, lowers his head, and listens to invisible voices that come wafting to him.

This store is like the box of an intent and inquisitive little boy who will one day become a professor of botany. This store has everything from buttons to dead butterflies, and its little owner is called Gedali. Everyone has left the bazaar, but Gedali has remained. He roams through his labyrinth of globes, skulls, and dead flowers, waving his cockerel-feather duster, swishing away the dust from the dead flowers.

We sit down on some empty beer barrels. Gedali winds and unwinds his narrow beard. His top hat rocks above us like a little black tower. Warm air flows past us. The sky changes color—tender blood pouring from an overturned bottle—and a gentle aroma of decay envelops me.

"So let's say we say 'yes' to the Revolution. But does that mean that we're supposed to say 'no' to the Sabbath?" Gedali begins, enmeshing me in the silken cords of his smoky eyes. "Yes to the Revolution! Yes! But the Revolution keeps hiding from Gedali and sending gunfire ahead of itself."

"The sun cannot enter eyes that are squeezed shut," I say to the old man, "but we shall rip open those closed eyes!"

"The Pole has closed my eyes," the old man whispers almost inaudibly. "The Pole, that evil dog! He grabs the Jew and rips out his beard, *oy*, the hound! But now they are beating him, the evil dog! This is marvelous, this is the Revolution! But then the same man who beat the Pole says to me, 'Gedali, we are requisitioning your gramophone!' 'But gentlemen,' I tell the Revolution, 'I love music!' And what does the Revolution answer me? 'You don't know what you love, Gedali! I am going to shoot you, and then you'll know, and I cannot *not* shoot, because I am the Revolution!'"

"The Revolution cannot *not* shoot, Gedali," I tell the old man, "because it is the Revolution."

"But my dear *Pan*! The Pole did shoot, because he is the counter-revolution. And you shoot because you are the Revolution. But Revolution is happiness. And happiness does not like orphans in its house. A good man does good deeds. The Revolution is the good deed done by good men. But good men do not kill. Hence the Revolution is done by bad men. But the Poles are also bad men. Who is going to tell Gedali which is the Revolution and which the counterrevolution? I have studied the Talmud. I love the commentaries of Rashi and the books of Maimonides. And there are also other people in Zhitomir who understand. And so all of us learned men fall to the floor and shout with a single voice, 'Woe unto us, where is the sweet Revolution?' "

The old man fell silent. And we saw the first star breaking through and meandering along the Milky Way.

"The Sabbath is beginning," Gedali pronounced solemnly. "Jews must go to the synagogue."

"*Pan* Comrade," he said, getting up, his top hat swaying on his head like a little black tower. "Bring a few good men to Zhitomir. *Oy*, they are lacking in our town, *oy*, how they are lacking! Bring good men and we shall give them all our gramophones. We are not simpletons. The International,* we know what the International is. And I want the International of good people, I want every soul to be accounted for and given first-class rations. Here, soul, eat, go ahead, go and find happiness in your life. The International, *Pan* Comrade, you have no idea how to swallow it!"

"With gunpowder," I tell the old man, "and seasoned with the best blood."

And then from the blue darkness young Sabbath climbed onto her throne.

"Gedali," I say to him, "today is Friday, and night has already fallen. Where can I find some Jewish biscuits, a Jewish glass of tea, and a piece of that retired God in the glass of tea?"

"You can't," Gedali answers, hanging a lock on his box, "you can't find any. There's a tavern next door, and good people used to run it, but people don't eat there anymore, they weep."

He fastened the three bone buttons of his green coat. He dusted himself with the cockerel feathers, sprinkled a little water on the soft palms of his hands, and walked off, tiny, lonely, dreamy, with his black top hat, and a large prayer book under his arm.

The Sabbath begins. Gedali, the founder of an unattainable International, went to the synagogue to pray.

* The Third Communist International, 1919–1943, an organization founded in Moscow by the delegates of twelve countries to promote Communism worldwide.

MY FIRST GOOSE

*S*avitsky, the commander of the Sixth Division, rose when he saw me, and I was taken aback by the beauty of his gigantic body. He rose—his breeches purple, his crimson cap cocked to the side, his medals pinned to his chest—splitting the hut in two like a banner splitting the sky. He smelled of perfume and the nauseating coolness of soap. His long legs looked like two girls wedged to their shoulders in riding boots.

He smiled at me, smacked the table with his whip, and picked up the order which the chief of staff had just dictated. It was an order for Ivan Chesnokov to advance to Chugunov-Dobryvodka with the regiment he had been entrusted with, and, on encountering the enemy, to proceed immediately with its destruction.

"... the destruction of which," Savitsky began writing, filling the whole sheet, "I hold the selfsame Chesnokov completely responsible for. Noncompliance will incur the severest punitive measures, in other words I will gun him down on the spot, a fact that I am sure that you, Comrade Chesnokov, will not doubt, as it's been quite a while now that you have worked with me on the front. . . ."

The commander of the Sixth Division signed the order with a flourish, threw it at the orderlies, and turned his gray eyes, dancing with merriment, toward me.

I handed him the document concerning my assignment to the divisional staff.

"See to the paperwork!" the division commander said. "See to the paperwork, and have this man sign up for all the amusements except for those of the frontal kind.* Can you read and write?"

"Yes, I can," I answered, bristling with envy at the steel and bloom of his youth. "I graduated in law from the University of Petersburg."

"So you're one of those little powder puffs!" he yelled, laughing. "With spectacles on your nose! Ha, you lousy little fellow, you! They send you to us, no one even asks us if we want you here! Here you get hacked to pieces just for wearing glasses! So, you think you can live with us, huh?"

"Yes, I do," I answered, and went to the village with the quartermaster to look for a place to stay.

The quartermaster carried my little suitcase on his shoulder. The village street lay before us, and the dying sun in the sky, round and yellow as a pumpkin, breathed its last rosy breath.

We came to a hut with garlands painted on it. The quartermaster stopped, and suddenly, smiling guiltily, said, "You see we have a thing about spectacles here, there ain't nothing you can do! A man of high distinguishings they'll chew up and spit out—but ruin a lady, yes, the most cleanest lady, and you're the darling of the fighters!"

He hesitated for a moment, my suitcase still on his shoulder, came up very close to me, but suddenly lunged away in despair, rushing into the nearest courtyard. Cossacks were sitting there on bundles of hay, shaving each other.

"Fighters!" the quartermaster began, putting my suitcase on the ground. "According to an order issued by Comrade Savitsky, you are required to accept this man to lodge among you. And no funny business, please, because this man has suffered on the fields of learning!"

The quartermaster flushed and marched off without looking back. I lifted my hand to my cap and saluted the Cossacks. A young fellow with long, flaxen hair and a wonderful Ryazan face walked up to my suitcase and threw it out into the street. Then he turned his backside toward me, and with uncommon dexterity began emitting shameless sounds.

"That was a zero-zero caliber!" an older Cossack yelled, laughing out loud. "Rapid-fire!"

* The division commander is punning, substituting the word *udovolstvie,* "amusements," for *prodovolstvie,* "provisions."

The young man walked off, having exhausted the limited resources of his artistry. I went down on my hands and knees and gathered up the manuscripts and the old, tattered clothes that had fallen out of my suitcase. I took them and carried them to the other end of the yard. A large pot of boiling pork stood on some bricks in front of the hut. Smoke rose from it as distant smoke rises from the village hut of one's childhood, mixing hunger with intense loneliness inside me. I covered my broken little suitcase with hay, turning it into a pillow, and lay down on the ground to read Lenin's speech at the Second Congress of the Comintern,* which *Pravda* had printed. The sun fell on me through the jagged hills, the Cossacks kept stepping over my legs, the young fellow incessantly made fun of me, the beloved sentences struggled toward me over thorny paths, but could not reach me. I put away the newspaper and went to the mistress of the house, who was spinning yarn on the porch.

"Mistress," I said, "I need some grub!"

The old woman raised the dripping whites of her half-blind eyes to me and lowered them again.

"Comrade," she said, after a short silence. "All of this makes me want to hang myself!"

"Goddammit!" I muttered in frustration, shoving her back with my hand. "I'm in no mood to start debating with you!"

And, turning around, I saw someone's saber lying nearby. A haughty goose was waddling through the yard, placidly grooming its feathers. I caught the goose and forced it to the ground, its head cracking beneath my boot, cracking and bleeding. Its white neck lay stretched out in the dung, and the wings folded down over the slaughtered bird.

"Goddammit!" I said, poking at the goose with the saber. "Roast it for me, mistress!"

The old woman, her blindness and her spectacles flashing, picked up the bird, wrapped it in her apron, and hauled it to the kitchen.

"Comrade," she said after a short silence. "This makes me want to hang myself." And she pulled the door shut behind her.

---

* The Third Communist International, 1919–1943, an organization founded in Moscow by the delegates of twelve countries to promote Communism worldwide.

In the yard the Cossacks were already sitting around their pot. They sat motionless, straight-backed like heathen priests, not once having looked at the goose.

"This fellow'll fit in here well enough," one of them said, winked, and scooped up some cabbage soup with his spoon.

The Cossacks began eating with the restrained grace of muzhiks who respect one another. I cleaned the saber with sand, went out of the courtyard, and came back again, feeling anguished. The moon hung over the yard like a cheap earring.

"Hey, brother!" Surovkov, the oldest of the Cossacks, suddenly said to me. "Sit with us and have some of this till your goose is ready!"

He fished an extra spoon out of his boot and handed it to me. We slurped the cabbage soup and ate the pork.

"So, what are they writing in the newspaper?" the young fellow with the flaxen hair asked me, and moved aside to make room for me.

"In the newspaper, Lenin writes," I said, picking up my *Pravda*, "Lenin writes that right now there is a shortage of everything."

And in a loud voice, like a triumphant deaf man, I read Lenin's speech to the Cossacks.

The evening wrapped me in the soothing dampness of her twilight sheets, the evening placed her motherly palms on my burning brow.

I read, and rejoiced, waiting for the effect, rejoicing in the mysterious curve of Lenin's straight line.

"Truth tickles all and sundry in the nose,"* Surovkov said when I had finished. "It isn't all that easy to wheedle it out of the pile of rubbish, but Lenin picks it up right away, like a hen pecks up a grain of corn."

That is what Surovkov, the squadron commander, said about Lenin, and then we went to sleep in the hayloft. Six of us slept there warming each other, our legs tangled, under the holes in the roof which let in the stars.

I dreamed and saw women in my dreams, and only my heart, crimson with murder, screeched and bled.

---

* A pun on "truth," *Pravda*, which is also the name of the Russian daily that the narrator is reading to the Cossacks.

THE RABBI

"All things are mortal. Only a mother is accorded eternal life. And when a mother is not among the living, she leaves behind a memory that no one has yet dared to defile. The memory of a mother nourishes compassion within us, just as the ocean, the boundless ocean, nourishes the rivers that cut through the universe."

These were Gedali's words. He uttered them gravely. The dying evening wrapped him in the rosy haze of its sadness.

"In the ardent house of Hasidism," the old man said, "the windows and doors have been torn out, but it is as immortal as a mother's soul. Even with blinded eyes, Hasidism still stands at the crossroads of the winds of history."

That is what Gedali said, and, after having prayed in the synagogue, he took me to Rabbi Motale, the last rabbi of the Chernobyl dynasty.

Gedali and I walked up the main street. White churches glittered in the distance like fields of buckwheat. A gun cart moaned around the corner. Two pregnant Ukrainian women came out through the gates of a house, their coin necklaces jingling, and sat down on a bench. A timid star flashed in the orange battles of the sunset, and peace, a Sabbath peace, descended on the slanted roofs of the Zhitomir ghetto.

"Here," Gedali whispered, pointing at a long house with a shattered facade.

We went into a room, a stone room, empty as a morgue. Rabbi Motale sat at a table surrounded by liars and men possessed. He was wearing a sable hat and a white robe, with a rope for a belt. The rabbi was sitting, his eyes closed, his thin fingers digging through the yellow fluff of his beard.

"Where have you come from, Jew?" he asked me, lifting his eyelids.

"From Odessa," I answered.

"A devout town," the rabbi said. "The star of our exile, the reluctant well of our afflictions! What is the Jew's trade?"

"I am putting the adventures of Hershele of Ostropol* into verse."

"A great task," the rabbi whispered, and closed his eyelids. "The jackal moans when it is hungry, every fool has foolishness enough for despondency, and only the sage shreds the veil of existence with laughter . . . What did the Jew study?"

"The Bible."

"What is the Jew looking for?"

"Merriment."

"Reb Mordkhe," the rabbi said, and shook his beard. "Let the young man seat himself at the table, let him eat on the Sabbath evening with other Jews, let him rejoice that he is alive and not dead, let him clap his hands as his neighbors dance, let him drink wine if he is given wine!"

And Reb Mordkhe came bouncing toward me, an ancient fool with inflamed eyelids, a hunchbacked little old man, no bigger than a ten-year-old boy.

"*Oy,* my dear and so very young man!" ragged Reb Mordkhe said, winking at me. "*Oy,* how many rich fools have I known in Odessa, how many wise paupers have I known in Odessa! Sit down at the table, young man, and drink the wine that you will not be given!"

We all sat down, one next to the other—the possessed, the liars, the unhinged. In the corner, broad-shouldered Jews who looked like fishermen and apostles were moaning over prayer books. Gedali in his green coat dozed by the wall like a bright bird. And suddenly I saw a youth behind Gedali, a youth with the face of Spinoza, with the powerful forehead of Spinoza, with the sickly face of a nun. He was smoking and twitching like an escaped convict who has been tracked down and brought back to his jail. Ragged Reb Mordkhe sneaked up on him

---

* In Yiddish folklore, a trickster.

from behind, snatched the cigarette from his mouth, and came running over to me.

"That is Ilya, the rabbi's son," Mordkhe wheezed, turning the bloody flesh of his inflamed eyelids to me, "the damned son, the worst son, the disobedient son!"

And Mordkhe threatened the youth with his little fist and spat in his face.

"Blessed is the Lord," the voice of Rabbi Motale Bratslavsky rang out, and he broke the bread with his monastic fingers. "Blessed is the God of Israel, who has chosen us among all the peoples of the world."

The rabbi blessed the food, and we sat down at the table. Outside the window horses neighed and Cossacks shouted. The wasteland of war yawned outside. The rabbi's son smoked one cigarette after another during the silent prayer. When the dinner was over, I was the first to rise.

"My dear and so very young man," Mordkhe muttered behind me, tugging at my belt. "If there was no one in the world except for evil rich men and destitute tramps, how would holy men live?"

I gave the old man some money and went out into the street. Gedali and I parted, and I went back to the railroad station. There at the station, on the propaganda train of the First Cavalry, I was greeted by the sparkle of hundreds of lights, the enchanted glitter of the radio transmitter, the stubborn rolling of the printing presses, and my unfinished article for the *Krasny Kavalerist.**

* The newspaper *The Red Cavalryman.*

THE ROAD TO BRODY

I mourn for the bees. They have been destroyed by warring armies. There are no longer any bees in Volhynia.

We desecrated the hives. We fumigated them with sulfur and detonated them with gunpowder. Smoldering rags have spread a foul stench over the holy republics of the bees. Dying, they flew slowly, their buzzing barely audible. Deprived of bread, we procured honey with our sabers. There are no longer any bees in Volhynia.

The chronicle of our everyday crimes oppresses me as relentlessly as a bad heart. Yesterday was the first day of the battle for Brody. Lost on the blue earth, we suspected nothing—neither I, nor my friend Afonka Bida. The horses had been fed grain in the morning. The rye stood tall, the sun was beautiful, and our souls, which did not deserve these shining, soaring skies, thirsted for lingering pain.

"In our Cossack villages the womenfolk tell tales of the bee and its kind nature," my friend began. "The womenfolk tell all sorts of things. If men wronged Christ, or if no wrong was done, other people will have to figure out for themselves. But if you listen to what the womenfolk of the Cossack villages tell, Christ is hanging tormented on the cross, when suddenly all kinds of gnats come flying over to plague him! And he takes a good look at the gnats and his spirits fall. But the thousands of little gnats can't see his eyes. At that moment a bee flies around Christ. 'Sting him!' a gnat yells at the bee. 'Sting him for us!'—'That I cannot do,' the bee says, covering Christ with her wings. 'That I cannot do, he belongs to the carpenter class.' One has to understand the bees," Afonka, my platoon commander, concluded. "I hope the bees hold out. We're fighting for them too!"

Afonka waved dismissively and started to sing. It was a song about a light bay stallion. Eight Cossacks in Afonka's platoon joined in the song.

The light bay stallion, Dzhigit was his name, belonged to a junior Cossack captain who got drunk on vodka the day of his beheading, sang Afonka sleepily, his voice taut like a string. Dzhigit had been a loyal horse, but on feast days the Cossack's carousing knew no bounds. He had five jugs of vodka on the day of his beheading. After the fourth jug, the junior Cossack captain mounted his steed and rode up to heaven. The climb was long, but Dzhigit was a true horse. They rode into heaven, and the Cossack reached for his fifth jug. But the last jug had been left back on earth. He broke down and wept, for all his efforts had been in vain. He wept, and Dzhigit pointed his ears, and turned to look at his master. Afonka sang, clinking and dozing.

The song drifted like smoke. We rode toward the sunset, its boiling rivers pouring over the embroidered napkins of the peasants' fields. The silence turned rosy. The earth lay like a cat's back, covered with a thick, gleaming coat of grain. The mud hamlet of Klekotov crouched on a little hill. Beyond the pass, the vision of deadly, craggy Brody awaited us. But in Klekotov a loud shot exploded in our faces. Two Polish soldiers peered out from behind a hut. Their horses were tied to a post. A light enemy battery came riding up the hill. Bullets unfurled like string along the road.

"Run for it!" Afonka yelled.

And we fled.

Brody! The mummies of your trampled passions have breathed their irresistible poison upon me. I had felt the fatal chill of your eye sockets filled with frozen tears. And now, in a tumbling gallop, I am being carried away from the smashed stones of your synagogues. . . .

THE *TACHANKA** THEORY

*H*eadquarters sent me a coachman, or, as we generally say here, a vehicular driver. His name is Grishchuk. He is thirty-nine years old.

He had spent five years in a German prison camp, escaped a few months ago, walked across Lithuania and northwest Russia, reached Volhynia, only, in Byelov, to fall into the hands of what must be the world's most brainless draft commission, which reconscripted him into active service. He had been a mere fifty versts from his home in the Kremenec District. He has a wife and children in the Kremenec District. He hasn't been home for five years and two months. The Draft Commission made him my vehicular driver, and now I am no longer a pariah among the Cossacks.

I have a *tachanka* and a driver for it. *Tachanka!* That word has become the base of the triangle on which our way of fighting rests: hack to pieces—*tachanka*—blood.

The simplest little open carriage, the *britzka*, the kind you would see some cleric or petty official riding in, has, through a whim of all the civil strife, become a terrible and fast-moving war machine, creating new strategies and tactics, twisting the traditional face of war, spawning *tachanka* heroes and geniuses. Such was Makhno,[†] who had made the *tachanka* the crux of his secretive and cunning strategy, abolishing infantry, artillery, even cavalry, and replaced that clumsy hodgepodge by

---

* An open carriage or buggy with a machine gun mounted on the back.

[†] The Ukrainian anarchist leader.

mounting three hundred machine guns onto *britzkas*. Such was Makhno, as innovative as nature: hay carts lined up in military formation to conquer towns. A wedding procession rolls up to the headquarters of a provincial executive committee, opens fire, and a frail little cleric, waving the black flag of anarchy, demands that the authorities immediately hand over the bourgeois, hand over the proletariat, hand over music and wine.

An army of *tachankas* is capable of unprecedented mobility.

Budyonny was just as adept at demonstrating this as Makhno was. To hack away at such an army is difficult, to corner it impossible. A machine gun buried under a stack of hay, a *tachanka* hidden in a peasant's shed, cease to be military targets. These hidden specks—the hypothetically existing but imperceptible components of a whole—when added up result in the new essence of the Ukrainian village: savage, rebellious, and self-seeking. Makhno can bring an army like this, its ammunition concealed in all its nooks and crannies, into military readiness within an hour, and can demobilize it even faster.

Here, in Budyonny's Red Cavalry, the *tachanka* does not rule so exclusively. But all our machine gun detachments travel only in *britzkas*. Cossack fantasy distinguishes two kinds of *tachanka*, "German settler" and "petty official," which is not fantasy but a real distinction.

The petty official *britzkas*, those rickety little carts built without love or imagination, had rattled through the wheat steppes of Kuban carrying the wretched, red-nosed civil servants, a sleep-starved herd of men hurrying to autopsies and inquests, while the settler *tachankas* came to us from the fat German settlements of the Volga regions of Samara and the Urals. The broad oaken seat backs of the settler *tachankas* are covered with simple paintings, plump garlands of rosy German flowers. The sturdy cart decks are reinforced with steel. The frame rests on soft, unforgettable springs. I can feel the ardor of many generations in these springs, now bouncing over the torn-up high roads of Volhynia.

I am experiencing the delight of first possession. Every day after we eat, we put on the harnesses. Grishchuk leads the horses out of the stable. They are becoming stronger with every passing day. With proud joy I notice a dull sheen on their groomed flanks. We rub the horses' swollen legs, trim their manes, throw Cossack harnesses—a tangled, withered mesh of thin straps—over their backs, and drive out of the yard at a fast trot. Grishchuk is sitting sideways on the box. My seat is covered with a bright sackcloth and hay smelling of perfume and tranquillity. The high wheels creak in the white, granular sand. Patches of blooming poppies color the earth, ruined churches glow on the hills. High above the road, in a niche wrecked by shells, stands the brown statue of Saint Ursula with bare round arms. And narrow, ancient letters form an uneven chain on the blackened gold of her pediment: "Glory Be to Jesus and the Mother of God."

Lifeless Jewish shtetls cluster around the foot of the Polish nobles' estates. The prophetic peacock, a passionless apparition in the blue vastness, glitters on brick walls. The synagogue, enmeshed in a tangle of huts, crouches eyeless and battered, round as a Hasidic hat, on the barren earth. Narrow-shouldered Jews hover sadly at crossroads. And the image of southern Jews flares up in my memory—jovial, potbellied, sparkling like cheap wine. There is no comparison between them and the bitter aloofness of these long bony backs, these tragic yellow beards. In their fervent features, carved by torture, there is no fat or warm pulse of blood. The movements of the Galician and the Volhynian Jew are abrupt, brusque, and offensive to good taste, but the power of their grief is filled with dark grandeur, and their secret contempt for the Polish masters is boundless. Looking at them, I understood the fiery history of these faraway hinterlands, the stories of Talmudists who leased out taverns, of rabbis who dabbled in moneylending, of girls who were raped by Polish mercenaries and for whom Polish magnates shot themselves.

DOLGUSHOV'S DEATH

The veils of battle swept toward the town. At midday, Korotchaev, the disgraced commander of the Fourth Division, who fought alone and rode out seeking death, flew past us in his black Caucasian cloak. As he came galloping by, he shouted over to me, "Our communications have been cut, Radzivillov and Brody are in flames!"

And off he charged—fluttering, black, with eyes of coal.

On the plain, flat as a board, the brigades were regrouping. The sun rolled through the crimson dust. Wounded men sat in ditches, eating. Nurses lay on the grass and sang in hushed voices. Afonka's scouts roamed over the field, looking for dead soldiers and ammunition. Afonka rode by two paces from me and, without turning his head, said, "We got a real kick in the teeth! Big time! They're saying things about our division commander—it looks like he's out. Our fighters don't know what's what!"

The Poles had advanced to the forest about three versts away from us, and set up their machine guns somewhere nearby. Flying bullets whimper and yelp; their lament has reached an unbearable pitch. The bullets plunge into the earth and writhe, quaking with impatience. Vytyagaichenko, the commander of the regiment, snoring in the hot sun, cried out in his sleep and woke up. He mounted his horse and rode over to the lead squadron. His face was creased with red stripes from his uncomfortable sleep, and his pockets were filled with plums.

"Son of a bitch!" he said angrily, spitting out a plum stone. "A damn waste of time! Timoshka, hoist the flag!"

"Oh, so we're going for it?" Timoshka asked, pulling the flagpole out of the stirrup, and unrolling the flag on which a star had been painted, along with something about the Third International.*

"We'll see what happens," Vytyagaichenko said, and suddenly shouted wildly, "Come on, girls, onto your horses! Gather your men, squadron leaders!"

The buglers sounded the alarm. The squadrons lined up in a column. A wounded man crawled out of a ditch and, shading his eyes with his hand, said to Vytyagaichenko, "Taras Grigorevich, I represent the others here. It looks like you're leaving us behind."

"Don't worry, you'll manage to fight them off," Vytyagaichenko muttered, and reared his horse.

"We sort of think we won't be able to fight them off, Taras Grigorevich," the wounded man called after Vytyagaichenko as he rode off.

Vytyagaichenko turned back his horse. "Stop whimpering! Of course I won't leave you!" And he ordered the carts to be harnessed.

At that very moment the whining, high-pitched voice of my friend Afonka Bida burst out, "Let's not set off at full trot, Taras Grigorevich! It's five versts. How are we supposed to hack them down if our horses are worn out? Why the rush? You'll be there in time for the pear pruning on St. Mary's Day!"

"Slow trot!" Vytyagaichenko ordered, without raising his eyes.

The regiment rode off.

"If what they're saying about the division commander is true," Afonka whispered, reining in his horse, "and they're getting rid of him, well then thank you very much—we might as well kill off the cattle and burn down the barn!"

Tears flowed from his eyes. I looked at him in amazement. He spun like a top, held his cap down, wheezed, and then charged off with a loud whoop.

Grishchuk, with his ridiculous *tachanka*,† and I stayed behind, rushing back and forth among walls of fire until the evening. Our divisional staff had disappeared. Other units wouldn't take us in. The reg-

* The Third Communist International, 1919–1943, an organization founded in Moscow by the delegates of twelve countries to promote Communism worldwide.

† An open carriage or buggy with a machine gun mounted on the back.

iments pushed forward into Brody but were repelled. We rode to the town cemetery. A Polish patrol jumped up from behind the graves, put their rifles to their shoulders, and started firing at us. Grishchuk spun his *tachanka* around. It shrieked with all its four wheels.

"Grishchuk!" I yelled through the whistling and the wind.

"What damn stupidity!" he shouted back morosely.

"We're done for!" I hollered, seized by the exhilaration of disaster. "We're finished!"

"All the trouble our womenfolk go to!" he said even more morosely. "What's the point of all the matchmaking, marrying, and in-laws dancing at weddings?"

A rosy tail lit up in the sky and expired. The Milky Way surfaced from under the stars.

"It makes me want to laugh!" Grishchuk said sadly, and pointed his whip at a man sitting at the side of the road. "It makes me want to laugh that women go to such trouble!"

The man sitting by the roadside was Dolgushov, one of the telephonists. He stared at us, his legs stretched out in front of him.

"Here, look," Dolgushov said, as we pulled up to him. "I'm finished . . . know what I mean?"

"I know," Grishchuk answered, reining in the horses.

"You'll have to waste a bullet on me," Dolgushov said.

He was sitting propped up against a tree. He lay with his legs splayed far apart, his boots pointing in opposite directions. Without lowering his eyes from me, he carefully lifted his shirt. His stomach was torn open, his intestines spilling to his knees, and we could see his heart beating.

"When the Poles turn up, they'll have fun kicking me around. Here's my papers. Write my mother where, what, why."

"No," I replied, and spurred my horse.

Dolgushov placed his blue palms on the ground and looked at his hands in disbelief.

"Running away?" he muttered, slumping down. "Then run, you bastard!"

Sweat slithered over my body. The machine guns hammered faster and faster with hysterical tenacity. Afonka Bida came galloping toward us, encircled by the halo of the sunset.

"We're kicking their asses!" he shouted merrily. "What're you up to here, fun and games?"

I pointed at Dolgushov and moved my horse to the side.

They spoke a few words, I couldn't hear what they said. Dolgushov held out his papers. Afonka slipped them into his boot and shot Dolgushov in the mouth.

"Afonka," I said, riding up to him with a pitiful smile. "*I couldn't have done that.*"

"Get lost, or I'll shoot you!" he said to me, his face turning white. "You spectacled idiots have as much pity for us as a cat has for a mouse!"

And he cocked his trigger.

I rode off slowly, without looking back, a feeling of cold and death in my spine.

"Hey! Hey!" Grishchuk shouted behind me, and grabbed Afonka's hand. "Cut the crap!"

"You damn lackey bastard!" Afonka yelled at Grishchuk. "Wait till I get my hands on him!"

Grishchuk caught up with me at the bend in the road. Afonka was not with him. He had ridden off in the opposite direction.

"Well, there you have it, Grishchuk," I said to him. "Today I lost Afonka, my first real friend."

Grishchuk took out a wrinkled apple from under the cart seat.

"Eat it," he told me, "please, eat it."

THE COMMANDER OF
THE SECOND BRIGADE

*G*eneral Budyonny, in his red trousers with the silver stripes, stood by a tree. The commander of the Second Brigade had just been killed. The general had appointed Kolesnikov to replace him.

Only an hour ago, Kolesnikov had been a regimental captain. A week ago Kolesnikov had been a squadron leader.

The new brigade commander was summoned to General Budyonny. The general waited for him, standing by the tree. Kolesnikov came with Almazov, his commissar.

"The bastards are closing in on us," the general said with his dazzling grin. "We win, or we die like dogs. No other options. Understood?"

"Understood," Kolesnikov answered, his eyes bulging from their sockets.

"You run for it, I'll have you shot," the general said with a smile, and he turned and looked at the commander of the special unit.

"Yes, General!" the commander of the special unit said.

"So start rolling, Koleso!"* one of the Cossacks standing nearby shouted cheerfully.

Budyonny swiftly turned on his heel and saluted his new brigade commander. The latter lifted five young red fingers to his cap, broke into a sweat, and walked along the plowed field. The horses were waiting for him fifty yards away. He hung his head, placing one long and

---

*A pun: Koleso, short for Kolesnikov, means "wheel."

crooked leg in front of the other with agonizing slowness. The fire of the sunset swept over him, as crimson and implausible as impending doom.

And suddenly, on the outstretched earth, on the yellow, harrowed nakedness of the fields, we saw nothing but Kolesnikov's narrow back, his dangling arms, and his hanging head with its gray cap.

His orderly brought him his horse.

He jumped into the saddle and galloped to his brigade without looking back. The squadrons were waiting for him on the main road, the high road to Brody.

A moaning hurrah, shredded by the wind, drifted over to us.

Aiming my binoculars, I saw the brigade commander on his horse circling through columns of thick dust.

"Kolesnikov has taken over the brigade," said our lookout, who was sitting in a tree above our heads.

"So he has," Budyonny answered, lighting a cigarette and closing his eyes.

The hurrahs faded. The cannonade died down. Pointless shrapnel burst above the forest. And we heard the great, silent skirmish.

"He's a good boy," Budyonny said, getting up. "Wants honors. Looks like he'll make it." And Budyonny had the horses brought over, and rode off to the battlefield. His Staff followed him.

As it happened, I was to see Kolesnikov again that very night, about an hour after the Poles had been finished off. He was riding in front of his brigade, alone, on a brown stallion, dozing. His right arm was hanging in a sling. A cavalry Cossack was carrying the unfurled flag about ten paces behind him. The men at the head of the squadron lazily sang bawdy ditties. The brigade stretched dusty and endless, like peasant carts heading to a market fair. At the rear, tired bands were gasping.

That evening, as Kolesnikov rode, I saw in his bearing the despotic indifference of a Tatar khan and saw in him a devotee of the glorified Kniga, the willful Pavlichenko, and the captivating Savitsky.

SASHKA CHRIST

*S*ashka, that was his real name, and Christ is what we called him because he was so gentle. He had been one of the shepherds of his Cossack village and had not done any heavy work since he was fourteen, when he had caught the evil disease.

This is what had happened. Tarakanich, Sashka's stepfather, had gone to the town of Grozny for the winter, and had joined a guild there. The guild was working well—it was made up of Ryazan muzhiks. Tarakanich did carpentry for them, and his income increased. When he realized that he could not manage the work alone anymore, he sent home for the boy to come and be his assistant—the village could survive the winter well enough without him. Sashka worked with his stepfather for a week. Then Saturday came, and they put their tools away and sat down to drink some tea. Outside it was October, but the air was mild. They opened the window, and put on a second samovar. A beggar woman was loitering near the windows. She knocked on the frame and said, "A good day to you! I see you're not from these parts. You can see what state I'm in, no?"

"What is it about your state?" Tarakanich said. "Come in, you old cripple!"

The beggar woman scrambled up and clambered into the room. She came over to the table and bowed deeply. Tarakanich grabbed her by her kerchief, pulled it off, and ruffled her hair. The beggar woman's hair was gray, ashy, and hanging in dusty tatters.

"Ooh, will you stop that, you naughty handsome man you!" she said. "You're a joke a minute, you are! But please, don't be disgusted by me just because I'm a little old woman," she quickly whispered, scampering onto the bench.

Tarakanich lay with her. The beggar woman turned her head to the side and laughed.

"Ooh, luck is raining on this little old woman's field!" she laughed. "I'll be harvesting two hundred *pood* of grain an acre!"

And she suddenly noticed Sashka, who was drinking his tea at the table, not looking up as if his life depended on it.

"Your boy?" she asked Tarakanich.

"More or less mine," Tarakanich answered. "My wife's."

"Ooh, look at him staring at us," the old woman said. "Hey, come over here!"

Sashka went over to her—and he caught the evil disease. But the evil disease had been the last thing on their minds. Tarakanich gave the beggar woman some leftover bones and a silver fiver, a very shiny one.

"Polish the fiver nicely with sand, holy sister," Tarakanich said to her, "and it'll look even better. If you lend it to the Almighty on a dark night, it will shine instead of the moon."

The old cripple tied her kerchief, took the bones, and left. And within two weeks the muzhiks realized what had happened. The evil disease made them suffer. They tried to cure themselves all winter long, dousing themselves with herbs. And in spring they returned to the Cossack village and their peasant work.

The village was about nine versts from the railroad. Tarakanich and Sashka crossed the fields. The earth lay in its April wetness. Emeralds glittered in the black ditches. Green shoots hemmed the soil with cunning stitches. A sour odor rose from the ground, as from a soldier's wife at dawn. The first herds trickled down from the hills, the foals played in the blue expanse of the horizon.

Tarakanich and Sashka walked along barely visible paths.

"Let me be one of the shepherds, Tarakanich," Sashka said.

"What for?"

"I can't bear that the shepherds have such a wonderful life."

"I won't allow it."

"Let me be one, Tarakanich, for the love of God!" Sashka repeated. "All the saints came from shepherds."

"Sashka the Saint!" the stepfather laughed. "He caught syphilis from the Mother of God!"

They passed the bend in the road by Red Bridge, then the grove and the pasture, and saw the cross on the village church.

The women were still puttering around in their vegetable gardens, and Cossacks were sitting among the lilacs, drinking vodka and singing. It was another half verst to Tarakanich's hut.

"Let us pray that everything is fine," Tarakanich said, crossing himself.

They walked over to the hut and peeked in the little window. Nobody was there. Sashka's mother was in the shed milking the cow. They crept over to her silently. Tarakanich came up behind her and laughed out loud.

"Motya, Your Excellency," he shouted, "how about some food for your guests!"

The woman turned around, began to shake, and rushed out of the shed and ran circling around the yard. Then she came back into the shed and, trembling, pressed her head on Tarakanich's chest.

"How silly and ugly you look," Tarakanich said, gently pushing her away. "Where are the children?"

"The children have left the yard," the woman said, her face ashen, and ran out again, throwing herself onto the ground.

"Oh, Aleshonka!" she shrieked wildly. "Our babies have gone, feet first!"

Tarakanich waved at her dismissively and went over to the neighbors. The neighbors told him that a week ago the Lord had taken the boy and the girl with typhus. Motya had written him a letter, but he probably hadn't gotten it. Tarakanich went back to the hut. The woman was stoking the oven.

"You got rid of them quite nicely, Motya," Tarakanich said. "Rip you to pieces, that's what I should do!"

He sat down at the table and fell into deep grief—and grieved till he fell asleep. He ate meat and drank vodka, and did not see to his work around the farm. He snored at the table, woke up, and snored again. Motya prepared a bed for herself and her husband, and another for Sashka to the side. She blew out the light, and lay down next to her husband. Sashka tossed and turned on the hay in his corner. His eyes were open, he did not sleep, but saw, as if in a dream, the hut, a star shining through the window, the edge of the table, and the horse collars under his mother's bed. A violent vision took hold of him; he surrendered to it and rejoiced in his waking dream. It was as if two silver strings hung from the sky, entwined into a thick rope to which a cradle was fastened, a rosewood cradle with carvings. It swung high above the earth but far from the sky, and the silver rope swayed and glittered. Sashka was lying in this cradle, fanned by the air. The air, loud as music, rose from the fields, and the rainbow blossomed above the unripe wheat.

Sashka rejoiced in his waking sleep, and closed his eyes so as not to see the horse collars under his mother's bed. Then he heard panting from the bed, and thought that Tarakanich must be pawing his mother.

"Tarakanich," he said loudly. "There's something I need to talk to you about."

"In the middle of the night?" Tarakanich yelled angrily. "Sleep, you fleabag!"

"I swear by the Holy Cross that there's something I need to talk to you about," Sashka said. "Come out into the yard!"

And in the yard, beneath the unfading stars, Sashka said to his stepfather, "Don't wrong my mother, Tarakanich, you're tainted."

"You should know better than to cross me, boy!" Tarakanich said.

"I know, but have you seen my mother's body? She has legs that are clean, and a breast that is clean. Don't wrong her, Tarakanich. We're tainted."

"Boy!" his stepfather said. "Avoid my blood and my wrath! Here are twenty kopeks, go to sleep and your head will be clearer in the morning."

"I don't need the twenty kopeks," Sashka muttered. "Let me go join the shepherds."

"I won't allow that," Tarakanich said.

"Let me join the shepherds," Sashka muttered, "or I'll tell Mother what we are. Why should she suffer with such a body?"

Tarakanich turned around and went into the shed to get an axe.

"Saint Sashka," he said in a whisper, "you wait and see, I'll hack you to pieces!"

"You'd hack me to pieces on account of a woman?" the boy said, barely audibly, and leaned closer to his stepfather. "Take pity on me and let me join the shepherds."

"Damn you!" Tarakanich said, and threw away the axe. "So go join the shepherds!"

And Tarakanich went back into the hut and slept with his wife.

That same morning Sashka went to the Cossacks to be hired, and from that day on he lived as a village shepherd. He became known throughout the whole area for his simple heart, and the people of the village gave him the nickname Sashka Christ, and he lived as a shepherd until he was drafted. The old men, who had nothing better to do, came out to the pasture to chat with him, and the women came running to Sashka for respite from their husbands' rough ways, and were not put off by Sashka's love for them or by his illness. Sashka's draft call came in the first year of the war. He fought for four years, and then returned to the village, where the Whites were running the show. Sashka was urged to go to the village of Platovskaya, where a detachment was being formed to fight the Whites. A former cavalry sergeant-major—Semyon Mikhailovich Budyonny—was running things in that detachment, and he had his three brothers with him: Emelian, Lukian, and Denis. Sashka went to Platovskaya, and there his fate was sealed. He joined Budyonny's regiment, his brigade, his division, and finally his First Cavalry Army. He rode to the aid of heroic Tsaritsyn,[*] joined with Voroshilov's Tenth Army, and fought at Voronezh, Kastornaya, and at the Generalsky Bridge on the Donets. In the Polish Campaign, Sashka joined the cavalry transport unit, because he had been wounded and was considered an invalid.

So that's how everything had come about. I had recently met Sashka Christ, and took my little suitcase and moved over to his cart. Many times we watched the sunrise and rode into the sunset. And whenever the obdurate will of war brought us together, we sat in the evenings on a sparkling earth mound,[†] or boiled tea in our sooty kettle in the woods, or slept next to each other on harvested fields, our hungry horses tied to our legs.

---

[*] Renamed Stalingrad in 1925 in honor of Joseph Stalin, who had played a major role in the defense of the city against General Denikin's White Russian Army. Today Volgograd.

[†] *Zavalinka:* a mound of earth around a Russian peasant hut that protects it from the weather and is often used for sitting outside.

THE LIFE OF MATVEY RODIONOVICH PAVLICHENKO

*D*ear comrades, brothers, fellow countrymen! Hear in the name of mankind the life story of Red General Matvey Pavlichenko. This general had been a mere swineherd, a swineherd on the estate of Lidino of which Nikitinsky was master, and, until life gave him battle stripes, this swineherd tended his master's pigs, and then with those battle stripes our little Matvey was given cattle to herd. Who knows— had he been born in Australia, my friends, our Matvey, son of Rodion, might well have worked his way up to elephants, yes, our Matyushka would have herded elephants, but unfortunately there are no elephants to be found in our district of Stavropol. To be perfectly honest, there is no animal larger than a buffalo in all the lands of Stavropol. And the poor fellow would not have had any fun with buffaloes—Russians don't enjoy taunting buffaloes. Give us poor orphans a mare on Judgment Day, and I guarantee you we will know how to taunt her till her soul goes tearing out of her sides.

So here I am, herding my cattle, cows crowding me from all sides, I'm doused in milk, I stink like a slit udder, all around me calves and mouse-gray bullocks roam. Freedom lies all around me in the fields, the grass of all the world rustles, the skies above me open up like a many-buttoned concertina, and the skies, my brothers, the skies we have in the district of Stavropol, can be very blue. So there I am, herding the beasts and playing my flute to the winds with nothing better to do, when an old man comes up to me and tells me, "Go, Matvey," he says to me, "go to Nastya."

"What for?" I ask him. "Or are you maybe pulling my leg, old man?"

"Go to her," he says. "She wants you."

So I go to her.

"Nastya!" I say to her, and all my blood runs dark. "Nastya," I say to her, "or are you making fun of me?"

But she does not speak a word, runs straight past me, running as fast as her legs can carry her, and she and I run together until we're out on the meadow, dead tired, flushed, and out of breath.

"Matvey," Nastya says to me at this point. "On the third Sunday before this one, when the spring fishing season began and the fishermen came back to shore, you were walking with them, and you let your head hang. Why did you let your head hang, or is it that a thought is squeezing down on your heart? Answer me!"

And I answer her.

"Nastya," I say to her. "I have nothing to tell you, my head is not a gun, it has neither a fore-sight nor back-sight, and you know my heart full well, Nastya, it is empty, completely empty, except perhaps for being doused in milk—it's a terrible thing how I stink of milk!"

And I can see that Nastya is about to burst into laughter at my words.

"I swear by the Holy Cross," she says, bursting into laughter, laughing loudly, laughing with all her might, her laughter booming across the steppes as if she were pounding a drum, "I swear by the Holy Cross, you sure know how to sweet-talk a girl!"

So we exchange a few foolish words, and soon enough we're married. Nastya and me began living together as best we could, and we did our best. We felt hot all night, we felt hot all winter, all night we went naked and tore the hide off each other. We lived it up like devils, until the day the old man came to me again.

"Matvey," he says. "The other day the master touched your wife in all those places, and the master is going to have her."

And I say to him, "No," I say to him, "it cannot be, and please excuse me, old man, or I shall kill you right here and now."

The old man rushed off without another word, and I must have marched a good twenty versts over land that day, yes, that day a good chunk of earth passed beneath my feet, and by evening I sprouted up in the estate of Lidino, in the house of my merry master Nikitinsky. The old man was sitting in his drawing room busy taking apart three saddles, an English, a dragoon, and a Cossack saddle, and I stood rooted by his door like a burdock, I stood rooted there for a good hour. Then he finally clapped eyes on me.

"What do you want?"

"I want to quit."

"You have a grudge against me?"

"I don't have a grudge, but I want to quit."

At this point he turned his eyes away, leaving the high road for the field path, put the red saddlecloths on the floor—they were redder than the Czar's banners, his saddlecloths were—and old Nikitinsky stepped on them, puffing himself up.

"Freedom to the free," he tells me, all puffed up. "Your mothers, all Orthodox Christian women, I gave the lot of them a good plowing! You can quit, my dear little Matvey, but isn't there one tiny little thing you owe me first?"

"Ho, ho!" I answer. "What a joker! May the Lord strike me dead if you're not a joker! It is *you* who still owes *me* my wage!"

"Your wage!" my master thunders, shoving me down onto my knees, kicking me and yelling in my ear, cursing the Father, the Son, and the Holy Ghost. "You want your wage, but the bull's yoke you ruined seems to have slipped your mind! Where is my bull's yoke? Give me back my bull's yoke!"

"I will give you back your bull's yoke," I tell my master, raising my foolish eyes up at him as I kneel there, lower than the lowest of living creatures. "I'll give you back your bull's yoke, but don't strangle me with debts, master, just wait awhile!"

So, my dear friends, my Stavropol compatriots, fellow countrymen, my comrades, my very own brothers: for five years the master waited with my debts, five years I lost, until, lost soul that I was, finally the year '18 came!* It rode in on merry stallions, on Kabardinian steeds! It brought big armies with it and many songs. O, my sweet year '18! O, for us to dance in each other's arms just one more time, my sweet darling year '18! We sang your songs, drank your wine, proclaimed your

*1918, the year following the Bolshevik Revolution.

truth, but all that's left of you now is a few scribblers! Yet, ah, my love, it was not the scribblers back then who came flying through Kuban, shooting the souls of generals to Kingdom Come! No! It was me, Matvey Rodionovich, who lay outside Prikumsk in a pool of my own blood, and from where I, Matvey Rodionovich, lay to the estate of Lidino was a mere five versts. And I rode to Lidino alone, without my regiment, and as I entered the drawing room, I entered peacefully. People from the local authorities were sitting there in the drawing room, Nikitinsky was serving them tea, groveling all over them. When he saw me his face tumbled to pieces, but I lifted my fur hat to him.

"Greetings," I said to the people there. "Greetings. May I come in, your lordship, or how shall we handle this?"

"Let's handle this nicely, correctly," one of the men says, who, judging by the way he speaks, must be a land surveyor. "Let us handle things nicely, correctly, but from what I see, Comrade Pavlichenko, it seems you have ridden quite a distance, and dirt has crossed your face from side to side. We, the local authorities, are frightened of such faces. Why is your face like that?"

"Because you are the local cold-blooded authorities," I answer. "Because in my face one cheek has been burning for five years now, burning when I'm in a trench, burning when I'm with a woman, and it will be burning at my final judgment! At my final judgment!" I tell him, and look at Nikitinsky with fake cheerfulness. But he no longer has any eyes—there are now two cannonballs in the middle of his face, ready and in position under his forehead, and with these crystal balls he winks at me, also with fake cheerfulness, but so abominably.

"My dear Matyusha," he says to me, "we've known each other so long now, and my wife Nadyezhda Vasilevna, whose mind has come unhinged on account of the times we're living in, she was always kind to you, Nadyezhda Vasilevna was, and you, my dear Matyusha, always looked up to her above all others! Wouldn't you like to at least see her, even though her mind has come unhinged?"

"Fine," I tell him, and follow him into another room, and there he started clasping my hands, the right one, then the left.

"Matyusha!" he says. "Are you my fate or are you not?"

"No," I tell him. "And stop using such words! God has dropped us lackeys and run. Our fate is a chicken with its head cut off, our life is not worth a kopeck! Stop using such words and let me read you Lenin's letter!"

"Lenin wrote me, Nikitinsky, a letter?"

"Yes, he wrote you a letter," I tell him, and take out the book of decrees, open it to an empty page, and read—though I'm illiterate to the bottom of my soul. "In the name of the people," I read, "for the establishment of a future radiant life, I order Pavlichenko—Matvey Rodionovich—to deprive, at his discretion, various persons of their lives."

"There we are," I tell him. "That is Lenin's letter to you!"

And he says to me, "No!"

"No," he says, "my dear Matyusha, even if life has gone tumbling to the devil, and blood has become cheap in Holy Mother Russia! But regardless of how much blood you want, you'll get it anyway, and you'll even forget my last dying look, so wouldn't it be better if I just show you my secret hideaway?"

"Show me," I tell him. "Maybe it'll be for the better."

And again we went through the rooms, climbed down into the wine cellar, where he pulled out a brick, and behind this brick lay a little case. In it, in this case, were rings, necklaces, medals, and a pearl-studded icon. He threw the case over to me and stood there rigidly.

"Take it!" he says. "Take what is most holy to the Nikitinskys, and go off to your den in Prikumsk!"

And here I grabbed him by the neck, by the hair.

"And what about my cheek?" I tell Nikitinsky. "How am I supposed to live with my cheek this way?"

And he burst out laughing for all he was worth, and stopped struggling to get away.

"A jackal's conscience," he says, and does not struggle. "I speak to you as to an officer of the Russian Empire, and you, you scum, were suckled by a she-wolf. Shoot me, you son of a bitch!"

But shoot him I did not—I did not owe him a shot. I just dragged him up to the sitting room. There in the sitting room Nadyezhda Vasilevna was wandering about completely mad, with a drawn saber in her hand, looking at herself in the mirror. And when I dragged Nikitinsky into the sitting room, Nadyezhda Vasilevna runs to sit in the chair, and she is wearing a velvet crown and feathers on her head. She sat in the chair and saluted me with the saber. Then I started kicking Nikitinsky, my master, I kicked him for an hour, maybe even more than an hour, and I really understood what life actually is. With one shot, let me tell you, you can only get rid of a person. A shot would have been a pardon for him and too horribly easy for me, with a shot you cannot get to a man's soul, to where the soul hides and what it looks like. But there are times when I don't spare myself and spend a good hour, maybe even more than an hour, kicking the enemy. I want to understand life, to see what it actually is.

THE CEMETERY IN
KOZIN

The cemetery in a shtetl. Assyria and the mysterious decay of the East on the overgrown, weed-covered fields of Volhynia.

Gray, abraded stones with letters three hundred years old. The rough contours of the reliefs cut into the granite. The image of a fish and a sheep above a dead man's head. Images of rabbis wearing fur hats. Rabbis, their narrow hips girded with belts. Beneath their eyeless faces the wavy stone ripple of curly beards. To one side, below an oak tree cleft in two by lightning, stands the vault of Rabbi Asriil, slaughtered by Bogdan Khmelnitsky's Cossacks. Four generations lie in this sepulcher, as poor as the hovel of a water carrier, and tablets, moss-green tablets, sing of them in Bedouin prayer:

> "Azriil, son of Anania, mouth of Jehovah.
> Elijah, son of Azriil, mind that fought oblivion hand to hand.
> Wolf, son of Elijah, prince taken from his Torah in his nineteenth spring.
> Judah, son of Wolf, Rabbi of Krakow and Prague.
> O death, O mercenary, O covetous thief, why did you not, albeit one single
>   time, have mercy upon us?"

PRISHCHEPA

I'm making my way to Leshniov, where the divisional staff has set up quarters. My traveling companion, as usual, is Prishchepa, a young Cossack from Kuban, a tireless roughneck, a Communist whom the party kicked out, a future rag looter, a devil-may-care syphilitic, an unflappable liar. He wears a crimson Circassian jacket made of fine cloth, with a ruffled hood trailing down his back. As we rode, he told me about himself.

A year ago Prishchepa had run away from the Whites. As a reprisal, they took his parents hostage and killed them at the interrogation. The neighbors ransacked everything they had. When the Whites were driven out of Kuban, Prishchepa returned to his Cossack village.

It was morning, daybreak, peasant sleep sighed in the rancid stuffiness. Prishchepa hired a communal cart and went through the village picking up his gramophone, kvas jugs, and the napkins that his mother had embroidered. He went down the street in his black cloak, his curved dagger in his belt. The cart rattled behind him. Prishchepa went from one neighbor's house to the next, the bloody prints of his boots trailing behind him. In huts where he found his mother's things or his father's pipe, he left hacked-up old women, dogs hung over wells, icons soiled with dung. The people of the village smoked their pipes and followed him sullenly with their eyes. Young Cossacks had gathered on the steppes outside the village and were keeping count. The count rose and the village fell silent. When he had finished, Prishchepa returned to his ransacked home. He arranged his reclaimed furniture the way he remembered it from his childhood, and ordered vodka to be brought to him. He locked himself in the hut and for two days drank, sang, cried, and hacked tables to pieces with his saber.

On the third night, the village saw smoke rising above Prishchepa's hut. Seared and gashed, he came staggering out of the shed pulling the cow behind him, stuck his revolver in her mouth, and shot her. The earth smoked beneath his feet, a blue ring of flame flew out of the chimney and melted away, the abandoned calf began wailing. The fire was as bright as a holy day. Prishchepa untied his horse, jumped into the saddle, threw a lock of his hair into the flames, and vanished.

THE STORY OF
A HORSE

One day Savitsky, our division commander, took for himself a white stallion belonging to Khlebnikov, the commander of the First Squadron. It was a horse of imposing stature, but with a somewhat raw build, which always seemed a little heavy to me. Khlebnikov was given a black mare of pretty good stock and good trot. But he mistreated the mare, hankered for revenge, waited for an opportunity, and when it came, pounced on it.

After the unsuccessful battles of July, when Savitsky was dismissed from his duties and sent to the command personnel reserves, Khlebnikov wrote to army headquarters requesting that his horse be returned to him. On the letter, the chief of staff penned the decision: "Aforementioned stallion is to be returned to primordial owner." And Khlebnikov, rejoicing, rode a hundred versts to find Savitsky, who was living at the time in Radzivillov, a mangled little town that looked like a tattered old whore. The dismissed division commander was living alone, the fawning lackeys at headquarters no longer knew him. The fawning lackeys at headquarters were busy angling for roasted chickens in the army commander's smiles, and, vying to outgrovel each other, had turned their backs on the glorious division commander.

Drenched in perfume, looking like Peter the Great, he had fallen out of favor. He lived with a Cossack woman by the name of Pavla, whom he had snatched away from a Jewish quartermaster, and twenty thoroughbreds which, word had it, were his own. In his yard, the sun was tense and tortured with the blindness of its rays. The foals were wildly suckling on their mothers, and stableboys with drenched backs were sifting oats on faded winnowing floors. Khlebnikov, wounded by the injustice and fired by revenge, marched straight over to the barricaded yard.

"Are you familiar with my person?" he asked Savitsky, who was lying on some hay.

"Something tells me I've seen you somewhere before," Savitsky said to him with a yawn.

"In that case, here is the chief of staff's decision," Khlebnikov said gruffly. "And I would be obliged, Comrade of the reserve, if you would look at me with an official eye!"

"Why not?" Savitsky mumbled appeasingly. He took the document and began reading it for an unusually long time. He suddenly called over the Cossack woman, who was combing her hair in the coolness under the awning.

"Pavla!" he yelled. "As the Lord's my witness, you've been combing your hair since this morning! How about heating a samovar for us!"

The Cossack woman put down her comb, took her hair in both hands, and flung it behind her back.

"You've done nothing but bicker all day, Konstantin Vasilevich," she said with a lazy, condescending smile. "First you want this, then you want that!"

And she came over to Savitsky; her breasts, bobbing on her high heels, squirmed like an animal in a sack.

"You've done nothing but bicker all day," the woman repeated, beaming, and she buttoned up the division commander's shirt.

"First I want this, then I want that," the division commander said, laughing, and he got up, clasped Pavla's acquiescing shoulders, and suddenly turned his face, deathly white, to Khlebnikov.

"I am still alive, Khlebnikov," he said, embracing the Cossack woman tighter. "My legs can still walk, my horses can still gallop, my hands can still get hold of you, and my gun is warming next to my skin."

He drew his revolver, which had lain against his bare stomach, and stepped closer to the commander of the First Squadron.

The commander turned on his heels, his spurs yelped, he left the yard like an orderly who has received an urgent dispatch, and once again rode a hundred versts to find the chief of staff—but the chief of staff sent him packing.

"I have already dealt with your matter, Commander!" the chief of staff said. "I ordered that your stallion be returned to you, and I have quite a few other things to deal with!"

The chief of staff refused to listen, and finally ordered the errant commander back to his squadron. Khlebnikov had been away a whole week. During that time we had been transferred to the Dubno forest to set up camp. We had pitched our tents and were living it up. Khlebnikov, from what I remember, returned on the twelfth, a Sunday morning. He asked me for some paper, a good thirty sheets, and for some ink. The Cossacks planed a tree stump smooth for him, he placed his revolver and the paper on it, and wrote till sundown, filling many sheets with his smudgy scrawl.

"You're a real Karl Marx, you are!" the squadron's military commissar said to him in the evening. "What the hell are you writing there?"

"I am describing various thoughts in accordance with the oath I have taken," Khlebnikov answered, and handed the military commissar his petition to withdraw from the Communist Party of the Bolsheviks.

· · ·

"The Communist Party," his petition went, "was, it is my belief, founded for the promotioning of happiness and true justice with no restrictings, and thus must also keep an eye out for the rights of the little man. Here I would like to touch on the matter of the white stallion who I seized from some indescribably counterrevolutionary peasants, and who was in a horrifying condition, and many comrades laughed brazenly at that condition, but I was strong enough to withstand that laughing of theirs, and gritting my teeth for the Common Cause, I nursed the stallion back to the desired shape, because, let it be said, Comrades, I am a white-stallion enthusiast and have dedicated to white stallions the little energy that the Imperial War and the Civil War have left me with, and all these stallions respond to my touch as I respond to his silent wants and needs! But that unjust black mare I can neither respond to, nor do I need her, nor can I stand her, and, as all my comrades will testify, there's bound to be trouble! And yet the Party is unable to return to me, according to the chief of staff's decision, that which is my very own, handing me no option but to write this here petition with tears that do not befit a fighter, but which flow endlessly, ripping my blood-drenched heart to pieces!"

*   *   *

This and much more was written in Khlebnikov's petition. He spent the whole day writing it, and it was very long. It took me and the military commissar more than an hour to struggle through it.

"What a fool you are!" the military commissar said to him, and tore it up. "Come back after dinner and you and I will have a little talk."

"I don't need your little talk!" Khlebnikov answered, trembling. "You and I are finished!"

He stood at attention, shivering, not moving, his eyes darting from one side to the other as if he were desperately trying to decide which way to run. The military commissar came up to him but couldn't grab hold of him in time. Khlebnikov lunged forward and ran with all his might.

"We're finished!" he yelled wildly, jumped onto the tree stump, and began ripping his jacket and tearing at his chest.

"Go on, Savitsky!" he shouted, throwing himself onto the ground. "Kill me!"

We dragged him to a tent, the Cossacks helped us. We boiled some tea for him, and rolled him some cigarettes. He smoked, his whole body shivering. And it was only late in the evening that our commander calmed down. He no longer spoke about his deranged petition, but within a week he went to Rovno, presented himself for an examination by the Medical Commission, and was discharged from the army as an invalid on account of having six wounds.

That's how we lost Khlebnikov. I was very upset about this because Khlebnikov had been a quiet man, very similar to me in character. He was the only one in the squadron who owned a samovar. On days when there was a break in the fighting, the two of us drank hot tea. We were rattled by the same passions. Both of us looked upon the world as a meadow in May over which women and horses wander.

KONKIN

So there we were making mincemeat of the Poles at Belaya Tserkov. So much so that the trees were rattling. I'd been hit in the morning, but managed to keep on buzzing, more or less. The day, from what I remember, was toppling toward evening. I got cut off from the brigade commander, and was left with only a bunch of five proletarian Cossacks tagging along after me. All around me everyone's hugging each other with hatchets, like priests from two villages, the sap's slowly trickling out of me, my horse has pissed all over itself. Need I say more?

Me and Spirka Zabuty ended up riding off a ways from the forest. We look—and yes, two and two does make four!—no less than a hundred and fifty paces away, we see a dust cloud which is either the staff or the cavalry transport. If it's the staff—that's great, if it's the cavalry transport—that's even better! The boys' tattered clothes hung in rags, their shirts barely covering their manhood.

"Zabuty!" I yell over to Spirka, telling him he's a son of a whore, that his mother is a you-know-what, or whatever (I leave this part up to you, as you're the official orator here). "Isn't that *their* staff that's riding off there?"

"You can bet your life it's their staff!" Spirka yells back. "The only thing is, we're two and they're eight!"

"Let's go for it, Spirka!" I shout. "Either way, I'm going to hurl some mud at their chasubles! Let's go die for a pickle and World Revolution!"

And off we rode. They were eight sabers. Two of them we felled with our rifles. I spot Spirka dragging a third to Dukhonin's headquarters to get his papers checked. And me, I take aim at the big King of Aces. Yes, brothers, a big, red-faced King of Aces, with a chain and a gold pocket watch. I squeezed him back toward a farm. The farm was full of apple and cherry trees. The horse that the Big Ace was riding was nice and plump like a merchant's daughter, but it was tired. So the general drops his reins, aims his Mauser at me, and puts a hole in my leg.

"Ha, fine, sweetheart!" I think to myself. "I'll have you on your back with your legs spread wide in no time!"

I got my wheels rolling and put two bullets in his horse. I felt bad about the horse. What a Bolshevik of a stallion, a true Bolshevik! Copper-brown like a coin, tail like a bullet, leg like a bowstring. I wanted to present him alive to Lenin, but nothing came of it. I liquidated that sweet little horse. It tumbled like a bride, and my King of Aces fell out of his saddle. He dashed to one side, then turned back again and put another little loophole in my body. So, in other words, I had already gotten myself three decorations for fighting the enemy.

"Jesus!" I think to myself. "Just watch him finish me off by mistake!"

I went galloping toward him, he'd already pulled his saber, and tears are running down his cheeks, white tears, the milk of man.

"You'll get me a Red Flag Medal!" I yell. "Give yourself up while I'm still alive, Your Excellency!"

"I can't do that, *Pan*!" the old man answers. "Kill me!"

And suddenly Spirka is standing before me like a leaf before a blade of grass.* His face all lathered up with sweat, his eyes as if they're dangling on strings from his ugly mug.

"Konkin!" he yells at me. "God knows how many I've finished off! But you have a general here, he's got embroidery on him, I'd like to finish him off myself!"

"Go to the Turk!" I tell Zabuty, and get furious. "It's my blood that's on his embroidery!"

---

* From the Russian folktale *The Little Humpbacked Horse*, in which the hero summons his magic horse with, "Appear before me like a leaf before a blade of grass!"

And with my mare I edge the general into the barn, where there was hay or something. It was silent in there, dark, cool.

"*Pan,* think of your old age!" I tell him. "Give yourself up to me, for God's sake, and we can both have a rest."

And he's against the wall, panting with his whole chest, rubbing his forehead with a red finger.

"I can't," he says. "Kill me, I will only hand my saber to Budyonny!"

He wants me to bring him Budyonny! O, Lord in Heaven! And I can tell the old man's on his last legs.

"*Pan!*" I shout at him, sobbing and gnashing my teeth. "On my proletarian honor, I myself am the commander-in-chief. Don't go looking for embroidery on me, but the title's mine. You want my title? I am the musical eccentric and salon ventriloquist of Nizhny . . . Nizhny, a town on the Volga!"

Then the devil got into me. The general's eyes were blinking like lanterns in front of me. The Red Sea parted before me. His snub enters my wound like salt, because I see that the old man doesn't believe me. So, my friends, what I did is, I closed my mouth, pulled in my stomach, took a deep breath, and demonstrated, in the proper way, our way, the fighter's way, the Nizhny way—demonstrated to this Polish nobleman my ventriloquy.

The old man went white in the face, clutched his heart, and sat on the ground.

"Do you now believe Konkin the Eccentric, commissar of the Third Invincible Cavalry Brigade?"

"A commissar?" he shouts.

"A commissar," I tell him.

"A Communist?" he shouts.

"A Communist," I tell him.

"At my hour of death," he shouts, "at my last breath, tell me, my dear Cossack friend, are you a Communist, or are you lying to me?"

"I am a Communist," I tell him.

So there's grandpa, sitting on the ground, kissing some kind of amulet or something, breaks his saber in half, and in his eyes two sparks flare up, two lanterns above the dark steppes.

"Forgive me," he says, "but I cannot give myself up to a Communist."

And he shakes my hand. "Forgive me," he says, "and finish me off like a soldier."

Konkin, the political commissar of the N. Cavalry Brigade and three-time Knight of the Order of the Red Flag, told us this story with his typical antics during a rest stop one day.

"So, Konkin, did you and the *Pan* come to some sort of an agreement in the end?"

"Can you come to an agreement with someone like that? He was too proud. I begged him again, but he wouldn't give in. So we took his papers, those he had with him, we took his Mauser, and the old fool's saddle, the one I'm sitting on right now. Then I see all my life flowing out of me in drops, a terrible tiredness grabs hold of me, my boots are full of blood, I lost interest in him."

"So you put the old man out of his misery?"

"Well, I guess I did."

BERESTECHKO

*W*e were advancing from Khotin to Berestechko. Our fighters were dozing in their saddles. A song rustled like a stream running dry. Horrifying corpses lay on thousand-year-old burial mounds. Muzhiks in white shirts raised their caps and bowed as we passed. The cloak of Division Commander Pavlichenko was fluttering ahead of the staff officers like a gloomy banner. His ruffled hood hung over his cloak, his curved saber at his side.

We rode past the Cossack burial mounds and the tomb of Bogdan Khmelnitsky. An old man with a mandolin came creeping out from behind a gravestone and with a child's voice sang of past Cossack glory. We listened to the song in silence, then unfurled the standards, and burst into Berestechko to the beat of a thundering march. The inhabitants had put iron bars over their shutters, and silence, a despotic silence, had ascended to the shtetl throne.

I happened to be billeted in the house of a redheaded widow, who was doused with the scent of widow's grief. I washed off the dirt of the road and went out into the street. An announcement was already nailed up on telegraph poles that Divisional Military Commissar Vinogradov would be giving a speech on the Second Congress of the Comintern.* Right outside the house a couple of Cossacks were getting ready to shoot an old silver-bearded Jew for espionage. The old man was screeching, and tried to break free. Kudrya from the machine gun

* The Third Communist International, 1919–1943, an organization founded in Moscow by the delegates of twelve countries to promote Communism worldwide.

detachment grabbed his head and held it wedged under his arm. The Jew fell silent and spread his legs. Kudrya pulled out his dagger with his right hand and carefully slit the old man's throat without spattering himself. Then he knocked on one of the closed windows.

"If anyone's interested," he said, "they can come get him. It's no problem."

And the Cossacks disappeared around the corner. I followed them, and then wandered through Berestechko. Most of the people here are Jewish, and only on the outskirts have a few Russian townspeople, mainly tanners, settled. The Russians live cleanly, in little white houses behind green shutters. Instead of vodka, they drink beer or mead, and in their front gardens grow tobacco which, like Galician peasants, they smoke in long curved pipes. That they are three diligent and entrepreneurial races living next to each other awakened in all of them an obstinate industriousness that is sometimes inherent in a Russian man, if he hasn't become louse-ridden, desperate, and besotted with drink.

Everyday life, which once flourished, has blown away. Little sprouts that had survived for three centuries still managed to blossom in Volhynia's sultry hotbed of ancient times. Here, with the ropes of profit, the Jews had bound the Russian muzhiks to the Polish *Pans* and the Czech settlers to the factory in Lodz. These were smugglers, the best on the frontier, and almost always warriors of the faith. Hasidism kept this lively population of taverners, peddlers, and brokers in a stifling grip. Boys in long coats still trod the ancient path to the Hasidic cheder, and old women still brought daughters-in-law to the *tsaddik* with impassioned prayers for fertility.

The Jews live here in large houses painted white or a watery blue. The traditional austerity of this architecture goes back centuries. Behind the houses are sheds that are two, sometimes three stories high. The sun never enters these sheds. They are indescribably gloomy and replace our yards. Secret passages lead to cellars and stables. In times of war, people hide in these catacombs from bullets and plunder. Over many days, human refuse and animal dung pile up. Despair and dismay fill the catacombs with an acrid stench and the rotting sourness of excrement.

Berestechko stinks inviolably to this day. The smell of rotten herring emanates from everyone. The shtetl reeks in expectation of a new era, and, instead of people, fading reflections of frontier misfortune wander through it. I had had enough of them by the end of the day, went beyond the edge of the town, climbed the mountain, and reached the abandoned castle of the Counts Raciborski, the recent owners of Berestechko.

The silence of the sunset turned the grass around the castle blue. The moon rose green as a lizard above the pond. Looking out the window, I could see the estate of the Raciborskis—meadows and fields of hops hidden beneath the crepe ribbons of dusk.

A ninety-year-old countess and her son had lived in the castle. She had tormented him for not having given the dying clan any heirs, and—the muzhiks told me this—she used to beat him with the coachman's whip.

A rally was gathering on the square below. Peasants, Jews, and tanners from the outlying areas had come together. Above them flared Vinogradov's ecstatic voice and the clanking of his spurs. He gave a speech about the Second Congress of the Comintern, and I roamed along the walls where nymphs with gouged eyes danced their ancient round dance. Then on the trampled floor, in a corner, I found the torn fragment of a yellowed letter. On it was written in faded ink:

*Berestechko, 1820, Paul, mon bien aimé, on dit que l'empereur Napoléon est mort, est-ce vrai? Moi, je me sens bien, les couches ont été faciles, notre petit héros achève sept semaines. . . .**

Below me, the voice of the divisional military commissar is droning on. He is passionately haranguing the bewildered townspeople and the plundered Jews: "You are the power. Everything here belongs to you. There are no masters. I shall now conduct an election for the Revolutionary Committee."

---

* Berestechko, 1820, my beloved Paul, I hear that Emperor Napoleon is dead. Is it true? I feel well; it was an easy birth, our little hero is already seven weeks old.

SALT

*D*ear Comrade Editor,
 I want to tell you of some ignorant women who are harmful to us. I set my hopes on you, that you who travel around our nation's fronts, have not overlooked the far-flung station of Fastov, lying afar beyond the mountains grand, in a distant province of a distant land, where many a jug of home-brewed beer we drank with merriment and cheer. About this aforementioned station, there is much you can write about, but as we say back home: you can shovel till the cows come home, but the master's dung heap never gets no smaller. So I will only describe what my eyes have seen in person.

It was a quiet, glorious night seven days ago when our well-deserved Red Cavalry transport train, loaded with fighters, stopped at that station. We were all burning to promote the Common Cause and were heading to Berdichev. Only, we notice that our train isn't moving in any way at all, our Gavrilka is not beginning to roll, and the fighters begin mistrusting and asking each other: "Why are we stopping here?" And truly, the stop turned out to be mighty for the Common Cause, because the peddlers, those evil fiends among whom there was a count-less force of the female species, were all behaving very impertinently with the railroad authorities. Recklessly they grabbed the handrails, those evil fiends, they scampered over the steel roofs, frolicked, made trouble, clutching in each hand sacks of contraband salt, up to five *pood* in a sack. But the triumph of the capitalist peddlers did not last long. The initiative showed by the fighters who jumped out of the train made it possible for the struggling railroad authorities to emit sighs from their breasts. Only the female species with their bags of salt stayed around. Taking pity, the soldiers let some of the women come into the railroad cars, but others they didn't. In our own railroad car of the Second Platoon two girls popped up, and after the first bell there comes an imposing woman with a baby in her arms: "Let me in, my dear Cossacks," she says. "I have been suffering through the whole war at train stations with a suckling baby in my arms, and now I want to meet my husband, but the way the railroad is, it is impossible to get through! Don't I deserve some help from you Cossacks?"

"By the way, woman," I tell her, "whichever way the platoon decides will be your fate." And, turning to the platoon, I tell them that here we have a woman who is requesting to travel to her husband at an appointed place and that she does, in fact, have a child with her, so what will your decision be? Let her in or not?

"Let her in," the boys yell. "Once we're done with her, she won't be wanting that husband of hers no more!"

"No," I tell the boys quite politely, "I bow to your words, platoon, but I am astonished to hear such horse talk. Recall, platoon, your lives and how you yourselves were children with your mothers, and therefore, as a result, you should not talk that way!"

And the Cossacks said, "How persuasive he is, this Balmashov!" And they let the woman into the railroad car, and she climbs aboard thankfully. And each of the fighters, saying how right I am, tumble all over each other telling her, "Sit down, woman, there in the corner, rock your child the way mothers do, no one will touch you in the corner, so you can travel untouched to your husband, as you want, and we depend upon your conscience to raise a new change of guard for us, because what is old grows older, and when you need youth, it's never around! We saw our share of sorrow, woman, both when we were drafted and then later in the extra service, we were crushed by hunger, burned by cold. So just sit here, woman, and don't be frightened!"

The third bell rang and the train pulled out of the station. The glorious night pitched its tent. And in that tent hung star lanterns. And the fighters remembered the nights of Kuban and the green star of Kuban. And thoughts flew like birds. And the wheels clattered and clattered.

With the passing of time, when night was relieved of its watch and the red drummers drummed in the dawn on their red drums, then the Cossacks came to me, seeing that I am sitting sleepless and am unhappy to the fullest.

"Balmashov," the Cossacks say to me, "why are you so horribly unhappy and sitting sleepless?"

"I bow to you deeply, O fighters, and would like to ask you the small favor of letting me speak a few words with this citizen."

And trembling from head to toe, I rise from my bunk from which sleep had run like a wolf from a pack of depraved dogs, and walk up to her, take the baby from her arms, rip off the rags it's swaddled in and its diaper, and out from the diaper comes a nice fat forty-pound sack of salt.

"What an interesting little baby, Comrades! It does not ask Mommy for titty, doesn't peepee on mommy's skirty, and doesn't wake people from their sleep!"

"Forgive me, my dear Cossacks," the woman cut into our conversation very coolly, "it wasn't me who tricked you, it was my hard life."

"I, Balmashov, forgive your hard life," I tell the woman. "It doesn't cost Balmashov much. What Balmashov pays for something, that is the price he sells it for! But address yourself to the Cossacks, woman, who elevated you as a toiling mother of the republic. Address yourself to these two girls, who are now crying for having suffered under us last night. Address yourself to our women on the wheat fields of Kuban, who are wearing out their womanly strength without husbands, and to their husbands, who are lonely too, and so are forced against their will to rape girls who cross their paths! And you they didn't touch, you improper woman, although you should have been the first to be touched! Address yourself to Russia, crushed by pain!"

And she says to me, "As it is I've lost my salt, so I'm not afraid of calling things by their real name! Don't give me that about saving Russia—all you care about is saving those Yids, Lenin and Trotsky!"

"Right now our topic of conversation is not the Yids, you evil citizen! And by the way, about Lenin I don't really know, but Trotsky is the dashing son of the Governor of Tambov who, turning his back on his high social rank, joined the working classes. Like prisoners sentenced to hard labor, Lenin and Trotsky are dragging us to life's road of freedom, while you, foul citizen, are a worse counterrevolutionary than that

White general waving his sharp saber at us from his thousand-ruble horse. You can see him, that general, from every road, and the worker has only one dream—to kill him! While you, you dishonest citizen, with your bogus children who don't ask for bread and don't run out into the wind, you one doesn't see. You're just like a flea, you bite and bite and bite!"

And I truthfully admit that I threw that citizen off the moving train and onto the embankment, but she, being brawny as she was, sat up, shook out her skirts, and went on her deceitful way. Seeing this uninjured woman and Russia all around her, the peasant fields without an ear of corn, the raped girls, and the comrades, many of whom were heading for the front but few of whom would ever return, I wanted to jump from the train and either kill myself or kill her. But the Cossacks took pity on me and said, "Just shoot her with that rifle."

And I took the loyal rifle from the wall and wiped that blot off the face of the working land and the republic.

And we, the fighters of the Second Platoon, swear before you, dear Comrade Editor, and before you, dear Comrades of the editorial office, that we will deal relentlessly with all the traitors who pull us into the pit and want to turn back the stream and cover Russia with corpses and dead grass.

In the name of all the fighters of the Second Platoon,

Nikita Balmashov, Fighter of the Revolution.

EVENING

*O*statutes of the RCP!* You have laid impetuous rails across the rancid dough of Russian prose. You have transformed three bachelors, their hearts filled with the passion of Ryazan Jesuses, into editors of the *Krasny Kavalerist.*† You have transformed them so that day after day they can churn out a rambunctious newspaper filled with courage and rough-and-ready mirth.

Galin with his cataract, consumptive Slinkin, and Sychev with his withered intestines shuffle through the barren soil of the rear lines, spreading the revolt and fire of their news sheet through the ranks of dashing, pensioned-off Cossacks, reserve cheats who have registered as Polish translators, and girls sent out to our Polit-otdel train** from Moscow for recuperation.

By evening the newspaper is ready—a dynamite fuse placed under the cavalry. The cross-eyed lantern of the provincial sun expires in the sky, the lights of the printing press scatter in all directions and burn uncontrollably like the passion of a machine. And then, toward midnight, Galin comes out of the railroad car shuddering from the bite of his unrequited love for Irina, our train's washerwoman.

"Last time," Galin says, pale and blind, his shoulders narrow, "last

* The Russian Communist Party
† *The Red Cavalryman,* the newspaper distributed to the Red Cavalry forces and for which Babel also wrote pieces.
** The train belonging to the Polit-otdel, the political organ of the new Soviet government charged with the ideological education of the military.

time, Irina, we discussed the shooting of Nicholas the Bloody, executed by the proletariat of Ekaterinburg. Now we will proceed to the other tyrants who died like dogs. Peter III was strangled by Orlov, his wife's lover. Paul was torn to pieces by his courtiers and his own son. Nikolai Palkin poisoned himself, his son perished March first, his grandson drank himself to death. It is important for you to know all this, Irina!"

And raising his blank eye, filled with adoration, to the washerwoman, Galin rummages relentlessly through the crypts of murdered emperors. He is standing stoop-shouldered, bathed in the rays of the moon hovering high above like a nagging splinter, the printing presses are hammering somewhere nearby, and the radio station is shining with clear light. Irina nestles against the shoulder of Vasily the cook as she stands listening to Galin's dull and nonsensical mutterings of love. Above her, the stars are dragging themselves through the black seaweed of the sky. The washerwoman yawns, makes the sign of the cross over her puffy lips, and stares wide-eyed at Galin.

Next to Irina, rough-faced Vasily yawns. Like all cooks he scorns mankind. Cooks: they constantly have to handle the meat of dead animals and the greed of the living, which is why, when it comes to politics, a cook always seeks things that have nothing to do with him. This goes for Vasily too. Hiking his pants up to his nipples, he asks Galin about the civil lists of various kings, the dowries of Czars' daughters. Then he yawns and says, "It's night, Irina, another day will be rolling in tomorrow. Let's go crush some fleas."

They closed the kitchen door, leaving Galin alone, with the moon hovering high above like a nagging splinter. I sat opposite the moon on the embankment by the sleeping pond, wearing my spectacles, with boils on my neck, my legs bandaged. My confused poetic brain was digesting the class struggle when Galin came up to me with his twinkling cataracts.

"Galin," I said, overcome with self-pity and loneliness, "I am sick, my end is near, I am tired of life in the Red Cavalry!"

"You're a wimp!" Galin said, and the watch on his bony wrist showed one in the morning. "You're a wimp, and we end up having to put up with wimps like you! We're cracking the nut for you, and soon enough you will be able to see the meat inside, at which point you'll take your thumb out of your mouth and sing the glories of the new life in striking prose—but for the time being, just sit where you are, nice and quiet, you wimp, and stop getting in the way with all your whimpering!"

He came closer to me, fixed the bandages which had slipped off my itching sores, and let his head loll onto his pigeon breast. The night comforted us in our anguish; a light breeze rustled over us like a mother's skirt, and the weeds below us glittered with freshness and moisture.

The roaring machines of the train's printing press screeched and fell silent. Dawn drew a line across the edge of the earth, the kitchen door creaked and opened a crack. Four feet with fat heels came thrusting out into the coolness, and we saw Irina's loving calves and Vasily's big toe with its crooked black nail.

"Vasilyok," the woman whispered in a throaty, expiring voice. "Get out of my bed, you troublemaker!"

But Vasily only jerked his heel and moved closer to her.

"The Red Cavalry," Galin said to me, "the Red Cavalry is a public conjuring trick pulled off by our Party's Central Committee. The curve of the Revolution has thrown the Cossack marauders, saddled with all kinds of prejudices, into the forefront, but the Central Committee is going to weed them out with its iron rake."

Then Galin began talking about the political education of the First Cavalry. He spoke long, in a dull voice, with complete clarity. His eyelid fluttered over his cataract.

AFONKA BIDA

*W*e were fighting by Leshniov. A wall of enemy cavalry rose all around us. The new Polish strategy was uncoiling like a spring, with an ominous whistle. We were being pushed back. It was the first time in our campaign that we felt on our own backs the devilish sharpness of flank attacks and breaches in the rear lines—slashes from the very weapons that had served us so well.

The front at Leshniov was being held by the infantry. Blond and barefoot, Volhynian muzhiks shuffled along crooked trenches. This infantry had been plucked from behind its plows the day before to form the Red Cavalry's infantry reserve. The peasants had come along eagerly. They fought with the greatest zeal. Their hoarse peasant ferocity amazed even the Budyonny fighters. Their hatred for the Polish landowners was built of invisible but sturdy material.

In the second phase of the war, when our whooping had lost its effect on the enemy's imagination, and cavalry attacks on our opponents, burrowed in their trenches, had become impossible, this ragtag infantry could have proved extremely useful to the Red Cavalry. But our poverty got the upper hand: there were three muzhiks to every rifle, and the cartridges that were issued didn't fit. The venture had to be dropped, and this true peasant home guard was sent back to its villages.

But back to the fighting at Leshniov. Our foot soldiers had dug themselves in three versts from the shtetl. A hunched youth with spectacles was walking up and down in front of them, a saber dangling at his side. He moved along in little hops, with a piqued look on his face, as if his boots were pinching him. This peasant *ataman*,* chosen and cherished by the muzhiks, was a Jew, a half-blind Jewish youth, with the sickly, intent face of a Talmudist. In battle, he showed circumspect and coolheaded courage that reflected the absentmindedness of a dreamer.

It was after two o'clock on a crystalline July day. A gossamer rainbow of heat glittered in the air. A festive stripe of uniforms and horse manes braided with ribbons came sparkling from behind the hills. The youth gave the signal for the men to take their positions. The muzhiks, shuffling in their bast sandals, ran to their posts and took aim. But it turned out to be a false alarm. It was Maslak's† colorful squadrons that came riding up the Leshniov high road, their emaciated but spirited horses trotting at a steady pace. In fiery pillars of dust, magnificent banners were fluttering on gilded poles weighed down by velvet tassels. The horsemen rode with majestic and insolent haughtiness. The tattered foot soldiers came crawling out of their trenches and, their mouths hanging open, watched the light-footed elegance of the unruffled stream.

In front of the regiment, riding a bowlegged steppe horse, was Brigade Commander Maslak, filled with drunken blood and the putridness of his fatty juices. His stomach lay like a big cat on the silver-studded pommel of his saddle. When Maslak saw the muzhik foot soldiers, his face turned a merry purple, and he beckoned Platoon Commander Afonka Bida to come over. We had given the platoon commander the nickname "Makhno"** because he looked so much like him. Maslak and Bida whispered for about a minute. Then Bida turned toward the First Squadron, leaned forward, and in a low voice ordered, "Charge!" The Cossacks, one platoon after another, broke into a trot. They spurred their horses and went galloping toward the trenches from which the muzhik foot soldiers were peering, dazzled by the sight.

"Prepare to engage!" sang Afonka's voice, dismal and as if he were calling from far away.

Maslak, wheezing and coughing, relishing the spectacle, rode off to

* Term for Cossack leader.
† Maslakov, commander of the First Brigade of the Fourth Division, a relentless partisan who was soon to betray the Soviet regime. [Footnote by Isaac Babel.]
** The Ukrainian anarchist leader.

the side, and the Cossacks charged. The poor muzhik foot soldiers ran, but it was too late. The Cossack lashes were already cutting across their tattered jackets as the horsemen circled the field, twirling their whips with exquisite artistry.

"What's all this nonsense about?" I shouted over to Afonka.

"Just a bit of fun," he shouted back, fidgeting in his saddle, and he dragged a young man out of the bushes in which he was hiding.

"Just a bit of fun!" he yelled, clobbering away at the terrified young man.

The fun ended when Maslak, tired and majestic, waved his plump hand.

"Foot soldiers! Stop gawking!" Afonka yelled, haughtily straightening his frail body. "Go catch some fleas!"

The Cossacks grinned at each other and gathered into formation. The foot soldiers vanished without a trace. The trenches were empty. And only the hunched Jewish youth stood in the same spot as before, eyeing the Cossacks haughtily through his spectacles.

The gunfire from the direction of Leshniov did not let up. The Poles were encircling us. We could see the single figures of their mounted scouts through our binoculars. They came galloping from the shtetl and disappeared again like jack-in-the-boxes. Maslak gathered together a squadron and divided it on either side of the high road. A sparkling sky hung above Leshniov, indescribably void as always in hours of danger. The Jew threw his head back and blew mournfully and loud on his metallic pipe. And the foot soldiers, the battered foot soldiers, returned to their positions.

Bullets flew thickly in our direction. Our brigade staff came under machine gun fire. We rushed into the forest and fought our way through the bushes on the right side of the high road. Branches, hit, cracked heavily above us. By the time we had managed to cut our way through the bushes, the Cossacks were no longer positioned where they had been. The division commander had ordered them to retreat toward Brody. Only the muzhiks sent a few snarling shots out of their trenches, and Afonka, trailing behind, went chasing after his platoon.

He was riding on the outermost edge of the road, looking around him and sniffing at the air. The shooting died down for a few moments. Afonka decided to take advantage of the lapse and began galloping at full speed. At that moment a bullet plunged into his horse's neck. Afonka galloped on another hundred paces or so, and then, right in front of our line, his horse abruptly bent its forelegs and sank to the ground.

Afonka casually pulled his wedged foot out of the stirrup. He sat on his haunches and poked about in the wound with his copper-brown finger. Then he stood up again and ran his agonized eyes over the glittering horizon.

"Farewell, Stepan," he said in a wooden voice, and, taking a step away from the dying horse, bowed deeply to it. "How will I return to my quiet village without you? Who am I to throw your embroidered saddle on? Farewell, Stepan!" he repeated more loudly, then choked, squeaked like a mouse in a trap, and began wailing. His gurgling howls reached our ears, and we saw Afonka frantically bowing like a possessed woman in a church. "But you'll see! I won't give in to goddamn fate!" he yelled, lifting his hands from his ashen face. "You'll see! From now on I'm going to hack those cursed Poles to pieces with no mercy at all! Right down to their gasping hearts, right down to their very last gasp, and the Mother of God's blood! I swear this to you, Stepan, before my dear brothers back home!"

Afonka lay down with his face on the horse's wound and fell silent. The horse turned its deep, sparkling, violet eye to its master, and listened to his convulsive wheezing. In tender oblivion it dragged its fallen muzzle over the ground, and streams of blood, like two ruby-red harness straps, trickled over its chest covered in white muscles.

Afonka lay there without moving. Maslak walked over to the horse, treading daintily on his fat legs, slid his revolver into its ear, and fired. Afonka jumped up and swung his pockmarked face to Maslak.

"Take the harness off, Afanasi, and go back to your unit," Maslak said to him gently.

And from our slope we saw Afonka, bent under the weight of the saddle, his face raw and red like sliced meat, tottering toward his squadron, boundlessly alone in the dusty, blazing desert of the fields.

Late that evening I saw him at the cavalry transport. He was sleeping on a cart which held all his "possessions"—sabers, uniform jackets, and pierced gold coins. His blood-caked head with its wrenched, dead mouth, lay as if crucified on the saddle's bow. Next to him lay the harness of the dead horse, the inventive and whimsical raiment of a Cossack racer: breastplates with black tassels, pliant tail cruppers studded with colored stones, and the bridle embossed with silver.

Darkness thickened around us. The cavalry transport crawled heavily along the Brody high road. Simple stars rolled through Milky Ways in the sky, and distant villages burned in the cool depths of the night. Orlov, the squadron subcommander, and big-mustached Bitsenko were sitting right there on Afonka's cart discussing his grief.

"He brought the horse all the way from home," long-mustached Bitsenko said. "Where's one to find another horse like that?"

"A horse—that's a friend," Orlov answered.

"A horse—that's a father," Bitsenko sighed. "The horse saves your life more times than you can count. Bida is finished without his horse."

In the morning Afonka was gone. The skirmishes near Brody began and ended. Defeat was replaced by fleeting victory, we had a change of division commander, but Afonka was still nowhere to be seen. And only a terrible rumbling from the villages, the evil and rapacious trail of Afonka's marauding, showed us his difficult path.

"He's off somewhere getting a horse," the men of the squadron said about him, and on the endless evenings of our wanderings I heard quite a few tales of this grim, savage pillaging.

Fighters from other units ran into Afonka about ten versts from our position. He lay in wait for Polish cavalrymen who had fallen behind, or scoured the forests looking for herds hidden by the peasants. He set villages on fire and shot Polish elders for hiding horses. Echoes of the frenzied one-man battle, the furtive ransacking robbery of a lone wolf attacking a herd, reached our ears.

Another week passed. The bitter events of the day crowded out the tales of Afonka's sinister bravado, and we began to forget our "Makhno." Then the rumor went round that Galician peasants had slaughtered him somewhere in the woods. And on the day we entered Berestechko, Yemelyan Budyak from the First Squadron went to the division commander to ask if he could have Afonka's saddle and the yellow saddlecloths. Yemelyan wanted to ride in the parade on a new saddle, but it was not to be.

We entered Berestechko on August 6. Fluttering in front of our division was our new division commander's Asiatic quilted jacket and his red Cossack coat. Lyovka, the division commander's brutal lackey, walked behind him leading his stud mare. A military march filled with protracted menace resounded through the pretentious, destitute streets. The town was a colorful forest of dead-end alleys and decrepit and convulsive planks and boards. The shtetl's heart, corroded by time, breathed its despondent decay upon us. Smugglers and philistines hid in their large, shadowy huts. Only *Pan* Ludomirski, a bell ringer in a green frock coat, met us at the church.

We crossed the river and entered deeper into the petit-bourgeois settlement. We were nearing the priest's house when Afonka suddenly came riding around the corner on a large stallion.

"Greetings," he called out in a barking voice, and, pushing the fighters apart, took his old position in the ranks.

Maslak stared into the colorless distance.

"Where did you get that horse?" he wheezed, without turning around.

"It's my own," Afonka answered, and rolled himself a cigarette, wetting the paper with a quick dart of his tongue.

One after the other, the Cossacks rode up to greet him. A monstrous pink pustule shone repugnantly in his charred face where his left eye had been.

The following morning Bida went carousing. He smashed Saint Valentine's shrine in the church and tried to play the organ. He was wearing a jacket that had been cut from a blue carpet and had an embroidered lily on its back, and he had combed his sweat-drenched forelock* over his gouged-out eye.

After lunch he saddled his horse and fired his rifle at the knocked-out windows of the castle of the Count Raciborski. Cossacks stood around him in a semicircle. They tugged at the stallion's tail, prodded its legs, and counted its teeth.

"A fine figure of a horse!" Orlov, the squadron subcommander, said.

"An exemplary horse," big-mustached Bitsenko confirmed.

* Ukrainian Cossacks shaved their heads, leaving only a forelock, known as a *chub*.

AT SAINT VALENTINE'S

O ur division occupied Berestechko yesterday evening. The headquarters have been set up in the house of Father Tuzynkiewicz.
Dressed as a woman, Tuzynkiewicz had fled Berestechko before our
troops entered the town. All I know about him is that he had dealt with
God in Berestechko for forty-five years, and that he had been a good
priest. The townspeople make a point of this, telling us he was even
loved by the Jews. Under Tuzynkiewicz, the old church had been ren-
ovated. The renovations had been completed on the day of the church's
three-hundredth anniversary, and the bishop had come from Zhitomir.
Prelates in silk cassocks had held a service in front of the church.
Potbellied and beatific, they stood like bells on the dewy grass. Faithful
streams flowed in from the surrounding villages. The muzhiks bent
their knees, kissed priestly hands, and on that day clouds never before
seen flamed in the sky. Heavenly banners fluttered in honor of the
church. The bishop himself kissed Tuzynkiewicz on the forehead and
called him the Father of Berestechko, *Pater Berestechkae*.

I heard this tale in the morning at the headquarters, where I was
checking over the report of our scout column that was on a reconnaissance
mission near Lvov in the district of Radziekhov. I read the documents.
The snoring of the orderlies behind me bespoke our never-ending home-
lessness. The clerks, sodden with sleeplessness, wrote orders to the
division, ate pickles, and sneezed. It wasn't until midday that I got away,
went to the window, and saw the church of Berestechko, powerful and
white. It shone in the mild sun like a porcelain tower. Flashes of mid-

day lightning sparkled on its shining flanks. The lightning's arcs began at the ancient green cupolas and ran lightly downward. Pink veins glimmered in the white stone of the portal, and above it were columns as thin as candles.

Then organ music came pouring into my ears, and that instant an old woman with disheveled yellow hair appeared outside the doors of the headquarters. She moved like a dog with a broken paw, hobbling in circles, her legs tottering. The pupils of her eyes, filled with the white liquid of blindness, oozed tears. The sounds of the organ, now drawn-out, now rapid, came fluttering over to us. Their flight was difficult, their wake reverberated plaintive and long. The old woman wiped her eyes with her yellow hair, sat on the floor, and began kissing the tops of my boots. The organ fell silent and then burst into a laughter of bass notes. I took the old woman by the arm and looked around. The clerks were pounding their typewriters and the orderlies snored ever louder, the spurs on their boots ripping the felt under the velvet upholstery of the sofas. The old woman kissed my boots tenderly, hugging them as she would an infant. I led her to the door and locked it behind me. The church towered strikingly before us, like a stage set. Its side doors were open, and on the graves of Polish officers lay horses' skulls.

We hurried into the churchyard, went through a dark corridor, and arrived in a square-shaped room, which had been built as an extension to the chancel. Sashka, the nurse of the Thirty-first Regiment, was puttering about in there, rummaging through a pile of silk that somebody had thrown on the floor. The cadaverous aroma of brocade, scattered flowers, and fragrant decay seeped into her nostrils, tickling and poisonous. Then Cossacks entered the room. They burst into guffaws, grabbed Sashka by the arms, and flung her with gusto onto a pile of cloth and books. Sashka's body, blossoming and reeking like the meat of a freshly slaughtered cow, was laid bare, her raised skirts revealing the legs of a squadron woman, slim, cast-iron legs, and dim-witted Kurdyukov, the silly fool, sat on top of Sashka, bouncing as if he were in a saddle, pretending to be in the grip of passion. She pushed him off and rushed out the door. We passed the altar, and only then did we enter the nave of the church.

The church was filled with light, filled with dancing rays, columns of air, and an almost cool exultation. How can I ever forget Apolek's painting, hanging over the right side-altar? In this painting twelve rosy *Paters* are rocking a cradle girdled with ribbons, with a plump infant Jesus in it. His toes are stretched out, his body lacquered with hot morning sweat. The child is writhing on his fat, wrinkly back, and twelve apostles in cardinals' miters are bending over the cradle. Their faces are meticulously shaven, flaming cloaks are billowing over their bellies. The eyes of the Apostles sparkle with wisdom, resolution, and cheer. Faint grins flit over the corners of their mouths, and fiery warts have been planted on their double chins—crimson warts, like radishes in May.

This church of Berestechko had its private and beguiling approach to the death agonies of the sons of man. In this church the saints marched to their deaths with the flair of Italian opera singers, and the black hair of the executioners shone like the beard of Holofernes. Here, above the altar, I saw the sacrilegious painting of John the Baptist, which had also sprung from Apolek's heretical, intoxicating brush. In this painting the Baptist was beautiful in the ambiguous and reticent way that drives the concubines of kings to shed their half-lost honor and their blossoming lives.

At first I did not notice the signs of destruction in the church, or didn't think they looked too bad. Only the shrine of Saint Valentine had been smashed. Lying around it were shreds of decayed wadding and the saint's ridiculous bones, which, if they resembled anything, looked like chicken bones. And Afonka Bida was still playing the organ. Afonka was drunk, wild, his body was lacerated. He had come back to us only yesterday with the horse he had seized from local farm-ers. Afonka was obstinately trying to play a march, and someone was badgering him in a sleepy voice, "Enough, Afonka, enough, let's go eat!" But Afonka wouldn't give up. Many more of Afonka's songs fol-lowed. Each sound was a song, and one sound was torn from the other. The song's dense tune lasted for a moment and then crossed over into another. I listened, looked around—the signs of destruction didn't look too bad. But *Pan* Ludomirski, the bell ringer of the Church of Saint Valentine and husband of the old blind woman, thought otherwise.

Ludomirsky had suddenly appeared out of nowhere. He walked through the church with measured steps, his head lowered. The old man could not bring himself to cover the scattered relics because a simple man, a lay person, may not touch what is holy. The bell ringer threw himself on the blue slabs of the floor, lifted his head, his blue nose jutting up above him like a flag above a corpse. His blue nose quivered above him and at that moment a velvet curtain by the altar swayed, rustled, and fell open. In the depths of the niche, against the backdrop of a sky furrowed with clouds, ran a bearded little figure wearing an orange Polish caftan—barefoot, his mouth lacerated and bleeding. A hoarse wail assailed our ears. The man in the orange caftan was being pursued by hatred, and his pursuer had caught up with him. The man lifted his arm to ward off the blow, and blood poured from it in a purple stream. The young Cossack standing next to me yelled out and, ducking, started to run, even though there was nothing to run from, because the figure in the niche was only Jesus Christ—the most unusual portrayal of the Son of God I have ever seen in my life.

Pan Ludomirski's Savior was a curly-headed Jew with a scraggly little beard and a low, wrinkled forehead. His sunken cheeks were tinted with carmine, and thin, red-brown eyebrows curved over eyes that were closed in pain.

His mouth was wrenched open, like a horse's mouth, his Polish caftan fastened with a precious girdle, and from under the caftan jutted crooked little porcelain feet, painted, bare, pierced by silver nails.

Pan Ludomirski stood under the statue in his green frock coat. He stretched his withered arm toward us and cursed us. The Cossacks stared at him with wide eyes and let their straw-colored forelocks hang. In a thundering voice, the bell ringer of the Church of Saint Valentine cursed us in the purest Latin. Then he turned away, fell to his knees, and clasped the feet of the Savior.

Back at the headquarters, I wrote a report to the division commander about the insult to the religious feelings of the local population. A decree was issued that the church be closed, and the guilty parties were charged with a breach of discipline and sent before the military tribunal.

SQUADRON COMMANDER
TRUNOV

*A*t noon we brought the bullet-ridden body of Trunov, our squadron commander, back to Sokal. He had been killed that morning in a battle with enemy airplanes. All the hits had caught Trunov in the face; his cheeks were riddled with wounds, his tongue torn out. We washed the dead man's face as best we could so that he would look less horrifying, placed his Caucasian saddle at the head of his coffin, and dug him a grave in a stately spot—in the public park in the middle of the town, right by the fence. Our squadron rode there on horseback. The regimental staff and the divisional military commissar were also present. And at two in the afternoon, by the cathedral clock, our rickety little cannon fired the first shot. The cannon saluted Squadron Commander Trunov with its timeworn three-inch bore, did a full salute, and we carried the coffin to the open pit. The coffin was open, the clean midday sun lit the lanky corpse, lit his mouth filled with smashed teeth and his carefully polished boots, their heels placed together as at a drill.

"Fighters!" Regimental Captain Pugachov said, as he eyed the dead man and walked up to the edge of the pit. "Fighters!" he said, standing at attention, shaking with emotion. "We are burying Pashka Trunov, an international hero! We are according Pashka the final honor!"

Pugachov raised his eyes, burning with sleeplessness, to the sky and shouted out his speech about the dead fighters of the First Cavalry, that proud phalanx which pounds the anvil of future centuries with the hammer of history. Pugachov shouted out his speech loudly, clenched the hilt of his curved Chechen saber, and scuffed the earth with his tattered boots and their silver spurs. After his speech the orchestra played the "Internationale," and the Cossacks took leave of Pashka Trunov. The whole squadron leaped onto their horses and fired a volley into the air, our three-inch cannon hissed toothlessly a second time, and we sent three Cossacks to find a wreath. They whirled off at full gallop, firing as they rode and plunging from their saddles in a display of acrobatics, and brought back armfuls of red flowers. Pugachov scattered the flowers around the grave, and we stepped up to Trunov for the last kiss. I touched my lips on an unblemished patch of forehead crowned by his saddle, and then left to go for a walk through the town, through gothic Sokal, which lay in its blue dust and in Galicia's dejection.

A large square stretched to the left of the park, a square surrounded by ancient synagogues. Jews in long, torn coats were cursing and shoving each other on this square. Some of them, the Orthodox, were extolling the teachings of Adassia, the Rabbi of Belz, which led the Hasidim of the moderate school, students of Rabbi Iuda of Husyatyn, to attack them. The Jews were arguing about the Kabbala, and in their quarrel shouted the name of Elijah, Gaon of Vilna, the persecutor of the Hasidim.

Ignoring war and gunfire, the Hasidim were cursing the name of Elijah, the Grand Rabbi of Vilna, and I, immersed in my sorrow over Trunov, joined in the jostling and yelled along with them to ease my pain, until I suddenly saw a Galician before me, sepulchral and gaunt as Don Quixote.

This Galician was wearing a white linen garment that reached down to his ankles. He was dressed as for burial or as for the Eucharist, and led a bedraggled little cow tied to a rope. Over its wide back darted the tiny wriggling head of a snake. On the snake's head was a teetering wide-brimmed hat made of village straw. The pitiful little cow tagged along behind the Galician. He led her with importance, and his lanky body cut into the hot brilliance of the sky like a gallows.

He crossed the square with a stately stride and went into a crooked little alley seasoned with sickeningly thick smoke. In the charred little hovels, in beggarly kitchens, were Jewesses who looked like old Negro women, Jewesses with boundless breasts. The Galician walked past them and stopped at the end of the alley before the pediment of a shattered building.

There by the pediment, near a crooked white column, sat a gypsy blacksmith shoeing horses. The gypsy was pounding the horses' hooves with a hammer, shaking his greasy hair, whistling, and smiling. A few Cossacks with horses were standing around him. My Galician walked up to the blacksmith, gave him a dozen or so baked potatoes without a word, and turned and walked off, not looking up at anyone. I was about to follow him, but one of the Cossacks, waiting for his horse to be shod, stopped me. This Cossack's name was Seliverstov. He had left Makhno* some time ago and was serving in the Thirty-third Cavalry Regiment.

"Lyutov," he said, shaking my hand, "you can't keep from picking quarrels with everyone! You've got the devil in you! Why did you finish off Trunov this morning?"

And from the scraps of gossip he had heard, Seliverstov yelled foolish gibberish at me, about how that very morning I had given Trunov, my squadron commander, a good beating. Seliverstov hurled all kinds of reproaches at me, reproached me in front of all the Cossacks, but there wasn't a grain of truth in what he said. It was true that Trunov and I had argued that morning, because Trunov wasted so much time dawdling with the prisoners. He and I had argued, but Pashka Trunov is dead, he will no longer be judged in this world, and I would be the last to do so. I will tell you why we quarreled.

We had taken some men prisoner at dawn today near the train station. There were ten of them. They were in their underwear when we took them. A pile of clothes lay next to the Poles—it was a trick, so that we couldn't tell the officers from the regular men by their uniforms. They had taken off their clothes themselves, but this time Trunov decided to find out the truth.

"All officers, step forward!" he commanded, walking up to the prisoners and pulling out his revolver.

Trunov had already been wounded in the head that morning. His head was bandaged with a rag, and blood trickled from it like rain from a haystack.

* The Ukrainian anarchist leader.

"Officers! Own up!" he repeated, and began prodding the Poles with the butt of his revolver.

Suddenly a thin old man with yellow cheekbones, a drooping mustache, and a large, bare bony back, came forward.

"End of this war!" the old man said with incomprehensible delight. "All officers run away, end of this war!"

And the Pole held out his blue hands to Trunov.

"Five fingers," he said, sobbing, twisting his large, wilted hands from side to side. "I raising with these five fingers my family!"

The old man gasped, swayed, and broke into tears of delight. He fell on his knees before Trunov, but Trunov pushed him back with his saber.

"Your officers are dogs!" Trunov said. "Your officers threw their uniforms here, but I'm going to finish off whoever they fit! We're going to have a little fitting!"

And Trunov picked out an officer's cap from the pile of rags and put it on the old man's head.

"It fits," Trunov murmured, stepping up closer to him, "it fits." And he plunged his saber into the prisoner's gullet.

The old man fell, his legs twitching, and a foamy, coral-red stream poured from his neck. Then Andryushka Vosmiletov, with his sparkling earring and his round villager's neck, sidled up to the dying man. Andryushka unbuttoned the dying Pole's trousers, shook him lightly, and pulled the trousers off. He flung them onto his saddle, grabbed another two uniforms from the pile, and then trotted off, brandishing his whip. At that moment the sun came out from behind the clouds. It nimbly enveloped Andryushka's horse, its cheerful trot, the carefree swish of its docked tail. Andryushka rode along the path to the forest— our cavalry transport was in the forest, the carters of the transport yelling and whistling, and making signs to Vosmiletov like to a deaf man.

The Cossack was already halfway there when Trunov, suddenly falling to his knees, hoarsely yelled after him.

"Andrei!" he shouted, lowering his eyes to the ground. "Andrei!" he repeated without looking up. "Our Soviet Republic is still alive, it's too early to be dealing out her property! Bring back those rags, Andrei!"

But Vosmiletov didn't even turn around. He rode at his amazing Cossack trot, his horse pertly swatting its tail, as if to shoo us away.

"Treason!" Trunov mumbled in disbelief. "Treason!" he said, quickly shouldering his gun and shooting, missing in his haste. This time Andrei stopped. He turned his horse toward us, bouncing on his saddle like a woman, his face red and angry, his legs jerking.

"Listen, countryman!" he yelled, riding closer, and immediately calming down at the sound of his own deep and powerful voice. "I should knock you to Kingdom Come to where your you-know-what mother is! Here you've caught a dozen Poles, and make a big song-and-dance of it! We've taken hundreds and didn't come running for your help! If you're a worker, then do your job!"

Andryushka threw the trousers and the two uniforms off his saddle, snorted, turned away from the squadron commander, and came over to help me draw up a list of the remaining prisoners. He loafed about and snorted unusually loudly. The prisoners howled and ran away from him. He ran after them and gathered them under his arms, the way a hunter grips an armful of reeds and pushes them back to see a flock of birds flying to the river at dawn.

Dealing with the prisoners, I exhausted my repertoire of curses, and somehow managed to write up eight of the men, the numbers of their units, the type of gun they carried, and moved on to the ninth prisoner. The ninth was a young man who looked like a German acrobat from a good circus, a young man with a white, German chest, sideburns, a tricot undershirt, and a pair of long woolen drawers. He turned the nipples on his high chest toward me, threw back his sweaty blond hair, and told me the number of his unit. Andryushka grabbed him by his drawers and sternly asked him, "Where did you get those?"

"My mama knitted them," the prisoner answered, suddenly tottering.

"She's a great knitter, that mama of yours," Andryushka said, looking more closely at the drawers, and ran his fingertips over the Pole's neat nails. "Yes, a great knitter—us, we never got to wear nothing like that."

He felt the woolen drawers again and took the ninth man by the hand in order to take him over to the other prisoners who were already on my list. But at that moment I saw Trunov creeping out from behind a mound. Blood was trickling from his head like rain from a haystack and the dirty rag had come undone and was hanging down. He crawled on his stomach holding his carbine in his hands. It was a Japanese carbine, lacquered and with a powerful shot. From a distance of twenty paces, Pashka shot the young Pole's skull to pieces and his brains spattered onto my hands. Trunov ejected the empty cartridges from his carbine and came over to me.

"Cross that one off," he said, pointing at my list.

"I'm not crossing him off," I answered, quaking. "From what I see, Trotsky's orders don't apply to you!"

"Cross that one off the list!" Trunov repeated, pressing his black finger down onto the paper.

"I'm not crossing him off!" I yelled with all my might. "There were ten of them, now there are eight—back at headquarters, Trunov, they're not going to let you get away with this!"

"At headquarters they'll chalk it up to the rotten life we live," Trunov said, coming up to me, all tattered, hoarse, and covered in soot. But then he stopped, raised his blood-drenched face to the sky, and said with bitter reproach, "Buzz, buzz! And there comes another one buzzing!"

And Trunov pointed to four dots in the sky, four bombers that came floating out from behind the shining, swanlike clouds. These were machines from the air squadron of Major Fauntleroy, large, armored machines.

"To horse!" the platoon commanders yelled when they saw the airplanes, and took the squadron at a fast trot into the woods. But Trunov did not ride with his squadron. He stayed back at the station building, huddled silently against the wall. Andryushka Vosmiletov and two machine-gunners, two barefoot fellows in crimson breeches, stood next to him, increasingly anxious.

"Run for it, boys!" Trunov said to them, and the blood began to drain from his face. "Here's a message to Pugachov from me."

And Trunov scrawled gigantic peasant letters on a crookedly torn piece of paper.

"As I have to perish today," he wrote, "I see it my duty to add two dead toward my possible shooting down of the enemy, and at the same time I am handing over my command to Platoon Commander Semyon Golov."

He sealed the letter, sat down on the ground, and took off his boots with great difficulty.

"For you," he said, handing the machine-gunners the message and his boots. "These boots are new."

"Good luck to you, Commander," the machine-gunners muttered back to him, shifting from one foot to the other, hesitating to leave.

"And good luck to you too," Trunov said, "whatever happens." And he went over to the machine guns that stood on a mound by the station hut. Andryushka Vosmiletov, the rag looter, was waiting for him there.

"Yes, whatever happens," Trunov said to him, and aimed his machine gun. "So you're staying with me, Andryushka?"

"Jesus Christ!" Andryushka answered, terrified, started sobbing, went white, and burst out laughing. "Damned Mother of Lord Jesus Christ!"

And he aimed the second machine gun at the airplanes.

The airplanes came flying over the station in tighter circles, rattled fussily high in the air, plunged, drew arcs, and the sun rested its pink rays on the sparkle of their wings.

In the meantime we, the Fourth Squadron, sat in the forest. There, in the forest, we awaited the outcome of the unequal battle between Pashka Trunov and Major Reginald Fauntleroy of the American forces. The major and three of his bombers proved their ability in this battle. They descended to three hundred meters, and first shot Andryushka and then Trunov. None of the rounds our men fired did the Americans any harm. The airplanes turned and flew away without even noticing our squadron hidden in the forest. And that was why, after waiting for half an hour, we were able to go pick up the bodies. Andryushka Vosmiletov's body was taken by two of his kinsmen who were serving in our squadron, and we took Trunov, our deceased squadron commander, to the gothic town of Sokal and buried him there in a stately spot— in a flower bed, in the public park in the middle of the town.

IVAN AND IVAN

*D*eacon Aggeyev had deserted from the front twice. For this he had been sent to Moscow's "regiment of the branded." Sergei Sergeyevich Kamenev,* the commander in chief, had inspected this regiment at Mozhaysk before it was to be sent to the front.

"I have no use for them," the commander in chief had said. "Send them back to Moscow to clean latrines."

In Moscow the branded regiment was somehow absorbed into an infantry company. The deacon also ended up in it. He arrived at the Polish front, where he claimed to be deaf. Barsutsky, the medical assistant from the first-aid detachment, after going back and forth with him for a week, was amazed at the deacon's obstinacy.

"To hell with that deaf man!" Barsutsky said to Soychenko, the medical orderly. "Go see if you can get a cart from the cavalry transport, we'll send the deacon to Rovno for a checkup."

Soychenko went to the transport and got three carts. Akinfiev was the driver of the first cart.

"Ivan," Soychenko said to him, "you're going to take the deaf man to Rovno."

"Take him I can," Akinfiev answered.

"Be sure to get me a receipt."

"Will do," Akinfiev said. "And what was it that caused it, this deafness of his?"

---

* Sergei Sergeyevich Kamenev, 1881–1963, was the commander in chief of the Eastern Front.

"To save his own goods and chattels a man will gladly set fire to another man's hide," Soychenko, the medical orderly, said. "That's what caused it. He's a damn freemason, that's what he is, not deaf!"

"Take him I can," Akinfiev repeated, and drove off after the other carts.

Three carts pulled up in front of the first-aid station. In the first cart sat a nurse who was being transferred to the rear lines, the second cart had been brought for a Cossack with an inflamed kidney, and in the third cart sat Ivan Aggeyev, the deacon.

Having arranged everything, Soychenko called the medical assistant.

"There goes that damn freemason," he said. "I'm putting him on the Revolutionary Tribunal cart* against receipt. They'll be off any minute now."

Barsutsky looked out the window, saw the carts, and went running out of the house, red-faced and hatless.

"Hey, I know you're going to cut his throat!" he yelled to Ivan Akinfiev. "I want the deacon in another cart!"

"Wherever you put him," the Cossacks standing nearby said, laughing, "our Ivan's going to get him."

Ivan Akinfiev, whip in hand, was also standing there next to his horses.

"Greetings, Comrade Medical Assistant," he said politely, taking off his cap.

"Greetings, my friend," Barsutsky answered. "You're going to have to put the deacon in another cart, you wild beast!"

"It would interest me to know," Akinfiev began in a whiny voice, and his upper lip shivered, slid up, and began quivering over his dazzling teeth, "it would interest me to know, if this is right behavior or behavior that is not right, that when the enemy is tormenting us unbelievably, when the enemy is pounding our last breath out of us, when the enemy is clinging to our legs like a lead weight and tying our hands with snakes, is it correct behavior for us to clog our ears at such a deadly hour?"

---

* The Revolutionary Tribunals were set up by the Bolsheviks after the October Revolution in 1918 to combat counterrevolutionary elements, abuse of power, speculation, and desertion from the Soviet army. The Revolutionary Tribunal carts were used to transport any personnel, prisoners, and supplies that connected with the tribunals' military work.

"Our Ivan thinks like a commissar!" Korotkov, the driver of the first cart, shouted.

"So what if he thinks like a commissar!" Barsutsky muttered, and turned away. "We all do. But we have to stick to the rules."

"But our deaf friend, he can hear perfectly well!" Akinfiev suddenly interrupted. He twirled his whip with his fat fingers, laughed, and winked at the deacon. The deacon sat on the cart, his large shoulders drooping, his head trembling.

"Well then, go with God!" the medical assistant yelled in desperation. "I hold you responsible, Ivan!"

"I'll gladly be held responsible," Ivan Akinfiev said slowly, and lowered his head. "Make yourself comfortable," he said to the deacon, without looking back at him. "Make yourself even more comfortable," he repeated, and took the reins in his hands.

The carts formed a line and hurried off one after the other along the high road. Korotkov drove in front and Akinfiev at the back, whistling a tune and waving the reins. They rode this way some fifteen versts, but as evening fell they came up against a sudden enemy attack.

On that day, July 22, the Poles in a swift maneuver had mangled the rear lines of our army, stormed the shtetl of Kozin, and had taken prisoner many of our fighters of the Eleventh Division. The squadrons of the Sixth Division rushed off to Kozin to counterattack the enemy. The lightning maneuvers of the units threw the cavalry transport into turmoil, and the Revolutionary Tribunal carts rolled through the raging throes of battle for two days and nights, and it was only on the third night that they came out onto the road along which the rearguard staff was retreating. It was on this road at midnight where I ran into the three carts.

Numb with despair, I ran into them after the battle at Khotin. In the battle at Khotin my horse had been killed. After I lost him, I climbed onto an ambulance cart, and gathered up wounded men until evening. Then all the able-bodied men were kicked off the ambulance cart, and I was left behind near a destroyed hut. Night came galloping toward me on swift steeds. The wailing of the transport carts deafened the universe; on the earth enveloped by screams the roads faded away. Stars slithered out of the cool gut of the sky, and on the horizon abandoned villages flared up. With my saddle on my shoulders I walked along a torn-up field path, stopping by a bend to answer the call of nature. Relieved, I buttoned myself up, but suddenly felt droplets falling on my hand. I switched on my flashlight, turned around, and saw lying on the ground the body of a Pole, drenched in my urine. A notebook and scraps of Pilsudski's proclamation* lay next to the corpse. The Pole's notebook had a list of his expenses, a schedule of performances at the Krakow Dramatic Theater, and an entry indicating the birthday of a woman by the name of Marie-Louisa. I picked up Pilsudski's proclamation, wiped the stinking liquid from my unknown brother's skull, and walked on, bent under the weight of my saddle.

At that moment, there was a groaning of wheels close by.

"Halt!" I yelled. "Who goes there?"

Night came galloping toward me on swift steeds, flames danced on the horizon.

"We're from the Revolutionary Tribunal," a voice smothered by darkness called back.

I rushed forward and ran right into the cart.

"They killed my horse!" I said loudly. "His name was Lavrik."

No one answered. I climbed onto the cart, put the saddle under my head, fell asleep, and slept till dawn, warmed by the rotting hay and the body of Ivan Akinfiev, my chance neighbor. In the morning, the Cossack woke up later than I did.

"Thank God it's light enough to see again," he said, took his revolver out from under his little trunk, and fired a shot next to the deacon's ear. The deacon was sitting right in front of us, driving the horses. Airy gray hair fluttered over his large, balding skull. Akinfiev fired another shot next to the deacon's other ear, and slipped the revolver back into its holster.

"Good day to you, Ivan!" he said to the deacon, grunting as he pulled on his boots. "So we'll grab a bite, huh?"

"Hey!" I yelled. "What the hell d'you think you're doing?"

"Not enough, that's what I'm doing!" Akinfiev answered, unpacking the food. "It's the third day now he's been pretending."

Then Korotkov, who I knew from the Thirty-first Regiment, yelled back from the first cart, telling me the whole story of the deacon from

* Jozef Klemens Pilsudski, 1867–1935, the first Chief of State of Poland after its independence from Russia in 1918, and commander in chief of the Polish army.

the beginning. Akinfiev listened carefully, cupping his ear, and then from under his saddle pulled out a roasted leg of ox. It was wrapped in a sackcloth and had straw all over it.

The deacon climbed over to us from the box, carved off a slice of green meat with his knife, and gave everyone a piece. After breakfast, Akinfiev wrapped the leg of ox in the sackcloth and slid it into the hay.

"Ivan," he said to Deacon Aggeyev, "let's drive out the devil. We have to stop anyway, since the horses need water."

He took a medicine bottle out of his pocket and a Tarnovsky syringe,* and gave them to the deacon. They climbed off the cart and walked about twenty paces into the field.

"Nurse!" Korotkov yelled from the first cart. "Adjust your eyes for distance, and you'll be dazzled by Akinfiev's endowment!"

"I you-know-what you and your endowments," the woman muttered, and turned away.

Akinfiev pulled up his shirt. The deacon knelt in front of him and gave him his injection. Then he wiped the syringe with a rag and held it up to the light. Akinfiev pulled his trousers up. He waited a moment, went behind the deacon, and fired another shot right next to his ear.

"My humblest thanks, Ivan," he said, buttoning up his trousers.

The deacon laid the medicine bottle on the grass and got up from his knees. His airy hair flew up.

"I will answer to a higher judge," he said dully. "You are not above me, Ivan."

"Nowadays everyone judges everyone else," the driver of the second cart, who looked like a boisterous little hunchback, interrupted. "They even sentence you to death, just like that!"

"Or even better," Deacon Aggeyev said, straightening up, "kill me, Ivan."

"Don't talk nonsense, Deacon!" Korotkov, whom I knew from before, said, coming up to him. "You should realize what kind of man you're riding with here. A lesser man would have shot you down like a duck, you wouldn't have had time to quack, yet he's trying to fish the truth out of you, and teach you a thing or two, you defrocked cleric!"

* A device for treating syphilis.

"Or even better," the deacon repeated obstinately, stepping forward, "kill me, Ivan."

"As it is, you'll kill yourself, you bastard," Akinfiev answered, going white and breaking into a lisp. "You're digging your own pit and burying yourself in it!"

Akinfiev waved his arms, tore his collar open, and fell down on the ground in a fit.

"O my dear little sweetheart!" he yelled wildly, and threw sand into his face. "O my bittersweet darling, my sweet darling Soviet power!"

"Ivan," Korotkov said, coming up to him, tenderly laying his hand on his shoulder. "Don't beat yourself, my dear friend, don't be sad. Come, we have to go now."

Korotkov filled his mouth with water and spat it into Akinfiev's face, and then carried him over to the cart. The deacon sat on the box again, and we drove off.

There were no more than two versts left to the shtetl of Verba. Countless transport carts had crowded into the town that morning. They were from the Eleventh, the Fourteenth, and the Fourth Divisions. Jews in waistcoats, with raised shoulders, stood in their doorways like bedraggled birds. Cossacks went from yard to yard collecting rags and eating unripe plums. The moment we arrived, Akinfiev curled up on the hay and fell asleep, and I took a blanket from his cart and went to look for some shade to lie down in. But the fields on both sides of the road were covered with excrement. A bearded muzhik in copper-rimmed spectacles and a Tyrolean hat was sitting by the wayside reading a newspaper. He waved to me and said, "We call ourselves human, but we make more filth than the jackals! One is ashamed to face the earth!"

And he turned away and went back to reading his newspaper through his large spectacles.

I headed for the forest to the left, and saw the deacon approaching me.

"Where are you off to, countryman?" Korotkov yelled to him from the first cart.

"To relieve myself," the deacon mumbled. He grabbed my hand, and kissed it. "You are a fine gentleman," he whispered with a grimace, shuddering and gasping for air. "I beg you, whenever you have a free moment, to write a letter to the town of Kasimov, so my wife can mourn for me."

"Are you deaf, Father Deacon, or not?" I shouted into his face.

"Excuse me?" he said. "Excuse me?" And he cupped his ear.

"Are you deaf, Aggeyev, or not?"

"That's exactly it, deaf!" he quickly said. "Three days ago I could hear perfectly well, but Comrade Akinfiev crippled my hearing with a shot. He was supposed to deliver me to Rovno, Comrade Akinfiev was, but I really doubt he'll deliver me there."

And the deacon fell to his knees and crawled headfirst between the carts, completely entangled in his disheveled, priestly hair. Then he got up from his knees, pulled himself free from in between the carts, and went over to Korotkov, who gave him some tobacco. They rolled cigarettes and lit them for each other.

"That's better," Korotkov said, and made some space next to him.

The deacon sat down, and both were silent.

Then Akinfiev woke up. He rolled the leg of ox out of the sackcloth, carved off a slice of green meat with his knife, and gave everyone a piece. At the sight of the festering meat I felt overcome by weakness and desperation, and gave my piece back.

"Farewell, boys!" I said. "Good luck to you all!"

"Farewell," Korotkov said.

I took my saddle from the cart and left. As I walked off, I heard the endless muttering of Akinfiev.

"Ivan, you made a big mistake, my friend," he was saying to the deacon. "You should have trembled at my name, but you just got into my cart without a second thought. You could still have escaped before you ran into me, but now I'm going to hurt you, Ivan, you can bet on it, I'm really going to hurt you!"

THE CONTINUATION
OF THE STORY OF
A HORSE

Four months ago, Savitsky, our former division commander, took away the white stallion belonging to Khlebnikov, commander of the First Squadron. Khlebnikov had left the army shortly after, and today Savitsky received a letter from him.

Khlebnikov to Savitsky

And no anger upon the Budyonny army can I have longer, my sufferings in that army I understand and keep within my heart purer than anything holy. But to you, Comrade Savitsky, as an international hero, the working masses of Vitebsk, where I am the chairman of the District Revolutionary Committee, send the proletarian cry: "Give us World Revolution!" And we hope that that white stallion will trot beneath you on soft paths for many a year to come in aid of Freedom so beloved by all, and the Brother Republics in which we must keep a sharp eye out for the provincial authorities and the district units in an administrative respect. . . .

Savitsky to Khlebnikov

My true and dear Comrade Khlebnikov,

Which letter you wrote me is very commendable for the Common Cause, all the more after your foolishness when the good of your own hide made your eyes blind and you de-joined our Communist Party of the Bolsheviks. Our Communist Party, Comrade Khlebnikov, is an iron column of fighters sacrificing their blood in the front lines, and when blood flows from iron, then it is no joke, Comrade, but victory or death. The same goes for the Common Cause, the dawn of which I do not expect to see because the fighting is heavy and I have to change commanding officers every two weeks. Thirty days I have been fighting in the rear guard, covering the retreat of the invincible First Red Cavalry, and finding myself facing powerful gunfire from airplanes and artillery. Tardy was killed, Likhmanikov was killed, Gulevoy was killed, Trunov was killed, and the white stallion is no longer under me, so with the change in our fortunes of war, Comrade Khlebnikov, do not expect to see your beloved Division Commander Savitsky ever again. To tell you the truth, we shall meet again in the Kingdom of Heaven, although, from what people say, the old man up there in heaven isn't running a kingdom, but an all-out whorehouse, and as it is we have enough clap down here on earth—so, who knows, we might not get to see each other after all. Farewell, Comrade Khlebnikov.

THE WIDOW

*S*hevelyov, the regimental captain, is dying in an ambulance cart. A woman is sitting at his feet. Night, pierced by the flashes of the cannonade, is stooping over the dying man. Lyovka, the division commander's driver, is warming up food in a pot. Lyovka's forelock is hanging over the fire, the hobbled horses are crackling in the bushes. Lyovka is stirring the pot with a twig and talking to Shevelyov, who is stretched out in the ambulance cart.

"I worked in the town of Temryuk, Comrade, as a circus rider and also as a lightweight wrestler. The women in a small town like that get very bored, so when the little ladies saw me, all the walls came tumbling down. 'Lev Gavrilich,' they'd say to me, 'surely you won't turn down a little à la carte appetizer—you won't find it a waste of your time.' So I went with one of them to a tavern. We order two portions of veal, we order a jug of vodka, we sit there nice and quiet, we drink, I look, and what do I see? Some sort of gentleman bustling over toward me, nicely dressed, clean, but I notice that he is full of himself, not to mention that he was two sheets to the wind.

" 'If you will pardon me,' he says to me, 'what, if I may ask, is your nationality?'

" 'For what reason are you touching me about my nationality when I am in the company of a lady?' I ask him.

"And he: 'You? You are an athlete?' he says. 'In French wrestling they'd finish you off in the twinkle of an eye. Show me your nationali—'
Yet I, believe it or not, still don't catch what's going on.

"So I ask him, 'Why do you—I don't even know your name—why do you try to provoke the kind of misunderstanding where one man or the other will have to lose his life, in other words, lie flat on his back awaiting his last breath?'"

"Lie flat on his back awaiting his last breath!" Lyovka repeats enthusiastically, stretching his arms up to the sky, letting the night envelop him like an aura. The tireless wind, the clean wind of the night, sings, fills itself with sound, and gently rocks the soul. The stars, blazing in the darkness like wedding rings, fall on Lyovka, become entangled in his hair, and expire on his tousled head.

"Lyovka, come here," Shevelyov suddenly whispers to him with blue lips. "The gold I have is for Sashka," the wounded man whispers. "The rings, the harness—everything's hers. We did our best to get by, I want to reward her. My clothes, my underwear, my medal for selfless heroism, are for my mother on the Terek. Send them to her with a letter and write in the letter: The regimental captain sends his regards, and don't cry. The house is yours, old woman, enjoy it. If anyone lays a finger on you, go straight to Budyonny and tell him, 'I'm Shevelyov's mama!' My horse, Abramka, I offer to the regiment, I am offering the horse in memory of my soul."

"Don't worry, I'll see to the horse," Lyovka mumbles. "Sashka!" he yells to the woman, waving to her. "You heard what he said? Swear before him—will you be sure to give the old woman what's hers or won't you?"

"I you-know-what the old woman!" Sashka says, and walks off into the bushes, holding her head high like a blind woman.

"Will you give her her miserable share?" Lyovka asks, catching up with her and grabbing her by the throat. "Say it here in front of him!"

"I'll give it to her, let me go!"

And then, having forced the declaration out of her, Lyovka grabbed the pot from the fire and began pouring soup into the dying man's rigid mouth. Cabbage soup trickled down Shevelyov's face, the spoon clanked against his sparkling, dead teeth, and bullets sang with growing mournfulness and force through the dense expanses of the night.

"They're shooting with rifles, the bastards," Lyovka said.

"The damn lackeys!" Shevelyov answered. "They're ripping open our right flank with their machine guns."

And Shevelyov, closing his eyes, stately as a corpse on a slab, listened to the battle with his large, waxen ears. Next to him, Lyovka was chewing meat, crunching and panting. When he had finished, Lyovka licked his lips and pulled Sashka into a ditch.

"Sash," he said, trembling, burping, his hands fidgeting. "Sash, as the Lord is my witness, we're covered in vice like yard dogs with lice. You only live once and then you die! Let me have you, Sash—I'll serve you, even if it's with my blood! His time's up, Sash, but the Lord has plenty more days in store for us!"

They sat down in the tall grass. The wavering moon crept from behind the clouds and stopped over Sashka's bare knee.

"You're warming each other," Shevelyov mumbled, "but it looks like the Fourteenth Division has been routed."

Lyovka crunched and panted in the bushes. The misty moon loitered in the sky like a beggar woman. Distant gunfire floated in the air. Feather grass rustled on the troubled earth onto which August stars fell.

Then Sashka returned to her previous place. She changed the wounded man's bandages and raised the flashlight over the festering wound.

"By tomorrow you'll be gone," Sashka said, wiping the cold sweat off Shevelyov. "By tomorrow you'll be gone. Death's already in your guts."

At that moment a heavy, many-voiced blast hit the earth. Four fresh enemy brigades, sent into battle under a unified command, had fired their first shell at Busk, lighting up the Bug watershed and severing our communications. Obedient blazes rose on the horizon, and heavy birds of cannon fire soared up from the flames. Busk was burning and Lyovka sped through the forest with the rattling cart of the commander of Division Six. He gripped the red reins tightly; the lacquered wheels banged against tree stumps. Shevelyov's ambulance cart came flying behind, Sashka checking the horses, which were straining at their harnesses.

They came to a clearing in the forest where there was a first-aid station. Lyovka unharnessed the horses and set out for the medical officer to ask for a horse blanket. He walked through the forest, which was filled with carts. Nurses' bodies jutted out from under their carts, timid dawn trudged over the soldiers' sheepskins. The sleeping men's boots lolled in a jumble, their pupils pointed to the sky, the black pits of their mouths askew.

The medical officer did have a horse blanket. Lyovka returned to Shevelyov, kissed his forehead, and pulled the blanket over his head. Then Sashka came up to the cart. She had knotted her kerchief under her chin and shaken the straw out of her dress.

"Pavlik," she said. "Jesus Christ in Heaven." And she lay herself against the dead man, covering him with her massive body.

"Her grief's killing her," Lyovka said. "Say what you want, she had it good with him. Now she'll have to take on the whole squadron again. It's tough."

And he drove off to Busk, where the headquarters of the Sixth Cavalry Division had been set up.

There, about ten versts from town, the battle against the Savinkov Cossacks was raging. The traitors were fighting us under the command of Cossack Captain Yakovlev, who had gone over to the Poles. They fought with courage. It was the second day our division commander was out with the troops, and as Lyovka did not find him at the headquarters, he went back to his hut, cleaned his horses, poured water over the wheels of his cart, and lay down to sleep on the threshing floor in the shed. The shed was filled with fresh hay, as arousing as perfume. Lyovka slept himself out, and then sat down to eat. His landlady boiled him some potatoes, which she doused in buttermilk. Lyovka was still sitting at the table when the funereal wail of trumpets and the clatter of many hooves resounded in the street. A squadron with bugles and banners rode along the winding Galician street. Shevelyov's body, covered with flags, was lying on a gun carriage. Sashka was riding behind the coffin on Shevelyov's stallion. A Cossack song came drifting from the back rows.

The squadron marched along the main street and turned toward the river. Lyovka, barefoot and without a cap, ran after the marching detachment and grabbed the reins of the squadron commander's horse.

Neither the division commander, who had stopped by the crossroads to salute the dead commander, nor his staff could hear what Lyovka was saying to the squadron commander.

"Drawers . . . mother on the Terek . . ." came wafting over to us in fragments on the breeze. Lyovka was shouting incoherently.

The squadron commander, without listening any further, freed his reins and pointed at Sashka. The woman shook her head and rode on. Lyovka jumped onto her horse behind her, grabbed her by the hair, pulled her head back, and slammed his fist into her face. Sashka wiped the blood away with the hem of her skirt and rode on. Lyovka slipped off her saddle, shook his forelock out of his face, and tied his red scarf around his hips. And the howling bugles led the squadron to the sparkling shore of the River Bug.

Lyovka came back to us later that day, his eyes glittering, and shouted, "I gave it to her! 'When the time comes,' she says, 'I'll send it to his mother. I won't forget him,' she says, 'I'll remember him.' 'You'd better remember him, you evil snake! If you forget, we'll come around and remind you! And if you forget a second time, we'll come around and remind you a second time!' "

ZAMOSC

The division commander and his staff were lying on a harvested field about three versts from Zamosc. The troops were going to attack the town that evening. Our orders were that we were to spend the night in Zamosc, and the division commander was waiting for a report of victory.

It was raining. Wind and darkness blew over the sodden earth. Stars were extinguished in the swelling ink of the clouds. Exhausted horses sighed and stamped their hooves in the darkness. We had nothing to give them to eat. I tied my horse's reins to my foot, wrapped myself in my cloak, and lay down in a waterlogged pit. The wet earth wrapped me in its comforting sepulchral embrace. The mare tugged at her reins, pulling at my leg. She found a tuft of grass and began nibbling at it. I fell asleep and dreamed of a threshing floor covered with hay. The dusty gold of threshed corn droned over it. Sheaves of wheat flew into the sky, the July day turned into evening, and the thickets of the sunset arched back over the village.

I lay stretched out on my silent bed of hay, and the hay caressing the nape of my neck drove me out of my mind. Then the barn doors opened with a whistle. A woman in a ball gown came up to me. She released one of her breasts from the black lace of her bodice and carefully offered it to me, like a wet nurse about to suckle an infant. She laid her breast on mine. An agonizing warmth shook the foundations of my soul, and drops of sweat—living, flowing sweat—seethed between our nipples.

"Margot!" I wanted to shout. "The earth is dragging me away with the rope of its wretchedness like a stubborn dog, and yet I have managed to see you again!"

I wanted to shout these words, but my jaws, clamped shut by a sudden frost, would not unclench.

Then the woman moved away from me and fell to her knees.

"Lord Jesus," she said, "take unto Thee the soul of Thy departed slave!"

She pressed two worn five-kopeck coins onto my lids and stuffed fragrant hay into the opening of my mouth. A moan tried in vain to flutter through my clenched jaws; my expiring pupils slowly rolled beneath the copper coins; I could not unclasp my hands, and . . . I awoke.

A muzhik with a tangled beard was lying in front of me. He held a rifle in his hands. My horse's back cut the sky like a black crossbeam. The reins gripped my foot in a tight noose, pulling it upward.

"You fell asleep, countryman," the muzhik said, and smiled with nocturnal, sleepless eyes. "That horse has dragged you a good half verst!"

I untied the reins and got up. Blood was trickling down my face, slashed by thistles.

Right there, not two paces away from me, lay the front line. I could see the chimneys of Zamosc, the thievish lights in the ravines of its ghetto, and the watchtower with its shattered lantern. The damp sunrise poured down on us like waves of chloroform. Green rockets soared over the Polish camp. They flashed in the air, came showering down like roses beneath the moon, and expired.

And in the silence I heard the distant breath of a moan. The smoke of a furtive murder encircled us.

"They're killing someone," I said. "Who is it they're killing?"

"The Pole's on a rampage," the muzhik told me. "The Pole is slashing the Yids' throats."

The muzhik moved the rifle from his right hand to his left. His beard had slid completely to one side. He looked at me fondly. "These nights on the front line are long," he said. "There's no end to these nights. One itches all over to talk to someone, but where d'you find this someone?"

The muzhik passed me his cigarette for me to light mine.

"It's all the fault of those Yids," he said. "They try to please every-body. After the war there'll be hardly any of them left. How many Yids you reckon there's in the world?"

"Around ten million," I answered, and began to bridle my horse.

"There'll be two hundred thousand of them left!" the muzhik yelled, grabbing me by the arm, afraid that I was about to leave. But I climbed onto my saddle and galloped off in the direction of our head-quarters.

The division commander was preparing to ride off. The orderlies were standing at attention before him, dozing on their feet. Squadrons of dismounted horsemen crept over wet hillocks.

"They've turned the screws on us," the division commander whis-pered, and rode off.

We followed him along the road to Sitaniec.

It began raining again. Dead mice floated down the roads. Autumn surrounded our hearts with traps. Trees, upright naked corpses, stood swaying at crossroads.

We arrived in Sitaniec in the morning. I was with Volkov, the staff quartermaster. He found us a hut at the edge of the village.

"Wine," I told the mistress of the house. "Wine, meat, and bread!"

The old woman sat down on the floor and fed the calf she had hid-den under her bed.

"*Nic niema*,"* she answered indifferently, "and I don't remember a time when there ever was anything."

I sat at the table, took off my revolver, and fell asleep. A quarter of an hour later I opened my eyes and saw Volkov hunched over the win-dowsill. He was writing a letter to his bride.

"Highly esteemed Valya," he wrote. "Do you remember me?"

I read the first line, and then took some matches out of my pocket and lit a pile of straw lying on the floor. Unfettered flames flashed up and came moving toward me. The old woman hurled herself chest-first onto the fire and extinguished it.

"What you doing, *Pan*?" the old woman gasped, staggering back in horror.

* Polish: "There's nothing."

Volkov turned around and stared at her with his empty eyes, and went back to writing his letter.

"I'm going to burn you, old woman," I muttered, drowsily. "I'm going to burn you and that stolen calf of yours."

"*Czekaj!*"* she shouted in a high-pitched voice. She ran out into the hall and came back with a jug of milk and some bread.

We had barely eaten half the bread when we heard shots rattling outside in the yard. There were many shots. They went on rattling and got on our nerves. We finished the milk, and Volkov went out into the yard to see what was going on.

"I've saddled your horse," he called through the window. "They've shot mine full of holes. The Poles have set up their machine guns less than a hundred paces from here!"

So the two of us ended up with one horse. She barely managed to take us out of Sitaniec. I sat in the saddle, and Volkov climbed on behind.

Transport carts rolled, roared, and sank in the mud. The morning seeped out of us like chloroform seeping over a hospital table.

"You married, Lyutov?" Volkov suddenly said, sitting behind me.

"My wife left me," I answered, dozing off for a few seconds, and I dreamed that I was sleeping in a bed.

Silence.

Our horse totters.

"Two more versts and this mare will be finished," Volkov says, sitting behind me.

Silence.

"We've lost the campaign," Volkov mutters, and begins to snore.

"Yes," I say.

---

* Polish: "Wait."

TREASON

*C*omrade Investigator Burdenko. Answering your question, my Party Membership Number is twenty-four zero-zero, issued to Nikita Balmashov by the Krasnodar Party Committee. My life history I would describe as domestic until 1914, as I worked on my father's fields, and I went from the fields into the ranks of the imperialists to defend Citizen Poincaré and the butchers of the German Revolution Ebert-Noske,* who, it looks like, were fast asleep one day and in their dreams saw how they could help St. Ivan, my Cossack village in the District of Kuban. And so the string kept unraveling all the way until Comrade Lenin, together with Comrade Trotsky, turned my beast of a bayonet to point it at new and better guts and paunches. From that time on I've been carrying number twenty-four zero-zero on the watchful tip of my bayonet, and I find it shameful and laughable to hear your words, Comrade Investigator Burdenko, this impossible sham about some unknown hospital in N. I neither fired at this hospital nor attacked it—I couldn't have. We were wounded, the three of us, in other words, Fighter Golovitsyn, Fighter Kustov, and me, not to mention that we had a fever in our bones and so didn't attack, but were crying, standing there in our hospital shirts out on the square among the free people of Jewish nationality! And as for the destruction of the three windowpanes, which we destroyed with an officer's revolver, I declare

---

*Raymond Poincaré, 1860–1932, president of France, supported the Imperialist Russian forces against the Bolsheviks in the Russian Civil War. Ebert and Noske were held responsible for the suppression of the Spartacus Rebellion in Germany.

from the bottom of my heart that these windowpanes did not corre-
spond to their purpose, as they were in the storeroom, which did not
need them. And Dr. Yaveyn, seeing our bitter gunshot, only laughed
with lots of chuckles, standing by the window of his hospital, and this
too can be corroborated by the aforementioned free Jews of the shtetl
of Kozin. As to Dr. Yaveyn, I also submit the following material,
Comrade Investigator, that he laughed when we, the three wounded
men, in other words Fighter Golovitsyn, Fighter Kustov, and me, initially presented ourselves for cure, and from his very first words, he
informed us far too roughly, 'You, fighters, will each take a bath in the
tub, and this very instant remove your weapons and clothes, as I'm worried they might be infectious—I want them out of here and dropped off
at the storeroom!' And as Fighter Kustov saw a beast before him and
not a man, he stepped forward with his broken leg and expressed himself, that the only people who need fear an infection from his sharp
Kuban saber are the enemies of our Revolution, and Fighter Kustov
also expressed an interest in knowing if at the storeroom one would find
among the things there a Party Fighter or, on the contrary, someone
from the partyless masses. And here Dr. Yaveyn obviously saw that we
were well able to recognize treason. He turned his back and without
another word and—again with lots of chuckles—sent us to the ward
where we also went, limping with broken legs, waving our crippled
arms, holding each other up, as the three of us are from the same
Cossack village of St. Ivan, in other words Fighter Golovitsyn, Fighter
Kustov, and me, we have the selfsame fate, and he who has a ripped-off
leg, he holds on to his comrade's arm, and he who is missing an arm,
he leans on his comrade's shoulder! Following the order issued, we went
to the ward where we expected to encounter Cultural and Educational
Work and devotion to the Cause, but what did we see in the ward? We
saw Red Army soldiers, only infantrymen, sitting on neat beds, playing
checkers, and with them nurses of tall build, smooth, standing by the
windows, fluttering their eyelashes. When we saw this, we stood there
as if lightning had struck us.

"You're done with fighting, boys?" I shout to the wounded.

"We're done with fighting," the wounded answer, and they move
their checkers made of bread pellets.

"Too soon," I tell the wounded, "too soon have you finished fighting, infantry, when the enemy walks on soft paws not fifteen versts from this town, and when you can read of our international situation in the *Krasny Kavalerist* newspaper, that it's one big disaster and that the horizon is full of black clouds!" But my words bounced off the heroic infantry like sheep dung from a regimental drum, and instead of a discussion the sisters of mercy led us off to some bunks and started all that drivel again about how we should hand in our weapons as if we had already been defeated! They agitated Kustov beyond words, and he began tearing at the wound on his left shoulder above his bleeding heart of a fighter and proletarian. Seeing his struggle, the nurses were quiet, but they only were quiet for the shortest time, and then again the partyless masses began making fun, and in the night the nurses sent volunteers ready to rip our clothes off us as we slept, or force us for Cultural and Educational Work to play theater roles in women's clothes, which is unseemly.

Unmerciful sisters! They tried more than once to trick us out of our clothes with sleeping powders, so that we started sleeping in shifts with one eye open, and we even went to the latrine in full uniform and with our revolvers. And suffering like this for a week and a day, so that we were already ranting and seeing visions, finally, waking on the accused morning of August 4, we noted on ourselves the following change: that we are lying there in shirts with numbers on them, like prisoners, without weapons and without the clothes sewn by our mothers, poor doddering old women from Kuban. And the sun, we see, is shining nice and bright, but the trench infantry, among who we three Red Cavalrymen are suffering, is hooliganizing us! And along with them the unmerciful sisters, who the night before gave us sleeping powders and now are wiggling their fresh breasts, bringing us trays with cococoa to drink, and milk enough in this cococoa to drown in! This whole frolicking merry-go-round makes the infantry bang their crutches on the ground so loud it's dreadful, and they pinch our bottoms like we're buyable females, yelling that Budyonny's First Cavalry has also finished fighting. But no, my curly-headed Comrades, you who have stuffed yourselves with such splendid paunches that rattle like machine guns in the night! Budyonny's First Cavalry has not yet finished fighting! So what we did was we excused ourselves as if we had to go answer a call of nature. Then the three of us went down into the courtyard and from the courtyard we went with our fevers and blue boils to Citizen Boyderman, the chairman of the Revolutionary Committee, without whom, Comrade Investigator Burdenko, it would never have come to this misunderstanding with the shooting—in other words, if it hadn't been for him, I mean if it hadn't been for the chairman of the Revolutionary Committee, who made us lose our senses completely. And even though we cannot present hard evidence about Citizen Boyderman, when we came in to the office of the chairman of the Revolutionary Committee, we noticed that he was a citizen of advanced years in a sheepskin coat, of Jewish nationality, sitting at the table, and the table is so full of papers that it is a terrible sight to see. And Citizen Boyderman's eyes dart first to one side, then to the other, and it is clear he has no idea what these papers are. These papers are a misery to him, even more so when unknown but deserving fighters come threatening, demanding rations, while one after the other local workers interrupt, informing him of the counterrevolution in the surrounding villages. And also regular workers suddenly appear who wish to get married at the Revolutionary Committee as soon as possible and without red tape. And we too announced with loud voices the incidents of treason at the hospital, but Citizen Boyderman only stared at us and his eyes darted again first to one side and then to the other, and he patted us on the shoulder, which already is not an Authority, and unworthy of an Authority! He didn't issue any resolution at all, and only announced, "Comrade Fighters, if you have compassion for the Soviet State, then leave these premises!" But we would not agree to do this, in other words, leave the premises, but demanded a full verification of his person, which, when he would not do that, we lost consciousness. And having lost consciousness, we went out onto the square in front of the hospital, where we disarmed the militia which was made up of one cavalry individual, and with tears in our eyes destroyed the three poor-quality windowpanes in the aforementioned storeroom. Dr. Yaveyn, during this unallowable action, made faces and chuckled, and all that at the very moment when four days later Comrade Kustov was to die of his illness!

In his short Red life, Comrade Kustov was endlessly distressed about treason, which one moment is winking at us from the window, the next is making fun of the coarse proletariat. But the proletariat,

Comrades, knows full well how coarse treason is, and we are pained by that, our soul is burning, and its fire tears our bodily prison to pieces.

Treason, I tell you, Comrade Investigator Burdenko, grins at us from the window, treason creeps in its socks through our house, treason has flung its boots over its shoulders, so that the floorboards of the house it is about to ransack will not creak.

CZESNIKI

The Sixth Division had gathered in the forest near the village of Czesniki and waited for the signal to attack. But Pavlichenko, commander of the Sixth Division, was waiting for the Second Brigade, and would not give the signal. So Voroshilov* rode up to the division commander and prodded his chest with the muzzle of his horse.

"We're dawdling, Division Commander," he said, "we're dawdling!"

"The Second Brigade is proceeding as you ordered at full trot to the place of engagement," Pavlichenko answered in a hollow voice.

"We're dawdling, Division Commander, we're dawdling!" Voroshilov repeated, tugging at his reins.

Pavlichenko took a step back.

"In the name of conscience," he shouted, wringing his clammy fingers, "in the name of conscience, do not rush me, Comrade Voroshilov."

"Do not rush me?" hissed Klim Voroshilov, the political representative of the Revolutionary War Council, closing his eyes. He sat on his horse, silent, his eyes closed, his lips moving. A Cossack wearing bast sandals and a bowler hat stared at him in amazement. The galloping squadrons went crashing through branches, roaring through the forest like the wind. Voroshilov combed his horse's mane with his Mauser.

"Army Commander!" he yelled, turning to Budyonny. "Say a few words to your troops before we ride! There he is, the Pole, standing on top of the hill like a pretty picture, laughing at you!"

* Kliment Yefremovich Voroshilov, 1881–1969, was a close friend and colleague of Stalin's, and cofounder with Budyonny of the Red Cavalry.

As a matter of fact, we could see the Poles through our binoculars. The army staff jumped onto their horses and the Cossacks streamed toward Budyonny from all sides.

Ivan Akinfiev, the former vehicular driver of the Revolutionary Tribunal, rode past sitting sidesaddle, and prodded me with his stirrup.

"What? You're with the troops now, Ivan?" I called out to him. "You've got no ribs left!"

"I you-know-what these ribs," Akinfiev called back. "Let's hear what the man has to say!"

He rode on and pushed his way through right up to Budyonny.

Budyonny shuddered, and said in a quiet voice: "Men! Our situations . . . well, it's . . . bad. A bit more liveliness, men!"

"To Warsaw!" the Cossack in the bast sandals and the bowler hat yelled, his eyes wild, and he slashed the air with his saber.

"To Warsaw!" Voroshilov shouted, rearing his horse and vaulting into the center of the squadrons.

"Fighters and Commanders!" he shouted passionately. "In Moscow, our ancient capital, there rages a power never before seen! A government of workers and peasants, the first in the world, orders you, fighters and commanders, to attack the enemy and bring back victory!"

"Draw your sabers!" Pavlichenko sang out from far behind the army commander, and his fat crimson lips glistened foam-speckled through the ranks. Pavlichenko's red Cossack coat hung in tatters, his repulsive, meaty face was twisted. He saluted Voroshilov with the blade of his precious saber.

"In accordance with my duty to the revolutionary pledge," said the commander of Division Six, wheezing, his eyes darting around, "I hereby report to the Revolutionary War Council that the Second Invincible Cavalry Brigade is at the present time moving at a fast trot to the place of engagement!"

"Well, get on with it," Voroshilov answered, waving him away. He tugged at his reins and rode off, with Budyonny at his side. On their long-limbed chestnut mares they rode next to each other in identical military jackets and glittering silver-embroidered trousers. The fighters, whooping, flocked after them, and pale steel gleamed in the purulence of the autumn sun. But I did not hear solidarity in the howls of the Cossacks, and, waiting for the attack, I went into the forest, into its heart, to our provision station.

A wounded Red Army soldier lay there in a delirium, and Styopka Duplishchev, a young, dim-witted Cossack, was rubbing down Hurricane, the division commander's thoroughbred stallion, which was descended from Lyulyusha, the Rostov record holder. The wounded man was rambling, reminiscing about Shuya, about a heifer and some sort of flax strands. Duplishchev, to drown out the pitiful muttering, was singing a song about an orderly and a fat general's wife. He sang louder and louder, waving his currycomb and patting the horse. But he was interrupted by Sashka, puffy Sashka, the lady of all the squadrons. She rode up to Duplishchev and jumped off her horse.

"So we'll do it, or what?" Sashka said to him.

"Get out of here," the young Cossack answered, turning his back to her, and began plaiting ribbons into Hurricane's mane.

"You stick to your word, Styopka!" Sashka told him. "Or are you just a lump of boot wax?"

"Get out of here!" Styopka answered. "I stick to my word."

He plaited all the ribbons into the horse's mane, and suddenly turned to me in despair. "Just look at that! See how she tortures me, Kiril Vasilich? For a whole month already you wouldn't believe what I've had to put up with! Wherever I turn to, she's there, wherever I run to, she blocks my path, always wanting me to let the stallion have a go. But the division commander tells me every day, 'Styopka,' he tells me, 'with a stallion like this one, many will be coming to ask you to let the stallion have a go, but don't let him, not before he's four!'"

"I bet you you won't be letting anyone before he's fifteen," Sashka muttered, and turned away. "And when he's fifteen, you'll be drooling bubbles, for all I know!"

She went over to her mare, tightened the saddle strap, and was about to ride off.

The spurs on her boots clattered, her lace stockings were full of straw and spattered with dirt, her monstrous breasts went swinging toward her back.

"And to think I brought a ruble with me," Sashka said to herself, shoving her spurred boot into the stirrup. "I brought it with me but now I'll have to take it away again."

She took out two fifty-kopeck coins, jingled them in her palm, and hid them again in her cleavage.

"So we'll do it, or what?" Duplishchev said, his eyes fixed on the silver, and he brought over the stallion.

Sashka went to a sloping place in the clearing and had her mare stand there.

"You'd be amazed, but you're the only one in these mudfields who's got a stallion," she said to Styopka, pushing Hurricane into position. "My mare's a frontline war horse, two years now she hasn't been humped, so I says to myself—why not get her some good blood?"

Sashka finished with the stallion, and then led her horse to the side.

"So, sweetie, we got our stuffing now," she whispered, kissing her mare's wet, skewbald lips from which slobbering strands of spittle hung. She rubbed her cheek against the mare's muzzle, and suddenly noticed the noise thudding through the forest.

"The Second Brigade's coming back," Sashka said sternly, turning to me. "We must go, Lyutov!"

"Coming back, not coming back, I don't give a damn!" Duplishchev shouted, the words getting stuck in his throat. "You've had your feast, now pay the priest!"

"My money's nice and fine where it is!" Sashka muttered, and leaped onto her mare.

I dashed after her, and we rode off in full gallop. Duplishchev's howl and the light thud of a gunshot rang out behind us.

"Just look at that!" the Cossack boy yelled as loudly as he could, running through the forest.

The wind hopped through the branches like a crazed rabbit, the Second Brigade went flying through the Galician oak trees, the placid dust of the cannonade rose above the earth as above a peaceful hut. And at a sign from the division commander, we launched our attack, the unforgettable attack on Czesniki.

AFTER THE BATTLE

*T*he story of my fight with Akinfiev is as follows:

On the thirty-first came the attack on Czesniki. The squadrons had gathered in the forest next to the village, and hurled themselves at the enemy at six in the evening. The enemy was waiting for us on a hill three versts away. We galloped the three versts on our totally exhausted horses, and when we got to the hill we saw a deadly wall of black uniforms and pale faces. They were Cossacks who had betrayed us at the beginning of the Polish Campaign and had been rounded up into a brigade by Cossack Captain Yakovlev. The Cossack captain formed his horsemen into a square formation, and waited with his saber unsheathed. A gold tooth flashed in his mouth and his black beard lay on his chest like an icon on the chest of a corpse. The enemy's machine guns fired at twenty paces; wounded men fell in our lines. We went trampling over them and hurled ourselves at the enemy, but his square formation did not waver, and we turned and ran.

So the Savinkov Cossacks gained a short-lived victory over the Sixth Division. They gained the victory because they did not turn their faces from the lava flow of our oncoming squadrons. The Cossack captain stood firm that time, and we ran without reddening our sabers with the traitors' contemptible blood.

Five thousand men, our whole division, poured down the slope with no one in pursuit. The enemy stayed on the hill, unable to believe their illogical victory and muster their wits to set out in pursuit after us. That is why we survived and went bounding into the valley unharmed, where we were met by Vinogradov, our military commissar. Vinogradov was dashing about on his crazed horse trying to send the fleeing Cossacks back into battle.

"Lyutov!" he yelled when he saw me. "Get those fighters to turn around or I'll rip your soul out!"

Vinogradov pounded his tottering stallion with the butt of his Mauser, howled, and tried rounding up the men. I got away from him and rode up to Gulimov, a Kirghiz, who was galloping past.

"Gulimov! Get back up there!" I yelled to him. "Turn back your horse!"

"Turn back your own damn horse!" Gulimov yelled back. His eyes darted about thievishly and he fired a shot, singeing the hair above my ear.

"Turn your own horse back," Gulimov hissed, grabbed my shoulder with one hand, and tried unsheathing his saber with the other. The saber was jammed in its sheath, the Kirghiz shuddered and looked around. He held my shoulder tightly and brought his head closer and closer.

"Yours first," he whispered almost inaudibly, "and mine will follow." And he tapped me lightly on the chest with the blade of his saber, which he had managed to unsheathe.

I felt a wave of nausea from death's closeness and its tight grip. With the palm of my hand I pushed away the Kirghiz's face, hot as a stone in the sun, and scratched it with all my might. Warm blood rippled under my nails, tickling them. I rode away from Gulimov, out of breath as after a long journey. My horse, my tormented friend, trotted slowly. I rode without looking where I was going, I rode without turning around, until I came across Vorobyov, the commander of the First Squadron. Vorobyov was looking for his quartermasters and couldn't find them. He and I made our way to Czesniki and sat down on a bench along with Akinfiev, the former vehicular driver of the Revolutionary Tribunal. Sashka, the nurse of the Thirty-first Cavalry Regiment, came by, and two commanders sat down on the bench with us. The commanders sat there in silence, dozing. One of them was shell-shocked, shaking his head uncontrollably and winking with one bloated eye. Sashka went to tell the people at the field hospital about him, and then came back to us, dragging her horse behind her by the reins. Her mare resisted, her hooves skidding in the wet mud.

"So where are you sailing off to?" Vorobyov asked the nurse. "Sit down here with us, Sash!"

"I'm not sitting with you!" Sashka answered, and slapped her mare on the belly. "No way!"

"What d'you mean?" Vorobyov shouted, laughing. "Or have you had second thoughts about drinking tea with men?"

"It's you that I've had second thoughts about!" she told the commander, hurling away the reins. "Yes, I've had second thoughts about drinking tea with you, after I saw you all today and saw what heroes you all are, and how disgusting you are, Commander!"

"So when you saw it," Vorobyov muttered, "how come you didn't join in the shooting?"

"Join in the shooting?" Sashka shouted in desperation, tearing off her nurse's band. "What am I supposed to shoot with? This?"

Here Akinfiev, the former vehicular driver of the Revolutionary Tribunal, with whom I still had some unfinished business to settle, came up to us.

"You've got nothing to shoot with, Sash," he said soothingly. "No one's blaming you for that! I blame those who get all mixed up in battle and forget to load cartridges in their revolvers!" A spasm suddenly shot over his face. "You rode in the attack!" he shouted at me. "You rode but didn't put any cartridges in! Why?"

"Back off, Ivan," I said to Akinfiev. But he wouldn't back off, and kept coming closer to me, an epileptic with a twisted spine and no ribs.

"The Pole shot at you, yes, but you didn't shoot at him!" he muttered, twisting and turning with his shattered hip. "Why?"

"The Pole did shoot at me," I told him brusquely, "but I didn't shoot at the Pole!"

"So you're a wimp, right?" Akinfiev whispered, stepping back.

"So I'm a wimp!" I said, louder than before. "What do you want?"

"What I want is for you to be aware," Akinfiev yelled in wild triumph, "aware that you're a wimp, because in my books all wimps should be shot dead, they believe in God!"

A crowd gathered, and Akinfiev yelled on about wimps without stopping. I wanted to walk away, but he ran after me, and caught up with me, and punched me in the back with his fist.

"You didn't put any cartridges in!" Akinfiev whispered in a breathless voice right next to my ear, and with his large thumbs began trying to wrench my mouth open. "You believe in God, you traitor!"

He tugged and tore at my mouth. I pushed the epileptic back and hit him in the face. He keeled over onto his side, hit the ground, and began to bleed.

Sashka went over to him with her dangling breasts. She poured water over him, and pulled out of his mouth a long tooth which was swaying in the blackness like a birch tree on a bare country road.

"These bantams know just one thing," Sashka said, "and that's how to belt each other in the mouth. With a day like this and everything, I just want to shut my eyes!"

There was anguish in her voice, and she took wounded Akinfiev with her, while I staggered off into the village of Czesniki, which was sliding around in the relentless Galician rain.

The village floated and bulged, crimson clay oozing from its gloomy wounds. The first star flashed above me and tumbled into the clouds. The rain whipped the willow trees and dwindled. The evening soared into the sky like a flock of birds and darkness laid its wet garland upon me. I was exhausted, and, crouching beneath the crown of death, walked on, begging fate for the simplest ability—the ability to kill a man.

THE SONG

When we were quartered in the village of Budziatycze, it was my lot to end up with an evil landlady. She was a widow, she was poor. I broke many locks on her storerooms, but found no provisions.

All I could do was to try and outsmart her, and one fine day, coming home early before dusk, I caught her closing the door of the stove, which was still warm. The hut smelled of cabbage soup, and there might well have been some meat in that soup. I did smell meat in her soup and laid my revolver on the table, but the old woman denied everything. Her face and black fingers were gripped by spasms, she glowered at me with fear and extraordinary hatred. Nothing would have saved her—I would have made her own up with my revolver if Sashka Konyayev, in other words Sashka Christ, hadn't suddenly turned up.

He came into the hut with his concertina under his arm, his exquisite legs shuffling in battered boots.

"How about a song?" Sashka said, looking at me, his eyes filled with blue and dreamy ice crystals. "How about a song?" he said, and sat down on the bench and played a prelude.

The pensive prelude came as if from far away. He stopped, and his blue eyes filled with longing. He turned away, and, knowing what I liked, started off on a song from Kuban.

"Star of the fields," he sang, "star of the fields over my native hut, and my mother's hand, so sorrowful. . . ."

I loved that song. Sashka knew this, because both of us, both he and I, had first heard this song back in '19 in the shallows of the Don in the Cossack village of Kagalnitskaya.

A hunter who poached in the protected waters there had taught it to us. There, in the protected waters, fish spawn and countless flocks of birds nest. The fish multiply in the shallows in incredible numbers, you can scoop them up with a ladle or even with your bare hands, and if you dip your oar in the water, it just stands there upright—a fish will have grabbed it and will carry it away. We saw this with our own eyes, we will never forget the protected waters of Kagalnitskaya. Every government has banned hunting there—a good ban—but back in '19 a war was raging in the shallows, and Yakov the hunter, who plied his forbidden trade right before our eyes, gave Sashka Christ, our squadron singer, a concertina as a present so that we would look the other way. He taught Sashka his songs. Many of them were soulful, old songs. So we forgave the roguish hunter, for we needed his songs: back then, no one could see the war ever ending, and Sashka covered our arduous paths with melody and tears. A bloody trail followed our paths. The songs soared over this trail. That is how it was in Kuban and on our campaigns against the Greens,* and that is how it was in the Urals and in the Caucasian foothills, and that is how it is to this very day. We need these songs, no one can see this war ever ending, and Sashka Christ, our squadron singer, is too young to die.

And this evening too, cheated of my landlady's cabbage soup, Sashka calmed me with his soft, wavering voice.

"Star of the fields," he sang, "star of the fields over my native hut, and my mother's hand, so sorrowful. . . ."

And I listened, stretched out in a corner on my rotting bedding. A dream broke my bones, the dream shook the putrid hay beneath me, and through the dream's burning torrent I could barely make out the old woman, who was standing by the wall, her withered cheek propped on her hand. She hung her ravaged head and stood fixed by the wall, not moving even after Sashka had finished playing. Sashka finished and put down his concertina, yawned, and burst out laughing as after a long

---

*Defectors from the Imperial army and later also from the new Soviet army, who banded together in guerrilla groups. They were called "Greens" because they hid in forests. Both the Whites and the Reds tried to organize them under their influence, creating bands of Red Greens and White Greens.

sleep, and then, noticing the chaos in the widow's hut, he wiped the debris from the bench and brought in a bucket of water.

"You see, deary, what your boss is up to?" the landlady said to him, pointing at me and rubbing her back against the door. "Your boss came in here, yelled at me, stamped his foot, broke all the locks in my house, and shoved his gun at me. It is a sin before the Lord to shove a gun at me—I'm a woman, after all!"

She rubbed her back against the door again and threw a sheepskin coat over her son. Her son lay snoring beneath an icon on a large bed covered with rags. He was a deaf-mute boy with a white, water-swollen head and gigantic feet, like those of a grown muzhik. His mother wiped the snot from his nose and came back to the table.

"Mistress," Sashka said to her, caressing her shoulder, "if you wish, I could be really nice to you."

But it was as if the woman hadn't heard what he had said.

"I didn't see no cabbage soup at all," she said, her cheek propped on her hand. "It ran away, my cabbage soup, and people shove their guns at me, so that even when a nice man comes along and I get a chance to tumble a little, I've ended up feeling so drab, I can't even enjoy sinning!"

She dragged out her mournful lament and, mumbling, rolled her deaf-mute son to the wall. Sashka lay with her on the rag-covered bed while I tried to sleep, conjuring up dreams so that I would doze off with pleasant thoughts.

THE RABBI'S SON

*D*o you remember Zhitomir, Vasily? Do you remember the River
Teterev, Vasily, and that night in which the Sabbath, the young
Sabbath, crept along the sunset crushing the stars with the heel of her
red slipper?

The thin horn of the moon dipped its arrows in the black waters of
the Teterev. Little, funny Gedali, the founder of the Fourth International,[*]
who took us to Rabbi Motale Bratslavsky for evening prayer. Little, funny
Gedali, shaking the cockerel feathers of his top hat in the red smoke of
the evening. The candles' predatory pupils twinkled in the rabbi's room.
Broad-shouldered Jews crouched moaning over prayer books, and the
old jester of the Chernobyl line of *tsaddiks* jingled copper coins in his
frayed pocket.

You remember that night, Vasily? Outside the window horses
neighed and Cossacks shouted. The wasteland of war yawned outside
and Rabbi Motale Bratslavsky, clutching his tallith with his withered
fingers, prayed at the eastern wall. Then the curtains of the cabinet fell
open, and in the funerary shine of the candles we saw the Torah scrolls
wrapped in coverings of purple velvet and blue silk, and above the
Torah scrolls hovered the humble, beautiful, lifeless face of Ilya, the
rabbi's son, the last prince of the dynasty.

And then, Vasily, two days ago the regiments of the Twelfth Army

---

[*] See the story "Gedali," in which Gedali envisions an ideal International that would supplant
the Third Communist International founded in Moscow in 1919 to promote Communism worldwide.

opened the front at Kovel. The victors' haughty cannonade thundered through the town. Our troops were shaken and thrown into disarray. The Polit-otdel train* crept along the dead spine of the fields. The typhoid-ridden muzhik horde rolled the gigantic ball of rampant soldier death before it. The horde scampered onto the steps of our train and fell off again, beaten back by rifle butts. It panted, scrambled, ran, was silent. And after twelve versts, when I no longer had any potatoes to throw to them, I threw a bundle of Trotsky leaflets at them. But only one of them stretched out a dirty, dead hand to grab a leaflet. And I recognized Ilya, the son of the Zhitomir rabbi. I recognized him straightaway, Vasily! It was so painful to see the prince, who had lost his trousers, his back snapped in two by the weight of his soldier's rucksack, that we broke the rules and dragged him up into the railroad car. His naked knees, clumsy like the knees of an old woman, knocked against the rusty iron of the steps. Two fat-breasted typists in sailor blouses dragged the dying man's timid, lanky body along the floor. We laid him out in the corner of the train's editorial compartment. Cossacks in red Tatar trousers fixed his slipped clothing. The girls, their bandy bovine legs firmly planted on the floor, stared coolly at his sexual organs, the withered, curly manhood of the emaciated Semite. And I, who had met him during one of my nights of wandering, packed the scattered belongings of Red Army soldier Ilya Bratslavsky into my suitcase.

I threw everything together in a jumble, the mandates of the political agitator and the mementos of a Jewish poet. Portraits of Lenin and Maimonides lay side by side—the gnarled steel of Lenin's skull and the listless silk of the Maimonides portrait. A lock of woman's hair lay in a book of the resolutions of the Sixth Party Congress, and crooked lines of Ancient Hebrew verse huddled in the margins of Communist pamphlets. Pages of *The Song of Songs* and revolver cartridges drizzled on me in a sad, sparse rain. The sad rain of the sunset washed the dust from my hair, and I said to the young man, who was dying on a ripped mattress in the corner, "Four months ago, on a Friday evening, Gedali the junk dealer took me to your father, Rabbi Motale, but back then, Bratslavsky, you were not in the Party."

* The train sent out by the Polit-otdel, the political organ of the new Soviet government charged with the ideological education of the military.

"I was in the Party back then," the young man answered, scratching his chest and twisting in his fever. "But I couldn't leave my mother behind."

"What about now, Ilya?"

"My mother is just an episode of the Revolution," he whispered, his voice becoming fainter. "Then my letter came up, the letter 'B,' and the organization sent me off to the front. . . ."

"So you ended up in Kovel?"

"I ended up in Kovel!" he shouted in despair. "The damn kulaks opened the front. I took over a mixed regiment, but it was too late. I didn't have enough artillery."

He died before we reached Rovno. He died, the last prince, amid poems, phylacteries, and foot bindings. We buried him at a desolate train station. And I, who can barely harness the storms of fantasy raging through my ancient body, I received my brother's last breath.

The Red Cavalry Cycle: Additional Stories

The seven additional RED CAVALRY stories in this section were not included in Babel's book KONARMIA (RED CAVALRY), published in 1926. Most of them appeared in magazines in the late 1920s and 1930s after the book had come out, while "And Then There Were Nine" and the fragment "And Then There Were Ten" were not published during Babel's lifetime. The last piece, "A Letter to the Editor," appeared in the magazine OKTYABR in October 1924. It was a response to General Budyonny's vitriolic article with the punning title "Babism Bablya" ("Babel's woman-ishness"), in which he condemned Babel's RED CAVALRY stories and their portrayal of himself and other real commanders.

MAKHNO'S BOYS

*T*he previous night, six Makhno* fighters raped a maid. When I heard this the following morning, I decided to find out what a woman looks like after being raped six times. I found her in the kitchen. She stood bent over a tub, washing clothes. She was a fat girl with blooming cheeks. Only a tranquil life on fertile Ukrainian soil can douse a Jewish girl in such bovine juices, lend her face such a lusty gloss. The girl's legs, fat, brick-red, bulging like globes, gave off the luscious stench of freshly carved meat, and it seemed to me that all that remained of yesterday's virginity were her cheeks, more flushed than usual, and her lowered eyes.

Young Kikin, the errand boy at Makhno's headquarters, was also in the kitchen. He was known at the headquarters as something of a simpleton—he had a tendency to walk about on his hands at the most unsuitable moments. More than once I found him in front of the mirror, stretching out his leg in his tattered trousers. He would wink at himself, slap himself on his bare, boyish stomach, sing marching tunes, and make triumphant grimaces which made even him guffaw. This boy's imagination worked with incredible vigor. Today I again found him busy on one of his special projects—he was sticking strips of gold paper on a German helmet.

"How many of them did you accommodate yesterday, Ruhlya?" he asked the girl, narrowing his eyes as he eyed the decorated helmet.

She remained silent.

* Nestor Ivanovich Makhno, 1889–1934, the Ukrainian anarchist leader.

"You accommodated six of them," he continued, "but there are girls who can accommodate up to twenty. Our boys did a Krapivno house-wife and they kept pounding and pounding away at her till they ran out of steam. But she was a good deal fatter than you are."

"Go get me some water," the girl said.

Kikin brought a bucket of water from the yard. He shuffled over to the mirror in his bare feet, put the helmet with the gold ribbons on his head, and carefully peered at his reflection. His image in the mirror fascinated him. He stuck his fingers in his nose and avidly watched it change shape under the pressure from within.

"I'll be going out on a mission," he said to the Jewess. "Don't you say a word to no one! Stetsenko's taking me into his squadron. At least they give you a real uniform, people respect you, and I'll have some real fight-er pals, not like here, where we're just some dinky little flea-ridden out-fit. Yesterday, when they grabbed you and I was holding you down by the head, I said to Matvey Vasilich, Hey, Matvey Vasilich, I said to him, four have already had a go, and I still get to keep holding and holding her down! You've already had her twice, Matvey Vasilich, and just because I'm underage and not in your gang, everyone can just push me around! And you yourself, Ruhlya, must have heard what he said to me—We, he said to me, don't push you around, Kikin! Once all my orderlies have had a go, it'll be your turn. He did say I could, and then, when they were already dragging you out into the woods, Matvey Vasilich tells me, You can do her now, Kikin, if you wish!—No way do I wish, Matvey Vasilich! I tell him, not after Vaska has had her, I'd never get over it till I die!"

Kikin grunted and fell silent. Barefoot, lanky, sad, his stomach bare, the glittering helmet on his straw-colored head, he lay down on the floor and stared into the distance.

"The whole world reckons the Makhno gang is all heroic and everything!" he said morosely. "But when you start hanging out with them, you soon see that they all harbor some grudge or other!"

The Jewess lifted her flushed face from the tub, glanced over at the boy, and left the kitchen with the heavy gait of a cavalryman whose numb legs have just touched the ground after a very long ride. Left alone, the boy looked dully around the kitchen, sighed, rested his palms on the floor, swung his legs in the air, and, with his heels together, quickly walked around on his hands.

A HARDWORKING
WOMAN

Three Makhno fighters—Gniloshkurov and two others—had come to an agreement with a woman about her love services. For two pounds of sugar, she agreed to take on the three of them, but when the third one's turn came, she couldn't hold out and went reeling around the room. The woman scrambled out into the yard, where she ran straight into Makhno.* He lashed her with his whip, tearing her upper lip, and Gniloshkurov got it too.

This happened in the morning, at nine o'clock. After that the day went by with much activity, and now it's night, the rain is drizzling, whispering and unyielding. It is rustling beyond the wall. In front of me, outside the window, hangs a single star. The town of Kamenka has drowned in the haze—the teeming ghetto is filled with teeming darkness and the inexorable bustling of the Makhno fighters. Someone's horse neighs softly like a pining woman; beyond the edge of the shtetl sleepless *tachankas*† creak, and the cannonade, falling silent, lies down to sleep on the black, wet earth.

Only Makhno's window is ablaze in a faraway street. It cuts through the gloom of the autumn night like an exhilarated searchlight, flashing, drenched with rain. There, in Makhno's headquarters, a brass band is playing in honor of Antonina Vasilevna, a nurse who was spending her first night with Makhno. The thick, melancholy trumpets blow louder and louder, and the partisans, huddled together beneath

---

* The anarchist leader.

† An open carriage or buggy with a machine gun mounted on the back.

---

my window, listen to the thundering of old marches. Three partisans are sitting beneath my window—Gniloshkurov and his comrades—and then Kikin, a crazed Cossack, comes rushing over to join them. He kicks his legs up in the air, does a handstand, chirps and sings, and has difficulty calming down, like an epileptic after a fit.

"Oat-head!" Gniloshkurov suddenly whispers to Kikin. "Oat-head," he repeats morosely. "How can it be that she let two more have a go after me without so much as batting an eyelash? There I was, putting my belt back on, and she looks at me and says to me, '*Merci* for spending some time with me, Papa, you are so charming! My name is Anelya—that's what I'm called, Anelya.' So you see, Oat-head, I think to myself she must have been chewing some bitter herbs since the morning, and then Petka wanted to have a go at her too!"

"Then Petka wanted to have a go at her too," fifteen-year-old Kikin chimes in, sitting down and lighting a cigarette. " 'Young man,' she tells Petka, 'would you please be kind enough, I'm at the end of my rope!' And she jumps up and starts spinning like a top, and the boys spread their arms and won't let her out the door, and she keeps begging and begging." Kikin stands up, his eyes flash, and he begins to laugh. "She escapes," Kikin continues, "and then right there at the door, who does she run into? Makhno himself. 'Halt!' he yells. 'I bet you have the clap! I'm going to hack you up here and now!' And he starts lashing her, and she—she still wants to give him some lip!"

"It must also be said," Petka Orlov's pensive and tender voice interrupts Kikin, "it must also be said, that there is greed among people, ruthless greed! I told her—'There's three of us, Anelya! Bring a girlfriend along, share the sugar with her, she'll help you!' 'No,' she says, 'I can cope well enough, I have three children to feed, it's not like I'm a virgin or something.' "

"A hardworking woman!" Gniloshkurov, still sitting beneath my window, assures Petka. "Hardworking to the last!"

And he falls silent. I can still hear the sound of water. The rain is continuing to stutter, bubble, and moan on the roofs. The wind grabs the rain and shoves it to the side. The triumphant blowing of the trumpets falls silent in Makhno's courtyard. The light in his room has dimmed by half. Gniloshkurov rises from the bench, splicing the dim glimmer of the moon. He yawns, tugs his shirt up, and scratches his remarkably white stomach, and then goes over to the shed to sleep. Petka Orlov's tender voice floats after him.

"In Gulya-Polye there was this out-of-town muzhik called Ivan Golub," Petka says. "He was a quiet muzhik—no drinking, he was cheerful when he worked, lifted too much of a load, got himself a rupture, and died. The people of Gulya-Polye mourned him and the whole village walked behind his coffin. They walked, even though he was a stranger."

And at the door of the shed, Petka begins muttering the story of the late Ivan, muttering more and more softly and tenderly.

"There is ruthlessness among people," Gniloshkurov says to him, yawning, "there really is, I tell you."

Gniloshkurov falls asleep, and the two others with him, and I remain alone by the window. My eyes explore the soundless dark, the beast of memory tears at me, and sleep will not come.

. . . She had sat in the main street selling berries since the morning. The Makhno fighters had paid her in abolished banknotes. She had the plump, airy body of a blonde. Gniloshkurov, his stomach jutting out, was sunning himself on a bench. He dozed, waited, and the woman, anxious to sell off her wares, gazed at him with her blue eyes, and blushed slowly and tenderly.

"Anelya," I whisper her name. "Anelya."

GRISHCHUK

*O*ur second trip to the shtetl ended badly. We had set out in the cart to find some fodder, and were heading back around midday. Grishchuk's back was bobbing gently up and down before my eyes. Right outside the village, he laid his reins carefully together, sighed, and slipped down from the box, crawled over my knees, and sprawled out across the cart. His cooling head rocked gently, the horses trotted on slowly, and a yellowing fabric of peace settled on his face like a shroud.

"Didn't eat nothing," he politely answered my cry of alarm, and wearily closed his eyelids.

That was how we rolled into the village—the coachman sprawled out across the cart.

At our lodgings I gave him some bread and a potato to eat. He ate sluggishly, dozing and shaking himself awake. Then he went out into the middle of the yard and lay down on his back, his arms spread wide.

"If you never tell me anything, Grishchuk," I said to him in exasperation, "how am I supposed to understand your pain?"

He said nothing and turned away. It was only that night, as we lay warming each other in the hay, that he shared with me a chapter from his mute novel.

Russian prisoners of war had worked building German fortifications along the North Sea coast. During the harvest season they were herded together and sent into the heart of Germany. A lone, crazed farmer took on Grishchuk. His madness consisted in his never speaking. He beat and starved Grishchuk until Grishchuk learned to communicate with him by hand signals. They lived together peacefully and in silence for four years. Grishchuk didn't learn the language because he never heard it spoken. After the German Revolution* he returned to Russia. His master had walked him to the edge of the village. They stopped at the side of the high road. The German pointed at the church, at his heart, at the boundless and empty blue of the horizon. He laid his gray, tousled head on Grishchuk's shoulder. They stood in a silent embrace. And then the German, throwing up his arms, ran back to his house with quick, faltering, stumbling steps.

---

*The abortive German November Revolution of 1918.

ARGAMAK

I decided to join the ranks at the front. The division commander grimaced when he heard this.

"Why the hell d'you want to go there? If you let your mouth hang open for a second, they shoot you point-blank!"

I held my ground. And that wasn't all. My choice fell on the most active division, the Sixth. I was assigned to the Fourth Squadron of the Twenty-third Cavalry Regiment. The squadron was commanded by Baulin, a Bryansk factory metalworker, who was a mere boy. He had grown a beard to inspire respect. Ash-blond tufts covered his chin. In his twenty-two years, Baulin had let nothing ruffle him. This quality, found in thousands of Baulins, proved an important element in the victory of the Revolution. Baulin was hard, taciturn, and headstrong. The path of his life had been decided. He had no doubts about the rightness of this path. Deprivation came easy to him. He could sleep sitting up. He slept pressing one arm against the other, and when he woke, his path from oblivion to full alertness was seamless.

One could expect no mercy under Baulin's command. My service started with an unusual omen of success—I was given a horse. There weren't any horses in the reserve stables or with the peasants. Chance helped. The Cossack Tikhomolov had killed two captured officers without authorization. He had been instructed to take them to the brigade headquarters, as enemy officers could give important information. Tikhomolov did not take them there. It was decided that he would be tried before the Revolutionary Tribunal,* but then they changed their minds. Squadron Commander Baulin came up with a punishment much harsher than anything the tribunal could have inflicted—he took Tikhomolov's stallion Argamak away from him, and sent Tikhomolov off to the transport carts.

The agony I had to suffer with Argamak was beyond what a man can endure. Tikhomolov had brought his horse from the Terek, where he was from. The stallion had been trained in the Cossack trot, that specific Cossack hard trot—dry, violent, sudden. Argamak's stride was long, extended, obstinate. With this devilish stride he carried me off, out of the lines, separating me from the squadron. I lost my sense of direction, roamed for days on end looking for my unit, ended up in enemy territory, slept in ravines, tried to tag along with other regiments but was chased away by them. My horsemanship was limited to the fact that in the Great War I had served with an artillery unit in the Fifteenth Infantry Division. Most of the time we had spent sitting on ammunition carts; we rarely rode out on raids. I didn't have an opportunity to get used to Argamak's cruel, bounding trot. Tikhomolov had bestowed on his horse all the devils of his downfall. I shook like a sack on the stallion's long, dry spine. I rode his back to pieces. Sores appeared on it. Metallic flies preyed upon these sores. Hoops of baked black blood girded the horse's flanks. Bad shoeing made Argamak trip, his hind legs became swollen at the breeching strap and turned elephantine. Argamak grew thin. His eyes filled with the fire one sees in tortured horses, the fire of hysteria and obstinacy. He no longer let me saddle him.

"You've liquidated that horse, four-eyes!" my platoon commander said.

The Cossacks said nothing in my presence, but behind my back plotted like plunderers in drowsy treachery. They didn't even ask me to write letters for them anymore.

The cavalry took Novograd-Volynsk. In a single day we had to cover seventy, eighty versts. We were getting close to Rovno. Rest days

---

* The Revolutionary Tribunals were the organs of military justice representing the Revolutionary Military Council. They investigated crimes committed by military personnel and dealt with prisoners of war. Revolutionary Tribunal detachments were present in each army division and brigade.

were annulled. Night after night I had the same dream: I am riding Argamak at full trot. Campfires are burning by the roadside. The Cossacks are cooking food. I ride past them, they don't even look up. A few call out a greeting, others don't even turn around, they're not interested in me. What does this mean? Their indifference indicates that there is nothing unusual in my horsemanship, I ride like everyone else, there's no reason for them to look at me. I gallop off and am happy. My thirst for peace and happiness was never quenched in my waking hours, which is why I dreamed these dreams.

There was no sign of Pashka Tikhomolov. He was watching me from somewhere on the fringes of the march, in the bumbling tail of carts crammed full with looted rags.

"Pashka keeps asking what's with you," my platoon commander said to me one day.

"Why, he has a problem with me?"

"It looks like he does."

"I reckon he feels I've done him wrong."

"Why, you reckon you didn't do him wrong?"

Pashka's hatred followed me through forests and over rivers. I felt it on my hide and shuddered. He nailed his bloodshot eyes on my path.

"Why did you saddle me with an enemy?" I asked Baulin.

Baulin rode past, yawning.

"Not my problem," he answered without looking back. "It's your problem."

Argamak's back healed a little, then his wounds opened up again. I put three saddlecloths under his saddle, but I could not really ride him, the wounds weren't healing. The knowledge that I was sitting on an open wound made me cringe.

A Cossack from our platoon, his name was Bizyukov, was Tikhomolov's countryman from the Terek, and he knew Pashka's father.

"His father, Pashka's father, he breeds horses for fun," Bizyukov told me one day. "A rough rider, sturdy. He comes to a herd, he picks out a horse on the spot, and they bring it to him. He stands face-to-face with the horse, his legs planted firm, glares at it. What does he want? This is what he wants: he waves his fist and punches the horse right between the eyes—the horse is dead. 'Why did you finish off the horse, Kalistrat?'—'I had a terrible desire for this horse, but I wasn't fated to ride it. The horse didn't take to me, but my desire for this horse was deadly!' He's a rough rider, let me tell you!"

And then Argamak, who had survived Pashka's father, who had been chosen by him, fell into my hands. How was this to end? I weighed many plans in my mind. The war had released me from other worries. The cavalry attacked Rovno. The town was taken. We stayed there for two days. The following night the Poles pushed us out. They engaged us in a skirmish to get their retreating units through. Their maneuver worked. The Poles were covered by a storm, lashing rain, a violent summer storm that tumbled onto the world in floods of black water. We cleared out of Rovno for a day. During the nocturnal battle we lost Dundic, the Serb, one of our bravest men. Pashka Tikhomolov also fought in this battle. The Poles attacked his transport carts. The area there was flat, without any cover. Pashka lined up his carts in a battle formation known only to him. It was, doubtless, how the Romans lined up their chariots. Pashka had a machine gun. He had probably stolen it and hidden it, for an emergency. With this machine gun he repelled the attack, saved his possessions, and led the whole transport to safety, except for two carts whose horses had been shot.

"What do you intend to do with your best fighters, marinate them?" they asked Baulin at headquarters a few days after the battle.

"If I'm letting them marinate, there must be a reason, right?"

"Careful, you'll run into trouble."

No amnesty was proclaimed for Pashka, but we knew that he was coming back. He came wearing galoshes on his bare feet. His toes had been hacked off, ribbons of black gauze hung from them. The ribbons dragged behind him like a train. In the village of Budziatycze, Pashka appeared at the square in front of the church where our horses stood tied to the hitching post. Squadron Commander Baulin was sitting on the church, steps, his feet soaking in a steaming bucket. His toes were rotting. They were pink, the way steel is pink before it is forged. Tufts of young straw-blond hair tumbled over Baulin's forehead. The sun burned on the bricks and tiles of the church. Bizyukov, standing next to Baulin, popped a cigarette into Baulin's mouth and lit it. Tikhomolov, dragging his tattered train behind him, went up to the hitching post. His galoshes shuffled. Argamak stretched his long neck and neighed to his master in greeting, a quiet, rasping neigh, like that of a horse in a desert. Pus coiled like lace between the strips of torn flesh on the horse's back. Pashka stood next to the horse. The dirty ribbons lay still on the ground.

"So that's how things stand," the Cossack said, barely audibly.

I stepped forward.

"Let's make peace, Pashka. I'm glad the horse is going back to you. I can't handle him. Let's make peace?"

"It's not Easter yet, for people to make peace," the platoon commander said from behind me, rolling a cigarette. His Tatar trousers loose, his shirt open over his copper chest, he was resting on the church steps.

"Kiss him three times, Pashka,"* mumbled Bizyukov, Tikhomolov's countryman, who knew Kalistrat, Pashka's father. "He wants to kiss three times."

I was alone among these men whose friendship I had not managed to win.

Pashka stood in front of the horse as if rooted there. Argamak, breathing strong and free, stretched his muzzle to him.

"So that's how things stand," the Cossack repeated. He turned to me sharply, and said emphatically, "I will not make peace with you."

He walked away, dragging his galoshes down the chalk-white, heat-baked street, his bandages sweeping the dust of the village square. Argamak walked behind him like a dog. The reins swung beneath his muzzle, his long neck hung low. Baulin continued soaking the reddish steel of his feet's rotting flesh in the tub.

"Why did you saddle me with an enemy?" I said to him. "None of this is my fault."

The squadron commander raised his head.

"I can see right through you!" he said. "Right through you! What you want is to live without enemies, you'll do anything not to have enemies."

"Kiss him three times," Bizyukov muttered, turning away.

A fiery spot burned on Baulin's forehead. His cheek twitched.

"You know what you end up with like that?" he said in a gasping voice. "You end up being bored! To goddamn hell with you!"

* A manifestation of friendship symbolizing the Holy Trinity.

It was obvious I had to leave. I got myself transferred to the Sixth Squadron. Things went better there. The long and the short of it was that Argamak had taught me some of Tikhomolov's horsemanship. Months passed. My dream had become a reality. The Cossacks' eyes stopped following me and my horse.

THE KISS

At the beginning of August, headquarters sent us to Budziatycze to regroup. The Poles had occupied it at the beginning of the war, but we had been quick to win it back. Our brigade entered the shtetl at dawn. I arrived later in the day. The best billets had already been taken, and I ended up at the schoolmaster's house. He was a paralyzed old man sitting in an armchair in a low-ceilinged room, among buckets with fruit-bearing lemon trees. On his head was a Tyrolean hat with a feather. His gray beard lay on his chest, which was covered with cigarette ash. Babbling, his eyes fluttering, he seemed to be asking me for something. I washed, went to the headquarters, and didn't come back until night. My orderly, Mishka Surovtsev, a cunning Cossack from Orenburg, gave me a full report: besides the paralyzed old man, there was also a daughter present, Elizaveta Alekseyevna Tomilina, and her five-year-old son who was also called Mishka, like Surovtsev. The daughter, the widow of an officer who had fallen in the Great War, was a respectable woman but, according to Surovtsev's information, would be willing to make herself available to a proper gentleman.

"I can arrange things," he told me, and went off to the kitchen, where he began clattering about with plates. The schoolmaster's daughter helped him. As they cooked, Surovtsev told her of my brave feats, how I had knocked two Polish officers out of their saddles in a battle, and how much the Soviet authorities respected me. He was answered by the restrained, soft voice of Tomilina.

"Where d'you sleep?" Surovtsev asked her as he left the kitchen. "You should come sleep closer to us, we're living, breathing people."

He brought me some fried eggs in a gigantic frying pan, and put it on the table.

"She's up for it," he said, sitting down. "She just hasn't come out and said it yet."

At that very instant we heard whispering, rattling, and heavy, careful steps. We didn't have time to finish eating our war meal, when some old men on crutches and old women with kerchiefs on their heads came hobbling through the house. They dragged little Mishka's bed into the dining room, into the lemon-tree forest, next to his grandfather's armchair. The feeble guests, readying themselves to defend Elizaveta Alekseyevna's honor, huddled together in a flock, like sheep in a storm, and, barricading the door, spent the whole night silently playing cards, whispering, "My trick," and falling silent at every sound. I was so mortified, so embarrassed, that I simply could not fall asleep behind that door, and could barely wait for the sun to rise.

"For your information," I told Tomilina when I ran into her in the hall, "for your information, I have a law degree and am a member of the so-called intelligentsia!"

Rigid, her arms dangling, she stood there in her old-fashioned housedress, which clung tightly to her slim body. Without blinking, she looked straight at me with widening blue eyes sparkling with tears.

Within two days we were friends. The schoolmaster's family, a family of kind, weak people, lived in boundless fear and uncertainty. Polish officials had convinced them that Russia had fallen in fire and barbarity, like Rome. They were overcome with a childlike, fearful joy when I told them of Lenin, the Moscow Arts Theater, of a Moscow in which the future was raging. In the evenings, twenty-two-year-old Bolshevik generals with scraggly red beards came to visit us. We smoked Moscow cigarettes, we ate meals that Elizaveta Alekseyevna prepared with army provisions, and sang student songs. Leaning forward in his armchair, the paralyzed old man listened avidly, his Tyrolean hat bobbing to the rhythm of our songs. Through all these days the old man was in the clutches of a sudden, stormy, vague hope, and, in order not to let anything darken his happiness, he did his best to overlook the foppish bloodthirstiness and loudmouthed simplicity with which in those days we solved all the problems of the world.

After our victory over the Poles—the family counsel decided—the Tomilins would move to Moscow. We would have a celebrated professor cure the old man, Elizaveta Alekseyevna would take classes, and we would put Mishka in the selfsame school that his mother had once gone to at Patriarkhy Prudy. The future seemed incontestably ours, and war was merely a stormy prelude to happiness, happiness, the core of our being. The only things that remained unresolved were the specific details, and nights passed in discussing these details, mighty nights, in which the candle end was mirrored in the dull bottle of our home-brewed vodka. Elizaveta Alekseyevna, blossoming, was our silent listener. I have never met a more impulsive, free, or timorous being. In the evenings, cunning Surovtsev, in the wicker cart he had requisitioned back in Kuban, drove us up the hill to where the abandoned house of the Counts Gasiorowski shone in the flames of the sunset. The horses, thin but long-bodied and thoroughbred, were running in step in their red reins. A carefree earring swayed on Surovtsev's ear. Round towers rose up from a pit that was overgrown with a yellow tablecloth of flowers. The ruined walls drew a crooked line flooded with ruby-red blood across the sky. A dog-rose bush hid its berries, and blue steps, the remains of the flight of stairs that Polish kings had once mounted, shone in the thickets. Once, as I sat there, I pulled Elizaveta Alekseyevna's head toward me and kissed her. She slowly pulled away, got up, and leaned against the wall, holding on to it with both hands. She stood there motionless, and around her, around her dazzled head, swirled a fiery dusty ray. Shuddering, as if she had just heard something, Tomilina raised her head and let go of the wall. She ran down the hill, her uncertain steps becoming faster. I called out to her, she didn't answer. Below, red-cheeked Surovtsev lay sprawled out in his wicker cart.

At night, when everyone was asleep, I crept to Elizaveta Alekseyevna's room. She sat reading, holding her book at arm's length. Her hand, lying on the table, seemed lifeless. She turned when I knocked, and rose.

"No," she said, looking me in the eyes, "please, dearest, no." And, embracing my head with her long, bare arms, she gave me an increasingly violent, never-ending, silent kiss.

The shrill ring of the telephone in the next room pushed us apart. An orderly was calling from headquarters.

"We're pulling out!" he said over the phone. "You are to report to the brigade commander now!"

I rushed out of the house without even putting on my hat, stuffing my papers into my bag as I ran. Horses were being brought out of yards, horsemen galloped yelling through the darkness. The brigade commander, tying his cloak, told us that the Poles had broken through our lines near Lublin, and that we had been ordered to execute a bypass maneuver. Both regiments pulled out an hour later. The old man, awoken from his sleep, anxiously followed me with his eyes through the leaves of a lemon tree.

"Promise me you will return," he kept saying, his head wagging.

Elizaveta Alekseyevna, a fur jacket over her batiste nightdress, accompanied us out onto the street. An invisible squadron raced past violently. At the curve in the road by the field I turned to look back— Elizaveta Alekseyevna was bending down to fix the jacket of little Mishka, who was standing in front of her, and the erratic light of the lamp burning on the windowsill streamed over the tender bones of her nape.

After riding a hundred kilometers without rest, we joined forces with the Fourteenth Cavalry Division and, fighting, we began our retreat. We slept in our saddles. At rest stops, we fell to the ground overwhelmed with exhaustion, and our horses, pulling at their reins, dragged us fast asleep through the harvested fields. It was the beginning of autumn and the soundless, drizzling Galician rain. Huddled together in a bristling silent herd, we dodged and circled, fell into the Poles' waiting net, but managed to slip out again just before they could close it. We lost all sense of time. When we were quartered in the church in Toscza, it did not even occur to me that we were only nine versts from Budziatycze. Surovtsev reminded me, we exchanged glances.

"The problem is that the horses are exhausted," he said cheerfully. "Otherwise we could go."

"We couldn't anyway," I replied. "They'd notice if we left in the middle of the night."

And we went. We tied gifts to our saddles—a clump of sugar, a fox-fur wrap, and a live, two-week-old goat kid. The road went through a swaying wet forest, a metallic star strayed through the crowns of the oaks. In less than an hour we arrived at the shtetl, its burned-out center filled with trucks, pale with flour dust, and with machine-gun-cart harnesses and broken shafts. Without dismounting, I knocked on the familiar window. A white cloud flitted through the room. Wearing the same batiste nightdress with its hanging lace, Tomilina came rushing out onto the porch. She took my hand in her hot hand and led me into the house. Men's underclothes were hanging out to dry on the broken branches of the lemon trees, and unknown men were sleeping in camp beds lined up in tight rows like in a field hospital. With crooked, hardened mouths they yelled out hoarsely in their sleep, breathing greedily and loud, their dirty feet jutting out. The house was occupied by our War Spoils Commission, and the Tomilins had been bundled off into a single room.

"When will you take us away from here?" Elizaveta Alekseyevna asked, clasping my hand.

The old man woke, his head wagging. Little Mishka cuddled the goat kid, and brimmed over with happy, soundless laughter. Above him stood Surovtsev, puffing himself up. Out of the pockets of his Cossack trousers he shook spurs, shot-through coins, and a whistle hanging on a yellow string. In this house occupied by the War Spoils Commission there was nowhere to hide, and Tomilina and I went to the wooden shed where the potatoes and beehive frames were kept in winter. There, in the shed, I saw what an inevitably pernicious path that kiss had been, the path that had begun by the castle of the Counts Gasiorowski.

Surovtsev came knocking shortly before dawn.

"When will you take us from here?" Elizaveta Alekseyevna asked, turning her head away.

I stood there silently, and then walked over to the house to say good-bye to the old man.

"The problem is we're running out of time," Surovtsev said, blocking my way. "Get on your horse, we've got to go!"

He jostled me out onto the street and brought me my horse. Elizaveta Alekseyevna gave me her chilled hand. As always, she held her head high. The horses, well rested overnight, carried us off at a brisk trot. The flaming sun rose through the black tangle of the oak trees. The rejoicing morning filled my whole being.

A glade in the forest opened up before us. I directed my horse toward it, and, turning back to Surovtsev, called out to him, "We could have stayed a bit longer. You came for me too early!"

"Too early?" he said, riding up closer to me, pushing away the wet branches that dropped their sparkling raindrops. "If it wasn't for the old man, I'd have come for you even earlier. He was trying to tell me something and suddenly was all nerves, started squawking, and keeled over. I rush to him, I look, he's dead, dead as a doornail!"

The forest came to an end. We rode over a plowed field without paths. Standing up in his stirrups, looking all around, whistling, Surovtsev sniffed out the right direction and, breathing it in with the air, hunched forward and went galloping toward it.

We arrived in time. The men of the squadron were just being awakened. The sun shone warmly, promising a hot day. That morning our brigade crossed the former border of the Kingdom of Poland.

AND THEN
THERE WERE NINE

*This story is an earlier variation of
"Squadron Commander Trunov."*

*N*ine prisoners of war are no longer alive. I know that in my heart. When Golov, a platoon commander from the Sormov workers,* killed the gangly Pole, I said to the chief of staff, "The example the platoon commander is setting is demoralizing our fighters. We must draw up a list of prisoners and then send them to headquarters for interrogation."

The chief of staff agreed. I took pencil and paper out of my bag and called Golov over.

"You look at the world through your spectacles," he told me, looking at me with hatred.

"Yes, through my spectacles," I said to him. "And what about you, Golov? How do you look at the world?"

"I look at it through the miserable life of a worker," he said, and went over to the prisoner who was holding a Polish uniform with dangling sleeves. The uniform had been too small for him. The sleeves had barely reached his elbows. Golov examined the prisoner's woolen drawers.

"You an officer?" Golov asked him, shielding his eyes from the sun.

"No," the Pole answered firmly.

"We never got to wear nothing like that!" Golov muttered, and fell silent. He stood there without saying a word, shuddered, looked at the prisoner, and his eyes paled and widened.

* The Sormov Steelworks (19,839 workers in 1917) played a key role in the Revolution and the Civil War.

"My mama knitted them," the prisoner said firmly. I turned around and looked at him. He was a slender young man. Long sideburns curled over his yellowish cheeks.

"My mama knitted them," he repeated, and lowered his eyes.

"She's a great knitter, that mama of yours," Andryushka Burak cut in. He was a young red-cheeked Cossack with silky hair, who earlier had dragged the trousers off a dying Pole. The trousers now lay thrown over his saddle. Laughing, Andryushka rode over to Golov, carefully scooped the uniform out of his hands, threw it over the trousers on his saddle, and, tapping his horse lightly with his whip, rode off.

At that moment the sun came pouring out from behind a cloud, enveloping with dazzling light Andryushka's horse, its lively trot, the carefree swish of its docked tail. In a daze, Golov watched the Cossack ride off. He turned and saw me drawing up the list of prisoners. He saw the young Pole with the curly sideburns. The Pole raised calm eyes filled with youthful arrogance and smiled at Golov's dismay. Golov cupped his hands to his mouth and yelled, "Our Republic is still alive, Andrei! It's too early to be dealing out her property! Bring back those rags!"

Andrei turned a deaf ear. He rode on at a trot, his horse pertly swatting its tail, as if it were shooing us away.

"Treason!" Golov mumbled, morose and rigid, pronouncing the word syllable by syllable. He kneeled, took aim, and fired, but missed. Andrei swerved his horse around and came galloping back toward Golov. His red-cheeked, blossoming face was filled with anger.

"Listen, countryman!" he yelled loudly, suddenly rejoicing in the sound of his powerful voice. "I should knock you to Kingdom Come, Platoon Commander! I should knock you to where your you-know-what mother is! You've got a dozen Poles on your hands, and you're making a big fuss! We've taken hundreds, and didn't come running for your help! If you're a worker, then do your job!"

And, glancing at us triumphantly, Andryushka rode off at a gallop. Platoon Commander Golov did not look up at him. He clutched his forehead. Blood was trickling from his head like rain from a haystack. He lay down on his stomach, crawled toward the stream, and for a long time held his smashed, blood-drenched head in the shallow water.

Nine prisoners of war are no longer alive. I know that in my heart.

Sitting on my horse, I made a list of them arranged in neat columns. In the first column I entered a row of numbers, in the second their names and surnames, and in the third column the units to which they had belonged. All in all there were nine names. The fourth name was Adolf Shulmeister, a clerk from Lodz, a Jew. He kept snuggling up to my horse and caressing my boots with tender, trembling fingers. His leg had been shattered by a rifle butt, and he left behind him a thin track, like a lame, wounded dog. The sun boiled the sparkling sweat on his orange, pockmarked, bald pate.

"You *Jude, Pane,*"* he whispered, frantically caressing my stirrup. "You Jude!" he whimpered, dribbling spittle, writhing with joy.

"Get back in line, Shulmeister," I yelled at the Jew, and suddenly, seized by deathly numbness, slipped off my saddle.

"How come you know?" I asked him breathlessly.

"Your eyes, their sweet Jewish look," he yelped, hopping on one leg, leaving his thin dog's track behind him. "Your sweet Jewish look, *Pane!*"

I barely managed to extricate myself from his condemned man's frenzy. I came back to my senses slowly, as after a concussion.

The chief of staff ordered me to take care of the details and rode off to the units.

The machine guns were dragged up onto the hill like calves on halters. They moved up side by side, like a well-ordered herd, clanking reassuringly. The sun played on their dusty muzzles. And I saw a rainbow on their steel. The Polish youth with the curly sideburns stared at them with village curiosity. He leaned his whole body forward, revealing a view of Golov, who was crawling out of a ditch pale and intent, his smashed head and his rifle raised. I stretched my hands out to Golov and yelled, but the sound choked and bulged in my throat. Golov quickly shot the prisoner in the back of the neck and jumped up to his feet. The surprised Pole turned to him, executing a half spin on his heel, as in a military exercise. With the slow movements of a woman giving herself to a man, he lifted both hands to his nape, slumped to the ground, and died instantly.

A smile of peace and relief flitted over Golov's face. A light flush returned to his cheeks.

*"You are a Jew, sir"—Shulmeister uses *vy*, the Russian polite form for "you," *Jude*, the German word for "Jew," and *Pane*, the Polish word for "sir."

"Our mothers don't knit drawers like that for us," he told me slyly. "Cross that one off, and give me a list for eight."

I gave him the list.

"You'll answer for that, Golov!" I said in desperation.

"I will answer for that!" he yelled in unbridled triumph. "But not to you, four-eyes, I'll answer to my own people from the Sormov factory. They know what's what!"

Nine prisoners of war are no longer alive. I know that in my heart. This morning I decided to hold a memorial service for the murdered men. In the Red Cavalry there is no one but me who can do it. Our unit stopped to rest on a ravaged Polish estate. I took out my diary and went into the flower garden, which had remained untouched. Hyacinths and blue roses were growing there.

I began writing about the platoon commander and the nine dead men, but a noise, a familiar noise, interrupted me. Cherkashin, the headquarters lackey, had launched a raid against the beehives. Mitya, a red-cheeked youth from Oryol, was following him, holding a smoking torch in his hand. Their heads were wrapped in their army coats. The slits of their eyes glowed. Swarms of bees charged their conquerors and died by their hives. And I put down my pen. I was horrified at the great number of memorial services awaiting me.

AND THEN
THERE WERE TEN

The following story fragment is an earlier variation of the two stories "Squadron Commander Trunov" and "And Then There Were Nine."

Zavadi Station. This happened yesterday. About thirty Poles were sitting tight in the stone building by the junction of the railroad tracks. The chief of staff himself got involved in this serious business. He strutted in front of our line of men with a revolver in his hand.

"How pointless it is to die at Zavady Station," I thought, and went over to the chief of staff.

The Poles ran [and broke through] our line of men. We brought back ten of them alive. We took them to the field. They looked like a striped blanket laid out on the ground. In front of them, Platoon Commander Golov, mounted, was standing in his stirrups.

"Officers! Own up!" he said, shaking his reins. Blood trickled from his head like rain from a haystack. He had been wounded on the forehead.

"All officers, step forward!" he repeated in a thicker voice, getting off his horse.

Suddenly a lanky man with a drooping little mustache stepped forward from the group.

"End of this war!" the man said with delight, and began crying. "All officers run away, end of this war!"

And the lanky man held out his blue hand to the squadron commander. On his face was an incomprehensible bliss.

"Five fingers," he muttered, sobbing, "I raising with these five fingers my family!"

And, with burning eyes, he slowly waved his large, wilted hand. Golov pushed it back with his saber.

"Your officers threw their uniforms here!" he yelled. "But we're going to have a little fitting now, and whoever the uniforms fit, I'm going to finish off!"

He picked out a cap without a brim from the pile of rags and put it on the lanky man's head.

"It fits," Golov whispered. He stepped up closer to the prisoner, looked him in the eyes, and plunged his saber into his gullet. The lanky man fell, shivered, his legs twitching in a frenzy. A foamy, coral-red stream poured from his neck. A young red-cheeked Cossack with silky hair knelt before the dying man. He unbuttoned the man's [trousers].

A LETTER TO THE EDITOR

This letter from Babel was published in 1924 in the literary magazine
Oktyabr, *issue no. 4, in answer to an article by General Budyonny, in*
which Budyonny attacked Babel for his portrayal of the Red Cavalry
and its fighters in his stories, accusing Babel, among other things, of
character assassination and "counterrevolutionary lies."

*I*n 1920, I served in the First Cavalry's Sixth Division, of which
Comrade Timoshenko was commander at the time. I witnessed his
heroic, military, and revolutionary work with much admiration. This
wonderful and pristine image of my beloved division commander long
ruled my imagination, and when I set about to write my memoirs of the
Polish Campaign, my thoughts often returned to him. But in the
process of writing, my aim of keeping within the parameters of historical truth began to shift, and I decided instead to express my thoughts
in a literary form. All that remained from my initial outline were a few
authentic surnames. Through an unforgivable oversight, however, I did
not undertake to remove these surnames, and, to my great consterna-
tion, these names have now appeared by mistake in print, as for
instance in the piece "Timoshenko and Melnikov,"* published in the
third volume of *Krasnaya Nov,* 1924. This oversight came about
because I was late handing in the materials for that volume, and the
editorial office, not to mention the typesetting department, had put me
under extreme pressure, and in this last-minute rush, I overlooked the
vital task of changing the original surnames in the final proofs. I need
not stress that Comrade Timoshenko has nothing whatsoever in common with the character in that piece, a fact clear to anyone who has
ever crossed paths with the former commander of Division Six, one of
the most courageous and selfless of our Red Commanders.

I. Babel

* In later editions of *Red Cavalry,* this piece was renamed "The Story of a Horse."

1920 Diary

On June 3, 1920, the day on which the first entry of the 1920 DIARY occurs (the first fifty-four pages of the diary are missing and believed lost), Isaac Babel was twenty-five years old, soon to be twenty-six. He had already made a name for himself as a promising writer and journalist and had, as a war correspondent, joined the Sixth Cavalry Division, commanded by the charismatic Timoshenko (Pavlichenko, in the RED CAVALRY stories), who was later to become a Marshal of the Soviet Union and Commissar of Defense.

The diary that Babel kept during his months with the Red Cavalry was a writer's diary. Babel noted quick impressions that he intended subsequently to develop as motifs and plot lines for the RED CAVALRY stories: "Describe the soldiers and women, fat, fed, sleepy"; "Describe the bazaar, the baskets of cherries"; "Describe what a horseman feels: exhaustion, the horse won't go on, the ride is long, no strength, the burned steppe, loneliness, no one there to help you, endless versts." At times the impressions appear in strings of telegraphic clauses that served Babel as a form of private shorthand, but when Babel is particularly taken by a scene or situation, he slips into the rich and controlled style that would mark the RED CAVALRY stories.

The RED CAVALRY stories that grew out of this diary shocked the world with their unforgiving depictions of the desperation and atrocities of the cavalrymen. Particularly daring was the way in which Babel depicted real people, their ranks and names unchanged, in realistic, savage, unflattering circumstances. In this diary, which was not intended for publication, Babel could afford even greater candor. The RED CAVALRY stories reveal that the heroic cavalry was made up of wild and ruthless Cossacks who had a skewed notion of Communist doctrine. They were clearly not the glorious harbingers of World Revolution that Soviet propaganda would have liked them to be. This contradiction might be suggested by the stories, but the 1920 DIARY states it in the clearest of terms. Babel asks, "What kind of men are our Cossacks? Many-layered: rag-looting, bravado, professionalism, revolutionary ideals, savage cruelty. We are the vanguard, but of what?"

The 1920 DIARY, by virtue of its privacy, is Babel's most sincere personal written testimony. His persona, so elusive in his fictional prose, is very clear in this private writing. We see his firm Socialist convictions, his sensitivity, his horror of the marauding ways of his Cossack companions, his ambiguous fascination with "the West and chivalrous Poland," his equivocal stance toward Judaism, with feelings that fluctuate between distaste and tenderness toward the Volhynian Jews, "the former (Ukrainian) Yids."

It is relatively late in the diary that Babel's optimism about the Soviet Union's chances of winning this war begins to fade. In the final entries, as Babel and his colleagues return to Russia on the fleeing propaganda train in mid-September of 1920, the war has been lost, the Soviet Union defeated.

Within days, the Red Cavalry was to go into reserve. Babel had chronicled its last great campaign.

JUNE 3, 1920. ZHITOMIR

Morning in the train,* came here to get my tunic and boots. I sleep

---

* The Polit-otdel train, equipped with a printing press and radio station, sent to the front for the ideological education of the troops.

with Zhukov, Topolnik,[*] it's dirty, in the morning the sun shines in my eyes, railroad car dirt. Lanky Zhukov, voracious Topolnik, the whole editorial crew unbelievably dirty people.

Bad tea in borrowed mess tins. Letters home, packages off to Yugrosta,[†] interview with Pollak, operation to seize Novograd, discipline is weakening in the Polish army, Polish White Guard literature, packets of cigarette paper, matches, former (Ukrainian) Yids, commissars—the whole thing stupid, malicious, feeble, talentless, and surprisingly unconvincing. Mikhailov copying out Polish articles word for word.

The train's kitchen, fat soldiers with flushed faces, gray souls, stifling heat in the kitchen, kasha, noon, sweat, fat-legged washerwomen, apathetic women—printing presses—describe the soldiers and women, fat, fed, sleepy.

Love in the kitchen.

Off to Zhitomir after lunch. A town that is white, not sleepy, yet battered and silent. I look for traces of Polish culture. Women well dressed, white stockings. The Catholic Church.

Bathe at Nuski in the Teterev, a horrible little river, old Jews in the bathing boxes with long, emaciated legs covered with gray hairs. Young Jews. Women are washing clothes in the Teterev. A family, beautiful woman, husband holds the child.

The bazaar in Zhitomir, old cobbler, bluing, chalk, laces.

The synagogue buildings, old architecture—how all this touches my soul.

Watch crystal, 1,200 rubles. Market. A small Jewish philosopher. An indescribable store: Dickens, brooms, and golden slippers. His philosophy: they all say they're fighting for truth yet they all plunder. If only one government at least were good! Wonderful words, his scant beard, we talk, tea and three apple turnovers—750 rubles. An interesting old woman, malicious, practical, unhurried. How greedy for money they all are. Describe the bazaar, the baskets of cherries, the inside of a tavern. A conversation with a Russian woman who came over to borrow a tub. Sweat, watery tea, I'm sinking my teeth into life again, farewell to you, dead men.

---

[*] Babel's colleagues, reporters for the *Krasny Kavalerist* (*The Red Cavalryman*).
[†] The Ukrainian division of ROSTA, the Soviet news service agency from 1918 to 1935.

Podolsky, the son-in-law, a half-starved intellectual, something about trade unions and service with Budyonny,* I, needless to say, am Russian, my mother a Jewess, what for?

The Zhitomir pogrom carried out by the Poles, and then, of course, by the Cossacks.

After our vanguard units appeared, the Poles entered the town for three days, Jewish pogrom, cut off beards, they always do, rounded up forty-five Jews in the market, took them to the slaughterhouses, torture, they cut out tongues, wailing over the whole town square. They torched six houses, the Konyukhovsky house, I went to take a look, those who tried to save them were machine-gunned down, they butchered the janitor into whose arms a mother had thrown an infant out of a burning window, the priest put a ladder against the back wall, and so they managed to escape.

The Sabbath is drawing to a close, we leave the father-in-law and go to the *tsaddik*. Didn't get his name. A stunning picture for me, though the decline and decadence are plain to see. Even the *tsaddik*—his broad-shouldered, gaunt body. His son, a refined boy in a long overcoat, I can see petit bourgeois but spacious rooms. Everything nice and proper, his wife a typical Jewess, one could even call her of the modern type.

The faces of the old Jews.

Conversations in the corner about rising prices.

I can't find the right page in the prayer book. Podolsky shows me. Instead of candles—an oil lamp.

I am happy, large faces, hooked noses, black, gray-streaked beards, I have many thoughts, farewell to you, dead men. The face of the *tsaddik*, a nickel-rimmed pince-nez.

"Where are you from, young man?"

"From Odessa."

"How is life there?"

"People are alive."

"Here it's terrible."

A short conversation.

I leave shattered.

---

* Semyon Mikhailovich Budyonny, the commander of the First Cavalry.

Podolsky, pale and sad, gives me his address, a marvelous evening. I walk, think about everything, quiet, strange streets. Kondratyev with a dark-haired Jewess, the poor commandant with his tall sheepskin hat, he doesn't succeed.

And then nightfall, the train, painted Communist slogans (the contrast with what I saw at the old Jews').

The hammering of the presses, our own electrical generator, our own newspapers, a movie is being shown, the train flashes, rumbles, fat-faced soldiers stand in line for the washerwomen (for two days).

JUNE 4, 1920. ZHITOMIR

Morning—packages off to Yugrosta, report on the Zhitomir pogrom, home, to Oreshnikov, to Narbut.

I'm reading Hamsun.* Sobelman tells me his novel's plot.

A new story of Job, an old man who has lived centuries, his students carried him off to feign a resurrection, a glutted foreigner, the Russian Revolution.

Schulz, what's most important, voluptuousness, Communism, how we are filching apples from the masters, Schulz is chatting away, his bald patch, apples hidden under his shirt, Communism, a Dostoyevskyan figure, there is something interesting there, must give it some thought, that inexhaustible overindulgence of his, Schulz in the streets of Berdichev.

Khelemskaya, she's had pleurisy, diarrhea, has turned yellow, dirty overcoat, applesauce. What're you doing here, Khelemskaya? You've got to get married, a husband, an engineer in a technical office, abortion or first child, that was what your life has been about, your mother, you took a bath once a week, your romance, Khelemskaya, that's how you should live, and you'll adapt to the Revolution.

The opening of a Communist club in the editorial office. That's the proletariat for you: incredibly feeble Jews and Jewesses from the underground. March forward, you pitiful, terrible tribe! Then describe the concert, women singing Ukrainian songs.

Bathing in the Teterev. Kiperman, and how we search for food.

* Knut Hamsun, the Norwegian novelist.

What kind of man is Kiperman? What a fool I am, he never paid me back. He sways like a reed, he has a large nose, and he is nervous, possibly insane, yet he managed to trick me, the way he puts off repaying me, runs the club. Describe his trousers, nose, and unruffled speech, torture in prison, Kiperman is a terrible person.

Night on the boulevard. The hunt for women. Four streets, four stages: acquaintance, conversation, awakening of desire, gratification of desire. The Teterev below, an old medical orderly who says that the commissars have everything, wine too, but he is nice about it.

Me and the Ukrainian editors.

Guzhin, whom Khelemskaya complained about today, they're looking for something better. I'm tired. And suddenly loneliness, life flows before me, but what is its significance?

JUNE 5, 1920. ZHITOMIR

Received boots, tunic on the train. Going to Novograd at sunrise. The automobile is a Thornicroft. Everything seized from Denikin. Sunrise in the monastery yard or the schoolyard. Slept in the automobile. Arrived in Novograd at 11. Travel farther in another Thornicroft. Detour bridge. The town is livelier, the ruins appear normal. I take my suitcase. The staff left for Korets. One of the Jewesses gave birth, in a hospital, of course. A gangly hook-nosed man asks me for a job, runs behind me with my suitcase. He promised to come again tomorrow. Novograd is Zvyagel.

A man from the supplies division in a white sheepskin hat, a Jew, and stoop-shouldered Morgan are on the truck. We wait for Morgan, he's at the pharmacy, our little friend has the clap. The automobile has come from Fastov. Two fat drivers. We're flying, a true Russian driver, all our insides thoroughly shook up. The rye is ripening, orderlies gallop by, miserable, enormous, dusty trucks, half-naked, plump, light-blond Polish boys, prisoners, Polish noses.

Korets: describe, the Jews outside the large house, a *yeshiva bokher**
in spectacles, what are they talking about, these old men with their yellow beards, stoop-shouldered merchants, feeble, lonely. I want to stay,

---

* Talmud student.

but the telephone operators roll up the wires. Of course the staff has left. We pick apples and cherries. Moved on at a wild pace. Then the driver, red sash, eats bread with his motor-oil-stained fingers. Six versts short of our goal the magneto floods with oil. Repairs beneath the scorching sun, sweat and drivers. I get there on a hay cart (I forgot: Artillery Inspector Timoshenko (?) [*sic*] is inspecting the cannons in Korets. Our generals.) Evening. Night. The park in Hoshcha. Zotov* and the staff rush on, transport carts go galloping by, the staff left for Rovno, damn it, what bad luck. The Jews, I decide to stay at Duvid Uchenik's, the soldiers try to talk me out of it, the Jews beg me to stay. I wash myself, bliss, many Jews. Are Uchenik's brothers twins? The wounded want to meet me. Healthy bastards, just flesh wounds on their legs, they get about on their own. Real tea, I eat supper. Uchenik's children, a small but shrewd girl with squinting eyes, a shivering six-year-old girl, a fat wife with gold teeth. They sit around me, there's anxiety in the air. Uchenik tells me the Poles were out plundering, then others raided, whooping and hollering, they carried off everything, his wife's things.

The girl: Aren't you a Jew? Uchenik sits watching me eat, the girl sits shivering on his lap. "She is frightened, the cellar and the shooting and your people." I tell them everything will be fine, what the Revolution means, I talk profusely. "Things are bad, we're going to be plundered, don't go to bed."

Night, a lantern in front of the window, a Hebrew grammar, my soul aches, my hair is clean, clean is my sorrow. Sweating from the tea. As backup: Tsukerman with a rifle. A radio-telegrapher. Soldiers in the yard, they chase everyone off to sleep, they chuckle. I eavesdrop on them, they hear something: Halt, who goes there? We'll mow you down!

The hunt for the woman prisoner. Stars, night over the shtetl. A tall Cossack with an earring and a cap with a white top. They had arrested mad Stasova, a mattress, she beckoned with her finger: Let's go, I'll let you have some, I can keep it working all night writhing, hopping, not running away! The soldiers chase everyone off to sleep. They eat supper—fried eggs, tea, stew—indescribable coarseness, sprawled

* Commander of the Cavalry Field Headquarters.

all over the table, Mistress, more! Uchenik in front of his house, he's on sentry duty, what a laugh, "Go off to sleep!" "I'm guarding my house!" A terrible situation with the fugitive madwoman. If they catch her, they'll kill her.

I can't sleep. I meddled, now they say everything's lost.

A difficult night, an idiot with a piglet's body—the radio-telegrapher. Dirty nails and refined manners. Discussion about the Jewish question. A wounded man in a black shirt, a milksop and lout, the old Jews are running, the women have been sent off. Nobody is asleep. Some girls or other on the porch, some soldier asleep on the sofa.

I write in my diary. There is a lamp. The park in front of the window, transport carts roll by. No one's going off to sleep. An automobile has arrived. Morgan is looking for a priest, I take him to the Jews.

Goryn, Jews and old women on the porches. Hoshcha has been ransacked, Hoshcha is clean, Hoshcha is silent. A clean job. In a whisper: Everything's been taken and they don't even weep, they're experts. The Horyn, a network of lakes and tributaries, evening light, here the battle for Rovno took place. Discussions with Jews, my people, they think I'm Russian, and my soul opens up to them. We sit on the high embankment. Peace and soft sighs behind me. I leave to defend Uchenik. I told them my mother is a Jewess, the story, Belaya Tserkov, the rabbi.

JUNE 6, 1920. ROVNO

Slept anxiously, just a few hours. I wake up, sun, flies, a good bed, pink Jewish pillows, feathers. The soldiers are banging their crutches. Again: Mistress, we want more! Roasted meat, sugar from a cut-glass chalice, they sit sprawled out, their forelocks* hanging down, dressed in riding gear, red trousers, sheepskin hats, leg stumps swinging boisterously. The women have brick-red faces, they run around, none of them slept. Duvid Uchenik is pale, in a vest. He tells me, Don't leave as long as they're still here. A cart comes by to pick them up. Sun, the cart is waiting across from the park, they're gone. Salvation.

The automobile arrived yesterday evening. At 1 P.M. we leave

---

* Ukrainian Cossacks shaved their heads, leaving only a forelock, known as a *chub*.

Hoshcha for Rovno. The River Horyn is sparkling in the sun. I go for a morning walk. It turns out the mistress of the house hadn't spent the night at home. The maid and her friends were sitting with the soldiers who wanted to rape her, all night till dawn the maid kept feeding them apples, quiet conversations: We've had enough of war, want to get married, go to sleep. The cross-eyed girl became talkative, Duvid puts on his vest, his *tallith*, prays solemnly, offers thanks, flour in the kitchen, dough is being kneaded, they're getting things under way, the maid is a fat, barefoot, thick-legged Jewess with soft breasts, tidying up, talking endlessly. The landlady's speech—what she wants is for everything to end well. The house comes to life.

I travel to Rovno in the Thornicroft. Two fallen horses. Smashed bridges, the automobile on wooden planks, everything creaks, endless line of transport carts, traffic jam, cursing, describe the transport carts in front of the broken bridge at noon, horsemen, trucks, two-wheelers with ammunition. Our truck drives with crazed speed, even though it is completely falling to pieces, dust.

Eight versts short of our goal, it breaks down. Cherries, I sleep, sweat in the sun. Kuzitsky, an amusing fellow, can immediately tell you your future, lays out cards, a medical assistant from Borodyanitsy, in exchange for treatment women offered him their services, roasted chicken, and themselves, he is constantly worried that the chief of the medical division won't let him go, shows me his genuine wounds, when he walks he limps, left a girl on the road forty versts from Zhitomir, go, she told him, because the divisional chief of staff was courting her. Loses his whip, sits half naked, babbles, lies without restraint, photograph of his brother, a former staff cavalry captain, now a division commander married to a Polish countess, Denikin's men shot him.

I'm a medical man.

Dust in Rovno, dusty molten gold flows over the dreary little houses.

The brigade rides past, Zotov at the window, the people of Rovno, the Cossacks' appearance, a remarkably peaceful, self-confident army. Jewish youths and maidens watch them with admiration, the old Jews look on indifferently. Describe the air in Rovno, something agitated and unstable about it, and there are Polish store signs and life.

Describe the evening.

The Khast family. A sly, black-haired girl from Warsaw takes us there. The medical orderly, malicious verbal stench, coquetry, You'll eat with us! I wash up in the hallway, everything is uncomfortable, bliss, I'm dirty and sweat-drenched, then hot tea with my sugar.

Describe this Khast, a complex fury of a man, unbearable voice, they think I don't understand Yiddish, they argue incessantly, animal fear, the father quite inscrutable, a smiling medical orderly, treats the clap (?) [*sic*], smiles, lies low, but seems hotheaded, the mother: We're intellectuals, we own nothing, he's a medical orderly, a worker, we don't mind having them here as long as they're quiet, we're exhausted! A stunning apparition: their rotund son with his cunning and idiotic smile behind the glass of his round spectacles, the fawning conversation, they scrape and bow to me, a gaggle of sisters, all vixens (?) [*sic*]. The dentist, some sort of grandson to whom they all talk with the same whining hysteria as to the old folk, young Jews come over, people from Rovno with faces that are flat and yellow with fear and fish eyes, they talk of Polish taunts, show their passports, there was a solemn decree of Poland annexing Volhynia as well, I recall Polish culture, Sienkiewicz, the women, the empire, they were born too late, now there is class consciousness.

I give my clothes to be laundered. I drink tea incessantly and sweat like a beast and watch the Khasts carefully, intently. Night on the sofa. Undressed for the first time since the day I set out. All the shutters are closed, the electric light burns, the stuffiness is unbearable, many people sleep there, stories of pillaging by Budyonny's men, shivering and terror, horses snort outside the window, transport carts roll down Shkolnaya Street, night. [The following twenty-one pages of the diary are missing.]

JULY 11, 1920. BELYOV

Spent the night with the soldiers of the staff squadron, in the hay. Slept badly, thinking about the manuscripts. Dejection, loss of energy, I know I'll get over it, but when will that be? I think of the Khasts, those worms, I remember everything, those reeking souls, and the cow eyes, and the sudden, high, screeching voices, and the smiling father. The main thing: his smile and he is hotheaded, and many secrets, reeking memories of scandals. The mother, a gigantic figure—she is malicious, cowardly, gluttonous, repugnant, her fixed, expectant stare. The daughter's repulsive and detailed lies, the son's eyes laughing behind his spectacles.

I roam about the village. I ride to Klevan, the shtetl was taken yesterday by the Third Cavalry Brigade of the Sixth Division. Our mounted patrols appeared on the Rovno-Lutsk high road, Lutsk is being evacuated.

8th–12th heavy fighting, Dundic killed, Shadilov, commander of the Thirty-sixth Regiment, killed, many horses fell, tomorrow we'll have the details.

Budyonny's orders concerning our loss of Rovno, the unbelievable exhaustion of the units, the frenzied attacks of our brigades which don't have the same results as before, incessant battles since May 27, if the army isn't given a breather, it will become unfit for battle.

Isn't it premature to issue such orders? No, they make sense: their objective is to rouse the rear lines—Klevan. Burial of six or seven Red Army fighters. I rode behind a *tachanka*. The funeral march, on the way back from the cemetery, a bravura infantry march, no sign of the funeral procession. A carpenter—a bearded Jew—is rushing around the shtetl, he's banging some coffins together. The main street is also Shossova.

My first requisition is a notebook. Menashe, the synagogue *shamas*, goes with me. I have lunch at Mudrik's, the same old story, the Jews have been plundered, their perplexity, they looked to the Soviet regime as saviors, then suddenly yells, whips, Yids. I am surrounded by a whole circle, I tell them about Wilson's note, about the armies of labor, the Jews listen, sly and commiserating smiles, a Jew in white trousers had come to the pine forests to recuperate, wants to go home. The Jews sit on earth mounds,* girls and old men, stillness, stifling, dusty, a peasant (Parfenty Melnik, the one who did his military service at Elizavetopol) complains that his horse has swollen up with milk, they took her foal away, sadness, the manuscripts, the manuscripts—that's what is clouding my soul.

Colonel Gorov, elected by the people, village headman—sixty years old—a pre-reform rat of a nobleman. We talk about the army, about Brusilov, if Brusilov set off, why shouldn't we? Gray whiskers, sputters,

---

* *Zavalinka:* a mound of earth around a hut that protects it from the weather and is often used for sitting on outside.

a man of the past, smokes homegrown tobacco, lives in the government building, I feel sorry for the old man.

The clerk of the district government, a handsome Ukrainian. Flawless order. Has relearned everything in Polish, shows me the books, the district statistics: 18,600 people, 800 of whom are Poles, wanted to be united with Poland, a solemn petition of unification with the Polish state.

The clerk is also a pre-reform figure in velvet trousers, with Ukrainian speech, touched by the new times, a little mustache.

Klevan, its roads, streets, peasants, and Communism are far from one another.

Hops-growing, many nurseries, rectangular green walls, sophisticated cultivation.

The colonel has blue eyes, the clerk a silken mustache.

Night, headquarters work at Belyov. What kind of man is Zholnarkevich? A Pole? His feelings? The touching friendship of two brothers.* Konstantin and Mikhail. Zholnarkevich is an old hand, exact, hardworking without overexerting himself, energetic without kicking up a fuss, Polish mustache, slim Polish legs. The headquarters staff is made up of Zholnarkevich and three other clerks toiling away till nightfall.

A colossal job, the positioning of the brigades, no provisions, the main thing: the operational itineraries are handled unobtrusively. The orderlies at the headquarters sleep on the ground. Thin candles burn, the divisional chief of staff in his hat wipes his forehead and dictates, ceaselessly dictates operational reports, orders to the artillery division, we are continuing our advance on Lutsk.

Night, I sleep on the hay next to Lepin,† a Latvian, horses that have broken from their tethers roam about, snatch away the hay from under my head.

July 12, 1920. Belyov

This morning I began my journal of military operations, analyzing the operational reports. The journal is going to be an interesting piece of work.

---

* Konstantin Karlovich Zholnarkevich was the divisional chief of staff, and his brother, Mikhail, was a staff officer.

† A staff officer in the Sixth Cavalry Division.

After lunch I go riding on the horse of Sokolov, the orderly. (He is ill with a relapse of typhus, he lies next to me on the ground in a leather jacket, thin, a man of breeding, a whip in his emaciated hand, he left the hospital, they didn't feed him, and he was bored, he lay there sick on that terrible night of our retreat from Rovno, he had been totally soaked in water, lanky, totters, talks to the people of the house with curiosity but also imperiously, as if all muzhiks were his enemy). Shpakovo, a Czech settlement. A rich region, lots of oats and wheat, I ride through the villages: Peresopnitsa, Milostovo, Ploski, Shpakovo. There is flax, they make sunflower oil out of it, and a lot of buckwheat.

Rich villages, hot noon, dusty roads, transparent sky without clouds, my horse lazy, when I whip it it moves. My first mounted ride. In Milostovo—I take a cart from Shpakovo—I'm going to get a *tachanka* and horses with an order from divisional headquarters.

I'm too softhearted. I look admiringly at the clean, hearty, un-Russian life of the Czechs. A good village elder, horsemen galloping in all directions, constantly new demands, forty cartloads of hay, ten pigs, the agents of the Requisitions Committee—grain, the elder is given a receipt—oats have been received, thank you. Reconnaissance commander of the Thirty-fourth Regiment.

The sturdy huts glitter in the sun, roof tiles, iron, stone, apples, the stone schoolhouse, a demi-urban type of woman, bright aprons. We go to Yuripov, the miller, the richest and best-educated man around here, a typical tall, handsome Czech with a Western European mustache. A wonderful courtyard, a dovecote—I'm touched by that—new mill machinery, former affluence, white walls, an extensive farm, a bright, spacious, single-story house and a nice room, and this Czech most probably has a good family, his father—a poor sinewy old man—all of them good people, a robust son with gold teeth, trim and broad-shouldered. A good wife, probably young, and his children.

The mill has, of course, been modernized.

The Czech has been stuffed full of receipts. They took four of his horses and gave him a note for the Rovno District Commissariat, they took a phaeton and gave him a broken *tachanka* in exchange, and three receipts for flour and oats.

The brigade arrives, red flags, a powerful, unified body, self-assured commanders, experienced, calm eyes of the forelocked Cossacks, dust, silence, order, marching band, they are swallowed into their billets, the brigade commander shouts over to me: We mustn't take anything from here, this is our territory. With worried eyes the Czech watches the dashing young brigade commander bustling about in the distance, chats politely with me, returns the broken *tachanka,* but it falls apart. I don't waste any energy. We go to a second, a third house. The village elder lets us know where there are things to be had. An old man actually does have a phaeton, his son keeps jabbering that it is broken, the front part is damaged—you have a bride, I think to myself, or you ride in it to church on Sundays—it's hot, I feel lazy and sorry for them, the horsemen scavenging through everything, this is what freedom initially looks like. I didn't take anything, even though I could have, I'll never be a true Budyonny fighter.

I'm back, it's evening, a Pole was caught in the rye, they hunted him down like an animal, wide fields, scarlet sun, golden fog, swaying grain, in the village they're driving cattle home, rosy, dusty streets, surprisingly tender forms, flaming tongues, orange flames shoot from the borders of the pearly clouds, the carts raise dust.

I work at the headquarters (my horse galloped nicely), I sleep next to Lepin. He is Latvian, his snout blunt, piglety, spectacles, he seems kind. A general staff man.

Cracks sudden, dull jokes. Hey, woman, when're you going to drop dead? And he grabs hold of her.

There's no kerosene at the headquarters. He says: We're striving toward enlightenment, but we have no light, I'm going to play with the village girls. Stretched out his arm, won't let go, his snout strained, his piggy lips quiver, his glasses shake.

JULY 13, 1920. BELYOV

My birthday. Twenty-six years old. I think of home, of my work, my life is flying past. No manuscripts. Dull misery, I will surmount it. I'm keeping my diary, it will be an interesting piece of work.

The clerks are handsome young men, the young Russians from headquarters sing arias from operettas, they are a little corrupted by the work there. Describe the orderlies, the divisional chief of staff and the others—Cherkashin, Tarasov—rag-looters, lickspittles, fawners, gluttons, loafers, products of the past, they know who their master is.

The work at the headquarters in Belyov. A well-oiled machine, a brilliant chief of staff, routine work, a lively man. They discovered that he is a Pole, relieved him of his duties, and then reinstated him on the order of the division commander. He is loved by all, gets on well with the division commander, what does he feel? He's not a Communist, he's a Pole, yet he is as loyal as a guard dog—try figuring that out!

About our operations.

The position of our units.

Our march on Lutsk.

The makeup of the division, the brigade commanders.

The work flow at headquarters: the directive, then the order, then the operational report, then the intelligence report, we drag the Polit-otdel along, the Revolutionary Tribunal,* the reserve horses.

I ride over to Yasinevichi to exchange my carriage for a *tachanka* and horses. Unbelievable dust, heat. We ride through Peresopnitsa, delight in the fields, my twenty-seventh year, I think the rye and barley are ripe, here and there the oats look very good, the poppies are past their bloom, there are no cherries, the apples aren't ripe, a lot of flax, buckwheat, many trampled fields, hops.

A rich land, but within bounds.

Dyakov, commander of the Reserve Cavalry: a fantastic apparition, red trousers with silver stripes, an embossed belt, a Stavropol Cossack, the body of an Apollo, a cropped gray mustache, forty-five years old, has a son and a nephew, outlandish cursing, things were sent over to him from the Supply Department, he had smashed a table to pieces there, but finally got what he wanted. Dyakov, his men love him: our commander is a hero. He was an athlete, can barely read and write, he says: I'm a cavalry inspector now, a general. Dyakov is a Communist, a daring old Budyonny fighter. He met a millionaire with a lady on his

---

* The polit-otdel was a political organ of the new Soviet government charged with the ideological education of the military during the Russian Civil War and the Russian-Polish War of 1920. The Revolutionary Tribunals, *Revtribunaly*, were the organs of military justice representing the Revolutionary Military Council. They investigated crimes committed by military personnel and dealt with prisoners of war. Detachments of the Revolutionary Tribunal were present in each army division and brigade.

arm: "I say, Mr. Dyakov, did we not meet at my club?"—"I have been in eight countries, when I come out on stage, I need only wink."

Dancer, concertina player, trickster, liar, a most picturesque figure. Has a hard time reading documents, he keeps losing them—all this paperwork, he says, has finished me off, if I walk out, what will they do without me?—cursing, chats with the muzhiks, their mouths hang open.

The *tachanka* and two emaciated horses, describe the horses.

People go to Dyakov with requests, phew, I'm being worn down to the bone, distribute underwear, one thing after the other, fatherly relationship, you (to one of the patients) will end up being the head cattle driver here. I go home. Night. Headquarters work.

We have been billeted in the house of the village elder's mother. The merry mistress of the house keeps up an endless babble, hitches up her skirts and works like a bee for her family and then seven people on top of that.

Cherkashin (Lepin's orderly) is rude and tiresome, won't leave her in peace, we're always asking for something or other, children are loafing about the house, we requisition hay, the hut is full of flies, some children, old people, a bride, soldiers jostle and holler. The old woman is sick. The old people drop by to visit her and are mournfully silent, the lamp.

Night, headquarters, the pompous telephone operator, K. Karlovich writes reports, orderlies, the clerks on duty are sleeping, the village pitch-black, a sleepy clerk is typing an order, K. Karlovich is precise as clockwork, the orderlies arrive silently.

The march on Lutsk. The Second Brigade is leading it, they still haven't managed to take it. Where are our advance units?

JULY 14, 1920. BELYOV

Sokolov has been billeted with us. He is lying on the hay, lanky, Russian, in leather boots. Misha is a nice, red-cheeked fellow from Oryol. Lepin* plays with the maid when no one is watching, he has a blunt, tense face, our landlady keeps up an endless babble, tells tales,

---

* A staff officer in the Sixth Cavalry Division.

works tirelessly, her old mother-in-law—a shriveled-up little old woman—loves her, Cherkashin, Lepin's orderly, eggs her on, she prattles on without stopping to catch her breath.

Lepin fell asleep at the headquarters, a completely idiotic face, he simply can't wake up. A wail over the village, the cavalrymen are trading in their horses, giving the villagers their worn-out nags, trampling the grain, taking their cattle, complaints to the chief of staff, Cherkashin is arrested for whipping a muzhik. Lepin spends three hours writing a letter to the tribunal, Cherkashin, he writes, had been influenced by the scandalously provocative behavior of the Red Officer Sokolov. My advice: don't put seven men in one hut.

Gaunt, angry Sokolov tells me: We're destroying everything, I hate the war.

Why are they all here in this war—Zholnarkevich, Sokolov? All this is subconscious, inert, unthinking. A nice system.

Frank Mosher.* A shot-down American pilot, barefoot but elegant, neck like a column, dazzlingly white teeth, his uniform covered with oil and dirt. He asks me worriedly: Did I maybe commit a crime by fighting against Soviet Russia? Our position is strong. O the scent of Europe, coffee, civilization, strength, ancient culture, many thoughts, I watch him, can't let him go. A letter from Major Fountleroy: things in Poland are bad, there's no constitution, the Bolsheviks are strong, the socialists the center of attention but not in power. One has to learn the new methods of warfare. What are they telling Western European soldiers? Russian imperialism is out to destroy the nationalities, customs, that's the main thing, to take over all the Slavic lands, what old and tired words these are! An endless conversation with Mosher, I sink into the past, they'll shake you up, Mosher, ha, Mr. Conan Doyle, letters to New York. Is Mosher being sly or not—he keeps asking frantically what Bolshevism is. A sad, heart-warming impression.

I'm getting used to the headquarters, I have what they call a vehicular driver, thirty-nine-year-old Grishchuk, a prisoner in Germany for six years, fifty versts from his home (he is from the Kremenets district), the army won't let him go, he says nothing.

---

* Frank Mosher, the assumed name of Captain Merian Caldwell Cooper, the shot-down American pilot whom Babel interrogated in Belyov. He later achieved fame as the creator and producer of the motion picture *King Kong*.

Division Commander Timoshenko is at headquarters. A colorful figure. A colossus, red half-leather trousers, a red cap, slender, a former platoon commander, a machine-gunner, an artillery warrant officer in the past. Legendary tales. The commissar of the First Brigade had been frightened by the fire—Boys, on your horses!—and Timoshenko had begun lashing at all his commanders with his whip: Kniga,* the regimental commanders, he shoots the commissar—On your horses, you sons of bitches!—goes charging after them, five shots—Comrades, help!—I'll show you!—Help!—a shot through the hand, in the eye, the revolver misfires, and I bawl out the commissar. He fires up the Cossacks, a Budyonny man, when you ride with him into battle, if the Poles don't kill you, he'll kill you.

The Second Brigade attacks Lutsk and withdraws toward evening, the enemy counterattacks, heavy forces, wants to break through to Dubno. We occupy Dubno.

Report: Minsk, Bobruisk, Molodechno, Proskurov, Sventsyany, Sarny, Staro-Konstantinov have been taken, they are entering Galicia where there will be a cav. maneuver—by the River Styr or the Bug. Kovel is being evacuated, heavy forces at Lvov, Mosher's deposition. There will be an assault.

The division commander's gratitude for the battle at Rovno. Issue a statement.

The village silent, a light at the headquarters, arrested Jews. The Budyonny fighters bring Communism, a little old woman weeps. Ha, what a gloomy life these Russians lead! Where is that Ukrainian mirth? The harvest is beginning. The poppies are ripening, I wonder where I can get some grain for the horses and cherry dumplings.

Which divisions are to our left?

Mosher barefoot, noon, dull Lepin.

July 15, 1920. Belyov

Interrogation of defectors. They show us our leaflets. Their power is great, the leaflets help the Cossacks.

---

* Vasily Ivanovich Kniga was the commander of the First Brigade of the Sixth Cavalry Division.

We have an interesting military commissar: Bakhturov,* a fighter, fat, foul-mouthed, always in the front lines.

Describe the job of a war correspondent, what exactly is a war correspondent?

I have to get the operational reports from Lepin, it's torture. The headquarters have been set up in the house of a converted Jew.

At night the orderlies stand in front of the headquarters building.

The harvest has begun. I am learning to tell the plants apart. Tomorrow is my sister's birthday.

A description of Volhynia. The muzhiks live revoltingly, dirty, we eat, poetic Matyash, a womanizer, even when he's talking to an old woman he is still mellifluous.

Lepin is courting the maid.

Our units are one-and-a-half versts from Lutsk. The army is preparing a cavalry attack, is concentrating its forces in Lvov, moving them up to Lutsk.

We've found a Pilsudski† proclamation: Warriors of the Rzecz Pospolita. A touching proclamation. Our graves are white with the bones of five generations of fighters, our ideals, our Poland, our happy home, your Motherland is relying on you, our young freedom is shuddering, one last stand, we will remember you, everything will be for you, Soldiers of the Rzecz Pospolita!

Touching, sad, without the steel of Bolshevik slogans, no promises and words like *order, ideals,* and *living in freedom.*

Victory will be ours!

JULY 16, 1920. NOVOSELKI

Received an army order: seize the crossings over the River Styr in the Rozhishche-Yalovichi sector.

The headquarters move to Novoselki, twenty-five versts. I ride with the division commander, the staff squadron, the horses gallop, forests, oak trees, forest paths, the division commander's red cap, his

---

* Pavel Vasilevich Bakhturov, the military commissar of the Sixth Cavalry Division from February to August 1920. He had just been decorated with a Red Flag Medal.

† Josef Pilsudski, the commander in chief of the Polish forces.

powerful frame, buglers, beauty, the new army, the division commander and the squadron—one body.

Our billet, our landlord and his wife, young and quite wealthy, they have pigs, a cow, all they ever say: *nemae.**

Zholnarkevich's tale of the sly medical orderly. Two women, he had to deal with them. He gave one of them castor oil—when it got to her, he dashed off to the other one.

A terrible incident, soldiers' love, two sturdy Cossacks came to an agreement with a woman—Can you hold out with two of us?—Yes, I can. One of them did it three times, the other one climbed onto her, she went running around the room dirtying the whole floor, they threw her out, didn't give her any money, she had been too hard-working.

About the Budyonny commanders: are they soldiers of fortune or future usurpers? They are of Cossack background, that's the main thing, describe the provenance of these detachments, all these Timoshenkos and Budyonnys had set up these detachments themselves, mainly with neighbors from their Cossack villages, now the detachments have been organized by the Soviet government.

The division is carrying out the order it was given, a powerful column is moving from Lutsk to Dubno, the evacuation of Lutsk has obviously been called off, troops and equipment are arriving there.

Our young landlord and his wife: she is tall with traces of village beauty, bustling about among her five children, who are rolling about on the bench. Interesting—each child looks after the next, Mama, give him titty. The mother, well built and flushed, lies sternly among her swarming brood of children. The husband is a good man. Sokolov: These pups should be shot, why keep breeding? The husband: Out of little ones big ones grow.

Describe our soldiers: Cherkashin (today he came back from the tribunal a little browbeaten), insolent, lanky, depraved, what an inhabitant of Communist Russia, Matyash, a Ukrainian, boundlessly lazy, keen on women, always torpid, his boots unlaced, lazy movements, Misha, Sokolov's orderly, has been to Italy, handsome, messy.

Describe: the ride with the division commander, a small squadron,

---

* Ukrainian: "there isn't any."

the division commander's retinue, Bakhturov, old Budyonny fighters, a march plays as we set off.

The divisional chief of staff is sitting on a bench, a peasant is choking with fury, points at a mare on her last legs that he has been given in exchange for a good horse. Dyakov comes riding in, the conversation is short, for a horse like this you can get fifteen thousand, for a horse like this, even twenty thousand. If it gets up, then it's a horse.

They are taking away the pigs, chickens, the village wails. Describe our provisions. I sleep in the hut. The horror of their lives. Flies. Research on flies, myriads of them. Five hollering, unhappy little children.

They hide provisions from us.

JULY 17, 1920. NOVOSELKI

I am beginning my war journal from 7/16. I go to Pozha [Pelcha]. The Polit-otdel,* they eat cucumbers there, sun, they sleep barefoot behind the haystacks. Yakovlev† promises to help. The day passes with work. Lepin's lip is swollen. He has round shoulders. He's tough to get along with. A new page: I am studying the science of military operations.

Next to one of the huts lies a slaughtered cow that has only recently calved. Her bluish teats lying on the ground, just skin. An indescribable pity! A murdered young mother.

JULY 18, 1920. NOVOSELKI—MALI DOROGOSTAI

The Polish army is gathering in the region of Dubno-Kremenets for a decisive attack. We are paralyzing their maneuver, we are a step ahead of them. The army launches an attack on the southern sector, our division is being held in reserve. Our task: to seize the crossings over the River Styr around Lutsk.

In the morning we arrive in Mali Dorogostai (north of Mlynov), we leave the transport carts behind, also the sick and the administrative staff, it is obvious that an operation is ahead.

---

* Charged with the ideological education of the military.
† The political commissar of the Sixth Cavalry Division.

We receive an order from the Southwestern Front,* when we cross into Galicia—it will be the first time that Soviet troops will cross the border—we are to treat the population well. We are not entering a conquered nation, the nation belongs to the workers and peasants of Galicia, and to them alone, we are only there to help them set up a Soviet power. The order is important and sensible—will the rag-looters stick to it? No.

We set out. Buglers. The division commander's cap glitters. A discussion with the division commander about the fact that I need a horse. We ride, forests, the fields are being harvested, but the harvest is poor, scanty, here and there two women and two old men. The centuries-old Volhynian forests, majestic green oaks and hornbeams, it is clear why the oak is king.

We ride along forest paths with two staff squadrons, they are always with the division commander, they are handpicked. Describe their horses' garb, sabers in red velvet, curved sabers, vests, carpets over their saddles. Dressed poorly, though each of them has ten service jackets—it's doubtless a matter of chic.

Fields, roads, sun, the wheat is ripening, we are trampling the fields, the harvest is weak, the grain stunted, there are many Czech, German, and Polish settlements. Different people, prosperity, cleanliness, marvelous gardens, we eat unripe apples and pears, everyone wants to be quartered with the foreigners, I also catch myself wishing for that, the foreigners are frightened.

The Jewish cemetery outside Malin, centuries old, the stones have toppled, almost all the same shape, oval at the top, the cemetery is overgrown with weeds, it saw Khmelnitsky,† now Budyonny, the unfortunate Jewish population, everything repeats itself, once again the same story of Poles, Cossacks, Jews is repeating itself with striking exactness, what is new is Communism.

More and more often we come across trenches from the last war, barbed wire everywhere, enough for fences for the next ten years,

---

* The Southwestern Front was formed on January 10, 1920, to fight the anti-Bolshevik White Polish Army in the Russian-Polish Campaign and the Imperialist forces of Generals Denikin and Wrangel.

† Bogdan Khmelnitsky, the legendary seventeenth-century Cossack leader whose brutal raids in the region were still remembered.

destroyed villages, they are being rebuilt again everywhere, but slowly, there's nothing, no materials of any kind, no cement.

With the Cossacks at the rest stops, hay for the horses, they all have long stories to tell: Denikin, their farms, their leaders, Budyonnys and Knigas, campaigns with two hundred men, plundering raids, the rich, free life of a Cossack, how many officers' heads they have chopped off. They read the newspaper, but the names just don't sink in, how easily they twist everything.

Wonderful camaraderie, unity, love of horses, a horse takes up a quarter of a day, incessant bartering and chatting. A horse's role and life.

Completely wayward attitude toward the leaders—they address them with the familiar "you."

M[ali] Dorogostai was completely destroyed, is being rebuilt.

We ride into the priest's garden. We take hay, eat fruit. A shady, sunny, wonderful garden, a little white church, there had been cows, horses, a priest with a little braid is wandering around in a daze collecting receipts. Bakhturov* is lying on his stomach eating yogurt with cherries, I'll give you a receipt, really, I will!

We've eaten enough of the priest's food to last us a whole year. Word has it he's ruined, is trying to get a position, do you have any openings for a regimental clergyman?

Evening at my quarters. Again *nemae*†—they're all lying, I write in my journal, they give us potatoes with butter. Night in the village, an enormous, crimson fiery circle before my eyes, yellow fields flee from the ravaged village. Night. Lights at the headquarters. There are always lights at headquarters, Karl Karlovich** dictates an order from memory, he never forgets anything, the telephone operators sit with hanging heads. Karl Karlovich served in Warsaw.

JULY 19, 1920. M[ALI] DOROGOSTAI—
SMORDVA—BEREZHTSY

Slept badly last night. Cramps in my stomach. We ate green pears yesterday. I feel dreadful. We're setting off at dawn.

---

* The military commissar of the Sixth Cavalry Division.
† Ukrainian: "there isn't any."
** Konstantin Karlovich Zholnarkevich, the chief of staff of the Sixth Cavalry Division.

The enemy is attacking us in the sector of Mlynov-Dubno. We pushed forward all the way to Radzivillov.

Today at dawn, the decisive attack by all the divisions—from Lutsk to Kremenets. The Fifth, the Sixth Division are concentrated in Smordva, we have reached Kozino.

In other words, we're heading south.

We're pulling out of M. Dorogostai. The division commander is greeting the squadrons, his horse is trembling. Music. We are stretched out along the road. The road is unbearable. We are going via Mlynov to Berezhtsy. A pity we can't enter Mlynov, it's a Jewish shtetl. We get to Berezhtsy, cannonade, the staff heads back, there's a smell of fuel oil, cavalry units are crawling over the slopes. Smordva, the priest's house, young provincial ladies in white stockings, their eyes red from weeping, it has been a long time since I have seen anything like it, the priest's wounded wife, limping, the sinewy cleric, a solid house, the divisional staff and the commander of Division Fourteen, we are waiting for the arrival of the brigades, our staff is on a hill, a truly Bolshevik staff: the division commander, Bakhturov, the military commissars. We're under gunfire, the division commander knows his stuff: he's clever, a go-getter, somewhat of a dandy, self-assured, the bypass movement toward Bokunin was his idea, the attack is held up, orders issued to the brigades. Kolesov and Kniga* came galloping over (the famous Kniga, why is he famous?). Kolesov's superb horse, Kniga has the face of a bakery sales clerk, a diligent Ukrainian. Swift orders, everyone confers, the gunfire gets stronger, shells are falling a hundred paces from us.

The commander of Division Fourteen is of a weaker mettle, a fool, talkative, an intellectual, wants to pass for a Budyonny fighter, curses incessantly—I've been fighting all night—likes to brag a bit. The brigades are winding in long ribbons along the opposite bank, the transport carts are under fire, columns of dust. Budyonny's regiments with their transport carts, carpets across their saddles.

I feel worse and worse. I have a temperature of 39.8. Budyonny and Voroshilov† arrive.

---

* Nikolai Petrovich Kolesov was commander of the Third Brigade, and Vasily Ivanovich Kniga was commander of the First Brigade of the Sixth Cavalry Division.

† The two founding members of the First Cavalry Army, Semyon Mikhailovich Budyonny, its commander, and Kliment Efremovich Voroshilov, its commissar.

There's a conference. The division commander goes flying past. The battle begins. I'm lying in the priest's garden. Grishchuk is completely impassive. What kind of a man is Grishchuk? Submissiveness, endless silence, boundless indolence. Fifty versts from home, hasn't been home in six years, doesn't run away.

He knows the meaning of authority, the Germans taught him that.

Wounded men start coming in, bandages, bare stomachs, forbearing, unbearable heat, incessant gunfire from both sides, can't doze off. Budyonny and Voroshilov on the porch. A picture of the battle, the cavalrymen return covered with dust, sweating, red, no traces of excitement, they've been slashing, they're professionals, everything done with the utmost calm, that's what sets them apart, self-assuredness, hard work, nurses go flying by on horses, a Zhguchy armored car. In front of us is Count Ledochowski's* mansion, a white building above the lake, not tall, not flamboyant, very noble, memories of my childhood, novels—many more memories. At the medical assistants': a pitiful, handsome young Jew, he might well have been on the count's payroll, gray with worry. If I may ask, what is the situation at the front? The Poles mocked and tormented, he thinks life is about to begin, but the Cossacks don't always behave well.

Echoes of battle—galloping horsemen, reports, the wounded, the dead.

I sleep in the churchyard. Some brigade commander or other is sleeping with his head resting on some young lady's stomach.

I have been sweating, I feel better. I ride to Berezhtsy, the headquarters office is there, a destroyed house, I drink cherry tea, lie down in the landlady's bed, sweat, aspirin powder. It would do me good to sleep a little. I remember—I have a fever, heat, some soldiers in the churchyard kicking up a fuss, others cool, they are coupling their stallions with mares.

Berezhtsy, Sienkiewicz, I drink cherry tea, I'm lying on a spring mattress, next to me lies a child gasping for breath. I dozed off for about two hours. They wake me. I'm drenched in sweat. At night we return to Smordva, from there we continue, a clearing in the forest. Night journey, moon, somewhere in front of us, the squadron.

* Ignacy Ledochowski, commander of the Polish Fourteenth Artillery Brigade.

A hut in the forest. The muzhiks and their womenfolk sleep along the walls. Konstantin Karlovich* is dictating. A rare picture: the squadron is sleeping all around, everything is steeped in darkness, nothing can be seen, a chill flows in from the forest, I bump into the horses, at the headquarters everyone's eating, I feel sick and lie down on the ground next to a *tachanka*, I sleep for three hours covered with Barsukov's shawl and coat, it feels good.

JULY 20, 1920. THE HEIGHTS NEAR SMORDVA. PELCHA.

We set out at five in the morning. Rain, damp, we stick to the forests. The operation is going very well, our division commander chose the right bypass maneuver, we're continuing to detour. We're soaked, forest paths. The bypass is taking us through Bokuika to Pelcha. Information: at 10 o'clock Dobryvodka was taken, at twelve o'clock, after negligible resistance, Kozin. We're pursuing the enemy, we go to Pelcha. Forests, forest paths, the squadrons are winding on ahead.

My health is better, for inexplicable reasons.

I am studying the flora of the province of Volhynia, there has been much logging, the clearing in the forest with felled trees, remains of the war, barbed wire, white trenches. Majestic green oaks, hornbeams, many pines, the willow is a majestic and gentle tree, rain in the forest, washed-out roads in the forest, ash trees.

To Pelcha along forest paths. We arrive around ten o'clock. Another village, lanky landlady, boring—*nemae,* very clean, son had been a soldier, gives us eggs, there's no milk, in the hut it's unbearably stuffy, it's raining, washes out all the roads, black squelching mud, it's impossible to get to the headquarters. Sitting all day in the hut, it's warm, there, outside the window, the rain. How boring and banal this kind of life is for me—chicks, a hidden cow, dirt, idiocy. An indescribable sadness lies over the earth, everything is wet, black, autumn, whereas back in Odessa . . .

In Pelcha we captured the transport carts of the Forty-ninth Polish Infantry Regiment. The spoils are being divided outside my window,

* Zholnarkevich, the chief of staff of the Sixth Cavalry Division.

completely idiotic cursing, nonstop, other words are boring, they avoid them, as for the cursing: the Mother of Christ, the Goddamn Mother, the peasant women cringe, the Mother of God, the children ask questions—the soldiers curse. Mother of God. I'll shoot you, damn it! I get a document bag and a saddlebag. Describe this dull life. The peasant doesn't go to work on the field. I sleep in the landlady's bed. We heard that England proposed that Sov. Russia and Poland make peace—is it possible this will end soon?

July 21, 1920. Pelcha—Boratin

We have taken Dubno. The resistance, regardless of what we say, has been insignificant. What is going on? The prisoners talk, and it is clear that it is the revolution of the little people. Much can be said about that, the beauty of the Polish pediments, there is something touching about it, Milady. Fate, slighted honor, Jews, Count Ledochowski. Proletarian Revolution. How I drink in the aroma of Europe that flows from over there.

We set out for Boratin by way of Dobryvodka, forests, fields, soft outlines, oak trees, again music and the division commander, and, nearby, the war. A rest stop in Zhabokriki, I eat white bread. Grishchuk sometimes seems dreadful to me—downtrodden. The Germans: that grinding jaw.

Describe Grishchuk.

In Boratin, a hardy, sunny village. Khmil, smiling at his daughter, he is a closemouthed but wealthy peasant, eggs fried in butter, milk, white bread, gluttony, sun, cleanliness, I am recuperating from my illness, to me all these peasants look alike, a young mother. Grishchuk is beaming, they gave him fried eggs with bacon, a wonderful, shadowy threshing shed, clover. Why doesn't Grishchuk run away?

A wonderful day. My interview with Konstantin Karlovich [Zholnarkevich]. What kind of men are our Cossacks? Many-layered: rag-looting, bravado, professionalism, revolutionary ideals, savage cruelty. We are the vanguard, but of what? The population is waiting for liberators, the Jews for freedom—but who arrives? The Kuban Cossacks. . . .

The army commander summons the division commander for a

meeting in Kozin. Seven versts. I ride. Sand. Every house remains in my heart. Clusters of Jews. Faces, ghetto, and we, an ancient people, tormented, we still have strength, a store, I drink excellent coffee, I pour balm on the storekeeper's soul as he listens to the rumpus in his store. The Cossacks are yelling, cursing, climbing up to the shelves, the poor store, the sweaty, red-bearded Jew. . . . I wander endlessly, I cannot tear myself away, the shtetl was destroyed, is being rebuilt, has existed for four hundred years, the ruins of a synagogue, a marvelous destroyed old temple, a former Catholic church, now Russian Orthodox, enchanting whiteness, three wings, visible from afar, now Russian Orthodox. An old Jew—I love talking with our people—they understand me. A cemetery, the destroyed house of Rabbi Azrail, three generations, the tombstone beneath the tree that has grown over it, these old stones, all of the same shape, the same contents, this exhausted Jew, my guide, some family of dim-witted, fat-legged Jews living in a wooden shed by the cemetery, the coffins of three Jewish soldiers killed in the Russian-German war.* The Abramoviches of Odessa, the mother had come to bury him, and I see this Jewess, who is burying her son who perished for a cause that to her is repulsive, incomprehensible, and criminal.

The old and the new cemetery, the shtetl is four hundred years old.

Evening, I walk among the buildings, Jews and Jewesses are reading the posters and proclamations: Poland is the dog of the bourgeoisie, and so on. Insects bring death, and don't remove heaters from the railroad cars.

These Jews are like paintings: lanky, silent, long-bearded, not like ours, fat and jovial. Tall old men hanging around with nothing to do. Most important: the store and the cemetery.

Seven versts back to Boratin, a marvelous evening, my soul is full, our landlord rich, sly girls, fried eggs, lard, our men are catching flies, the Russo-Ukrainian soul. All in all, uninteresting.

JULY 22, 1920. BORATIN

Before lunch, a report to army field headquarters. Nice, sunny weather, rich, solid village, I go to the mill, describe what a water mill

* The First World War.

is like, Jewish workman, then I bathe in the cold, shallow stream beneath the weak sun of Volhynia. Two girls are playing in the water, a strange, almost irrepressible urge to talk dirty, rough slippery words.

Sokolov is doing badly. I give him horses to get him to the hospital. The staff leaves for Leshniov (Galicia, we cross the border for the first time). I wait for the horses. It is nice here in the village, bright, stomach full.

Two hours later I leave for Khotin. The road goes through the forest, anxiety. Grishchuk is dull-witted, frightening. I am on Sokolov's heavy horse. I am alone on the road. Bright, clear, not hot, a light warmth. A cart up ahead, five men who look like Poles. A game: we ride, we stop, where are you from? Mutual fear and anxiety. By Khotin we can see our troops, we ride off, gunfire. A wild gallop back, I yank the horse's reins. Bullets buzz, howl. Artillery fire. At times Grishchuk gallops with dark and taciturn energy, and then at dangerous moments he is unfathomable, limp, black, a heavy growth of beard on his jaw. There's no longer anyone in Boratin. Our transport carts have passed beyond it, a mess begins. The transport-cart saga, aversion and vileness. Gusev is in charge. We wait outside Kozin half the night, gunfire. We send out a scout, nobody knows anything, horsemen ride about the place with an intent air, tall German fellow from the district commander's, night, want to sleep, the feeling of helplessness—you don't know where they're taking you, I think it's the twenty or thirty men we chased into the woods, an assault. But where did they get the artillery from? I sleep for half an hour, they say there was an exchange of fire, a line of our men advanced. We move farther. The horses are exhausted, a terrible night, we move in a colossal train of transport carts through the impenetrable darkness, we don't know which villages we're passing through, there's a great blaze to one side, other trains of transport carts cross our path. Has the front collapsed or is this just a transport-cart panic?

Night drags on endlessly, we fall into a ditch. Grishchuk drives strangely, we're rammed from behind by a shaft, there are yells from somewhere far away, we stop every half verst and stand around futilely and for an agonizingly long time.

A rein tears, our *tachanka* no longer responds, we drive off into a field, night, Grishchuk has an attack of savage, blunt, hopeless despair that infuriates me: O may these reins burn in hell, burn, burn! Grishchuk is blind, he admits it, at night he can't see a thing. The train of transport carts leaves us behind, the roads are harsh, black mud, Grishchuk, clutching the remnants of the reins, with his surprising jangling tenor: We're done for, the Poles are going to catch up with us, they're shelling us from all around, our cavalry transport is surrounded. We drive off at random with torn reins. Our *tachanka* screeches, in the distance a heavy gloomy dawn, wet fields. Violet streaks in the sky with black voids. At dawn the shtetl of Verba. Railroad tracks—dead, frail— the smell of Galicia. 4 o'clock in the morning.

JULY 23, 1920. IN VERBA

Jews, who have been up all night, stand pitiful, like birds, blue, disheveled, in vests and without socks. A wet and desolate dawn, all of Verba crammed with transport carts, thousands of them, all the drivers look alike, first-aid units, the staff of the Forty-fifth Division, depressing rumors and doubtless absurd, and these rumors are circulating despite our chain of victories. . . . Two brigades of the Eleventh Division have been taken prisoner, the Poles have captured Kozin, poor Kozin, I wonder what will happen there? The strategic position is interesting, the Sixth Division is at Leshniov, the Poles are at Kozin, at Boratin, at our rear lines, we are like squashed pies. We are waiting on the road from Verba. We stand there for two hours, Misha in a tall white cap with a red ribbon gallops over the field. Everyone eats bread with straw, green apples, with dirty fingers and reeking mouths. Dirty, disgusting food. We drive on. Amazing, we come to a standstill every five steps, an endless line of provision carts of the Forty-fifth and the Eleventh Divisions, at times we lose our transport unit, then we find it again. The fields, the trampled rye, villages stripped of food and others not yet completely stripped of food, a hilly region, where are we going? The road to Dubno. Forests, wonderful, ancient, shadowy forests. Heat, shade in the forest. Many trees have been felled for military purposes, a curse upon them, the bare forest clearings with their protruding stumps. The ancient Volhynian forests of Dubno—must find out where they get that fragrant black honey.

Describe the forests.

Krivikha: ruined Czechs, a tasty-looking woman. The horror that follows, she cooks for a hundred men, flies, the commissar's moist and rattled woman, Shurka, wild game with potatoes, they take all the hay, reap the oats, potatoes by the ton, the girl at the end of her tether, the vestiges of a prosperous farm. The pitiful, lanky, smiling Czech, the nice, fleshy foreign woman, his wife.

A bacchanalia. Gusev's tasty-looking Shurka with her retinue, the Red Army scum, cart drivers, everyone tramping about in the kitchen, grabbing potatoes, ham, pies are being baked for them. The heat is unbearable, you can't breathe, clouds of flies. The tortured Czechs. Shouting, coarseness, greed. And yet my meal is marvelous: roast pork with potatoes and marvelous coffee. After the meal I sleep under the trees—a quiet, shady slope, swings are swaying before my eyes. Before my eyes lie quiet green and yellow hills drenched in sunlight, and forests. The forests of Dubno. I sleep for about three hours. Then we're off to Dubno. I ride with Prishchepa, a new acquaintance, caftan, white hood, illiterate Communist, he takes me to see Zhenya. Her husband—*a grober mensh**—rides on his little horse from village to village buying up produce from the peasants. The wife a tasty-looking, languorous, sly, sensual young Jewess, married five months, doesn't love her husband, and, by the way, she's flirting with Prishchepa. I'm the center of attention—*er ist ein* [illegible]†—she keeps staring at me, asks me my surname, doesn't take her eyes off me, we drink tea, I'm in an idiotic bind, I am quiet, slack, polite, and thank her for every gesture. Before my eyes: the life of a Jewish family, the mother comes by, some young ladies or other, Prishchepa is quite the ladies' man. Dubno has changed hands quite a few times. Our side, it seems, didn't plunder it. So once again they are all shivering, once again degradation without end and hatred toward the Poles who tear out their beards. The husband: Will there be freedom to trade, to buy a few things and then sell them right away, no speculating? I tell him yes, there will, everything will be for the better—my usual system—in Russia wondrous things are happening: express trains, free food for children, theaters, the International.** They listen

* Yiddish: "an uncouth individual."

† German: "he is a . . ."

** The Third Communist International, 1919–1943, an organization founded in Moscow by the delegates of twelve countries to promote Communism worldwide.

with delight and mistrust. I think to myself: a sky full of diamonds will be yours, everything will be turned upside down, everyone will be uprooted yet again, I feel sorry for them.

The Dubno synagogues. Everything destroyed. Two small anterooms remain, centuries, two minute little rooms, everything filled with memories, four synagogues in a row, and then the pasture, the fields, and the setting sun. The synagogues are pitiful, squat, ancient, green and blue little buildings, the Hasidic one, inside, no architecture whatsoever. I go into the Hasidic synagogue. It's Friday. What stunted little figures, what emaciated faces, for me everything that existed for the past 300 years has come alive, the old men bustle about the synagogue, there is no wailing, for some reason they all run back and forth, the praying is extremely informal. It seems that Dubno's most repulsive-looking Jews have gathered. I pray, rather, I almost pray, and think about Hershele,* this is how I should describe him. A quiet evening in the synagogue, this always has an irresistible effect on me, four synagogues in a row. Religion? No decoration at all in the building, everything is white and plain to the point of asceticism, everything is incorporeal and bloodless to a monstrous degree, to grasp it fully you have to have the soul of a Jew. But what does this soul consist of? Is it not bound to be our century in which they will perish?

A little nook in Dubno, four synagogues, Friday evening, Jews and Jewesses by the ruined stones—all etched in my memory. Then evening, herring, I am sad because there's no one to copulate with. Prishchepa and the teasing and exasperating Zhenya, her sparkling Jewish eyes, fat legs, and soft breasts. Prishchepa, his hands slip deeper, and her unyielding gaze, while her fool of a husband is out in the tiny shed feeding his commandeered horse.

We stay the night with other Jews, Prishchepa asks them to play some music, a fat boy with a hard, idiotic face, gasping with terror, says that he is not in the mood. The horse is nearby in the yard. Grishchuk is only fifty versts from home. He does not run away.

The Poles attack in the area of Kozin-Boratin, they are at our rear lines, the Sixth Division is in Leshniov, Galicia. We're marching to

---

* In Yiddish folklore, a trickster.

Brody, Radzivillov is in front and one brigade is in the rear. The Sixth Division is in hard fighting.

JULY 24, 1920

Morning at army headquarters. The Sixth Division is annihilating the enemy assaulting us in Khotin, the area of battle is Khotin-Kozin, and I think to myself, poor Kozin.

The cemetery, round stones.

Prishchepa and I ride from Krivikha to Leshniov by way of Demidovka. Prishchepa's soul—an illiterate fellow, a Communist, the Kadety* killed his parents, he tells me how he went about his Cossack village collecting his belongings. Colorful, wearing a hood, as simple as grass, will turn into a rag-looter, despises Grishchuk because he doesn't love or understand horses. We ride through Khorupan, Smordva, and Demidovka. Remember the picture: transport carts, horsemen, half-wrecked villages, fields and forests, oak trees, now and then wounded men and my *tachanka*.

We arrive in Demidovka toward evening. A Jewish shtetl, I am on guard. Jews in the steppes, everything is destroyed. We are in a house with a horde of women. The Lyachetskys and the Shvevels,† no, this isn't Odessa. Dora Aronovna, a dentist, is reading Artsybashev,** a Cossack rabble loitering about. She is proud, angry, says that the Poles destroyed all sense of self-respect, despises the Communists for their plebianism, a horde of daughters in white stockings, devout father and mother. Each daughter distinctly individual: one is pitiful, black-haired, bowlegged, the other fleshy, a third housewifely, and all, doubtless, old maids.

The main friction: today is the Sabbath. Prishchepa wants them to roast potatoes, but tomorrow is a day of fasting, *Tishah b'Ab*,‡and I

---

* Members of the Constitutional Democratic Party, liberal monarchists who were in favor of a more moderate bourgeois revolution as opposed to a proletarian revolution. After the October Revolution, the Kadety actively fought the Bolsheviks.

† Shevel was Babel's mother's maiden name. His aunt, Katya Aronovna, had married into the Lyakhetsky family.

** The author Mikhail Petrovich Artsybashev, 1878–1927.

‡ The ninth day of the month Ab, a Jewish day of mourning commemorating the destruction of the First and Second Temples in Jerusalem.

say nothing because I am Russian. The dentist, pale with pride and self-respect, announces that nobody will dig up potatoes because it is a holy day.

I manage to restrain Prishchepa for quite a while, but then he explodes: Yids, sons-of-bitches, a whole arsenal of curses, all of them hate us and me, dig up potatoes, frightened in the garden that isn't theirs, they blame the Christians, Prishchepa is outraged. How painful it all is—Artsybashev, the orphaned schoolgirl from Rovno, Prishchepa in his hood. The mother wrings her hands: the stove has been lit on the Sabbath, curses fly. Budyonny was here and left again. An argument between a Jewish youth and Prishchepa. A youth with spectacles, black-haired, highly strung, scarlet, inflamed eyelids, inaccurate Russian speech. He believes in God, God is the ideal we carry in our souls, every person has their own God in their soul, if you act badly, God grieves, this nonsense is proclaimed with rapture and pain. Prishchepa is offensively idiotic, he talks of religion in ancient times, mixes Christianity and Paganism, his main point, in ancient times there was the commune, needless to say nothing but rubbish—you have no education whatsoever—and the Jew with his six years of Rovno high-school education quotes Platonov—touching and comical—the clans, the elders, Perun, paganism.

We eat like oxen, fried potatoes, and five glasses of coffee each. We sweat, they serve us everything, it's all terrible, I tell fairy tales about Bolshevism, its blossoming, the express trains, the Moscow textile mills, the universities, the free food, the Revel Delegation, and, to crown it all, my tale about the Chinese, and I enthrall all these poor tortured people. *Tishah b'Ab*. The old woman sobs sitting on the floor, her son, who worships her, says that he believes in God to make her happy, he sings in a pleasant tenor and tells the story of the destruction of the Temple. The terrible words of the prophets: they will eat dung, the maidens will be defiled, the menfolk slaughtered, Israel crushed, angry and dejected words. The lamp smokes, the old woman wails, the youth sings melodiously, the girls in their white stockings, outside the window Demidovka, night, Cossacks, everything just as it had been in the days when the Temple was destroyed. I go to sleep in the wet, reeking yard.

It's a disaster with Grishchuk, he is in a daze, hovering around like a sleepwalker, he is feeding the horses badly, informs me about problems *post factum,* favors the muzhiks and their children.

Machine-gunners have come in from the front lines, they come over to our yard, it is night, they are wrapped in their cloaks. Prishchepa is courting a Jewess from Kremenets, pretty, fleshy, in a smooth dress. She blushes tenderly, her one-eyed father-in-law is sitting nearby, she blossoms, it's nice talking with Prishchepa, she blossoms and acts coquettish—what are they talking about?—then, he wants to go to bed, spend some time with her, she is tormented, who understands her soul better than I? He: We will write to each other. I wonder with a heavy heart: surely she won't give in. Prishchepa tells me she agrees (with him they all agree). I suddenly remember that he seemed to have had syphilis, I wonder: was he fully cured?

The girl later on: I will scream. Describe their initial pussyfooting conversation—how dare you—she is an educated person, she served on the Revolutionary Committee.*

God almighty, I think, the women are hearing all these curses now, they live like soldiers, what happened to their tenderness?

At night rain and storm, we run over to the stable, dirty, dark, damp, cold, the machine-gunners will be sent back to the front lines at dawn, they assemble in the pouring rain, cloaks and freezing horses. Miserable Demidovka.

JULY 25, 1920

We pull out of Demidovka in the morning. A tortured two hours, they woke the Jewesses at four o'clock in the morning and had them boil Russian meat,† and that on *Tishah b'Ab.* Half-naked and disheveled girls run through wet gardens, Prishchepa is in the grip of lust, he throws himself on the bride of the one-eyed man's son while their cart is being requisitioned, an incredible bout of cursing, the soldiers are eating meat out of the pots, she, I will scream, her face, he pushes her against the wall, a shameless spectacle. Under no circumstances does she want to hand over the cart, they had hidden it in the

* Local organs of the Soviet government.
† Nonkosher.

loft, she will make a good Jewess. She wrangles with the commissar, who says that the Jews do not want to help the Red Army.

I lost my briefcase and then found it at the headquarters of the Fourteenth Division in Lishnya.

We head for Ostrov—fifteen versts, there is a road from there to Leshniov, it's dangerous there, Polish patrols. The priest, his daughter looks like Plevitskaya* or a merry skeleton. She is a Kiev student, everyone yearns for civility, I tell my fairy tales, she cannot tear herself away. Fifteen dangerous versts, sentries gallop past, we cross the border, wooden planks. Trenches everywhere.

We arrive at the headquarters. Leshniov. The little town half destroyed. The Russians have fouled up the place pretty badly. A Catholic church, a Uniate church, a synagogue, beautiful buildings, miserable life, a few spectral Jews, a revolting landlady, a Galician woman, flies and dirt, a lanky, shy blockhead, second-grade Slavs. Convey the spirit of destroyed Leshniov, its enfeeblement and its depressing, semi-foreign dirt.

I sleep in the threshing shed. A battle is raging at Brody and at the Tsurovitse crossing. Leaflets about Soviet Galicia. Pastors. Night in Leshniov. How unimaginably sad this all is, and these pitiful Galicians gone wild, and the destroyed synagogues, and trickles of life against a backdrop of horrifying events, of which only reflections come through to us.

JULY 26, 1920. LESHNIOV

The Ukraine in flames. Wrangel† has not been annihilated. Makhno** is launching raids in the districts of Ekaterinoslav and Poltava. New gangs have appeared, a rebellion near Kherson. Why are they rebelling? Is the Communist jacket too short for them?

What's going on in Odessa? Longing.

Much work, I'm remembering the past. This morning Brody was taken, again the surrounded enemy managed to get out, a sharp order

* Nadyezhda Plevitskaya, a celebrated Russian singer and actress.
† Baron Pyotr Nikolaevich Wrangel was the commander of the anti-Bolshevik armies in southern Russia.
** The Ukrainian anarchist leader.

from Budyonny, we've let them get away four times now, we are able to shake them loose but we don't have the strength to hold them.

A meeting in Kozin, Budyonny's speech: We've stopped all maneuvering, from now on frontal attacks, we are losing contact with the enemy, no reconnaissance, no defense, the division commanders show no initiative, lifeless operations.

I talk with Jews, for the first time uninteresting Jews. Nearby, the destroyed synagogue, a red-haired man from Brody, some countrymen of mine from Odessa.

I move in with a legless Jew, affluence, cleanliness, quiet, marvelous coffee, clean children, the father lost both legs on the Italian Front, new house, they're still building, the wife has an eye for profit but is decent, polite, a small shady room, I recover from the Galicians.

I am distressed, I must think things through: Galicia, the World War, and my own fate.

Life in our division. About Bakhturov,* about our division commander, the Cossacks, the marauding, the vanguard's vanguard. I don't belong.

In the evening panic: the enemy pushed us back out of Churovitse, they were a verst and a half away from Leshniov. The division commander went galloping off and came galloping back. And our wanderings begin again, another night without sleep, transport carts, enigmatic Grishchuk, the horses walk quietly; cursing, forests, stars, we stop somewhere. Brody at dawn, all this is horrifying: barbed wire everywhere, burned-out chimneys, a bloodless city, drab houses, word has it there are goods to be had, our men won't hold back, there were factories here, a Russian military cemetery, and, judging by the nameless lonely crosses on the graves, these were Russian soldiers.

The road is completely white, cut-down forests, everything disfigured, Galicians on the road, Austrian uniforms, barefoot with pipes in their mouths, what is in their faces, what mystery of insignificance, commonplaceness, submissiveness.

Radzivillov is worse than Brody, barbed wire on poles, pretty buildings, dawn, pitiful figures, fruit trees plucked bare, bedraggled, yawning Jews, destroyed roads, defiled crucifixes, sterile earth, shattered

---

* The military commissar of the Sixth Cavalry Division.

Catholic churches, where are their priests, smugglers used to be here, and I can see how life used to be.

KHOTIN. JULY 27, 1920

After Radzivillov—endless villages, horsemen charging on, difficult after a sleepless night.

Khotin is the same village where we had been under fire. My quarters are horrifying: abject poverty, bathhouse, flies, an unruffled, gentle, well-built muzhik, a crafty woman, she won't give a thing, I get some lard, potatoes. They live absurdly, wild, the dingy room and the myriad flies, the terrible food, and they don't strive for anything better—and the greed, and the repulsive, immutable way their dwelling is set up, and the hides reeking in the sun, the limitless dirt, exasperate me.

There was a landowner here—Sveshnikov—the factory is destroyed, his manor is destroyed, the majestic skeleton of the factory, a red brick-building, cobbled paths, now no trace of them, the muzhiks indifferent.

Artillery supplies are lagging, I'm immersing myself in headquarters work: the vile work of murder. What is to Communism's credit: at least it doesn't advocate animosity toward the enemy, only toward Polish soldiers.

Prisoners were brought in, a Red Army fighter wounded a perfectly healthy man with two gunshots for no reason whatsoever. The Pole doubles over, moans, they put a pillow under his head.

Zinoviev was killed, a young Communist in red trousers, a rattle in his throat and blue eyelids.

Astonishing rumors are going around—on the 30th, discussions for an armistice will begin.

Night in a reeking hole they call a yard. I can't sleep, it's late, I go over to the headquarters, the situation with the crossings is not all that good.

Late night, red flag, silence, Red Army fighters thirsting for women.

JULY 28, 1920. KHOTIN

The skirmish for the crossing at Churovitse. The Second Brigade is bleeding to death in Budyonny's presence. The whole infantry battalion is wounded, almost completely destroyed. The Poles are in old reinforced trenches. Our men weren't successful. Is the Poles' resistance growing stronger?

There is no sign of slackening due to the prospect of peace.

I'm staying in a poor hut where a son with a big head plays the violin. I terrorize the mistress of the house, she won't give me anything. Grishchuk, sullen as a stone, does not take good care of the horses, it turns out he was schooled by hunger.

A ruined estate, Sveshnikov the landowner, the majestic, destroyed distillery (the symbol of the Russian landed gentry?), when the alcohol was handed out all the fighters drank themselves into a stupor.

I am exasperated, I can't contain my indignation: the dirt, the apathy, the hopelessness of Russian life are unbearable, the Revolution will do some good work here.

The mistress of the house hides the pigs and the cow, talks fast, sugary, and with impotent hatred, is lazy, and I have the impression she is running their household into the ground, her husband believes in a strong government, is charming, gentle, passive, resembles Stroyev.

The village is boring, living here is dreadful. I'm immersing myself in headquarters work. Describe the day, the reverberations of the battle raging only a few versts away from us, the orderlies, Lepin's* hand is swollen.

The Red Army fighters sleep with the women.

A story: How a Polish regiment had laid down its weapons four times, but then each time began defending itself again as we hacked them down.

Evening, quiet, a discussion with Matyazh, he is boundlessly lazy, indolent, snot-nosed, and somehow pleasantly, affectionately lustful. The terrible truth is that all the soldiers have syphilis. Matyazh is almost cured (with practically no treatment). He had syphilis, got treatment for two weeks, he and a fellow countryman were to pay ten silver kopecks in Stavropol, his fellow countryman died, Misha had it many times, Senechka and Gerasya have syphilis, and they all go with women, and back home they have brides. The soldier's curse. Russia's curse—it's horrifying. They swallow ground crystal, at times they drink

---

* A staff officer in the Sixth Cavalry Division.

either carbolic acid or crushed glass. All our fighters: velvet caps, rapes, Cossack forelocks, battle, Revolution, and syphilis. The whole of Galicia is infected.

A letter to Zhenya,* I long for her and home.

Must keep an eye on the Osobotdel† and the Revolutionary Tribunal.**

Will there really be peace talks on the 30th?

An order from Budyonny. We've let the enemy escape a fourth time, we had completely surrounded them at Brody.

Describe Matyazh, Misha. The muzhiks, I want to fathom them. We have the power to maneuver, to surround the Poles, but, when it comes down to it, our grip is weak, they can break free, Budyonny is furious, reprimands the division commander. Write the biographies of the division commander, the military commissar, Kniga,‡ and so on.

JULY 29, 1920. LESHNIOV

In the morning we set out for Leshniov. Again the same landlord as before, black-bearded, legless Froim. During my absence he was robbed of four thousand guldens, they took his boots. His wife, a smooth-tongued bitch, is colder to me, now that she has realized she can't make any money off me, how greedy they are. I talk with her in German. Bad weather begins.

Froim has lame children, there are many of them, I can't tell them apart, he has hidden his cow and his horse.

Galicia is unbearably gloomy, destroyed churches and crucifixes, overcast low-hanging sky, the battered, worthless, insignificant population. Pitiful, inured to the slaughter and the soldiers and the disarray, matronly Russian women in tears, the torn-up roads, stunted crops, no sun, Catholic priests with wide-brimmed hats, without churches. An oppressive anguish emanates from all who are struggling to survive.

---

* Evgenia Borisovna Babel, née Gronfein, Babel's wife.

† Osobii Otdel ("Special Section") was formed in December 1918 to identify and eradicate counterrevolutionary elements in the Red Army.

** The Revolutionary Tribunals were the organs of military justice representing the Revolutionary Military Council.

‡ The commander of the First Brigade of the Sixth Cavalry Division, who had been decorated with a Red Flag Medal.

Are the Slavs the manure of history?

The day passes full of anxiety. The Poles broke through the Fourteenth Division's position to the right of where we are, they've again occupied Berestechko. No information whatsoever, quite a quadrille, they are moving behind our rear lines.

The mood at headquarters. Konstantin Karlovich* is silent. The clerks, that band of gorged, impudent, venereal ruffians, are worried. After a hard, monotonous day, a rainy night, mud—I'm wearing low shoes. And now a really powerful rain is setting in, the real victor.

We trudge through the mud, a fine, penetrating rain.

Cannon and machine gun fire closer and closer. I have an unbearable urge to sleep. There's nothing to feed the horses with. I have a new coachman: a Pole, Gowinski, tall, adept, talkative, bustling, and, needless to say, impudent.

Grishchuk is going home, at times he explodes—"I'm worn out"— he did not manage to learn German because his master had been a severe man, all they did was quarrel, but they never talked.

It also turns out he had starved for seven months, and I didn't give him enough food.

The Pole: completely barefoot, with haggard lips, blue eyes. Talkative and happy-go-lucky, a defector, he disgusts me.

An insurmountable urge to sleep. It's dangerous to sleep. I lie there fully clothed. Froim's two legs are standing on a chair next to me. A little lamp is shining, his black beard, the children are lying on the floor.

I get up ten times—Gowinski and Grishchuk are asleep—anger. I fall asleep around four o'clock, a knock at the door: we must go. Panic, the enemy is right outside the shtetl, machine gun fire, the Poles are getting nearer. Pandemonium. They can't bring the horses out, they break down the gates, Grishchuk with his repulsive despair, there's four of us, the horses haven't been fed, we have to go get the nurse, Grishchuk and Gowinski want to leave her behind, I yell in a voice not my own—the nurse? I'm furious, the nurse is foolish, pretty. We fly up the high road to Brody, I rock and sleep. It's cold, penetrating wind and rain. We have to keep an eye on the horses, the harness is unreliable, the Pole is singing, I'm shivering with cold, the nurse is chattering away

---

* Zholnarkevich, the chief of staff of the Sixth Cavalry Division.

foolishly. I rock and sleep. A new sensation: I can't keep my eyelids open. Describe the inexpressible urge to sleep.

Again we are fleeing from the Pole. There you have it: the cavalry war. I wake up, we have stopped in front of some white buildings. A village? No, Brody.

JULY 30, 1920. BRODY

A gloomy dawn. I've had enough of that nurse. We dropped Grishchuk off somewhere. I wish him good luck.

Where do we go from here? Tiredness is stifling me. It's six o'clock in the morning. We end up with some Galician. The wife is lying on the floor with a newborn baby. He is a quiet little old man, children are lying with his naked wife, there are three or four of them.

There's some other woman there too. Dust soaked down with rain. The cellar. A crucifix. A painting of the Holy Virgin. The Uniates are really neither one thing nor the other. A strong Catholic influence. Bliss—it is warm, some kind of hot stench from the children, from the women. Silence and dejection. The nurse is sleeping, but I can't, bedbugs. There is no hay, I yell at Gowinski. The landlord doesn't have any bread, milk.

The town is destroyed, looted. A town of great interest. Polish culture. An old, rich, distinctive, Jewish population. The terrible bazaars, the dwarves in long coats, long coats and *peyes*, ancient old men. Shkolnaya Street, nine synagogues, everything half destroyed, I take a look at the new synagogue, the architecture [one word illegible, the kondesh/kodesh], the *shamas*, a bearded, talkative Jew: If only there were peace, then we'd have trade. He talks about the Cossacks' looting of the town, of the humiliations inflicted by the Poles. A wonderful synagogue, how lucky we are that we at least have some old stones. This is a Jewish town, this is Galicia, describe. Trenches, destroyed factories, the Bristol, waitresses, "Western European" culture, and how greedily we hurl ourselves onto it. Pitiful mirrors, pale Austrian Jews—the owners. And the stories: there had been American dollars here, oranges, cloth.

The high road, barbed wire, cut-down forests, and dejection, boundless dejection. There's nothing to eat, there's nothing to hope for, war, everyone's as bad as the next, as strange as the next, hostile, wild, life had been quiet and, most important, full of tradition.

Budyonny fighters in the streets. In the shops nothing but lemon fizz, and also the barbershops have opened. At the bazaar the shrews are only selling carrots, constant rain, ceaseless, penetrating, smothering. Unbearable sorrow, the people and their souls have been killed.

At the headquarters: red trousers, self-assuredness, little souls puffing themselves up, a horde of young people, Jews also among them, they are at the personal disposal of the army commander and are in charge of food.

Mustn't forget Brody and the pitiful figures, and the barbershop, and the Jews from the world beyond, and the Cossacks in the streets.

It's a disaster with Gowinski, there's absolutely no fodder for the horses. The Odessan hotel Galpernia, there is hunger in town, nothing to eat, good tea in the evening, I comfort my landlord, pale and panicky as a mouse. Gowinski found some Poles, he took their army caps, someone helped Gowinski. He is unbearable, doesn't feed the horses, is wandering about somewhere, is constantly jabbering away, can't get his hands on anything, is frightened they might arrest him, and they've already tried to arrest him, they came to me.

Night in the hotel, next door a married couple and their conversation, and words and [blacked out] coming from the woman's lips. Oh, you Russians, how disgustingly you spend your nights, and what voices your women have now! I listen with bated breath and feel despondent.

A terrible night in tortured Brody. Must be on the alert. I haul hay for the horses at night. At the headquarters. I can sleep, the enemy is advancing. I went back to my billet, slept deeply with a deadened heart, Gowinski wakes me.

JULY 31, 1920. BRODY, LESHNIOV

In the morning before we leave, my *tachanka* is waiting on Zolotaya Street, an hour in a bookstore, a German store. All marvelous uncut books, albums, the West, here it is, the West and chivalrous Poland, a chrestomathy, a history of all the Boleslaws,* and for some reason this

---

* A dynasty of medieval Polish kings.

seems to me so beautiful: Poland, glittering garments draped over a decrepit body. I rummage like a madman, leaf through books, it is dark, then a horde pours in and rampant pillaging of office supplies begins, repulsive young men from the War Spoils Commission with a super-military air. I tear myself away from the bookstore in despair.

Chrestomathies, Tetmajer,* new translations, a heap of new Polish national literature, textbooks.

The headquarters are in Stanislavchik or Koziuzkov. The nurse served with the Cheka, very Russian, tender and shattered beauty. She lived with all the commissars, that's my impression, and suddenly: her album from the Kostroma Gymnasium, the schoolmistresses, idealistic hearts, the Romanoff boarding school, Aunt Manya, skating.

Again Leshniov and my old landlord, terrible dirt, the thin veneer of hospitality and respect for the Russians. Despite my kindness there is an air of unfriendliness emanating from these ruined people.

The horses, there's nothing to feed them with, they are growing thin, the *tachanka* is falling apart because of stupid little things, I hate Gowinski, he is such a happy-go-lucky, gluttonous walking disaster. They're no longer giving me any coffee.

The enemy has circumvented us, pushed us back from the river crossings, ominous rumors about a breach of the Fourteenth Division's lines, orderlies gallop off. Toward evening—Grzhimalovka (north of Churovitse). A destroyed village, we got oats, ceaseless rain, my shoes can't make the shortcut to headquarters, a torturing journey, the front line is moving closer to us, I drank some marvelous tea, boiling hot, at first the mistress of the house pretended to be ill, the village has con-tinually been within the range of the battles to secure the crossing. Darkness, anxiety, the Pole is stirring.

Toward evening the division commander came, a marvelous figure of a man, gloves, always out in the front lines, night at the headquar-ters, Konstantin Karlovich's work.

AUGUST 1, 1920. GRZHIMALOVKA, LESHNIOV

God, it's August, soon we shall die, man's brutality is indestructible. The situation is getting worse at the front. Gunfire right outside the

---

* Kazimierz Przerwa Tetmajer, 1865–1940, Polish poet and writer.

village. They are forcing us back from the crossing. Everyone's left, a few staff people have remained, my *tachanka* is standing by the head-quarters, I am listening to the sounds of battle, for some reason I feel good, there are only a few of us, no transport carts, no administrative staff, it's peaceful, simple, Timoshenko's* tremendous sangfroid. Kniga is impassive, Timoshenko—if he doesn't kick them out I'll shoot him, tell him that from me!—and yet he smiles. In front of us the road bloated by rain, machine guns flare up here and there, the invisible presence of the enemy in this gray and airy sky. The enemy has advanced all the way to the village. We are losing the crossing over the Styr. How many times have we headed back to ill-fated Leshniov?

The division commander is off to the First Brigade. It is terrible in Leshniov, we are stopping for two hours, the administrative staff is flee-ing, the enemy wall is rising all around.

The battle near Leshniov. Our infantry is in the trenches, this is amazing: barefoot, semi-idiotic Volhynian fellows—the Russian village, and they are actually fighting the Poles, the *Pans*† who oppressed them. Not enough weapons, the cartridges don't fit, the boys are moping about in the stifling hot trenches, they are moved from one clearing to another. A hut by the clearing, an obliging Galician makes some tea for me, the horses are standing in a little hollow.

I went over to a battery, precise, unhurried, technical work.

Under machine gun fire, bullets shriek, a dreadful sensation, we creep along through the trenches, some Red Army fighter is panicking, and, of course, we are surrounded. Gowinski had gone to the road, want-ed to dump the horses, then drove off, I found him at the clearing, my *tachanka* destroyed, peripeteia, I look for somewhere to sit, the machine-gunners push me away, they are bandaging a wounded young man, his leg is up in the air, he is howling, a friend whose horse was killed is with him, we strap the *tachanka* together, we drive off, the *tachanka* is screech-ing, won't turn. I have the feeling that Gowinski will be the death of me, that's fate, his bare stomach, the holes in his shoes, his Jewish nose, and the endless excuses. I move to Mikhail Karlovich's** cart, what a relief,

---

* Commander of the Sixth Cavalry Division.

† Polish: "Lords."

** Mikhail Karlovich Zholnarkevich, staff officer, and brother of Konstantin Karlovich, the divisional chief of staff.

I doze, it's evening, my soul is shaken, transport carts, we come to a halt on the road to Bielavtsy, then go along a road bordered by the forest, evening, cool, high road, sunset, we are rolling toward the front lines, we bring Konstantin Karlovich [Zholnarkevich] some meat.

I am greedy and pitiful. The units in the forest have left, typical picture, the squadron, Bakhturov* is reading a report on the Third International, about how people from all over the world came together, a nurse's white kerchief is flashing through the trees, what is she doing here? We drive back, what kind of man is Mikhail Karlovich? Gowinski's run off, no horses. Night, I sleep in the cart next to Mikhail Karlovich. We're outside Bielavtsy.

Describe the people, the air.

The day has passed, I saw death, white roads, horses between trees, sunrise and sunset. The main thing: Budyonny fighters, horses, troop movements, and war, through the wheat fields walk solemn, barefoot, spectral Galicians.

Night in the wagon.

I chatted with some clerks by their *tachanka* on the edge of the forest.

AUGUST 2, 1920. BIELAVTSY

The problem with my *tachanka*. Gowinski drives toward the shtetl, needless to say he hasn't found a blacksmith. My shouting match with the blacksmith, he jostled a woman, shrieks and tears. The Galicians don't want to fix the *tachanka*. A whole arsenal of devices, persuasion, threats, begging, what proved most effective was the promise of sugar. A long story, one smith is ill, I drag him over to another one, tears, they drag him home. They don't want to wash my clothes, nothing will induce them to.

Finally they fix the *tachanka*.

I am tired. Alarm at the headquarters. We leave. The enemy is closing in, I run to warn Gowinski, heat, I'm afraid of being late, I run through sand, manage to warn him, catch up again with the headquarters staff outside the village, no one will take me, they leave, dejection, I ride for a while with Barsukov, we are rolling toward Brody.

* The military commissar of the Sixth Cavalry Division.

I am given an ambulance *tachanka* from the Second Squadron, we drive to the forest, my driver Ivan and I wait there. Budyonny arrives, Voroshilov, it is going to be a decisive battle, no more retreating, all three brigades turn around, I speak with the staff commandant. The atmosphere at the start of a battle, a large field, airplanes, cavalry maneuvers on the field, our cavalry, explosions in the distance, the battle has begun, machine guns, the sun, somewhere the two armies clash, muffled shouts of "Hurrah!" Ivan and I move back, deadly danger, I do not feel fear, but passivity, he seems to be frightened, which way should we drive, Korotchayev's* group turns to the right, we, for some reason, go left, the battle is raging, wounded men on horses catch up with us, one of them, deathly pale—"Brother, take me with you!"—his trousers soaked with blood, he threatens to shoot us if we don't take him, we rein in our horses, he is in a terrible state, Ivan's jacket becomes soaked with blood, a Cossack, we stop, I will bandage him, his wound is light, in the stomach, a rib has been hit, we take another one whose horse has been killed. Describe the wounded man. For a long time we go roving through the fields under fire, we can't see a thing, these indifferent roads, the weeds, we send out horsemen, we come to a high road—which way should we go, Radzivillov or Brody?

The administrative staff is supposed to be at Radzivillov along with all the transport carts, but in my opinion, Brody would be more interesting, the battle is being fought for Brody. Ivan's opinion prevails, some of the cart drivers are saying the Poles are in Brody, the transport carts are fleeing, the army staff has left, we drive to Radzivillov. We arrive in the night. All this time we've been eating carrots and peas, penetrating hunger, we're covered in dirt, haven't slept. I took a hut on the outskirts of Radzivillov. Good choice, my knack for this sort of thing is getting better. An old man, a girl. The buttermilk is marvelous, we had all of it, they're making tea with milk, Ivan is going to get some sugar, machine gun fire, the thunder of carts, we run out of the house, the horse is suddenly limping, that's how things are sometimes, we are running in panic, we're being shot at, we have no idea what's going on, they'll catch us any moment now, we make a dash for the bridge, pandemonium, we fall into the marshes, wild panic, a dead man lying

* A brigade commander of the Sixth Cavalry Division.

there, abandoned carts, shells, *tachankas*. Traffic jam, night, terror, carts standing in an endless line, we are moving, a field, we stop, we sleep, stars. What upsets me most in all of this is the lost tea, I'm so upset, it's peculiar. I think about it all night and hate the war.

What a crazy life.

AUGUST 3, 1920

Night in the field, we are rolling toward Brody in a buggy. The town keeps changing hands. The same horrifying picture, the town, half destroyed, is waiting once more. The provision station, I run into Barsukov at the edge of town. I drive over to the headquarters. Deserted, dead, dismal. Zotov* is sleeping stretched out on some chairs, like a corpse. Borodulin and Pollak are also asleep. The building of the Bank of Prague, ransacked and gutted, water closets, those bank cashier windows, mirror glass.

Word has it that the division commander is in Klyokotovo, we spent about two hours in devastated Brody with its ominous air, tea in a barbershop. Ivan is standing outside the headquarters. Should we leave, shouldn't we leave. We leave for Klyokotovo, we turn off the Leshniov high road, we don't know—is it ours or Polish, we drive on feeling our way, the horses are exhausted, one of them is limping harder, we eat potatoes in the village, brigades show up, indescribable beauty, a frightful force is moving, endless lines, a big farm, everything in ruins, a thresher, a Clenton locomobile, a tractor, the locomobile is still working, it's a hot day.

The battlefield, I meet the division commander, where is the staff, we've lost Zholnarkevich. The battle begins, artillery cover, explosions nearby, a grim moment, the decisive battle over whether we will stem the Polish offensive or not, Budyonny to Kolesnikov† and Grishin: "I'll shoot you!" They leave on foot, pale.

Before that, the terrible field sown with hacked-up men, an inhuman cruelty, inconceivable wounds, crushed skulls, young, white, naked bodies are gleaming in the sun, notebooks lying around, single pages, military booklets, Bibles, bodies in the rye.

---

* Commander of the Cavalry Field Headquarters.
† Actually Nikolai Petrovich Kolesov, commander of the Third Brigade.

I absorb these impressions mainly with my mind. The battle begins, I'm given a horse. I see columns forming, chains, they attack, I feel sorry for these poor men—they are not men, they are columns— the gunfire reaches maximum intensity, the carnage is carried out in silence. I ride on, rumors that the division commander is being recalled?

The beginning of my adventures, I ride with the transport carts toward the high road, the battle is growing fiercer, I find the provision station, we're being fired at on the high road, the whistling of shells, explosions a mere twenty paces away, the feeling of hopelessness, the transport carts are flying at full gallop, tag along with the Twentieth Regiment of the Fourth Division, wounded men, the querulous commander: No, he says, not wounded, just a little bang on the head. They're professionals. And everywhere fields, sun, bodies, I sit by the field kitchen, hunger, peas, nothing to feed my horse with.

Field kitchen, talking, we sit on the grass, the regiment suddenly pulls out, I have to go to Radzivillov, the regiment heads for Leshniov and I feel helpless, I am afraid of getting cut off from them. An endless journey, dusty roads, I move to a cart, a Quasimodo, two donkeys, a grim spectacle: the hunchbacked driver, silent, his face dark like the forests of Murom.

We drive, I have a terrible feeling—I am getting farther and farther from the division. Hope flutters up—then suddenly the opportunity to take a wounded man to Radzivillov, the wounded man has a pale, Jewish face.

We ride into the forest, we're fired at, shells a hundred paces away, endless rushing back and forth along the forest edge.

Thick sand, impassable. The ballad of the tortured horses.

An apiary, we search the hives, four huts in the forest—nothing there, everything ransacked, I ask a Red Army fighter for bread, he answers me, "I don't want anything to do with Jews." I'm an outsider, in long trousers, not one of them, I am lonely, we ride on, I am so tired I can barely stay on my mare, I have to look after her myself, we arrive at Konyushkovo, we steal some barley, they tell me: Go take whatever you want, take everything. I go through the village looking for a nurse, the womenfolk are hysterical, within five minutes of our arrival the looting begins, some women are beating their breasts, lamenting, sobbing unbearably, these never-ending horrors are hard to bear, I look for a nurse, insuperable sorrow, I swipe a jug of milk from the regimental commander, snatch a dough-bun out of the hands of a peasant woman's son.

Ten minutes later, we're off. Who'd have thought it! The Poles are somewhere nearby. Back we go again, I don't think I can bear this for much longer, and at a fast trot at that, at first I ride with the commander, then I tag along with the transport carts, I want to move over onto a cart, they all give me the same answer: The horses are tired. You want me to get off so you can sit here, huh? Well, so get yourself up here, just mind the corpses! I look at the sackcloth, corpses are lying under it.

We come to a field, there are many transport carts from the Fourth Division, a battery, again a field kitchen, I look for some nurses, a difficult night, I want to sleep, I have to feed my horse, I lie down, the horses are eating the excellent wheat, Red Army fighters in the wheat, ashen, at the end of their tether. My mare is tormenting me, I run after her, I join a nurse, we sleep on a *tachanka*, the nurse is old, bald, most probably a Jewess, a martyr, unbearable cursing, the vehicular driver keeps trying to push her off, the horses roam about, the vehicular driver won't wake up, he is rough and foulmouthed, she says: Our heroes are terrible people. She covers him, they sleep in each other's arms, the poor old nurse, that driver should be shot, the foul language, the cursing, this is not the nurse's world—we fall asleep. I wake up two hours later—our bridle has been stolen. Despair. Dawn. We are seven versts away from Radzivillov. I ride off willy-nilly. The poor horse, all of us are poor, the regiment moves on. I get going.

For this day, the main thing is to describe the Red Army fighters and the air.

AUGUST 4, 1920

I am heading alone to Radzivillov. A difficult road, nobody on it, the horse is tired, with every step I'm afraid of running into Poles. Things turned out well, in the area around Radzivillov there are no units, in the shtetl uneasiness, they send me to the station, the townspeople devastated and completely used to change. Sheko* in the auto-

---

* Yakov Vasilevich Sheko, the new chief of staff of the Sixth Cavalry Division, who replaced Konstantin Karlovich Zholnarkevich.

mobile. I'm in Budyonny's billet. A Jewish family, young ladies, a group from the Bukhteyev Gymnasium, Odessa, my heart skips a beat.

O joy, they give me cocoa and bread. The news: we have a new division commander, Apanasenko, and a new divisional chief of staff, Sheko. Wonder of wonders.

Zholnarkevich arrives with his squadron, he is pitiable, Zotov informs him he has been replaced: I'll go sell buns on Sukharevka! Of course you're of the new school, he says, you know how to set up units, in the old days I could do that too, but now, without any reserves, I can't.

He has a high fever, he says things that would be better left unsaid, a shouting match with Sheko, he immediately raises his voice: "The general chief of staff ordered you to report to headquarters!"— "I don't have to pass any tests, I'm not some little boy who hangs out at headquarters!" He leaves the squadron and goes off. The old guard is leaving, everything is falling apart, now Konstantin Karlovich [Zholnarkevich] is gone too.

Another impression, both harsh and unforgettable, is the arrival of the division commander on his white horse, along with his orderlies. The whole ragtag from the headquarters comes running with chickens for the army commander, they are patronizing, loutish, Sheko, haughty, asks about the operations, the division commander tells him, smiles, a marvelous, statuesque figure of a man, and despair. Yesterday's battle— the Sixth Division's brilliant success—1,000 horses, three regiments chased back into the trenches, the enemy routed, pushed back, the division headquarters are in Khotin. Whose success is this, Timoshenko's or Apanasenko's?* Comrade Khmelnitsky: a Jew,† a guzzler, a coward, insolent, but for the army commander a chicken, a piglet, corn on the cob. The orderlies detest him, the insolent orderlies, their only interest: chickens, lard, they eat like pigs, they're fat, the chauffeurs stuff themselves with lard, all this on the porch in front of the house. My horse has nothing to eat.

The mood has changed completely, the Poles are retreating, even

---

* Timoshenko had been the commander of the Sixth Cavalry Division from November 1919 to August 1920, and Apanasenko from August to October 1920.

† R. P. Khmelnitsky, Voroshilov's aide-de-camp, was a Jew, who happened to have the same name as Bogdan Khmelnitsky, the legendary seventeenth-century Cossack leader.

though they are still occupying Brody, we're beating them again, Budyonny's pulled us through.

I want to sleep, I can't. The changes in the life of the division will have a significant effect. Sheko in a cart. Me with the squadron. We are riding to Khotin, again at a trot, we've put fifteen versts behind us. I'm billeted with Bakhturov. He is devastated, the division commander is out and he feels he will be next.* The division is shaken, the fighters walk around in silence, what will come next? Finally I have had some supper: meat, honey. Describe Bakhturov, Ivan Ivanovich, and Petro. I sleep in the threshing shed, finally some peace.

AUGUST 5, 1920. KHOTIN

A day of rest. We eat, I wander through the sun-drenched village, we rest, I had some lunch, supper—there is honey, milk.

The main thing: internal changes, everything is topsy-turvy.

I feel so sorry for our division commander it hurts, the Cossacks are worried, a lot of hushed talk, an interesting sight, they gather in groups, whisper to one another, Bakhturov is crestfallen, our division commander was a hero, the new commander won't let him into the room, from 600–6,000, a harsh humiliation, they hurled it in his face, "You are a traitor!" Timoshenko laughed.† Apanasenko is a new and colorful figure of a man, ugly, pockmarked, passionate, haughty, ambitious, he sent an appeal to headquarters at Stavropol and the Don about the disorder in the rear lines, in order to let them know back home that he was a division commander. Timoshenko was more pleasant, cheerful, broad-minded, and, perhaps, worse. The two men—I suppose they didn't like each other. Sheko is showing his true colors, unbelievably heavy-handed orders, haughtiness. Work at headquarters now completely changed. There is no transport or administrative staff. Lepin is raising his head—he is hostile, idiotic, answers back to Sheko.**

In the evening music, and dance—Apanasenko trying to be popu-

---

* Bakhturov, the military commissar of the Sixth Cavalry Division, was to be relieved of his duties the following day.

† Timoshenko's tenure as commander of the Sixth Cavalry Division ended with the battle near Brody. He was held responsible for the battle's failure.

** Lepin, as a staff officer, now had to report to Sheko, the new chief of staff.

lar—the circle widens, he chooses a horse for Bakhturov from the Polish ones, now everyone is riding Polish horses, they are marvelous, narrow-chested, tall, English, chestnut horses—I mustn't forget this. Apanasenko has the horses paraded.

All day long, talk of intrigues. A letter to the rear lines.

Longing for Odessa.

Remember the figure, face, cheerfulness of Apanasenko, his love of horses, chooses one for Bakhturov.

About the orderlies who throw their lot in with the "masters." What will Mikheyev, lame Sukhorukov, all the Grebushkos, Tarasovs, and Ivan Ivanoviches do with Bakhturov?* They all follow blindly.

About the Polish horses, about the squadrons galloping through the dust on the tall, golden, narrow-chested, Polish horses. Forelocks, chains, suits tailored out of carpets.

Six hundred horses got stuck in the marshes, unlucky Poles.

AUGUST 6, 1920. KHOTIN

The exact same place. We get ourselves in order, shoe the horses, eat, there is a break in operations.

My landlady is a small, timorous, fragile woman with tortured, meek eyes. Lord, how the soldiers torment her, the endless cooking, we steal honey. Her husband came home, bombs from an airplane chased his horses away. The old man hasn't eaten for five days, now he is going off into the wide world to look for his horses, a saga. An ancient old man.

A sultry day, thick, white silence, my soul rejoices, the horses are standing, oats are being threshed for them, the Cossacks sleep next to them all day long, the horses are resting, that's our top priority.

From time to time Apanasenko flits by, unlike the reserved Timoshenko he is one of us, he is our fatherly commander.

In the morning Bakhturov leaves, his retinue follows, I watch the new military commissar's work, a dull but polished Moscow worker, this is where his strength lies: humdrum but grand visions, three military commissars, absolutely must describe limping Gubanov, the

---

* Now that Bakhturov, their former "master," has lost his tenure.

scourge of the regiment, a desperate fighter, a young, twenty-three-year-old youth, modest Shiryayev, cunning Grishin. They are sitting in the garden, the military commissar is asking them questions, they gossip, talk pompously about World Revolution, the mistress of the house is shaking apples from the trees because all her apples have been eaten, the military commissar's secretary, lanky, with a ringing voice, goes looking for food.

New trends at the headquarters: Sheko* is issuing special orders, bombastic and highfalutin, but short and energetic, he gives the Revolutionary Council his opinion, he acts on his own initiative.

Everyone is pining for Timoshenko,† there won't be a mutiny.

Why am I gripped by a longing that will not pass? Because I am far from home, because we are destroying, moving forward like a whirlwind, like lava, hated by all, life is being shattered to pieces, I am at a huge, never-ending service for the dead.

Ivan Ivanovich is sitting on a bench, talking of the days when he spent twenty thousand, thirty thousand. Everyone has gold, everyone ransacked Rostov, threw sacks of money over their saddles and rode off. Ivan Ivanovich dressed and kept women. Night, threshing shed, fragrant hay, but the air is heavy, I am smothered by something, by the sad senselessness of my life.

AUGUST 7, 1920. BERESTECHKO

It is evening now, 8. The lamps in the shtetl have just been lit. There is a funeral service in the room next door. Many Jews, the doleful chants of home, they rock, sit on benches, two candles, the eternal light on the windowsill. The funeral service is for the landlady's granddaughter, who died of fright after their house was looted. The mother is crying, tells me the story as she prays, we stand at the table, I have been pounded by sorrow for two months now. The mother shows me a photograph tattered by teardrops, and they all say what an uncommon beauty she was, some commander ran amok, banging on the door in the night, they dragged them out of bed, the Poles ransacked the house,

---

* The new chief of staff of the Sixth Cavalry Division.
† The former commander of the Sixth Cavalry Division.

then the Cossacks, ceaseless vomiting, she wasted away. The main thing for the Jews—she was a beauty, no other like her in all the shtetl.

A memorable day. In the morning we went from Khotin to Berestechko. I ride with Ivanov, the military commissar's secretary, a lanky, voracious, spineless fellow, a lout—and, believe it or not, he is the husband of Komarova, the singer, "We used to do concerts, I'll write to her to come." A Russian maenad.

The corpse of a slaughtered Pole, a terrible corpse, naked and bloated, monstrous.

Berestechko has changed hands quite a few times. There are historic sites outside Berestechko, Cossack graves. And this is the main thing, everything is repeating itself: Cossack against Pole, or rather serf against *Pan*.

I won't forget this shtetl, covered courtyards, long, narrow, stinking, everything 100–200 years old, the townsfolk more robust than in other places, the main thing is the architecture, the white and watery blue little houses, the little backstreets, the synagogues, the peasant women. Life is almost back on track again. People had led a good life here— respected Jewry, rich Ukrainians, market fairs on Sundays, a specialized class of Russian artisans: tanners trading with Austria, contraband.

The Jews here are less fanatical, better dressed, heartier, they even seem more cheerful, the very old men in long coats, the old women, everything exudes the old days, tradition, the shtetl is saturated in the bloody history of the Polish Jewish ghetto. Hatred for the Poles is unanimous. They looted, tortured, scorched the pharmacist's body with white-hot iron pokers, needles under his nails, tore out his hair, all because a Polish officer had been shot at—sheer idiocy! The Poles have gone out of their minds, they are destroying themselves.

An ancient church, the graves of Polish officers in the churchyard, fresh burial mounds, ten days old, white birch crosses, all this is terrible, the house of the Catholic priest has been destroyed, I find ancient books, precious Latin manuscripts. The priest, Tuzynkiewicz, I find a photograph of him, he is short and fat, he worked here for forty-five years, he lived in one place, a scholar, the assortment of books, many of them in Latin, editions of 1860, that was when Tuzynkiewicz lived. His living quarters are old-fashioned, enormous, dark paintings, photographs of the prelate conventions at Zhitomir, portraits of Pope Pius

X, a nice face, an exquisite portrait of Sienkiewicz*—here he is the essence of the nation. Blanketing all this is the stench of Sukhin's pitiful little soul. How new all this is for me, the books, the soul of the Catholic *Pater*, a Jesuit, I want to fathom the heart and soul of Tuzynkiewicz, and I have. Lepin suddenly plays the piano, touchingly. He sometimes sings in Latvian. Remember: his little bare feet, so droll you could die. What a funny creature.

A terrible incident: the looting of the church, they've ripped down the chasubles, the precious, glittering material is torn and lying on the floor, a sister of mercy dragged off three bundles, they are tearing the linings, the candles have been taken, the receptacles smashed open, the papal bulls thrown out, the money taken—this magnificent church, what its eyes have seen these past 200 years (Tuzynkiewicz's manuscripts), how many counts and serfs, magnificent Italian art, rosy *Paters* rocking the infant Jesus, the magnificent dark Jesus, Rembrandt, a Madonna like that of Murillo, maybe even by Murillo, and the main thing: the pious, well-fed Jesuits, the eerie Chinese figurine behind a veil, Jesus, a little bearded Jew in crimson Polish raiment, a bench, the shattered shrine, the figure of St. Valentine. The beadle, shivering like a bird, squirms, speaks in a jumble of Russian and Polish, I mustn't touch these things, he sobs. These animals are only here to plunder. It's very clear, the old gods are being destroyed.

An evening in the town. The church has been closed. In the late afternoon I go to the castle of Count Raciborski. A seventy-year-old man, his mother ninety. It was just the two of them, they were mad, people say. Describe the two of them. An old, aristocratic Polish house, most probably over a hundred years old, antlers, old bright paintings on the ceilings, remains of antlers, small rooms for the servants upstairs, flagstones, corridors, excrement on the floors, little Jewish boys, a Steinway piano, sofas slashed down to the springs, remember the white, delicate oak doors, French letters dated 1820, *notre petit héros achève 7 semaines.*† My God, who wrote that, when, the letters have been trampled on, I took some relics, a century, the mother is a countess, Steinway piano, park, pond.

---

* Henryk Sienkiewicz, 1846–1916, Polish novelist, author of *Quo Vadis?*
† French: "our little hero is already seven weeks old."

I cannot tear myself away—I think of Hauptmann, *Elga*.*

A rally in the castle park, the Jews of Berestechko, dull Vinokurov,†
children running around, a Revolutionary Committee is being elected,
the Jews twirl their beards, the Jewesses listen to words about the
Russian paradise, the international situation, about the uprising in
India.

A night filled with anxiety, someone said we should be on the alert,
all alone with feeble *mishures*,** unexpected eloquence, what did he talk
about?

AUGUST 8, 1920. BERESTECHKO

I am settling down in the shtetl. There were fairs here. The peasants sell pears. They are paid with long-abolished banknotes. This place
had been bubbling over with life, Jews had exported grain to Austria,
human and commodity contraband, the closeness of the border.

Unusual barns, cellars.

I've been billeted with the proprietress of a coach inn, a gaunt, redheaded bitch. Ilchenko bought some cucumbers, reads the *Zhurnal dlya
Vsekh*,‡ and is pontificating about economic policy, the Jews are to
blame for everything, a blunt, Slavic creature who filled his pockets
during the plundering of Rostov. Some adopted children, the mother
recently died. The tale of the pharmacist under whose nails the Poles
stuck needles, people gone berserk.

A hot day, the townsfolk are roaming about, they are coming alive
again, there will be trade.

Synagogue, Torahs, built thirty-six years ago by an artisan from
Kremenets, they paid him fifty rubles a month, gold peacocks, crossed
arms, ancient Torahs, the *shamases* show no enthusiasm whatever, wiz-
ened old men, the bridges of Berestechko, how they shook, the Poles
gave all this a long-faded tint. The little old man at whose house

---

* Gerhart Hauptmann, 1862–1946, German dramatist. His play Elga was first performed in
1905.

† Aleksander Nikolayevich Vinokurov was the military commissar of the Sixth Cavalry
Division. He replaced Bakhturov.

** Yiddish: "servant."

‡ *Magazine for All*, a popular monthly magazine.

Korotchayev, the demoted division commander,* and his Jewish subaltern, are billeted. Korotchayev was chairman of the Cheka somewhere in Astrakhan, rotten to the core. Friendship with the Jew. We drink tea at the old man's. Silence, placidity. I roam about the shtetl, there is pitiful, powerful, undying life inside the Jewish hovels, young ladies in white stockings, long coats, so few fat people.

We are sending out scouts to Lvov. Apanasenko† sends dispatches to the Stavropol Executive Committee, heads will roll on the home front, he is delighted. The battle outside Radzivillov, Apanasenko acts heroically—instantaneous disposition of the troops, he almost opened fire on the retreating Fourteenth Division. We're nearing Radzikhov. Moscow newspapers of July 29. The commencement of the Second Congress of the Third International, finally the unification of all peoples has been realized, everything is clear: two worlds, and a declaration of war. We will be fighting endlessly. Russia has thrown down a challenge. We will march to Europe to subjugate the world. The Red Army has become an international factor.

I have to take a closer look at Apanasenko. *Ataman.***

The quiet old man's funeral service for his granddaughter.

Evening, performance in the count's garden, the theatergoers of Berestechko, an idiot of an orderly, the young ladies of Berestechko, silence descends, I would like to stay here awhile and get to know it.

AUGUST 9, 1920. LASHKOV

The move from Berestechko to Lashkov. Galicia. The division commander's carriage, the division commander's orderly is Lyovka—the one who chases horses like a gypsy. The tale of how he whipped his neighbor Stepan, a former constable under Denikin who had harassed the people, when Stepan came back to the village. They wouldn't just "butcher" him, they beat him in prison, slashed his back, jumped up and down on him, danced, an epic exchange: "Are you feeling good, Stepan?" "I'm feeling bad." "And the people you harassed, did they feel

---

* D. D. Korotchayev had been the provisional commander of the Fourth Cavalry Division from May 1 to June 20, 1920.

† The new commander of the Sixth Cavalry Division.

** Also *hetman*, a Cossack leader.

good?" "No, they felt bad." "And did you think that someday you might be feeling bad?" "No, I didn't." "You should have thought about that, Stepan, because what we think is that if we'd fallen into your hands, you'd have butchered us, so f— it, now, Stepan, we will kill you." When they finally left him he was already getting cold. Another tale about Shurka the nurse. Night, battle, regiments form, Lyovka in the phaeton, Shurka's lover is heavily wounded, gives Lyovka his horse, they take away the wounded man and return to the battle. "Shurka, we only live once, and then we die!" "Well, okay, then." She went to a boarding school in Rostov, gallops with the regiment, she can do fifteen. "But now, Shurka, let's go, we're retreating." The horses got caught up in the barbed wire, he galloped four versts, a village, he sits down, cuts through the barbed wire, the regiment rides through, Shurka leaves the formation. Lyovka prepares supper, they want food, they ate, chatted, go on, Shurka, one more time. Well, okay. But where?

She went galloping after the regiment, he went to sleep. If your wife comes, I'll kill her.

Lashkov is a green, sunny, quiet, rich Galician village. I've been billeted at the deacon's house. His wife has just given birth. Downtrodden people. A clean, new hut, but there's nothing in the hut. Next door typical Galician Jews. They think—he must be Jewish, no? The story: they came plundering, one of them chopped off the heads of two chickens, found the things in the threshing shed, dug up things from the earth, herded everyone together in the hut, the usual story, remember the young man with sideburns. They tell me that the head rabbi lives in Belz, they finished off the rabbis.

We rest, the First Squadron is in my front garden. Night, a lamp is standing on my table, the horses snort quietly, everyone here is a Kuban Cossack, they eat, sleep, cook together, marvelous, silent camaraderie. They're all peasants, in the evenings they sing with rich voices songs that sound like hymns, devotion to horses, small bundles, saddle, bridle, ornate sabers, greatcoat, I sleep surrounded by them.

I sleep in the field during the day. No operations, rest—what a marvelous and necessary thing it is. The cavalry, the horses are recuperating after this inhuman work, people are recuperating from all the cruelty, living together, singing songs with quiet voices, they are telling each other things.

The headquarters are in the school. The division commander at the priest's.

AUGUST 10, 1920. LASHKOV

Our rest continues. Scouts to Radzikhov, Sokolovka, Stoyanov, all in the direction of Lvov. News has come that Aleksandrovsk was taken, gigantic complications in the international situation, will we have to go to war against the whole world?

A fire in the village. The priest's threshing shed is burning. Two horses, thrashing around with all their might, burned. You can't lead a horse out of a fire. Two cows broke out, the hide of one of them split, blood is coming out of the crack, touching and pitiful.

The smoke envelops the entire village, bright flames, plump black billows of smoke, a mass of wood, hot in the face, everything carried out of the priest's house and the church, thrown into the front garden. Apanasenko in a red Cossack jacket, a black coat, clean-shaven face, a terrifying apparition, an ataman.

Our Cossacks, a sad sight, dragging loot out over the back porch, their eyes burning, all of them looking uneasy, ashamed, this so-called habit of theirs is ineradicable. All the church banners, ancient saints' books,* icons are being carried out, strange figures painted whitish pink, whitish blue, monstrous, flat-faced, Chinese or Buddhist, heaps of paper flowers, will the church catch fire, peasant women are wringing their hands in silence, the townspeople, frightened and silent, are running barefoot, everyone sits in front of their hut with a bucket. They are apathetic, cowed, remarkably numb, but they'd drop everything to put out their own fires. They've come to terms with the plundering—the soldiers are circling around the priest's trunks like rapacious, overwrought beasts, they say there's gold in there, one can take it away from a priest, a portrait of Count Andrzej Szceptycki, the Metropolitan of Galicia. A manly magnate with a black ring on his large, aristocratic hand. The lower lip of the old priest, who has served in Lashkov for thirty-five years, is constantly trembling. He tells me about Szceptycki, that he is not "educated" in the Polish spirit, comes from Ruthenian

---

* *Chet'i Menie*, anthologies of Old Church Slavonic writings about the lives of saints, organized by month and date.

grandees, "The Counts of Szceptycki," then they went over to the Poles, his brother is commander in chief of the Polish forces, Andrzej returned to the Ruthenians. His ancient culture, quiet and solid. A good, educated priest who has laid in a supply of flour, chickens, wants to talk about the universities, Ruthenians, the poor man, Apanasenko with his red Cossack jacket is staying with him.

Night—an unusual sight, the high road is brilliantly lit, my room is bright, I'm working, the lamp is burning, calm, the Kuban Cossacks are singing with feeling, their thin figures by the campfires, the songs are totally Ukrainian, the horses lie down to sleep. I go to the division commander. Vinokurov tells me about him—a partisan, an ataman, a rebel, Cossack freedom, wild uprising, his ideal is Dumenko,* an open wound, one has to submit oneself to the organization, a deadly hatred for the aristocracy, clerics, and, most of all, for the intelligentsia, which he cannot stomach in the army. Apanasenko will graduate from a school—how is it different from the times of Bogdan Khmelnitsky?

Late at night. Four o'clock.

August 11, 1920. Lashkov

A day of work, sitting at the headquarters, I write to the point of exhaustion, a day of rest. Toward evening, rain. Kuban Cossacks are staying the night in my room, strange: peaceful and warlike, domestic, and peasants of obvious Ukrainian origin, not all that young.

About the Kuban Cossacks. Camaraderie, they always stick together, horses snort beneath the windows night and day, the marvelous smell of horse manure, of sun, of sleeping Cossacks, twice a day they boil large pails of soup and meat. At night Kuban Cossacks come to visit. Ceaseless rain, they dry themselves and eat their supper in my room. A religious Kuban Cossack in a soft hat, pale face, blond mustache. They are decent, friendly, wild, but somehow more sympathetic, domestic, less foulmouthed, more calm than the Cossacks from Stavropol and the Don.

The nurse came, how clear it all is, must describe that, she is worn

---

* Boris Mokeyevich Dumenko had been the legendary commander of the Fourth Cavalry Divison in 1918, and fought with Stalin, Budyonny, and Voroshilov at the Battle of Tsaritsyn.

out, wants to leave, everyone has had her—the commandant, at least that's what they say, Yakovlev,* and, O horror, Gusev. She's pitiful, wants to leave, sad, talks gibberish, wants to talk to me about something and looks at me with trusting eyes, she says I am her friend, the others, the others are scum. How quickly they have managed to destroy a person, debase her, make her ugly. She is naive, foolish, receptive even to revolutionary phrases, and the silly fool talks a lot about the Revolution, she worked in the Cheka's Culture and Education Division, how many male influences.

Interview with Apanasenko. This is very interesting. Must remember this. His blunt, terrible face, his hard body, like Utochkin's.†

His orderlies (Lyovka), magnificent golden horses, his hangers-on, carriages, Volodya, his adopted son—a small Cossack with an old man's face, curses like a grown man.

Apanasenko, hungry for fame, here we have it: a new class of man. Whatever the operational situation might be, he will always go off and come back again, an organizer of units, totally hostile to officers, four George Crosses, a career soldier, a noncommissioned officer, an ensign under Kerensky, chairman of the Regimental Committee, stripped officers of their stripes, long months on the Astrakhan steppes, indisputable authority, a professional soldier.

About the atamans, there had been many there, they got themselves machine guns, fought against Shkuro and Mamontov,** merged into the Red Army, a heroic epic. This is not a Marxist Revolution, it is a Cossack uprising that wants to win all and lose nothing. Apanasenko's hatred for the rich, an unquenchable hatred of the intelligentsia.

Night with the Kuban Cossacks, rain, it's stuffy, I have some sort of strange itch.

AUGUST 12, 1920. LASHKOV

The fourth day in Lashkov. A completely downtrodden Galician village. They used to live better than the Russians, good houses, strong

---

* The political commissar of the Sixth Cavalry Division.
† Sergey Utochkin, a celebrated Russian aviation pioneer from Odessa.
** Andrei Grigorevich Shkuro and Konstantin Konstantinovich Mamontov were counterrevolutionary Cossack generals.

sense of decency, respect for priests, the people honest but blood-drained, my landlord's deformed child, how and why was he born, not a drop of blood left in the mother, they are continually hiding something somewhere, pigs are grunting somewhere, they have probably hidden cloth somewhere.

A day off, a good thing—my correspondence, mustn't neglect that.

Must write for the newspaper, and the life story of Apanasenko.

The division is resting, a kind of stillness in one's heart, and people are better, songs, campfires, fire in the night, jokes, happy, apathetic horses, someone reads the newspaper, they stroll around, shoe their horses. What all this looks like, Sokolov is going on leave, I give him a letter home.

I keep writing about pipes, about long-forgotten things, so much for the Revolution, that's what I should be concentrating on.

Don't forget the priest in Lashkov, badly shaven, kind, educated, possibly mercenary: a chicken, a duck, his house, lived well, droll etchings.

Friction between the military commissar and the division commander. He got up and left with Kniga* while Yakovlev, the divisional political commissar, was giving a report, Apanasenko went to the military commissar.

Vinokurov: a typical military commissar, always wants things done his way, wants to put the Sixth Division on track, struggle with the partisan attitude, dull-witted, bores me to death with his speeches, at times he's rude, uses the informal "you" with everyone.

AUGUST 13, 1920. NIVITSA

At night the order comes: head for Busk, thirty-five versts east of Lvov.

We set out in the morning. All three brigades are concentrated in one place. I'm on Misha's horse, it was taught to run and won't go at a walking pace, it goes at a trot. The whole day on horseback with the division commander. The farm at Porady. In the forest, four enemy airplanes, a volley of fire. Three brigade commanders: Kolesnikov,

---

* Vasily Ivanovich Kniga, commander of the First Brigade of the Sixth Cavalry Division.

Korotchayev, Kniga. Vasily Ivanovich [Kniga]'s sly move, headed for Toporov (Chanyz) in a bypass maneuver, didn't run into the enemy anywhere. We are at the Porady farm, destroyed huts, I pull an old woman out of a hatch door, dovecotes. Together with the lookout on the battery. Our attack by the woods.

A disaster—swamps, canals, the cavalry can't be deployed anywhere, attacks in infantry formation, inertia, is our morale flagging? Persistent and yet light fighting near Toporov (in comparison to the Imperialist carnage), they're attacking on three sides, cannot overpower us, a hurricane of fire from our artillery, from two batteries.

Night. All the attacks failed. Overnight the headquarters move to Nivitsa. Thick fog, penetrating cold, horse, roads through forests, campfires and candles, nurses on *tachankas,* a harsh journey after a day of anxiety and ultimate failure.

All day long through fields and forests. Most interesting of all: the division commander, his grin, foul language, curt exclamations, snorting, shrugs his shoulders, is agitated, responsibility for everything, passion—if only he had been there everything would have been fine.

What can I remember? The night ride, the screams of the women in Porady when we began (I broke off writing here, two bombs thrown from an airplane exploded a hundred paces from us, we're at a clearing in the forest west of St[ary] Maidan) taking away their linen, our attack, something we can't quite make out, not frightening at a distance, some lines of men, horsemen riding over a meadow, at a distance this all looks like it is done haphazardly, it does not seem in the least bit frightening.

When we advanced close to the little town, things began to heat up, the moment of the attack, the moment when a town is taken, the feverish, frightening, mounting rattle of the machine guns driving one to hopelessness and despair, the ceaseless explosions and, high up over all of this, silence, and nothing can be seen.

The work of Apanasenko's headquarters, every hour there are reports to the army commander, he is trying to ingratiate himself.

We arrive frozen through, tired, at Nivitsa. A warm kitchen. A school.

The captivating wife of the schoolmaster, she's a nationalist, a sort of inner cheerfulness about her, asks all kinds of questions, makes us tea, defends her *mowa*,* your *mowa* is good and so is my *mowa*, and always laughter in her eyes. And this in Galicia, this is nice, it's been ages since I've heard anything like this. I sleep in the classroom, in the straw next to Vinokurov.†

I've got a cold.

AUGUST 14, 1920

The center of operations—the taking of Busk and the crossing of the Bug. All day long attacking Toporov, no, we've stopped. Another indecisive day. The forest clearing by St[ary] Maidan. The enemy has taken Lopatin.

Toward evening we throw them out. Once again Nivitsa. Spend the night at the house of an old woman, in the yard together with the staff.

AUGUST 15, 1920

Morning in Toporov. Fighting near Busk. Headquarters are in Busk. Force our way over the Bug. A blaze on the other side. Budyonny's in Busk.

Spend the night in Yablonovka with Vinokurov.

AUGUST 16, 1920

To Rakobuty, a brigade made it across.

I'm off to interrogate the prisoners.

Once again in Yablonovka. We're moving on to N[ovy] Milatin, St[ary] Milatin, panic, spend the night in an almshouse.

AUGUST 17, 1920

Fighting near the railroad tracks near Liski. The butchering of prisoners.

Spend the night in Zadvurdze.

---

* Ukrainian: "language."
† The military commissar of the Sixth Cavalry Division.

AUGUST 18, 1920

Haven't had time to write. We're moving on. We set out on August 13. From that time on we've been on the move, endless roads, squadron banners, Apanasenko's horses, skirmishes, farms, corpses. Frontal attack on Toporov, Kolesnikov* in the attack, swamps, I am at an observation point, toward evening a hurricane of fire from two batteries. The Polish infantry is waiting in the trenches, our fighters go, return, horse-holders are leading the wounded, Cossacks don't like frontal attacks, the cursed trenches cloud with smoke. That was the 13th. On the 14th, the division moves to Busk, it has to get there at all cost, by evening we had advanced ten versts. That's where the main operation has to take place: the crossing of the Bug. At the same time they're searching for a ford.

A Czech farm at Adamy, breakfast in the farmhouse, potatoes with milk, Sukhorukov thrives under every regime, an ass-kisser, Suslov dances to his tune, as do all the Lyovkas. The main thing: dark forests, transport carts in the forests, candles above the nurses, rumbling, the tempos of troop movement. We're at a clearing in the forest, the horses are grazing, the airplanes are the heroes of the day, air operations are on the increase, airplane attacks, five-six planes circle endlessly, bombs at a hundred paces, I have an ash-gray gelding, a repulsive horse. In the forest. An intrigue with the nurse: Apanasenko made her a revolting proposition then and there, they say she spent the night with him, now she speaks of him with loathing. She likes Sheko,[†] but the divisional military commissar likes her, cloaking his interest in her with the pretext that she is, as he says, without protection, has no means of transport, no protector. She talks of how Konstantin Karlovich[**] courted her, fed her, forbade others to write her letters, but everyone kept on writing to her. She found Yakovlev[‡] extremely attractive, and the head of the Registration Department, a blond-haired boy in a red hood asked for her hand and her heart, sobbing like a child. There was also some other story but I couldn't find out anything about it. The saga of the nurse, and the main thing: they talk a lot about her and everyone

---

* Kolesov, commander of the Third Brigade.
[†] The chief of staff of the Sixth Cavalry Division.
** Zholnarkevich, the former chief of staff of the Sixth Cavalry Division.
[‡] The political commissar of the Sixth Cavalry Division.

looks down on her, her own coachman doesn't talk to her, her little boots, aprons, she does favors, Bebel brochures.

*Woman and Socialism.**

One can write volumes about the women in the Red Army. The squadrons set off into battle—dust, rumbling, the baring of sabers, savage cursing—they gallop ahead with hitched-up skirts, dust-covered, fat-breasted, all of them whores, but comrades too, and whores because they are comrades, that's the most important thing, they serve in every way they can, these heroines, and then they're looked down upon, they give water to the horses, haul hay, mend harnesses, steal things from churches and from the townsfolk.

Apanasenko's agitation, his foul language, is it willpower?

Night again in Nivitsa, I sleep somewhere in the straw, because I can't remember anything, everything in me is lacerated, my body aches, a HUNDRED versts by horse.

I spend the night with Vinokurov. His attitude toward Ivanov.[†] What kind of man is this gluttonous, pitiful, tall youth with a soft voice, wilted soul, and sharp mind? The military commissar is unbearably rough with him, swears at him ceaselessly, finds fault with everything: What's up with you—curses fly—You didn't do it? Go pack your things, I'm kicking you out!

I have to fathom the soul of the fighter, I am managing, this is all terrible, they're animals with principles.

Overnight the Second Brigade took Toropov in a nocturnal attack. An unforgettable morning. We move at a fast trot. A terrible, uncanny shtetl, Jews stand at their doors like corpses, I wonder about them: what more are you going to have to go through? Black beards, bent backs, destroyed houses, here there's [illegible], remnants of German efficiency and comfort, some sort of inexpressible, commonplace, and burning Jewish sadness. There's a monastery here. Apanasenko is radiant. The Second Brigade rides past. Forelocks, jackets made out of carpets, red tobacco pouches, short carbines, commanders on majestic horses, a Budyonny brigade. Parade, marching bands, we greet you, Sons of the Revolution. Apanasenko is radiant.

We move on from Toporov—forests, roads, the staff on the road,

---

* *Die Frau und der Sozialismus* (*Woman and Socialism*) by August Bebel.
† Vinokurov's secretary.

orderlies, brigade commanders, we fly on to Busk at a fast trot, to its eastern part. What an enchanting place (on the 18th an airplane is flying, it will now drop bombs), clean Jewesses, gardens full of pears and plums, radiant noon, curtains, in the houses the remnants of the petite bourgeoisie, a clean and possibly honest simplicity, mirrors, we have been billeted at the house of a fat Galician woman, the widow of a schoolmaster, wide sofas, many plums, unbearable exhaustion from overstrained nerves (a shell came flying, didn't explode), couldn't fall asleep, lay by the wall next to the horses remembering the dust and the horrible jostle in the transport cart, dust—the majestic phenomenon of our war.

Fighting in Busk. It's on the other side of the bridge. Our wounded. Beauty—over there the shtetl is burning. I ride to the crossing, the sharp experience of battle, have to run part of the way because it's under fire, night, the blaze is shining, the horses stand by the huts, a meeting with Budyonny is under way, the members of the Revolutionary War Council* come out, a feeling of danger in the air, we didn't take Busk with our frontal attack, we say good-bye to the fat Galician woman and drive to Yablonovka deep in the night, the horses are barely moving ahead, we spend the night in a pit, on straw, the division commander has left, the military commissar and I have no strength left.

The First Brigade found a ford and crossed the Bug by Poborzhany. In the morning with Vinokurov at the crossing. So here is the Bug, a shallow little river, the staff is on a hill, the journey has worn me out, I'm sent back to Yablonovka to interrogate prisoners. Disaster. Describe what a horseman feels: exhaustion, the horse won't go on, the ride is long, no strength, the burned steppe, loneliness, no one there to help you, endless versts.

Interrogation of prisoners in Yablonovka. Men in their underwear, exhausted, there are Jews, light-blond Poles, an educated young fellow, blunt hatred toward them, the blood-drenched underwear of a wounded man, he's not given any water, a fat-faced fellow pushes his papers at me. You lucky fellows—I think—how did you get away. They crowd around me, they are happy at the sound of my benevolent voice, miser-

* *Revvoensoviet,* founded in 1918, were councils in which military commanders and political representatives of the Bolshevik government conferred on military tactics.

able dust, what a difference between the Cossacks and them, they're spineless.

From Yablonovka I return by *tachanka* to the headquarters. Again the crossing, endless lines of transport carts crossing over (they don't wait even a minute, they are right on the heels of the advancing units), they sink in the river, trace-straps tear, the dust is suffocating, Galician villages, I'm given milk, lunch in a village, the Poles have just pulled out of here, everything is calm, the village dead, stifling heat, midday silence, there's no one in the village, it is astounding that there is such light, such absolute and unruffled silence, peace, as if the front were well over a hundred versts away. The churches in the villages.

Farther along the road is the enemy. Two naked, butchered Poles with small, slashed faces are glittering through the rye in the sun.

We return to Yablonovka, tea at Lepin's, dirt, Cherkashin* denigrates him and wants to get rid of him. If you look closely, Cherkashin's face is dreadful. In his body, tall as a stick, you can see the muzhik—he is a drunkard, a thief, and a cunning bastard.

Lepin is dirty, dim-witted, touchy, incomprehensible.

Handsome Bazkunov's long, endless tale, a father, Nizhny-Novgorod, head of a chemistry department, Red Army, prisoner under Denikin, the biography of a Russian youth, his father a merchant, an inventor, dealt with Moscow restaurants. Chatted with him during the whole trip. We are heading for Milatin, plums along the road. In St[ary] Milatin there is a church, the priest's house, the priest lives in a luxurious house, unforgettable, he keeps squeezing my hand, sets off to bury a dead Pole, sits down with us, asks whether our commander is a good man, a typical Jesuitical face, shaven, gray eyes dart around—a pleasure to behold—a crying Polish woman, his niece, begging that her heifer be returned to her, tears and a coquettish smile, all very Polish. Mustn't forget the house, knickknacks, pleasant darkness, Jesuitical, Catholic culture, clean women, and the most aromatic and agitated *Pater*, opposite him a monastery. I want to stay here. We wait for the order for where we are to stay—in Stary Milatin or in Novy Milatin. Night. Panic. Some transport carts, the Poles have broken through somewhere, pandemonium on the road, three rows of transport carts,

* Lepin's orderly.

I'm in the Milatin schoolhouse, two beautiful old maids, it's frightening how much they remind me of the Shapiro sisters from Nikolayev, two quiet, educated Galician women, patriots, their own culture, bedroom, possibly curlers, in thundering, war-torn Milatin, outside these walls transport carts, cannons, fatherly commanders telling tales of their heroic feats, clouds of orange dust, the monastery is enveloped by them. The sisters offer me cigarettes, they breathe in my words of how everything will be marvelous—it's like balm, they have blossomed out, and we speak elegantly about culture.

A knock at the door. The commandant wants me. A fright. We ride over to Novy Milatin. *N. Milatin.* With the military commissar in the almshouse, some sort of town house, sheds, night, vaults, the priest's maid, dark, dirty, myriads of flies, tiredness beyond compare, the tiredness of the front.

Daybreak, we depart, the railroad has to be breached (this all takes place on August 17), the Brody-Lvov railroad.

My first battle, I saw the attack, they gather in the bushes, the brigade commanders ride up to Apanasenko—careful Kniga,* all slyness, rides up, talks up a storm, they point to the hills, there beneath the forest, there over the hollow, they've spotted the enemy, the regiments ride to attack, sabers in the sun, pale commanders, Apanasenko's hard legs, hurrah.

What happened? A field, dust, the staff in the plains, Apanasenko curses in a frenzy, brigade commander—destroy those bastards, f—ing bandits.

The mood before the battle, hunger, heat, they gallop in attack, nurses.

A thunder of hurrahs, the Poles are crushed, we ride out onto the battlefield, a little Pole with polished nails is rubbing his pink, sparsely haired head, answers evasively, prevaricating, hemming and hawing, well, yes, Sheko,† roused and pale, answer, who are you—I'm, he ducks the question, a sort of ensign, we ride off, they take him, a good-looking fellow behind him loads his gun, I shout—"Yakov Vasilevich [Sheko]!" He acts like he didn't hear, rides on, a shot, the little Pole in

---

* Vasily Ivanovich Kniga, commander of the First Brigade of the Sixth Cavalry Division.
† The chief of staff of the Sixth Cavalry Division.

his underwear falls on his face and twitches. Life is disgusting, murderers, it's unbearable, baseness and crime.

They are rounding up the prisoners, undressing them, a strange
picture—they undress incredibly fast, shake their heads, all this in the
sun, mild embarrassment, all the command personnel is there, embarrassment, but who cares, so cover your eyes. I will never forget that "sort
of" ensign who was treacherously murdered.

Ahead—terrible things. We crossed the railroad tracks by
Zadvurdze. The Poles are fighting their way along the railroad tracks to
Lvov. An attack in the evening at the farm. Carnage. The military commissar and I ride along the tracks, begging the men not to butcher the
prisoners, Apanasenko* washes his hands of it. Sheko's tongue ran away
with him: "Butcher them all!" It played a horrifying role. I didn't look
into their faces, they impaled them, shot them, corpses covered with
bodies, one they undress, another they shoot, moans, yells, wheezing,
our squadron led the attack, Apanasenko stands to the side, the
squadron has dressed up, Matusevich's horse was killed, his face frightening, dirty, he is running, looking for a horse. This is hell. How we
bring freedom—terrible. They search a farm, men are dragged out,
Apanasenko: Don't waste bullets, butcher them. Apanasenko always
says—butcher the nurse, butcher the Poles.

We spend the night in Zadvurdze, bad quarters, I'm with Sheko,
good food, ceaseless skirmishes, I'm living a soldier's life, completely
worn out, we are waiting in the forest, nothing to eat all day, Sheko's
carriage arrives, brings something, I'm often at the observation point,
the work of the batteries, the clearings, hollows, the machine guns are
mowing, the Poles are mainly defending themselves with airplanes,
they are becoming a menace, describe the air attacks, the faraway and
seemingly slow hammering of the machine guns, panic in the transport
carts, it's harrowing, they are incessantly gliding over us, we hide from
them. A new use of aviation, I think of Mosher, Captain Fauntleroy in
Lvov, our wanderings from one brigade to the next, Kniga only likes
bypass maneuvers, Kolesnikov† frontal attacks, I ride with Sheko on
reconnaissance, endless forests, deadly danger, on the hills, bullets are
buzzing all around before the attack, the pitiful face of Sukhorukov

*The commander of the Sixth Cavalry Division.
† Actually Nikolai Petrovich Kolesov, commander of the Third Brigade.

with his saber, I tag along behind the staff, we await reports, but they advancing, doing bypass maneuvers.

The battle for Barshchovitse. After a day of fluctuations, Polish columns manage in the evening to break through to Lvov. When Apanasenko saw this, he went mad, he is shaking, the brigades are going full force even though they are dealing with a retreating enemy, and the brigades stretch out in endless ribbons, three cavalry brigades are hurled into the attack, Apanasenko is triumphant, snorts, sends out Litovchenko as the new commander of the Third Brigade to replace Kolesnikov, who's been wounded, you see them, there they are, go finish them off, they're running. He meddles in the artillery action, interferes with the orders of the battery commanders, feverish, they were hoping to repeat what had happened at Zadvurdze, but it wasn't to be. Swamps on one side, ruinous fire on the other. March to Ostrov, the Sixth Cavalry Division is supposed to take Lvov from the southeast.

Gigantic losses among the command personnel: Korotchayev, heavily wounded, his adjutant, a Jew, was killed, the commander of the Thirty-fourth Regiment wounded, all the commissars of the Thirty-first Regiment out of action, all the chiefs of staff wounded, above all Budyonny's commanders.

The wounded crawl onto *tachankas*. This is how we're going to take Lvov, the reports to the army commander are written in the grass, brigades gallop, orders in the night, again forests, bullets buzz, artillery fire chases us from one place to another, miserable fear of airplanes, get down off your horse, a bomb's about to explode, there's a revolting sensation in your mouth. Nothing to feed the horses with.

I see now what a horse means to a Cossack and a cavalryman.

Unhorsed cavalrymen on the hot dusty roads, their saddles in their arms, they sleep like corpses on other men's carts, horses are rotting all around, all that's talked about is horses, the customs of barter, the excitement, horses are martyrs, horses are sufferers—their saga, I myself have been gripped by this feeling, every march is an agony for the horse.

Apanasenko's visits to Budyonny with his retinue. Budyonny and Voroshilov at a farm, they sit at a table. Apanasenko's report, standing at attention. The failure of the special regiment: they had planned an attack on Lvov, set out, the special regiment's sentry post was, as always, asleep, it was taken down, the Poles rolled their machine guns within a hundred paces, rounded up the horses, wounded half the regiment.

The Day of the Transfiguration of Our Savior Jesus Christ—19 August—in Barshchovitse, a butchered, but still breathing, village, peace, a meadow, a flock of geese (we dealt with them later—Sidorenko or Yegor chopped up the geese on a block with their sabers), we eat boiled goose. That day, white as they were, they beautified the village, on the green meadows the villagers, festive but feeble, spectral, barely able to crawl out of their hovels, silent, strange, dazed, and completely cowed.

There is something quiet and oppressive about this holiday.

The Uniate priest in Barshchovitse. A ruined, defiled garden, Budyonny's headquarters had been here, and smashed, smoked-out beehives, this is a terrible, barbaric custom—I remember the broken frames, thousands of bees buzzing and fighting by the destroyed hives, their panicking swarms.

The priest explains to me the difference between the Uniate and the Russian Orthodox faith. Sheptitsky is a tall man, he wears a canvas cassock. A plump man, a dark, chubby face, shaved cheeks, sparkling little eyes with a sty.

The advance on Lvov. The batteries are drawing nearer and nearer. A rather unsuccessful skirmish by Ostrov, but still the Poles withdraw. Information on Lvov's defenses—schoolmasters, women, adolescents. Apanasenko will butcher them—he hates the intelligentsia, with him it's deep-rooted, he wants an aristocracy on his own terms, a muzhik and Cossack state.

August 21, a week of battle has passed, our units are four versts outside Lvov.

An order: the whole Red Cavalry is being put under the command of the Western Front.* They are moving us north to Lublin. There will be an attack there. They are withdrawing the army, now four versts from the town, even though it took so much time for them to get there. The Fourteenth Army will replace us. What is this? Madness, or the impossibility of a town being taken by the cavalry? I will remember the forty-five-verst ride from Barshchovitse to Adamy for the rest of my life. I on my little piebald horse, Sheko† in his carriage, heat and dust,

---

* *Zapfront* (Zapadnii Front), February 1919 to January 1921, was the central Red Army command of western and northwestern strategic points in Soviet Russia.

† The chief of staff of the Sixth Cavalry Division.

the dust of the Apocalypse, stifling clouds, endless lines of transport carts, all the brigades are on the move, clouds of dust from which there is no escape, one is afraid of suffocating, shouting all around, movement, I ride with a squadron over fields, we lose Sheko, the most horrendous part of it begins, the ride on my little horse which can't keep up, we ride endlessly and always at a trot, I am completely exhausted, the squadron wants to overtake the transport carts, we overtake them, I am afraid of being left behind, my horse is drifting along like a bit of fluff, to the point of inertia, all the brigades are on the move, all the artillery, they've each left one regiment behind as a covering force, and these regiments are to reunite with the division at the onset of darkness. In the night we ride through silent, dead Busk. What is special about Galician towns? The mixture of the dirty, ponderous East (Byzantium and the Jews) with the beer-drinking German West. Fifteen km. from Busk. I can't hold out anymore. I change my horse. It turns out that there is no covering on the saddle. Riding is torture. I keep constantly changing position. A rest stop in Kozlov. A dark hut, bread with milk. A peasant, a warm and pleasant person, was a prisoner of war in Odessa, I lie on the bench, mustn't fall asleep, I'm wearing another man's service jacket, the horses in the dark, it's stuffy in the hut, children on the floor. We arrived in Adamy at four in the morning. Sheko is asleep. I leave my horse somewhere, there is hay, and I lie down to sleep.

AUGUST 21, 1920. ADAMY

Frightened Ruthenians. Sun. Nice. I'm ill. Rest. The whole day in the threshing shed. I sleep, feel better toward evening, my head pounds, aches. I'm billeted with Sheko. Yegor, the chief of staff's lackey. We eat well. How we get our food. Vorobyov took over the Second Squadron. The soldiers are pleased. In Poland, where we are heading, there's no need to hold back—with the Galicians, who are completely innocent, we had to be more careful. I'm resting, I'm not in the saddle.

Conversation with Artillery Division Commander Maksimov, our army is out to make some money, what we have is not revolution but an uprising of renegade Cossacks.

They are simply an instrument the party is not above using.

Two Odessans, Manuilov and Boguslavsky,* operational air force military commissar, Paris, London, a handsome Jew, a big talker, articles in a European magazine, the divisional chief of staff's adjutant, Jews in the Red Cavalry, I tell them what's what. Wearing a service jacket, the excesses of the Odessan bourgeoisie, painful news from Odessa. They're being smothered there. What about my father? Have they really taken everything away from him? I have to give some thought to the situation back home.

I'm turning into a sponger.

Apanasenko has written a letter to the officers of the Polish army: You bandits, stop fighting, surrender, you *Pans*, or we will butcher you all!

Apanasenko's letter to the Don headquarters, to Stavropol, there they are making things difficult for our fighters, for the Sons of the Revolution, we are heroes, we have no fear, we will march ahead.

A description of the squadron's rest, they steal hens, the squealing of pigs, agents, musical flourishes on the town square. They wash clothes, thresh oats, come galloping with sheaves. The horses, wiggling their ears, eat oats. The horse is everything. Horse names: Stepan, Misha, Little Brother, Old Girl. Your horse is your savior, you are aware of it every moment, even if you might beat it inhumanly. No one takes care of my horse. They barely take care of it.

AUGUST 22, 1920. ADAMY

Manuilov, the divisional chief of staff's adjutant, has a stomachache. I'm not surprised. Served with Muravyov,† in the Cheka, something to do with military investigation, a bourgeois, women, Paris, air force, something to do with his reputation, and he's a Communist. Boguslavsky, the secretary, frightened, sits silently and eats.

A peaceful day. We march on northward.

I'm billeted with Sheko. I can't do anything. I'm tired, battered. I

---

* Manuilov was the adjutant to Sheko, the divisional chief of staff, and Boguslavsky was staff secretary.

† Mikhail Artemevich Muravyov, a legendary figure who in 1918, during his tenure as commander of the Western Front, instigated the counterrevolutionary Muravyov Revolt for which he was executed.

sleep and eat. How we eat. The system. The provisions depot men and the foragers won't give us anything. The arrival of the Red Army fighters in the village, they search through everything, cook, all night the stoves sputter, the household daughters suffer, the squealing of pigs, they come to the military commissar with receipts. The pitiful Galicians.

The saga of how we eat. We eat well: pigs, hens, geese.

Those who don't take part are "rag-looters" and "wimp."

AUGUST 23/24, 1920. VIKTOV

Ride on to Vitkov in a cart. System of using civilian carts, poor civilians, they are harassed for two, three weeks, are let go, given a pass, are snatched up by other soldiers, are harassed again. An episode: where we are billeted a boy comes back from the transport carts. Night. His mother's joy.

We march into the Krasnostav-Lublin district. We've overtaken the army, which is four versts from Lvov. The cavalry did not manage to take it.

The road to Vitkov. Sun. Galician roads, endless transport carts, factory horses, ravaged Galicia, Jews in shtetls, somewhere an unscathed farm, Czech we imagine, we attack the unripe apples, the beehives.

More details about the beehives another time.

On the road, in the cart, I think, I mourn the fate of the Revolution.

The shtetl is unusual, rebuilt on a single plan after its destruction, little white houses, tall wooden roofs, sadness.

We are billeted with the divisional chief of staff's aides, Manuilov knows nothing about staff work, the hassles of trying to get horses, no one will give us any, we ride on the civilians' carts, Boguslavsky wears lilac-colored drawers, a great success with the girls in Odessa.

The soldiers ask for a theatrical show. They're fed *His Orderly Let Him Down.*

The divisional chief of staff's night: where's the Thirty-third Regiment, where did the Second Brigade go, telephone, orders from army headquarters to the brigade commander, 1, 2, 3!

The orderlies on duty. The setup of the squadrons—Matusevich and Vorobyov,* a former commandant, an unalterably cheerful and, from what I can see, a foolish man.

The divisional chief of staff's night: the division commander wants to see you.

AUGUST 25, 1920. SOKAL

Finally, a town. We ride through the shtetl of Tartakuv, Jews, ruins, cleanliness of a Jewish kind, the Jewish race, little stores.

I am still ill, I've still not gotten back on my feet after the battles outside Lvov. What stuffy air these shtetls have. The infantry had been in Sokal, the town is untouched, the divisional chief of staff is billeted with some Jews. Books, I saw books. I'm billeted with a Galician woman, a rich one at that, we eat well, chicken in sour cream.

I ride on my horse to the center of town, it's clean, pretty buildings, everything soiled by war, remnants of cleanliness and originality.

The Revolutionary Committee. Requisitions and confiscation. Interesting: they don't touch the peasantry, all the land has been left at its disposal. The peasantry is left alone.

The declarations of the Revolutionary Committee.

My landlord's son—a Zionist and *ein ausgesprochener Nationalist.*† Normal Jewish life, they look to Vienna, to Berlin, the nephew, a young man, is studying philosophy, wants to go to the university. We eat butter and chocolate. Sweets.

Friction between Manuilov and the divisional chief of staff.** Sheko tells him to go to—

"I have my pride," they won't give him a billet, no horse, there's the cavalry for you, this isn't a holiday resort. Books—*polnische, Juden.*‡

In the evening, the division commander in his new jacket, well fed, wearing his multicolored trousers, red-faced and dim-witted, out to have some fun, music at night, the rain disperses us. It is rain-

---

* Now demoted to the rank of squadron commander.
† German: "a vehement nationalist."
** Manuilov was the divisional chief of staff's adjutant, and Sheko, his boss, was the divisional chief of staff.
‡ German: "Polish ones, Jews."

ing, the tormenting Galician rain, it pours and pours, endlessly, hopelessly.

What are our soldiers up to in this town? Dark rumors.

Boguslavsky has betrayed Manuilov. Boguslavsky is a slave.

AUGUST 26, 1920. SOKAL

A look around town with the young Zionist. The synagogues: the Hasidic one is a staggering sight, it recalls three hundred years ago, pale, handsome boys with *peyes,* the synagogue as it was two hundred years ago, the selfsame figures in long coats, rocking, waving their hands, howling. This is the Orthodox party, they support the Rabbi of Belz, the famous Rabbi of Belz, who's made off to Vienna. The moderates support the Rabbi of Husyatin. Their synagogue. The beauty of the altar made by some artisan, the magnificence of the greenish chandeliers, the worm-eaten little tables, the Belz synagogue—a vision of ancient times. The Jews ask me to use my influence so they won't be ruined, they're being robbed of food and goods.

The Yids hide everything. The cobbler, the Sokal cobbler, is a proletarian. His apprentice's appearance, a red-haired Hasid—a cobbler.

The cobbler has been waiting for Soviet rule—now he sees the Yid-killers and the looters, and that there'll be no earnings, he is shaken, and looks at us with distrust. A hullabaloo over money. In essence, we're not paying anything, 15–20 rubles. The Jewish quarter. Indescribable poverty, dirt, the boxed-in quality of the ghetto.

The little stores, all of them open, whiting and resin, soldiers ransacking, swearing at the Yids, drifting around aimlessly, entering homes, crawling under counters, greedy eyes, trembling hands, a strange army indeed.

The organized looting of the stationery store, the owner in tears, they tear up everything, they come up with all kinds of demands, the daughter with Western European self-possession, but pitiful and red-faced, hands things over, is given some money or other, and with her storekeeper's politeness tries to act as if everything were as it should be, except that there are too many customers. The owner's wife is so full of despair that she cannot make head or tail of anything.

At night the town will be looted—everyone knows that.

Music in the evening—the division commander is out to have some fun. In the morning he wrote some letters to Stavropol and the Don. The front will not tolerate the disgraceful goings-on in the rear lines. The same old story.

The division commander's lackeys lead his magnificent horses with their breastplates and cruppers back and forth.

The military commissar and the nurse. A Russian man—a sly muzhik—coarse and sometimes insolent and confused. Has a high opinion of the nurse, sounds me out, asks me all kinds of questions, he is in love.

The nurse goes to say good-bye to the division commander, and this after everything that's happened. Everyone's slept with her. That boor Suslov is in the adjoining room—the division commander is busy, he's cleaning his revolver.

I'm given boots and underwear. Sukhorukov received them and dealt them out himself, he's a super-lackey, describe him.

A chat with the nephew who wants to go to university.

Sokal: brokers and artisans—Communism, they tell me, isn't likely to strike root here.

What battered, tormented people these are.

Poor Galicia, poor Jews.

My landlord has eight doves.

Manuilov has a sharp confrontation with Sheko, he has many sins in his past. A Kiev adventurer. He came to us demoted from having been chief of staff of the Third Brigade.

Lepin. A dark, terrifying soul.

The nurse—twenty-six men and one woman.*

August 27, 1920

Skirmishes near Znyatin, Dluzhnov. We ride northwest. Half the day with the transport carts. Heading to Laszczow, Komarow. In the morning we set off from Sokal. A regular day with the squadrons: we wander through forests and glades with the division commander, the brigade commanders come, sun, for five hours I haven't gotten off my

* A reference to Maxim Gorky's story, "Twenty-six Men and One Woman."

horse, brigades ride past. Transport cart panic. I left the carts at a clearing in the forest, rode over to the division commander. The squadrons
on a hill. Reports to the army commander, a cannonade, there are no
airplanes, we ride from one place to another, a regular day. Heavy
exhaustion toward evening, we spend the night in Wasylow. We didn't
reach Laszczow, our target destination.

The Eleventh Division is in Wasylow or somewhere near there,
pandemonium, Bakhturov*—a tiny division, he has lost some of his
sparkle. The Fourth Division is mounting successful battles.

AUGUST 28, 1920. KOMAROW

I rode off from Wasylow ten minutes after the squadrons. I am riding with three horsemen. Earth mounds, glades, destroyed farms,
somewhere in the greenery are the Red Columns, plums. Gunfire, we
don't know where the enemy is, we can't see anybody, machine guns are
hammering quite near and from different directions, my heart tenses,
and so every day single horsemen are out looking for their field headquarters, they are carrying reports. Toward noon I found my squadron
in a ravaged village with all the villagers hiding in their cellars, under
trees covered in plums. I ride with the squadrons. I ride into Komarow
with the division commander, red hood. A magnificent, unfinished, red
church. Before we entered Komarow, after the gunfire (I was riding
alone), silence, warm, a bright day, a somewhat strange and translucent
calm, my soul ached, all alone, nobody getting on my nerves, fields,
forests, undulating valleys, shady roads.

We stop opposite the church.

The arrival of Voroshilov and Budyonny. Voroshilov blows up in
front of everyone: "Lack of energy!" He gets heated, a heated individual, the whole army restless, he rides and yells, Budyonny is silent,
smiles, white teeth. Apanasenko defends himself: "Let's go inside"—
"Why do we keep letting the enemy get away?" Voroshilov shouts.
"Without contact you can't strike."

Is Apanasenko worthless?

---

* Pavel Vasilevich Bakhturov, the former military commissar of the Sixth Cavalry Division, had
become the military commissar of the Eleventh Division on August 8.

The pharmacist who offers me a room. Rumors of atrocities. I go into the shtetl. Indescribable fear and desperation.

They tell me what happened. Hiding in a hut, they are frightened that the Poles will return. Last night Captain Yakovlev's* Cossacks were here. A pogrom. The family of David Zis, in their home, the old prophet, naked and barely breathing, the butchered old woman, a child with chopped-off fingers. Many of these people are still breathing, the stench of blood, everything turned topsy-turvy, chaos, a mother over her butchered son, an old woman curled up, four people in one hut, dirt, blood under a black beard, they're just lying there in their blood. Jews in the town square, the tormented Jew who shows me everything, a tall Jew takes his place. The rabbi has gone into hiding, everything has been smashed to pieces in his house, he doesn't leave his burrow until evening. Fifteen people have been killed: Hasid Itska Galer, 70 years old, David Zis, synagogue *shamas*, 45 years old, his wife and his daughter, 15 years old, David Trost, his wife, the butcher.

At the house of a raped woman.

Evening—at my landlord's, a conventional home, Sabbath evening, they didn't want to cook until the Sabbath was over.

I look for the nurses, Suslov laughs. A Jewish woman doctor.

We are in a strange, old-fashioned house, they used to have everything here—butter, milk.

At night, a walk through the shtetl.

The moon, their lives at night behind closed doors. Wailing inside. They will clean everything up. The fear and horror of the townsfolk. The main thing: our men are going around indifferently, looting where they can, ripping the clothes off the butchered people.

The hatred for them is the same, they too are Cossacks, they too are savage, it's pure nonsense that our army is any different. The life of the shtetls. There is no escape. Everyone is out to destroy them, the Poles did not give them refuge. All the women and girls can scarcely walk. In the evening a talkative Jew with a little beard, he had a store, his daughter threw herself out of a second-floor window, she broke both arms, there are many like that.

What a powerful and magnificent life of a nation existed here. The

* A Cossack captain fighting on the Polish side.

fate of the Jewry. At our place in the evening, supper, tea, I sit drinking in the words of the Jew with the little beard who asks me plaintively if it will be possible to trade again.

An oppressive, restless night.

AUGUST 29, 1920. KOMAROW, LABUNYE, PNEVSK

We pull out of Komarow. During the night our men looted, in the synagogue they threw away the Torah scrolls and took the velvet coverings for their saddles. The military commissar's orderly eyes the phylacteries, wants to take the straps. The Jews smile obsequiously. That is religion.

Everyone is greedily looking at what hasn't yet been taken. They rummage through bones and ruins. They've come here to make some money.

My horse is limping, I take the divisional chief of staff's horse, want to trade, I am too soft, a talk with the village elder, nothing comes of it.

Labunye. A vodka distillery. A hundred thousand liters of spirits. Under guard. Rain, penetrating and incessant. Autumn, everything points to autumn. The Polish family of the bailiff. The horses under a canopy, the Red Army fighters drinking in spite of the prohibition. Labunye is a threatening peril for the army.

Everything is secretive and simple. The people are silent, as if nothing out of the ordinary were going on. Oh, you Russians! Everything breathes secrecy and menace. Sidorenko has calmed down.

The operation to take Zamosc. We are ten versts from Zamosc. There I will ask about R.Y.

The operation, as always, is uncomplicated. Bypass via the west and the north, and then take the town. Alarming news from the Western Front.* The Poles have taken Bialystok.

We ride on. The looted estates of Kulaczkowski near Labunki. White columns. An enchanting, even if manorial, setup. The destruction is beyond belief. The real Poland: bailiffs, old women, white-blond children, rich, semi-European villages with elders, local headmen, all

---

* The central Red Army command of western and northwestern strategic points in Soviet Russia.

Catholic, beautiful women. Our men are dragging away oats on the estate. The horses stand in the drawing room, black horses. Well—after all, we do have to keep them out of the rain. Extremely precious books in a chest, they didn't have time to take them along: the constitution approved by the Sejm* at the beginning of the eighteenth century, old folios from the times of Nicholas I, the Polish code of laws, precious bindings, Polish manuscripts of the sixteenth century, the writings of monks, old French novels.

There is no destruction upstairs, it was merely searched, all the chairs, walls, sofas have been slashed open, the floors ripped up—not destroyed, just searched. Delicate crystal, the bedroom, the oak beds, powder case, French novels on the tables, many French and Polish books about child care, smashed intimate feminine toiletries, remnants of butter in a butter dish, newlyweds?

A settled way of life, gymnastic equipment, good books, tables, bottles of medicine—everything sacrilegiously besmirched. An unbearable feeling of wanting to run away from the vandals, but they walk about, search, describe how they walk, their faces, hats, their cursing: Goddamn, f—ing Mother of God, the Holy Virgin. They drag sheaves of oats through the impassable mud.

We near Zamosc. A terrible day. The rain is the victor, not letting up even for a minute. The horses can barely pull the carts. Describe this unendurable rain. We wander deep into the night. We are soaked to the bone, tired, Apanasenko's red hood. We bypass Zamosc, the units are three to four versts away from it. The armored trains won't let us pass, they shower us with artillery fire. We stay in the fields, wait for reports, dull rivulets flow. Brigade Commander Kniga in a hut, a report. Our fatherly commander. We cannot do a thing against the armored train. It turns out we didn't know that there was a railroad here, it's not marked on the map, a mix-up, so much for our reconnaissance.

We roam around and keep waiting for them to take Zamosc. Damn it to hell. The Poles keep fighting better and better. Horses and men are shivering. We spend the night in Pnevsk. A fine Polish peasant family. The difference between Poles and Russians is striking. The Poles live more cleanly, cheerfully, play with their children, beautiful icons, beautiful women.

* The Polish Parliament.

AUGUST 30, 1920

In the morning we leave Pnevsk. The operation to take Zamosc continues. The weather is as bad as before, rain, slush, impassible roads, we barely slept: on the floor, in the straw, wearing our boots—on constant alert.

Again roaming around. We go with Sheko to the Third Brigade. He goes with his revolver drawn to attack the Zavadi Train Station. Lepin and I stay in the forest. Lepin is squirming. The skirmish at the station. Sheko has a doomed look on his face. Describe the "rapid fire." The station has been taken. We ride along the railroad tracks. Ten prisoners, one of them we arrive too late to save.* A revolver wound? An officer. Blood is flowing out of his mouth. Thick, red, clotting blood is drenching his whole face, it looks terrible, red, covered in his thick blood. The prisoners are all undressed. Trousers have been slung over the squadron leader's saddle. Sheko makes him give them back. They try to make the prisoners put on their clothes, but they won't put anything on. An officer's cap. "And then there were nine." Foul words all around. They want to kill the prisoners. A bald, lame Jew in his drawers who can't keep up with the horse, a terrible face, an officer no doubt, gets on everyone's nerves, he can't walk, they are all in the grip of animal fear, pitiful, unfortunate people, Polish proletarians, one of the Poles is stately, calm, with sideburns, wearing a knitted jersey, he comports himself with dignity, everyone keeps asking if he's an officer. They want to butcher them. A dark cloud gathers over the Jew. A frenzied Putilov worker—They should all be butchered, the scum—the Jew is hopping after us, we always drag prisoners along, and then hand them over to the authorities of the military escort. What happens to them. The rage of the Putilov worker, foaming at the mouth, his saber: I will butcher the scum and won't have to answer for it.

We ride over to the division commander, he is with the First and Second Brigades. We are always within sight of Zamosc, we can see its chimneys, houses, we are trying to take it from all sides. A night attack

---

* See the stories "And Then There Were Nine" and "And Then There Were Ten," in which the Cossacks capture Polish prisoners at the Zavadi Station. Babel and Lepin arrive too late to stop the Cossacks from murdering one of the prisoners.

is in preparation. We are three versts from Zamosc, are waiting for the town to be seized, will spend the night there. Field, night, rain, penetrating cold, we are lying on the wet earth, there's nothing to feed the horses with, it's dark, men ride with messages. The First and the Third Brigades will lead the attack. Kniga and Levda*—a semiliterate Ukrainian who is commander of the Third Brigade—arrive the way they always do. Tiredness, apathy, the unquenchable thirst for sleep, almost desperation. A line advances briskly in the dark, a whole brigade on foot. Next to us a cannon. An hour later the infantry advances. Our cannon is firing continuously, a soft, cracking sound, flames in the night, the Poles are firing rockets, crazed shooting from rifles and machine guns, this is hell, we wait, it's three in the morning. The battle ebbs. Nothing came of it. For us more and more often now things come to nothing. What does this mean? Is the army giving up?

We ride ten versts to Sitaniec to lodge for the night. The rain is getting stronger. An indescribable fatigue. My one and only dream—a billet. My dream becomes a reality. A dismayed old Pole with his wife. The soldiers, needless to say, clean him out. Extreme fear, they've all been hiding in cellars. Heaps of noodles, butter, milk, bliss. I keep unearthing more and more food. A tortured, nice old woman. Delightful melted butter. Suddenly gunfire, bullets whistling about the stables, about the horses' legs. We up and run. Despair. We ride to the other end of the village. Three hours of sleep interrupted by reports, debriefings, anxiety.

AUGUST 31, 1920. CZESNIKI

A meeting with the brigade commanders. A farm. A shady glade. The destruction total. Not even any clothes left. We clean out the last of the oats. An orchard, an apiary, the destruction of the hives, terrible, the bees buzz around in desperation, the hives are detonated with gunpowder, the men wrap themselves in their greatcoats and launch an attack on the hives, a bacchanalia, they drag out the frames with their sabers, the honey streams onto the ground, the bees sting, they are

* Kniga was the commander of the First Brigade of the Sixth Cavalry Division, and Levda was commander of the Third Brigade of the Fourteenth Cavalry Division.

smoked out with tarred rags, burning rags. Cherkashin.* In the apiary
there is chaos and complete destruction, smoke rises from the ruins.

I am writing in the garden, a glade, flowers, I feel sorrow for all
this.

The military order to leave Zamosc, to go to the rescue of the
Fourteenth Division, which is being forced back from Komarow. The
shtetl has again been taken by the Poles. Poor Komarow. We ride along
the flanks and the brigades. Before us, the enemy cavalry—nothing to
hold us back, whom should we butcher if not the Cossacks of Captain
Yakovlev.† An attack is imminent. The brigades are gathering in the
forest—two versts from Czesniki.

Voroshilov and Budyonny are with us all the time. Voroshilov,
short, graying, in red trousers with silver stripes, always goading, getting on everyone's nerves, keeps hounding Apanasenko about why the
Second Brigade hasn't arrived. We are waiting for the arrival of the
Second Brigade. Time is dragging with torturing slowness. Do not rush
me, Comrade Voroshilov. Voroshilov: Everything is ruined, f— it to
hell.

Budyonny is silent, at times he smiles, showing his dazzling white
teeth. We must send the brigade first, and then the regiment.
Voroshilov's patience snaps, he sends everyone he has into the attack.
The regiment marches past Voroshilov and Budyonny. Voroshilov pulls
out his enormous revolver, show the Polish *Pans* no mercy, his cry is
met with joy. The regiment flies off helter-skelter, hurrah, go for it,
some gallop off, others hold back, others again move in a trot, the horses balk, bowler hats and carpets.** Our squadron launches an attack. We
gallop about four versts. They are waiting for us in columns on the hill.
Amazing: none of them so much as move. Sangfroid, discipline. An
officer with a black beard. I'm being shot at. My sensations. Flight. The
military commissars turn. Nothing helps. Luckily, the enemy doesn't
pursue us, otherwise we would have had a catastrophe on our hands. We
try to gather a brigade together for a second attack, nothing comes of it.
Manuilov is threatened with revolvers. The nurses are the heroines.

---

* An orderly at the Sixth Cavalry Division headquarters.
† The Cossack captain fighting on the Polish side.
** Babel is referring to the colorful attire of the Cossacks, some of whom are wearing bowler
hats and clothes cut out of carpets, and have draped carpets looted from houses over their saddles.

We ride back. Sheko's* horse is wounded, Sheko has a concussion, his terrible, rigid face. He doesn't understand what is happening, he is crying, we lead his mare. She is bleeding.

The nurse's story: there are nurses who are only out for sympathy, we help the fighters, go through thick and thin with them, I would shoot, but what can I shoot with, a f—ing dick, I don't even have that.

The command staff is crushed, menacing signs of our army's disintegration. Cheerful, foolish Vorobyov† recounts his heroic feats, he went galloping up, four shots point-blank. Apanasenko suddenly turns around: You ruined the attack, you bastard.

Apanasenko in a black mood, Sheko pitiful.

There is talk about how the army isn't in the shape it used to be, it's high time for a rest. What next? We spend the night in Czesniki, we are frozen through, tired, silent—impassable, all-engulfing mud, autumn, destroyed roads, dejection. Before us somber prospects.

September 1, 1920. Terebin

We set out from Czesniki in the night. We stopped there for two hours. Night, cold, on our horses. We are shivering. The military order to retreat, we are surrounded, we have lost contact with the Twelfth Army,** we don't have contact with anybody. Sheko is crying, his head shaking, his face that of a hurt child, he is pitiful, crushed. What bastards people are. Vinokurov‡ wouldn't give him the military order to read—he is not on active duty. Apanasenko gives him his carriage, but I'm not their driver.

Endless conversations about yesterday's attack, lies, sincere regrets, the fighters are silent. That idiot Vorobyov keeps shooting his mouth off. The division commander cuts him off.

The beginning of the end of the First Cavalry Army. Rumors of retreat.

Sheko is a man deep in misfortune.

---

* The chief of staff of the Sixth Cavalry Division.
† Commander of the Second Squadron of the Sixth Cavalry Division.
** The infantry, the main force in the Russian-Polish campaign.
‡ The military commissar of the Sixth Cavalry Division.

Manuilov has a temperature of 40°C, fever, everyone hates him, Sheko harasses him, why? He doesn't know how to comport himself. Borisov, the orderly, cunning, ingratiating, secretive, no one has any pity for him, that's what's dreadful. A Jew?

The Fourth Division saves the army. And that with Timoshenko—the traitor.*

We arrive in Terebin, a half-destroyed village, cold. It's autumn, during the day I sleep in the threshing shed, at night together with Sheko.

My talk with Arzam Slyagit. Riding next to me. We spoke about Tiflis, fruit, sun. I think about Odessa, my soul is torn.

We are dragging Sheko's bleeding horse behind us.

SEPTEMBER 2, 1920. TEREBIN—METELIN

Pitiful villages. Unfinished huts. Half-naked villagers. We ruin them once and for all. The division commander is with the troops. The military order: delay the enemy's advance on the Bug, attack in the area of Wakijow-Hostyne. We fight but without success. Rumors about the weakening of the army's fighting efficiency are becoming more persistent. Desertion. Masses of reports of men going on leave, illness.

The main illness of the division is the absence of command staff, all the commanders are from the ranks, Apanasenko hates the democrats,† they don't understand a thing, there's no one who can lead a regiment into an attack.

Squadron commanders are leading regiments.

Days of apathy, Sheko is recovering, he is depressed. Life is tough in the atmosphere of an army whose side has split open.

SEPTEMBER 3, 4, 5, 1920. MALICE

We have moved on to Malice.

Orlov is the new chief of staff's adjutant. A figure from Gogol. A

---

* An ironic comment. After Timoshenko had been relieved of his command of the Sixth Cavalry Division on August 5, 1920, he became the division commander (August 25) of the Fourth Cavalry Division. He was awarded his second Red Flag Medal for his leadership in the Battle for Zamosc.

† Russian Social Democratic Workers Party, of which there was a Leninist and a non-Leninist wing.

pathological liar, his tongue always wagging, a Jewish face, the main thing: the terrifying ease, when you think about it, with which he talks, chatters, lies, he's in pain (he limps), a partisan, a Makhno* fighter, he went to high school, commanded a regiment. His ease frightens me, what is behind it.

Finally Manuilov has fled, and not without scandal—he was threatened with arrest, how addle-brained Sheko is, they had sent him to the First Brigade, sheer idiocy, Army headquarters sent him to the air force. Amen.

I'm billeted with Sheko. Dull, amiable if you know how to stay on his good side, inept, does not have a strong will. I grovel—and so I get to eat. Boguslavsky, languid, half Odessan, dreams of "Odessan girls," from time to time will ride out at night to collect an army order.

The First Platoon of the First Squadron. Kuban Cossacks. They sing songs. Staid. They smile. They're not rowdy.

Levda† reported sick. A cunning Ukrainian. "I have rheumatism. I am too weak to work." Three report sick from the brigades, they're in cahoots. If we're not given any leave, the division will go under, there's no ardor, the horses won't go on, the men are impassive, the Third Brigade, two days in the field, cold, rain.

A sad country, impassable mud, no muzhiks to be seen anywhere, they hide their horses in the forests, women sobbing quietly.

A report from Kniga: Unable to execute my duties without a command staff.

All the horses are in the forests, the Red Army fighters exchange them, a science, a sport.

Barsukov is falling apart. He wants to go to school.

There are skirmishes. Our side is trying to advance on Wakijow-Honiatycki. Nothing comes of it. A strange weakness.

The Pole is slowly but surely pushing us back. The division commander is useless, he has neither the initiative nor the necessary tenacity. His purulent ambition, philandering, gluttony, and probably feverish activity should it be needed.

Our way of life.

---

* The Ukrainian anarchist leader.
† Commander of the Third Brigade of the Fourteenth Cavalry Division.

Kniga writes: The previous ardor no longer exists, the fighters are dragging their feet.

Dispiriting weather all the time, destroyed roads, terrible Russian village mud in which your boots get stuck, there is no sun, it is raining, gloomy, what a cursed land.

I am ill, angina, fever, I can barely move, terrible nights in stifling, smoke-filled huts in the straw, my whole body torn to pieces, flea-bitten, itching, bleeding, there's nothing I can do.

Our operations continue sluggishly, a period of equilibrium in which, however, the ascendancy is beginning to shift to the Poles.

The command staff is passive, doesn't even exist anymore.

I rush over to the nurse to pick up bandages, I have to go through kitchen gardens, impassable mud. The nurse is staying with a platoon. A heroine, even though she copulates with many. A hut, everyone smoking, cursing, changing foot wrappings, a soldier's life, and another person, the nurse. Anyone too squeamish to drink from the same mug as the rest gets thrown out.

The enemy advances. We took Lot, have to give it up again, the enemy pushes us back, not a single attack of ours has brought results, we send off the transport carts, I ride to Terebin on Barsukov's cart, from there on rain, slush, misery, we cross the Bug, Budyatichi. So—it has been decided to relinquish the Bug line.

SEPTEMBER 6, 1920. BUDYATICHI

Budyatichi is occupied by the Forty-fourth Division. Clashes. They are startled by our division pouring in like a wild horde. Orlov:* Hand this place over to us and get out!

The nurse—a proud woman, pretty and somewhat dim-witted—is in tears, the doctor is outraged at the shouts of "Down with the Yids, save Russia!" They are stunned, the quartermaster was thrashed with a whip, the field hospital demolished, pigs are requisitioned and dragged off without receipts or anything, and before everything had been well ordered, all sorts of representatives go to see Sheko to complain. There you have the Budyonny fighters.

---

* The adjutant of the chief of staff of the Sixth Cavalry Division.

The proud nurse, a kind we've never seen before, in white shoes and stockings, a full, shapely leg, they have things nicely organized, respect for human dignity, quick, thorough work.

We are billeted with Jews.

My thoughts of home are becoming increasingly persistent. I see no way out.

SEPTEMBER 7, 1920. BUDYATICHI

We are occupying two rooms. The kitchen is full of Jews. There are refugees from Krylow, a pitiful little bunch of people with the faces of prophets. They sleep side by side. All day long they are boiling and baking, the Jewess works like a slave, sewing, laundering. They pray there too. Children, young girls. The damn bastards, the lackeys, they are continually stuffing themselves, drinking vodka, guffawing, growing fat, hiccuping with lust for women.

We eat every two hours.

A unit is placed on the opposite shore of the Bug, a new phase in the operation.

It's been two weeks now that everyone's been saying more and more doggedly that the army has to be pulled out for a rest. A rest!— our new battle cry.

A delegation turns up, the division commander entertains them, they're constantly eating, his stories about Stavropol, Suslov is growing fatter, the bastard has gotten himself a good deal.

Terrible tactlessness: Sheko, Suslov, Sukhorukov have been put up for a Red Flag Medal.

The enemy is trying to cross over to our side of the Bug, the Fourteenth Division acted quickly and pushed them back.

I am issuing certificates.

I've gone deaf in one ear. The result of my cold? My body is all scratched up, cuts everywhere, I don't feel well. Autumn, rain, everything is depressing, deep mud.

SEPTEMBER 8, 1920. VLADIMIR-VOLYNSK

In the morning I head to the administrative headquarters on a civilian cart. I have to testify, some song and dance about money. Some demi-rearguard sordidness: Gusev, Nalyotov, money at the Revolutionary Tribunal. Lunch with Gorbunov.

Off to Vladimir with the same nags. An arduous ride, insurmountable mud, the roads impassable. We arrive at night. A squabble about the billet, a cold room in a widow's house. Jews—storekeepers. Mama and Papa are old.

Poor Grandma. The gentle, black-bearded husband. The redheaded, pregnant Jewess is washing her feet. The girl has diarrhea. It is cramped, but there is electricity, it's warm.

For supper there are dumplings with sunflower oil—pure bliss. There you have it: Jewish abundance. They think I don't understand Yiddish, they are as cunning as flies. The town is destitute.

Borodin* and I sleep on a featherbed.

SEPTEMBER 9, 1920. VLADIMIR-VOLYNSK

The town is destitute, dirty, hungry, you can't buy anything with money, sweets cost twenty rubles and cigarettes. Dejection. Army headquarters. Gloomy. A council of trade unions, young Jews. I go to the economic councils and the trade unions, dejection, the military members make demands, act like louts. Sickly young Jews.

Magnificent meal—meat, kasha. Our only pleasure is food.

The new military commissar at headquarters—a monkey's face.

My landlord wants to barter for my shawl. I'm not going to let him hoodwink me.

My driver, barefoot with bleary eyes. *Oy* Russia!†

A synagogue. I pray, bare walls, some soldier or other is swiping the electric light bulbs.

The bathhouse. A curse on soldiering, war, the cramming together of young, tormented, still-healthy people gone crazy.

The home life of my landlord and his wife, they are taking care of a few things, tomorrow is Friday, they are already preparing themselves, the old woman is good, the old man a little underhanded, they are only pretending to be poor. They say: Better to starve under the Bolsheviks than to eat fancy bread under the Poles.

---

* An orderly at the headquarters of the Sixth Cavalry Division.
† Babel uses "Rasseya," an archaic folksy name for Russia.

SEPTEMBER 10, 1920. KOVEL

Half the day in the shattered, doleful, terrible train station in Vladimir-Volynsk. Dejection. The black-bearded Jew is working. We arrive in Kovel at night. Unexpected joy: The Polit-otdel train.* Supper with Zdanevich,† butter. I spend the night in the radio station. Blinding light. A miracle. Khelemskaya is having an affair. Lymph glands. Volodya. She took off all her clothes. My prophecy came true.

SEPTEMBER 11, 1920. KOVEL

The town has kept traces of European-Jewish culture. They won't accept Soviet money, a glass of coffee without sugar: fifty rubles. A disgusting meal at the train station: 600 rubles.

Sun, I go from doctor to doctor, have my ear treated, itching.

I visit Yakovlev,** quiet little houses, meadows, Jewish alleys, a quiet hearty life, Jewish girls, youths, old men at the synagogues, perhaps wigs. Soviet power does not seem to have ruffled the surface, these quarters are across the bridge.

Dirt and hunger in the train. Everyone's emaciated, louse-ridden, with sallow faces, they all hate one another, sit locked up in their cubicles, even the cook is emaciated. A striking change. They are living in a cage. Khelemskaya, dirty, puttering about in the kitchen, her connection to the kitchen, she feeds Volodya, a Jewish wife "from a good home."

All day I look for food.

The district in which the Twelfth Army is located. Luxurious establishments: clubs, gramophones, conscientious Red Army fighters, cheerful, life is bubbling up, the newspapers of the Twelfth Army, Central Military News Service, Army Commander Kuzmin‡ who writes articles. As far as work goes, the Polit-otdel seems to be doing well.

---

* A train for the ideological education of the troops, equipped with a printing press and radio station.
† V. Zdanevich, the editor-in-chief of the Red Cavalry newspaper *Krasny Kavalerist*, for which Babel wrote articles.
** The political commissar of the Sixth Cavalry Division.
‡ Nikolai Nikolayevich Kuzmin was the provisional commander of the Twelfth Army from August to November 1920.

The life of the Jews, crowds in the streets, the main street is Lutskaya Street, I walk around on my shattered feet, I drink an incredible amount of tea and coffee. Ice cream: 500 rubles. They have no shame. Sabbath, all the stores are closed. Medicine: five rubles.

I spend the night at the radio station. Blinding light, sassy radio-telegraphers, one of them is struggling to play a mandolin. Both read avidly.

SEPTEMBER 12, 1920. KIVERTSY

In the morning, panic at the train station. Artillery fire. The Poles are in town. Unimaginably pitiful flight, carts in five rows, the pitiful, dirty, gasping infantry, cavemen, they run over meadows, throw away their rifles, Borodin the orderly already sees the butchering Poles. The train moves out quickly, soldiers and carts come dashing, the wounded, their faces contorted, jump up into our train cars, a gasping political worker, his pants have fallen down, a Jew with a thin, translucent face, possibly a cunning Jew, deserters with broken arms jump on, sick men from the field hospital.

The institution that calls itself the Twelfth Army. For every fighter there are four rear-line men, two ladies, two trunks filled with things—and even the actual fighter doesn't fight. The Twelfth Army is ruining the front and the Red Cavalry, it exposes our flanks and then sends us to stop up those holes with ourselves. One of their units, the Urals Regiment or the Bashkir Brigade, surrendered, leaving the front open. Disgraceful panic, the army is unfit for combat. The soldier types: The Russian Red Army infantryman is barefoot, not only not modernized, but the embodiment of "wretched Russia," hungry and squat muzhiks, tramps, bloated, louse-ridden.

At Goloby all the sick, the wounded, and the deserters are thrown off the train. Rumors, and then facts: the Provision Unit of the First Cavalry sent into the cul-de-sac of Vladimir-Volynsk has been captured by the enemy, our headquarters has moved to Lutsk, a mass of fighters and equipment of the Twelfth Army has been captured, the army is fleeing.

In the evening we arrive in Kivertsy.

Life in the railway car is hard. The radio-telegraphers keep plotting to get rid of me, one of them still has an upset stomach, he plays the mandolin, the other keeps taunting him because he is an idiot.

Life in the railway car, dirty, malicious, hungry, animosity toward one another, unhealthy. Moscow women smoking, eating like pigs, faceless, many pitiful people, coughing Muscovites, everyone wants to eat, everyone is angry, everyone has an upset stomach.

SEPTEMBER 13, 1920. KIVERTSY

A bright morning, the forest. The Jewish New Year. Hungry. I go into the shtetl. Boys wearing white collars. Ishas Khakl offers me bread and butter. She earns her money "herself," a hardy woman, a silk dress, she has tidied up the house. I am moved to tears, here the only thing that helped was talking things through, we spoke for a long time, her husband is in America, a shrewd, unhurried Jewess.

A long stop at the station. Dejection, like before. We get books from the club, we read avidly.

SEPTEMBER 14, 1920. KLEVAN

We stop in Klevan for a day and a night, the whole time at the station. Hunger, dejection. The town of Rovno won't allow us passage. A railroad worker. We bake shortbread and potatoes at his place. A railroad watchman. They eat, say kind things, don't give us anything. I am with Borodin, his light gait. All day long we look for food, from one watchman to the next. I spend the night in the radio station in the blinding light.

SEPTEMBER 15, 1920. KLEVAN

The third day of our agonizing stop in Klevan begins, the same hunt for food, in the morning we had a lot of tea with shortbread. In the evening I rode to Rovno on a cart of the First Cavalry's Air Force Department. A conversation about our air force, it doesn't exist, all the machines are broken, the pilots don't know how to fly, the planes are old, patched up, completely worthless. The Red Army fighter with a swollen throat—quite a type. He can barely speak, his throat must be completely blocked, inflamed, sticks in his fingers to scrape away the film in his gullet, they told him salt might help, he pours salt down his throat, he hasn't eaten for four days, he drinks cold water because nobody will give him hot. His talk is garbled, about the attack, about the commander, about the fact that they were barefoot, some advanced, others didn't, he beckons with his finger.

Supper at Gasnikova's.

Sketches for the
Red Cavalry Stories

The notebooks that Isaac Babel kept while he worked as a war correspondent in the Russian-Polish Campaign of 1920 are the most significant documentation of his writing process. They are terse, quick jottings of incidents and impressions that he wished to use and develop, first in his diary and later in the RED CAVALRY stories. Like his diary, his drafts and sketches are reminders of how he wished to present incidents: "Very simple, A FACTUAL ACCOUNT, no superfluous descriptions. . . . Pay no attention to continuity in the story." Babel was very interested in keeping an accurate account of specific details, such as an individual's military rank or the dates and tactical implications of incidents—so much so, that he made the dangerous choice of threading real figures and incidents into his stories, not always showing them in a favorable light. Commander Budyonny was to become Marshal of the Soviet Union, Voroshilov was Stalin's right-hand man, and Timoshenko became a Marshal of the Soviet Union and Commissar of Defense.

As becomes clear from these jottings, Babel's ultimate aim in the stories he intended to write about the Polish Campaign was literary effect. As he experienced these events, he was already arranging them as they were to appear, first in his diary, and later in finished prose: "THE SEQUENCE: Jews. Airplane. Grave. Timoshenko. The letter. Trunov's burial, the salute."

The battle near Br[ody]

Pil[sudski's] pro[clamations] 2.

Killed, butchered men, sun, wheat, military booklets, Bible pages. Pilsudski's proclamation?

The battle near Br[ody]

No discussions.—Painstaking choice of words.—Konkin— proverbs: If the Lord does not decree, the bladder will not burst.—His beard is that of Abraham, his deeds are those of an evil man—we're covered in vice like yard dogs with lice.—Gnats will chew at you till their dying breath.—To save his own goods and chattels a man will gladly set fire to another man's hide.

The battle near Br[ody]

1. Decamp from Bielavtsy. The battle by Brody.—I bandage men.— Description of the battle.—Korotchayev.* The death of a wounded man in my arms. Radzivillov. Ivan shoots a horse, the horseman runs away.—On the bridge.—It's a pity about the buttermilk.
2. Departure from Brody. An untouched steam contraption. Farm. I go to answer the call of nature . . . A corpse. A sparkling day. The place is littered with corpses, completely unnoticeable in the rye. Pilsudski's proclamations. Battle, butchery in silence.—The division commander.—I move away. Why? I don't have the strength to bear this.
3. Going around in circles. First I went to . . . [written over: Konkin]. Konyushkovo.—The nurse.
4. Radzivillov.

The battle near Br[ody]

1. On the Radzivillov high road. Battle. In Radzivillov. Night. The movement of the horses is the main thing.

---

* A brigade commander of the Sixth Cavalry Division who had been demoted after his provisionary tenure as commander of the Fourth Cavalry Division.

2. Night in Brody. The synagogue is next door.
3. (Briefly). Departure from Brody. A corpse. A field littered with corpses. Pilsudski's proclamations. Battle. Kolesnikov and Grishin. I go away.—The wounded platoon commander. A special insert.
4. Konkin. We're going around in circles.—Anti-Semites.
5. The nurse. Night. Desperation. Dawn.
The length of the episodes—half a page each.
Battle.
1. Wounded men in the *tachanka*. The heroism of the Cossack. I will shoot him. The death of the wounded man.
2. Night, horses are moving.
3. Brody. Next door.
4. Departure from Brody. Corpses. Pilsudski's proclamations. The battle begins. Kolesnikov and Grishin. The beginning of wandering in circles.
5. Lyovka.
6. Konkin.
7. The nurse.

The battle near Brody II

On Ivan's *tachanka*. Wounded men. Lyovka? Brody or Radzivillov. Buttermilk manqué.

The battle by Klyokotovo. Budyonny with his staff. Got cut off from my unit. Roaming about with the Fourth Division.—The nurse.

The end of the battle. A new division commander* with his retinue. K.K.† in Radzivillov.

Lyovka.

Short chapters?
1. On Ivan's *tachanka*. Death.—Describe the wounded.—Budyonny. Kolesnikov. Grishin.—Roaming about in circles. [. . .]

---

* Iosif Rodionovich Apanasenko took over as commander of the Sixth Cavalry Division on August 5, 1920, from Semyon Konstantinovich Timoshenko.
† Konstantin Karlovich Zholnarkevich was the chief of staff of the Sixth Cavalry Division until August 5, 1920, during the period when Timoshenko was the division commander.

Immediately a description of the battle—dust, sun, details, a picture of a Budyonny battle.—Specifics—the killing of the officer, and so on.—After that we are on our *tachanka*, dead men.—Brody or Radzivillov.

II. The field. Waiting to move to our night camp. The nurse.—The horses are pulling the men.

1. Decamp from Belavtsy. The battle near Brody. On Ivan's *tachanka*.
2. Radzivillov.
3. Entry into Brody. The field by Klyokotovo. A farm. A field sown with corpses. Pilsudski's declarations.—A meeting with the division commander.
4. The battle by Klyokotovo.—Konkin.—The death of the Polish general.
5. Roaming around in circles with the Fourth Division. Night in the field.—The Jewish nurse.
6. In Radzivillov. K.K. [Zholnarkevich]. Sheko.

August 3. The battle near B[rody]. The battle near Brody. My roaming around.

1. The Jewish nurse. What does this mean? I sleep in the field tying the stirrup to my foot. I want to kill my vehicular driver!—The main thing: about the nurse.
2. In Radzivillov.—The visit of K.K. and Timoshenko,* The battle ended with a change in the command staff.
3. Rest. New men. Night in the field. The horses, I tie myself to the stirrup.—Night, corn on the cob, nurse. Dawn. Without a plot.

Dialogues. The battle near Brody

Rest stops. Hay. Threshing sheds. Horses.
Topics?
The cunning orderly.—Arrival at the night camp. Feeding the horses. We drag away the peasants' hay.

Night.—We rested for two hours. On our horses. *The battle near Brody.*—Our bridle has been stolen.

---

* Timoshenko, the commander of the Sixth Division, and his chief of staff, K. K. Zholnarkevich.

Chapter about Brody—in separate fragments—I've been cut off from my division, what that means.

Vasili Rybochkin.

Style: "In Belyov."—Short chapters saturated with content.

Konkin. I find the brigade waiting in suspense. Introduction at the priest's place. What do you want, Moseika? News of heroic Vasili Rybochkin. The army commander's order. The other Rybochkin.—Plays the Cossack.—Then, returning from battle: a gold watch, trunks, a horse.—When I get to Nizhny, ha, will I show them . . . The sister of mercy on the horse. A bitch. The commissar has made a nice profit.—His picture as a clown.—Greetings from Nizhny.—The internationally renowned miracle clown and overseas circus rider.—The procession moves off.

The battle near Lvov

Day by day. Briefly. Dramatic.—Include: the Polish air force. Zadvurdze.

The Polish air force. The battle near Lvov.

The Red Cavalry is retreating. What from? From twenty airplanes.

The secret is out in the open, the cure has been found. Mosher* was right. The airplanes are having a strong demoralizing effect. The wounding of Korotchayev.†—Major Fauntleroy's letter to his headquarters in New York.—First encounter with Wes[tern] European technology.—The planes take off in the mornings.

The battle near Lvov.—Describe the battle with the airplanes.—Then development.—The battle.—The air squadron sends us packing, follows us, we squirm, relocate from one place to another. The battle near Lvov.—Describe the day.—Development after the story.—The two phases of war.—Our victories, the fruitlessness of our efforts, but the failure is not obvious.

Brody

I have never seen a sadder town.—The origins of Jewry, an impres-

---

* Frank Mosher, the assumed name of Captain Merian Caldwell Cooper, the shot-down American pilot that Babel interrogated in Belyov.

† A brigade commander of the Sixth Cavalry Division.

sion that will last my whole life. The Brodsky synagogue in Odessa, aristocracy.—Friday evening. The town—a quick walk around the center, it is destroyed. The outskirts, a Jewish town.—A description of the synagogues: the main thing.

1. At the Galician's. Polite death. 2. Synagogues. 3. Night, in the room next door. Talmudists.—Hasidism with blind eye sockets. A vision of ancient times: for the Rabbi of Belz and for the Rabbi of Husyatin. Chandeliers, old men, children. Talmudists.—I have lived through many nights shivering in corridors, but never have I lived through such a damp, boring, dirty night.—She is a nurse, he is from the quartermaster's office.—Through the crack. The woman's foul language.—The history of the synagogue.—Find out about the history of Brody.—They are hiding a shriveled-up little old man—The Rabbi of Belz. [. . .]. Without comparison or historical counterpart.—Simply a story.

Sokal 1.

In the square in front of the synagogue. The quarreling of the Jews. The Cossacks digging a grave. Trunov's body. Timoshenko. An airplane?—An airplane chased the Jews away, then I went up to Tim[oshenko]. A phrase from Melnikov's* letter—and I understand the suffering felt within this army.

The sequence: Jews. Airplane. Grave. Timoshenko. The letter. Trunov's burial, the salute.

The Orthodox Jews, the Rabbi of Belz. I've lost you, Sasha.— Religious carnage, you'd think you were in the eighteenth century, Ilya-Gaon, Baal Shem, if the Cossacks didn't dig the grave (description). The Uniate cleric, his leg like an arc.—The Uniate cleric, what ruin, what ruin, say I there are more important things to think about, an airplane is coming, a spot in the distance, the Cossacks, and you won't even have to go out. Do you all remember Melnikov, his white stallion? His petition to the army. He sends you his greetings and his love.

---

* Parfenti Melnikov, commander of the First Squadron of the Sixth Cavalry Division, who appears as Khlebnikov in "The Story of a Horse" and "The Continuation of the Story of a Horse."

Tim[oshenko] rests his military notebook on the coffin cover to write in it.

Sokal 2.

Go to hell with your "what ruin," we have more important things to deal with here.—Trunov's body with his neatly placed legs and his carefully polished boots.—His head on the saddle, the stirrups around his chest.
—I have lost you, Pava—
Very simple, *a factual account,* no superfluous descriptions.—Stand to attention. We are burying Pavel Trunov. Military commissar, give your speech. And the military commissar gave a speech about Soviet power, about the constitution of the Union of Soviet Republics, and about the blockade.

The past.

I remember, said Tim[oshenko], right now is when we could use him.—We are burying Pavel Trunov, the international hero.—The military commissar, honor the memory of this hero in the presence of the fighters.

Trunov's death

I too would believe in the resurrection of Elijah if it weren't for that airplane that came floating toward us, etc. It dropped bombs with soft thuds. Art[illery] harnesses.
The airplane, the Cossack from inside the grave: I inform you, Comr. Division Commander, that it is highly possible that we will all end up here.—Right you are.—and he went to get the dead man ready. His saddle, stirrups, the band and the delegations from the regiments. We are burying Trunov, the international hero, the military commissar gives a speech that expresses this.
Com[rades], the Communist Party is an iron column, pouring out its blood in the front line. And when blood flows from iron, that is no laughing matter, Comrades, but victory or death. A subject: the military commissar's speech.

Gowinski

A Polish deserter. Where in the world is there an army like ours?

They took him in and sent him right over to me as my coachman. He is shaken, then suddenly whips the horses and sings at the top of his voice.

Rev. chapter.—Af[onka] Bida. They caught him, wanted to kill him—the main thing: why didn't they kill him?—Then they forgot about him, then they put him on the rations list. A subject: how Gowinski was placed on the rations list.

The fire in Lashkov

Galician culture.—The cler[gyman] Szeptycki, description of the icons, chasubles, the womenfolk, how they bury, the church.—Apanasenko at the fire, he looks like Utochkin.*—The Cossacks are ransacking.—All night long my room is brightly lit.—My landlord in Lashkov.—Kuban Cossacks beneath my window.—Also there—the band—the nurse. A proposal? The Galicians are putting out the fire with detestable slackness, they cannot.—Burned horses, singed cows.—The Galicians' apathy.—Apanasenko.

Briefly.—Immediately the fire, Ap[anasenko], the Galicians, the Cossacks.—The pile outside the church, the conversation with the clergyman, Count Szeptycki.—The Metropolitan of Galicia.

Page 1. A miniature.

The books.

Style, scope.—The cemetery in Kozin . . .

The estate of Kulaczkowski, horses in the drawing room—a listing of the books.

A poem in prose.

Books—I grabbed as many as I could, they keep calling me—I cannot tear myself away.—We gallop off—I keep throwing books away—a piece of my soul—I've thrown them all away.—The core—a listing of the books.—Books and battle—Heloise and Abelard. Napoleon.—Anatole France.

LESHNIOV. JULY 29, 1920

The vicissitudes of a cavalry campaign.—Rain is the victor, a

---

* Sergei Utochkin, a celebrated Russian aviation pioneer from Odessa.

Gal[ician] shtetl through a sheet of rain.—Night at Froim's.—A night of anxiety.—Gowinski and Grishchuk.—The highroad to Brody.

Describe the night simply. Beginning: the night will be one of anxiety. The condition of waiting and fatigue.

Milatin

Right away a description of the monastery.—The Catholic priest. Burials. The Polish woman.—Korotchayev. Remembering the days of marching. The horses chomping, the sky shimmers through, we are lying in the hay.—Then at the Jew's. Korotchayev acts like a country squire. The Jew has no revolutionary tendencies.—The demoted division commander.—Then, Korotchayev's star—the Jewish adjutant of the squadron commander.—Kniga.—A tall, immovable man, bulky, like the inspector in Korolenko,* he sits on the sofa, is silent, vodka—a mute scene—a figure behind the enclosure, a Basilian monastery, the monk in a gray cassock, tall, broad-shouldered, fingers his rosary—I stand there—bewitched—then noise, the thunder of transport carts.— A Pole lying in a coffin.—Two orderlies—one of them, Borisov, tiptoes through the yard, his head down, the other—a Kirghiz . . . the body is slashed—uncovered—covered again.—I feel sorry for the Polish woman—I want to be graceful, gallant.—They return from battle—a special calm, their usual way of riding, professionalism! Separate: Milatin, Korotchayev. [. . .]

Milatin 2.

The maid—a tiny, brown, ugly Polish woman—a cow with teats, a young mother. The cool luxury of the room.—The empty, shriveled teats.

The sequence: A sultry, dusty, golden evening.—Transport carts.— Right away a description of the monastery. The *Pater* and his niece, the roads to the monastery.—He conducts burials in secret . . . I make my way to the monastery. The masterful voice of the Catholic priest. (Pay no attention to continuity in the story.) The funeral rites.—A new military order, the arrival of the Cossacks, I leave.—The Cossacks return from battle in businesslike fashion.

* A figure in Vladimir Korolenko's autobiographical novel *The History of My Contemporary*.

Second chapter about Korotchayev.

The maid by the gate—the main figure of trust.

Belyov—Boratin.

A four-day march. Diary. A simple, lengthy narration.—Begin—a marvelous march?—I saw, I remembered—marching in the forests with the division commander, rest stop with Germans, then with the cleric. The regimental clergyman. K[onstantin] K[arlovich Zholnarkevich]. Nighttime at headquarters . . . Headquarters, symbol . . . A battle by Smordva.—My illness. Night in Smordva. A rest stop in Zhabokriki.— Grishchuk.—A meeting in Kozin.

Apanasenko's life story.

Noncommissioned officer. Four St. George Crosses. Son of a swineherd.—Got the village together. He stuck out his neck.—He joined forces with Budyonny.—The Astrakhan campaign.

His epistle to the Poles, which starts out like this: You damn bastards. Compose his epistle.

Lepin

His soul rebels. Wanted to go to the Latvians.* His petition.

Demidovka

Briefly.—Naked Prishchepa.—The blood-drenched pig.— Barsukov.—The synagogue.—The kitchen.

I ride with Prishchepa, Prishchepa's tale, a Jewish shtetl, I prick up my ears (my father is in the Brodsky Synagogue, surrounded by merchants in the choir. Women weep). The father deaf.—A stately old man. The anxious stateliness of the deaf.

Prishchepa, argument with the high school student or with Ida Aronovna.

Chapters: Prishchepa.—The old woman, prayer, the pig.—Ida Aronovna. The rape.—The synagogue.

The form?

---

* Lepin, one of the staff officers, was Latvian.

Demidovka

The beginning: a description of the family, an analysis of their feelings and beliefs.—How do I come to find out all this? A universal phenomenon. (Their) political Weltanschauung. They have orphans in their house.

2. Our arrival. Potatoes, coffee. Prishchepa's argument with the youth. My tale about Soviet power.—Evening. The shtetl beyond the windows. *Tishah b'Ab.*—The destruction of Jerusalem. A description of the girl from Kremenets. In the house of her *future* father-in-law. In the morning she is in complete disarray, ashen, she defends the cart, a conversation with the commissar. Prishchepa walks around her, presses against her, our girls cook pork, the Kremenets girl is sewing.—Demidovka medical externs.— A dentist—the pride of the family. A description of the family—the father is of the old school, a venerable Jew, new shoots, [. . .], listens to modern ideas, does not interfere, the mother a go-between, the children disperse, life filled with tradition, there's a hunchbacked one, a proud one (the dentist), there's a plump one (married), one has dedicated herself to her family and the household, another is a midwife helping the womenfolk, she will grow old in Demidovka.—Describe each sister separately. (Chekhov's *Three Sisters?*).—A lyrical prelude.—Into this family, which still hasn't broken up, Prishchepa and I have intruded.—The hunchbacked one serves us, then toward morning Dora Aronovna softens up too, how painful it is to see this broken feminine pride. A pretty girl, the only beautiful one, which is why it is so hard for her to get married—she is a blend of shtetl health, very black, moist eyes, Polish slyness, and Warsaw slippers, her ever-anxious parents conceived her in a simple moment of joy, the rest are complex, proud—the only son, sixteen years old, in other words six years of war, is nervous, a dreamer, his mother's favorite.—The wailing of Jeremiah.—The son is reading, the daughters lie on their beds in white stockings.—They bring us everything.—About *Tishah b'Ab*— build on the correspondence of the prayers with what is going on outside the walls.—Shots—the lock, machine-gunners returning from their positions, the Cossacks are out and about.—Dora Aronovna—for us this is a holiday—she is pale with pride.—Prishchepa—we will spill blood.—I capture their attention with a tale—the longest to resist is Dora Aronovna.

1. Description of the family. 2. Potatoes, scandal, we eat,

Prishchepa with eyes clouded with caresses. They are pitiful. We speak about the Poles. Dora Aronovna dreams of W[estern] Eu[rope], in Kiev she had been part of various circles, I tell fairytales,—Prishchepa and the high-school boy.—Evening. The weather is a little gloomy. The shtetl is inexpressibly sad, the bent father-in-law, machine-gunners come, Prishchepa courts the girl, the high-school boy goes to the synagogue.—3. *Tishah b'Ab.*—The wailing of Jeremiah. Night in the yard. Morning. The machine-gunners leave, carts, the girl from Kremenets. Ida Aronovna's pride is crushed.—What is read on *Tishah b'Ab?*

Simple. Briefly. A description of the damp evening.—A description of the shtetl.—Fright in the synagogue.—Prishchepa's courting.

About the bees. A story? The figure of the old Czech. He died—stung all over.

The division commander's day: A conference day. Narrative.
1. The Frenchman. 2. The dispatch bag from the Economic Council. 3. The division commander's morning. At the headquarters. The division commander's lackeys.

Budyatichi. The meeting with the Forty-fourth Div[ision]. The doctor, the nurse [. . .] A proud nurse, good organization of medical setup, the brigade is well organized. Orlov. Get out of here . . . At that moment, elegant Sheko. A scandal with Orlov. The nurse, like a greeting from Russia, things have changed there if such women are coming to the army. A new army, a real one.—A characterization of Orlov. He throws things away.—They pack their things—culture—thermos, blanket, fold-up cots.

❧

ISAAC EMMANUELOVICH BABEL

A CHRONOLOGY

by Gregory Freidin

1894   Isaac Babel is born (June 30) in Moldavanka, a poor district near the harbor of Odessa, to Feiga and Man Yitzkhovich Bobel, a dealer in agricultural machinery. Soon after, the family, now under the name Babel, relocates to Nikolayev (150 kilometers from Odessa). Babel studies English, French, and German; private Hebrew lessons.

1899   Babel's sister, Meriam, born on July 16.

1905   The October Manifesto of Czar Nicholas II establishes a constitutional monarchy. Pogroms in southern Russia, including Nikolayev, witnessed by Babel. But the family is untouched.

1906   Babel's family, now considerably more prosperous, moves back to Odessa and settles in the residential center of the city. Babel enrolls in the Nicholas I Commercial School in Odessa; begins writing stories in French.

1911   After an unsuccessful attempt to enroll at the University of Odessa (due to the restrictions on Jews), Babel enters the Institute of Finance and Business Studies in Kiev. Meets Evgenia Borisovna Gronfein, his future wife.

1913   First publication: the story "Old Shloyme."

1914   World War I begins.

1915   Babel follows his institute's evacuation from Kiev to Saratov.

1916   After graduating from the institute, moves to St. Petersburg, meets Maxim Gorky, and begins to contribute stories and sketches to Gorky's journal *Letopis* and other periodicals (stories: "Mama, Rimma, and Alla," "Elya Isaakovich and Margarita Prokofievna"). Babel's stories receive a favorable response from reviewers.

1917   Charged with writing pornography (story "The Bathroom Window"), but the charge is made moot by the political turmoil.

        The February Revolution.* Czar Nicholas II abdicates. Russia is ruled by the provisional government. Babel briefly volunteers for the Rumanian front.

        Bolshevik coup d'état in October.†

        Babel abandons the disintegrating front in November, returns to Odessa, and takes a dangerous journey to Petrograd** (his story "The Road," 1932). Reaches Petrograd in December 1917 and joins the newly organized Cheka for a brief stint as a translator for the counterintelligence department.

1918   In March, Babel becomes a regular contributor of sketches about life in the city to Maxim Gorky's anti-Leninist newspaper *Novaya zhizn* until the publication is shut down by the Bolsheviks on July 6 (Babel's last contribution is in the July 2 issue).

        Contributes stories to newspaper *Zhizn iskusstva* (Petrograd) in November.

1918–19 Serves in the food requisitioning detachments during the Civil War; returns to Odessa. Marries Evgenia Gronfein (August 9, 1919).

1920   Odessa Party Committee issues Babel the credentials of a war correspondent under the name of Kiril Vasilievich Lyutov, assigned to Budyonny's Cavalry Army on the Polish front. Babel spends June through September with the Budyonny Cavalry.‡

        Returns to Odessa severely ill (lifelong asthma). Travels with his wife in Georgia and the Caucasus, contributes to local periodicals.

1921   End of the Civil War. The tolerant New Economic Policy replaces War Communism.

        Babel does editorial work for a publishing house, contributing stories and essays to Odessa periodicals.

---

* March, according to the Gregorian calandar, adopted subsequently.

† November 7, according to the Gregorian calandar.

** Formerly St. Petersburg.

‡In August 1920, the Red Army reaches the outskirts of Warsaw but is soon after repelled and by September defeated by Pilsudski's troops, aided by the Western powers; an armistice is signed in October 1921; the Treaty of Riga, finalizing the Russian-Polish border and ceding parts of the Ukraine and Belarus to Poland, is signed on March 18, 1921.

1923   Most of the Benya Krik stories (the Odessa stories) written and published in Odessa.

       Father dies (July 13).

1923–24 After finishing the Odessa stories, Babel begins work on the *Red Cavalry* stories (June 1923), the publication of his stories in the avant-garde *Lef* and the fellow traveler *Krasnaya Nov*; the beginning of Babel's fame.

1924   Lenin dies on January 21; Stalin, the Communist Party's General Secretary since 1922, begins his ascent to power.

       Budyonny's first attack on *Red Cavalry* stories (March).

       Babel publication in the first issue of Evgeny Zamiatin's independent journal *Russkii sovremennik*.

       Meriam Chapochnikoff (Babel's sister) emigrates to Brussels.

1925   First two childhood stories (the cycle *The Story of My Dovecote*) are published with a dedication to Maxim Gorky.

       Evgenia Babel (Gronfein), Babel's wife, emigrates to Paris.

1926   *Red Cavalry* is published as a book. Babel's mother emigrates to Brussels. Babel is Russia's "most famous writer."

1925–27 Babel's liaison with Tamara Kashirina (later, Mrs. Vsevolod Ivanov).

1926   Mikhail (Ivanov) is born to Babel and Tamara Kashirina in July.

       Babel finishes his play *Sunset* in August.

       Works on the film script of *Benya Krik*; the beginning of Babel's career as a screenwriter (script based on Shalom Aleichem's *Roaming Stars* and others).

1927   The film *Benya Krik* is released and soon taken out of circulation. In subsequent publications of the script, Babel disowns the film.

       Babel is in Kiev on family business; possibly works on *The Jewess* (a novel) of which only the beginning is extant. Plans a work on the French Revolution, hints that he is working on a novel about the Cheka; continues work on the "childhood" story cycle (referred to by Babel as "my true legacy").

       Babel leaves Russia for Paris in July; a brief affair with E. Khaiutina (future Mrs. Nikolai Yezhov) in Berlin; rejoins his wife in Paris.

       Sunset staged successfully in Baku (October 23), in two theaters in Odessa (October 25 and December 1).

1928   Moscow production of *Sunset* at the Moscow Art Theater II (February 28) fails.

       The Shakhty Trial. End of the liberal New Economic Policy era and beginning of the Stalin Revolution.

       Babel returns to Russia in October. General Budyonny resumes attacks on the *Red Cavalry* stories. Gorky comes to Babel's defense.

       The Chinese Mill, a film comedy based on a script by Babel, premieres in July.

       Continues work on the childhood story cycle (according to Babel, "part of a larger whole").

       Critic Alexander Voronsky, an early patron and admirer of Babel, chides him in print for his low productivity, or "silence."

       Completes the story "My First Fee" (1922–28); plans *Kolya Topuz*, a long narrative about an Odessa bandit who is reformed during the period of socialist construction (late 1920s–early 1930s).

1929   Trotsky is exiled from Soviet Russia in January.

Babel's daughter, Nathalie, born in Paris to Evgenia Borisovna Babel on July 17.

Red Cavalry is published in English translation in the United States (following German and French editions), preceded by the appearance of some stories in literary magazines.

1929–30 "In search of new material," Babel, like many other Soviet writers, travels in the industrial heartland to observe "socialist construction"; witnesses the brutal collectivization and famine in the Ukraine (February–summer 1930).

1930   Babel is publicly accused of granting an anti-Soviet interview to a Polish newspaper while on the French Riviera. He insists, apparently successfully, that the interview was a fabrication. Attempts to receive permission to return to Paris fail in part due to the author's continued "silence."

1931   Resumes contacts with Khaiutina.

Spends early spring in the Ukraine.

Publishes two more childhood stories (the *Dovecote* cycle) and a "collectivization" story, "Gapa Guzhva."

Impending publication of a series of stories is announced at the end of the year, only one of them subsequently published.

1932   Publication of the story "Guy de Maupassant." Babel lives in Molodenovo, a village outside Moscow, close to Gorky's summer estate.

Babel meets Antonina Nikolayevna Pirozhkova, a young engineer.

After many pleas, Babel finally is allowed to return to his family in France.

1932–33 In Paris, Babel sees his daughter for the first time. Collaborates on a script about a famous socialist-revolutionary double agent, Yevno Azef, for a French movie studio (continues this work later in Russia). Close friendship with Ilya Ehrenburg, who introduces Babel to André Malraux. Babel visits Gorky in Sorrento. Travels through France, Italy, Germany.

Returns to Moscow in August in response to Gorky's request for assistance in organizing the First Congress of Soviet Writers.

In the fall, Babel travels, with Antonina Pirozhkova, through the Caucasus on the way to Kabardino-Balkaria (a small Caucasus republic).

1934   Babel travels to the Donbass region (January).

During the 17th Communist Party Congress, "The Congress of Victors," opposition to Stalin becomes manifest, but is ultimately defeated.

Publication of Babel's story "Dante Street."

Osip Mandelstam recites his anti-Stalin verses to his friends and is arrested in May.

At the First Congress of Soviet Writers (August), Babel obliquely criticizes the cult of Stalin. Speaking about his modest output, Babel calls himself "a great master of the genre [of literary silence]." He is grateful to the Soviet establishment for being able to enjoy the high status of a writer despite his "silence," which, in the West, would have forced him to abandon writing and "sell haberdashery." Babel spends time with André Malraux, who attended the congress.

Assassination of Sergei Kirov on December 1. Beginning of the great purges.

1935   Babel attends the Congress of Soviets in Moscow (February).

Babel completes *Maria,* his second play, which is published in March.

Babel and Pasternak are dispatched, on the insistence of André Malraux and André Gide, to the anti-Fascist International Congress of Writers for the Defense of Culture and Peace in Paris (June).

On July 14, Babel witnesses huge demonstrations in Paris (Popular Front and the pro-Fascist Croix de Feu*), seeing in them the signs of an impending revolution.

Along with his wife and daughter, Babel visits his mother and sister in Brussels (July). Babel makes plans to bring his entire family back to the Soviet Union. These plans do not materialize.

Babel returns to the Soviet Union (August) and travels, with Antonina Pirozhkova, to the Kiev region and on to Odessa. After returning to Moscow, Babel and Pirozhkova establish a household.

Ilya Ehrenburg, on a visit to Moscow from Paris, queries Babel about the mounting repression and the purges of the old Bolshevik intellectuals from the leadership. Babel attributes the changes to the preparations for war, which calls for a more decisive, military-style government and a kind of art that could best serve the goals of total mobilization of society.

Babel collaborates with Sergei Eisenstein on the film *Bezhin Meadow,* about a young peasant Communist who is murdered for denouncing his father as a kulak (winter 1935–36).

1936   Attack on Dmitri Shostakovich's opera *Lady Macbeth of the Mtsensk District* (January) inaugurates the "Campaign against Formalism," a purge in the cultural sphere.

Together with André and Roland Malraux, Babel visits Gorky in the Crimea and, along with Mikhail Koltsov, serves as Malraux's interpreter (March). Afterward Gorky complains to Stalin that the "Campaign against Formalism" represents a harmful cultural policy.

Babel spends time with André Gide in Moscow and occasionally interprets for him.

Maxim Gorky dies on June 18.

As one of the leading figures in the Writers' Union, Babel receives a country house (dacha) in Peredelkino.

Spanish Civil War begins in July.

The trial of Lev Kamenev, Grigory Zinoviev, and other famous party and military leaders, including several Civil War heroes (some friends of Babel's) takes place in August. The accused are sentenced to death.

Nikolay Yezhov (now the husband of E. Khaiutina) replaces Genrikh Yagoda in September as the head of the NKVD (Stalin's secret police).

According to an NKVD informer, Babel is critical of the trials, saying that the prosecution failed to make a convincing case against the accused.

* Ilya Ehrenburg, *Memoirs: 1914–1941,* translated by Tatyana Shebunina (NY: Grosset & Dunlap, 1966), p. 317.

1937   Daughter Lydia is born to Babel and Antonina Pirozhkova (January).

Babel publishes stories "Sulak," "Di Grasso" (thematically, part of the childhood story cycle), and "The Kiss" (a new concluding story of *Red Cavalry*).

Show trials of political and military leaders continue.

1938   In a meeting with Ilya Ehrenburg, Babel recounts how banned books are pulped in a Moscow factory. Ehrenburg, who has just been recalled to Moscow from Spain, suggests to Babel that if Fascism wins in Spain, the repressive USSR would be the only place left for people like Babel and himself, and "so much the worse for us."*

Last meeting with Ehrenburg (May).

Yezhov is replaced by Lavrenty Beria as the head of the NKVD and is soon afterward arrested. He gives evidence against Babel.

Babel publishes a story "The Trial" (August).

Collaborates on scripts for the film version of Gorky's autobiographical trilogy (he is chiefly responsible for the script of the volume *My Universities*, released in 1939–40).

Signs a contract for an edition of his collected works.

1939   Babel completes a film script for a military-industrial spy thriller, *Number 4 Staraya Square* (the title referring to the address of the Communist Party Central Committee Headquarters in Moscow).

Babel is arrested on May 15 and is soon charged with spying for France and Austria. The accusation is based, in part, on the evidence provided by Yezhov and Babel's fellow writers Boris Pilnyak and Mikhail Koltsov, who had been arrested earlier.

Molotov-Ribbentrop Pact is signed in Moscow in August. In September, the armies of Germany and the Soviet Union invade and partition Poland.

1940   Babel is executed in the Lubyanka prison on January 27.

1941   Germany invades the Soviet Union on June 22.

1948   Rumors circulate about Babel's imminent release from prison.

1953   Stalin dies (March 5).

1954   Babel is officially exonerated on December 23. The death certificate misleadingly states that he died under unknown circumstances on March 17, 1941.

1955   *Collected Stories by Isaac Babel*, with an introduction by Lionel Trilling, is published in New York.

1956   Nikita Khrushchev denounces Stalin at the 20th Party Congress (February).

1957   A volume of selected stories is published in Moscow with the introduction by Ilya Ehrenburg, at last opening the way for subsequent editions, albeit censored and incomplete.

1964   *Isaac Babel, The Lonely Years: 1925–1939: Unpublished Stories and Correspondence*, edited and introduced by Nathalie Babel. Revised edition published in 1995.

* S. Povartsov, *Prichina smerti—rasstrel* (*Cause of Death: Execution by the Firing Squad*), M. 1966, p. 130.

1966   *You Must Know Everything,* edited by Nathalie Babel, published in New York.

1989   *Vospominania o Babele* (*Babel Remembered*), edited by Antonina Pirozhkova, is published in Moscow, including Pirozhkova's essay "Years Spent Together (1932–1939)."

1990   The two-volume *Sochineniia* (*Works*) edition is published in Moscow, the most comprehensive uncensored edition of Babel to date, albeit incomplete.

        Details of Babel's interrogation and death begin to reach Soviet press (publications by Arkady Vaksberg and Vitaly Shentalinsky based on their research in the KGB archives).

1994   The centenary of Babel's birth is marked by international conferences in Russia and the United States.

1996   Pirozhkova publishes *At His Side: The Last Years of Isaac Babel,* translated by Anne Frydman and Robert L. Busch (Royalton, Vermont).

GREGORY FREIDIN

NOTES

THE *RED CAVALRY* STORIES

The stories are presented in the order in which they appeared in the first edition of the book *Konarmiya* (*Red Cavalry*), May 1926, by which time all the stories had been published in magazines and newspapers as indicated below.

CROSSING THE RIVER ZBRUCZ
Original title: *Perekhod cherez Zbruch*. First published in *Pravda,* August 3, 1924. Dated Novograd-Volynsk, July 1920.

Savitsky: The altered name Babel used in his later editions of the *Red Cavalry* stories for Semyon Konstantinovich Timoshenko, 1895–1970, the commander of the Sixth Division of the Red Cavalry. He was later to become a Marshal of the Soviet Union and Commissar of Defense. He appears as Savitsky in the *Red Cavalry* stories "My First Goose," "The Commander of the Second Brigade," "The Story of a Horse," and "The Continuation of the Story of a Horse," and as Timoshenko throughout the *1920 Diary*. In the original publication of the stories, Babel used Timoshenko's name.

THE CHURCH IN NOVOGRAD
Original title: "*Kostel v Novograde.*" First published in *Izvestiya Odesskovo Gubispolkoma,* February 18, 1923.

See also *1920 Diary* entry for July 15.

A LETTER
Original title: "*Pismo.*" First published in *Izvestiya Odesskovo Gubispolkoma,* February 11, 1923. Dated Novograd-Volynsk, June 1920.

See also *1920 Diary* entry of August 9, 1920.

Pavlichenko: The altered name of Iosif Rodionovich Apanasenko, 1890–1943, who took over the command of Division Six after Timoshenko. Mentioned throughout the *1920 Diary* and in the *Red Cavalry* stories "The Life of Matvey Rodionovich Pavlichenko" and "Czesniki." In the original publication of the stories, Babel used Apanasenko's name.

THE RESERVE CAVALRY COMMANDER
First published in *Lef 4,* 1923. Babel changed the original title "*Dyakov*" to

"*Nachalnik konzapasa*" ("The Reserve-Cavalry Commander") in later story editions. Dated Belyov, July 1920.

See also *1920 Diary* entries for July 13, 14, and 16.

PAN APOLEK
Original title: "*Pan Apolek.*" First published in *Krasnaya nov* 7, 1923.

ITALIAN SUN
First published in *Krasnaya nov* 3, 1923. Babel changed the original title "*Sidorov*" to "*Solntse Italii*" ("Italian Sun") in later story editions. Dated Novograd-Volynsk, July 1920.

GEDALI
Original title: "*Gedali.*" First published in *Krasnaya nov* 4, 1924. Dated Zhitomir, June 1920.

See also *1920 Diary* entries for June 6 and July 7.

MY FIRST GOOSE
Original title: "*Moi pervii gus.*" First published in *Izvestiya Odesskovo Gubispolkoma*, May 4, 1924. Dated July 1920.

See also *1920 Diary* entry for August 9.

THE RABBI
Original title: "*Rabbi.*" First published in *Krasnaya nov* 1, 1924.

See also *1920 Diary* entry for June 3.

THE ROAD TO BRODY
Original title: "*Put v Brody.*" First published in *Izvestiya Odesskovo Gubispolkoma*, June 17, 1923. Dated Brody, August 1920.

See also *1920 Diary* entries for August 18 and 31.

THE *TACHANKA* THEORY
Original title: "*Ucheniye o tachanke.*" First published in *Izvestiya Odesskovo Gubispolkoma*, February 23, 1923.

DOLGUSHOV'S DEATH
Original title: "*Smert Dolgusheva.*" First published in *Izvestiya Odesskovo Gubispolkoma*, May 1, 1923. Dated Brody, August 1920.

Korotchayev: Was demoted by General Budyonny from provisional commander of the Fourth Cavalry Division to one of the brigade commanders of the Sixth Cavalry Division. See also *1920 Diary* entries for August 2, 8, and 13.

THE COMMANDER OF THE SECOND BRIGADE
First published in *Lef* 4, 1923. Babel changed the original title "*Kolesnikov*" to "*Kombrig 2*" ("The Commander of the Second Brigade"). Dated Brody, August 1920.

See also *1920 Diary* entry for August 3, in which Budyonny threatens to shoot Kolesnikov and Grishin. In the original edition of this story in *Lef*, Babel had used Grishin's name, which in later editions Babel changed to Almazov.

SASHKA CHRIST
Original title: "*Sashka Khristos.*" First published in *Krasnaya nov* 1, 1924.

See also *1920 Diary* entry for July 28.

THE LIFE OF MATVEY RODIONOVICH PAVLICHENKO
Original title: "*Zhiznyeopisaniye Pavlichenki, Matveya Rodionicha.*" First published in *Shkval* 8, 1924.

Matvey Rodionovich Pavlichenko: the altered name of Iosif Rodionovich Apanasenko, 1890–1943, who took over the command of the Sixth Cavalry Division in August 1920. Mentioned throughout the *1920 Diary*, particularly the entries for August 5, 8–13. See also Sketches for the *Red Cavalry* Stories, "Apanasenko's Life Story" (p. 304).

THE CEMETERY IN KOZIN

Original title: "*Kladbishche v Kozine.*" First published in *Izvestiya Odesskovo Gubispolkoma*, February 23, 1923.

See also *1920 Diary* entries for July 18 and 21.

PRISHCHEPA

Original title: "*Prishchepa.*" First published in *Izvestiya Odesskovo Gubispolkoma*, June 17, 1923. Dated Demidovka, July 1920.

See also *1920 Diary* entries for July 23, 24. See also the two sections on Demidovka in Sketches for the *Red Cavalry* Stories (pp. 304–6).

THE STORY OF A HORSE

First published in *Izvestiya Odesskovo Gubispolkoma*, April 13, 1923. Babel changed the original title "*Timoshenko i Melnikov*" ("Timoshenko and Melnikov") to "*Istoriya odnoi loshadi*" ("The Story of a Horse") in later editions. Dated Radzivillov, July 1920. The story was republished in *Krasnaya nov* 3, 1924.

In a letter to the editor, Parfenti Melnikov denied that he had ever written a letter renouncing his membership in the Communist Party. Babel wrote an apology, published in the literary magazine *Oktyabr*. See "A Letter to the Editor" (p. 198).

KONKIN

Original title: "*Konkin.*" First published in *Krasnaya nov* 3, 1924. Dated Dubno, August 1920.

See also *1920 Diary* entry for July 13.

BERESTECHKO

Original title: "*Berestechko.*" First published in *Krasnaya nov* 3, 1924. Dated Berestechko, August 1920.

See also *1920 Diary* entries for August 7 and 8.

SALT

Original title: "*Sol.*" First published in *Izvestiya Odesskovo Gubispolkoma*, November 25, 1923.

EVENING

First published in *Krasnaya nov* 3. Babel changed the original title "*Galin*" to "*Vecher*" ("Evening") in later editions. Dated Kovel, 1920.

See also *1920 Diary* entries for September 10 and 11.

AFONKA BIDA

Original title: "*Afonka Bida.*" First published in *Krasnaya nov* 1, 1924.

See also *1920 Diary* entry for August 1.

AT SAINT VALENTINE'S

Original title: "*U Svyatogo Valentina.*" First published in *Krasnaya nov* 3, 1924. Dated Berestechko, August 1920.

See also *1920 Diary* entry for August 7.

SQUADRON COMMANDER TRUNOV
Original title: *"Eskadronnii Trunov."* First published in *Krasnaya nov* 2, 1925.
See also "And Then There Were Nine," "And Then There Were Ten," and the *1920 Diary* entry for August 30. See also "Sokal 1" and "Sokal 2" in Sketches for the *Red Cavalry* Stories (pp. 300–301).

IVAN AND IVAN
Original title: *"Ivany."* First published in *Russkii Sovremenik* 1, 1924.
See also *1920 Diary* entry for August 3.

A CONTINUATION OF THE STORY OF A HORSE
First published in *Krasnaya nov* 3, 1924 as part of the story *"Timoshenko i Melnikov"* ("Timoshenko and Melnikov"), which Babel changed to *"Prodolzhenie istorii odnoi loshadi"* ("A Continuation of the Story of a Horse") in later editions.

THE WIDOW
First published in *Izvestiya Odesskovo Gubispolkoma* 15, 1923. Babel changed the original title *"Shevelyov"* to *"Vdova"* ("The Widow") in later editions.
See also *1920 Diary* entry for August 9.

ZAMOSC
Original title: *"Zamostye."* First published in *Krasnaya nov* 3, 1924. Dated Sokal, September 1920.
See also *1920 Diary* entries for August 29 and 30.

TREASON
Original title: *"Izmena."* First published in *Izvestiya Odesskovo Gubispolkoma*, March 20, 1923.

CZESNIKI
Original title: *"Chesniki."* First published in *Krasnaya nov* 3, 1924.
See also *1920 Diary* entries for August 28–31.

AFTER THE BATTLE
Original title: *"Posle boya."* First published in *Prozhektor* 20, 1924. Dated Galicia, September 1920.
See also *1920 Diary* entry for August 31.

THE SONG
First published in *Krasnaya nov* 3, 1925. Babel changed the original title *"Vecher"* ("Evening") to *"Pesnya"* ("The Song"). Dated Sokal, August 1920.

THE RABBI'S SON
Original title: *Syn Rabbi.* First published in *Krasnaya nov* 1, 1924.
See also *1920 Diary* entry for September 12.

THE *RED CAVALRY* CYCLE:
ADDITIONAL STORIES

MAKHNO'S BOYS
Original title: *"U batko nashego Makhno."* First published in *Krasnaya nov* 4, 1924, dated 1923.

A HARDWORKING WOMAN
Original title: "*Staratelnaya zhenshchina*." First published in *Pereval* 6, 1926.
  See also *1920 Diary* entry for July 16.

GRISHCHUK
Original title: "*Grishchuk*." First published in *Izvestiya Odesskovo Gubispolkoma*, February 23, 1923, subtitled "From the *Red Cavalry*," dated July 16, 1920.
  See also *1920 Diary* entries for July 14, 19, and 21–29.

ARGAMAK
Original title: "*Agarmak*." First published in *Novii mir* 3, 1932, subtitled "An Unpublished Chapter of the *Red Cavalry*," dated 1924–1930.

THE KISS
Original title: "*Potselui*." First published in *Krasnaya nov* 7, 1937

AND THEN THERE WERE NINE
Original title: "*Ikh bylo devyat*." First published in *Novii Zhurnal* 95, New York, June 1969.
  See also "And Then There Were Ten," "Squadron Commander Trunov," and the *1920 Diary* entry for August 30.

AND THEN THERE WERE TEN
Original title: "*Ikh bylo desyat*." First published in *Petersburg 1918*, 1989, Michigan, Ardis Publishers.

A LETTER TO THE EDITOR
First published in *Oktyabr* 4, 1924.

1920 DIARY

First full publication in *Isaak Babel: Sochineniya v dvukh tomakh*, Moscow 1990.

JUNE 3
"Love in the kitchen": see the *Red Cavalry* story "Evening."
  "The Bazaar in Zhitomir": see the *Red Cavalry* stories "Gedali" and "The Rabbi's Son."

JULY 13
Dyakov: see the *Red Cavalry* story "The Reserve Cavalry Commander."

JULY 14
Grishchuk: see the *Red Cavalry* stories "The Tachanka Theory" and "Dolgushov's Death."
  Semyon Konstantinovich Timoshenko: Appears as Savitsky in the *Red Cavalry* stories "My First Goose," "The Commander of the Second Brigade," "The Story of a Horse," and "The Continuation of the Story of a Horse."

JULY 16
"A terrible incident, soldiers' love": see "A Hardworking Woman" from the additional stories.
  "If it gets up, then it's a horse": see the *Red Cavalry* story "The Reserve Cavalry Commander," and "Grishchuk" from the additional stories.

JULY 18
"The Jewish cemetery outside Malin": see the *Red Cavalry* story "The Cemetery in Kozin."

JULY 19

Nikolai Petrovich Kolesov (also referred to as Kolesnikov in the diary entries for August 3, 13, and 18, and in the Sketches for the Red Cavalry Stories) appears as Kolesnikov in the *Red Cavalry* story "The Commander of the Second Brigade."

JULY 21

"A cemetery, the destroyed house of Rabbi Azrail": see the *Red Cavalry* story "The Cemetery in Kozin."

JULY 23

Prishchepa: See the *Red Cavalry* story "Prishchepa" and the two sections on Demidovka in Sketches for the *Red Cavalry* Stories (pp. 304–06).

JULY 24

"My tale about the Chinese": Babel's friend Viktor Shklovsky wrote in an essay volume (*Gamburgsky shchet*, 1928) that throughout 1919 Babel "talked of nothing but two Chinese men in a brothel."

AUGUST 1

"Our infantry is in the trenches": See the *Red Cavalry* story "Afonka Bida."

AUGUST 2

Korotchayev: See the *Red Cavalry* story "Dolgushov's Death."

AUGUST 3

"Budyonny to Kolesnikov and Grishin: 'I'll shoot you!' "—see the *Red Cavalry* story "The Commander of the Second Brigade."

AUGUST 4

"We have a new division commander, Apanasenko"—appears in the *Red Cavalry* stories as Pavlichenko. See "A Letter," "The Life of Matvey Rodionovich Pavlichenko," and "Czesniki."

AUGUST 7

"The looting of the church": See also the *Red Cavalry* story "At Saint Valentine's."

"*Notre petit héros achève 7 semaines*": See also the *Red Cavalry* story "Berestechko."

AUGUST 8

"Scorched the pharmacist's body with white-hot iron pokers": See the *1920 Diary* entry for August 8.

AUGUST 9

"The tale of how he whipped his neighbor Stepan": See the *Red Cavalry* story "The Letter."

"Shurka's lover is heavily wounded": See the *Red Cavalry* story "The Widow."

Alexander Nikolayevich Vinokurov: Appears as Vinogradov in the *Red Cavalry* stories "Berestechko" and "After the Battle."

AUGUST 11

"Must write . . . the life story of Apanasenko": See the *Red Cavalry* story: "The Life of Matvey Rodionovich Pavlichenko."

AUGUST 18

"Interrogation of prisoners": See stories "Squadron Commander Trunov," "And Then There Were Nine," and "And Then There Were Ten."

"Smashed, smoked-out beehives": See "The Road to Brody."

AUGUST 30
"And then there were nine": See stories "Squadron Commander Trunov," "And Then There Were Nine," and "And Then There Were Ten."

AUGUST 31
Captain Yakovlev: See "The Widow" and "After the Battle."

SEPTEMBER 12
"Panic at the train station": See "The Rabbi's Son."
   "The nurse's story": See "After the Battle."

SKETCHES FOR THE *RED CAVALRY* STORIES

First published in *Literaturnoe Nasledstvo* 74, 1965.